CASTLES

A *Just Cause Universe* Novel

Ian Thomas Healy

Local Hero Press Edition

Castles: A *Just Cause Universe* Novel
Published by Local Hero Press, LLC

1st Printing
Local Hero Press: trade paperback, April 1, 2015
Printed in the United States of America

ISBN-13: 9781971445076

Cover art by Irshad Karim
Book design by Local Hero Press, LLC

Books by Local Hero Press

The *Just Cause Universe*

Just Cause
The Archmage
Day of the Destroyer
Deep Six
Jackrabbit
Champion
Castles
The Lion and the Five Deadly Serpents
Tusks
The Neighborhood Watch
Jackrabbit: Big In Japan
Arena
Hero Academy
The Path
Cinco de Mayo
Search and Rescue
Rooftops
Plague
Soldiers of Fortune
Just Cause Universe Compendium
Destroyer of Earth
Flint and Steel
The Club
Jackrabbit: Rinse and Repeat
Posse
Extinction Event
Rain Must Fall

Pariah of Verigo

Pariah's Moon
Pariah's War

Three Flavors of Tacos

The Guitarist
Making the Cut
The Scene Stealers

Collections

Airship Lies
High Contrast
The Good Fight
The Good Fight 3: Sidekicks
The Good Fight 4: Homefront
The Good Fight 5: The Golden Age
Muddy Creek Tales
Caped

Other Novels

Assassin
Blood on the Ice
Funeral Games
Hope and Undead Elvis
Horde
The Murder Squad (2026)
Roast Wyvern (and Other Recipes)
Starf*cker
Strings
The Oilman's Daughter
Troubleshooters

Nonfiction

Action! Writing Better Action Using Cinematic Techniques

This book, like so many before it, represents the work of a talented team. I may have written these words, but it took my editors Alicia Howie and Allison M. Dickson to make them better. I may have created these characters, but Irshad Karim and Justin Wasson brought them to life with their artwork, both for the cover and the art used in the book trailer. Special thanks go out to the members and officers of the Pen & Cape Society for their continued support and tireless promotion of the superhero fiction genre. I can't thank my family enough for their support in the selfish act of writing, and as always, I am grateful to all you readers out there for encouraging me to keep telling you stories.

INTRODUCTION

Superheroes are messy. Yeah, I mean, they're cool and everything. We love the costumes and the powers, and we all like to fantasize about what superpower we wish we had. Me? I want to teleport and have the ability to manipulate time and space. Basically, I want to be a human TARDIS, but I digress. Superheroes, if they existed in real life, would be a nightmare of human rights and basic infrastructure. Think of how all the buildings would have to be reinforced just in case some brick lost his temper. Think of all the riders business owners would need to carry on their insurance policies. Think of the current nightmare of airport security and amplify it by a thousand. Think of all the taxes that would go toward just the cleanup costs after a couple of them have a fight in a populated area. Did Superman get a bill after Man of Steel? Even the Ghostbusters got sued and forced out of business after they took down Gozer and blasted the Stay Puft Marshmallow Man, so I would say such there has to be some kind of bureaucratic red tape action happening, even if we don't see it on the screen.

So yeah, superheroes are messy. But not a lot of people want to talk about that, because we'd rather see them kicking butt, not testifying in congressional committee hearings about their potential threat to public safety. Right?

Well, actually, I think that's exactly what we need to see. We've become more than a little weary these days of displays of wanton destruction just for the sake of spectacle. It was a major part of the discussion following movies like *The Avengers*, *Man of Steel*, and the most recent *Godzilla* remake. If we're really to suspend disbelief, should there not be at least some accountability for the aftereffects of a fight between two god-like entities? In 2001, our real world equivalent of super villains took down two skyscrapers filled with people in the middle of Manhattan. Nearly fifteen years later, we can still say we know all too well what such trauma does to a nation.

In *CASTLES*, perhaps more than any other volume in the Just Cause series, Mr. Healy begins to answer a call to accountability. Or, rather, he sends his heroes in to do it for him, and it's not always pretty or fun. Because if anything else were to exist in an actual world populated by super-powered humans, it would be politicians looking to stake a career on building policies to either help elevate these people or break their backs. Shades of fascism, and perhaps even war and genocide, are inevitable. And you would be forced to ask yourself what side you would stand on. It would not be an easy answer, I'm afraid. Because parahumans, as Healy calls them, are capable of so much, and they don't always come in tidy packages with a virtuous hearts and healthy consciences. We can't even have a reasonable conversation about guns today. Imagine if someone could shut down a power grid with his mind, or fully inhabit any secure computer system in the world, or could absorb any bullet or rocket you shoot at him. It's the stuff of nightmares, and is one reason why I think the superhero genre is within kissing distance of the dystopian one.

Humanity would be bitterly divided in a world filled with parahumans. But there is a glimmer of hope. If Healy can answer the nearly impossible questions he raises in this book, perhaps there is still hope for us in our simpler world to figure things out. Because superheroes are messy, but so are we.

Allison M. Dickson
February, 2015

Playboy Interview of James Forsythe, PRA Director

January 2009, reprinted with permission

James "Juice" Forsythe was appointed by President George W. Bush to head up the brand-new Parahuman Resources Agency in December of 2006. After two years on the job, he used the canny leadership he exhibited as the leader of Just Cause to transform the PRA from a small office in the unfashionable wing of the Pentagon into a powerful administration in its own right, helping the world keep tabs on the ever-growing population of parahumans and using that intelligence to dispatch them to where they could do the most good.

We sent reporter Cheryl Bradley, who interviewed Jack "Crackerjack" Raymond in the October 2006 issue, to talk with Forsythe. She tells us:

"I met with Forsythe over two days in a Lower Manhattan tavern where we could look out across the Bay to see Fort Justice being renovated under its bright lights and scaffolding. Forsythe is a giant of a man, nearly having to duck and turn sideways through doorways so his shoulders don't get wedged. Despite being nearly fifty, he's in phenomenal shape and has been known to play pick-up basketball with a certain President-Elect. I asked him to demonstrate his parahuman powers and he said it wasn't really appropriate for the tavern, so we went to the alley out back. He took the battery from his own car and brushed the naked terminals. Sparks shot out as if we were using jumper cables. He drained the battery dry, then picked up a piece of rebar we found in the alley and bent it into a pretzel as easily as if it were actual dough. I offered to replace his battery myself but he wouldn't hear of it."

How is running the PRA different than leading Just Cause?

The hours are longer and the coffee isn't nearly as good. *[laughs]*

Honestly, I thought I was busy when I was in law school, and then I thought that was nothing. Being busy was running a superhero team. Now that I'm behind a desk, I look back at my years in costume and think how great it was to be able to just hit people who needed it.

The PRA is a challenging job, but it's one America has needed for a long time. After 9/11 and the loss of so many of our teammates, it only made sense for Just Cause to leave the private sector. With the resources of Homeland Security behind us, Just Cause could become a more effective force for good in America, and Mr. Bush was always a great fan of the team. I'm sure that's why he tapped me for the PRA position.

Now that there are so many new parahumans, and more of them turning up almost on a daily basis, there really needs to be an organization to help keep track of everyone. Names change, costumes change, but parahuman powers don't. It's been said the only thing that can stop a parahuman criminal is a parahuman cop, and the PRA exists to help those cops do a better job. Think of us like the FBI, but focused upon parahuman-related issues.

Those issues include the Champions. Talk a bit about that.

The idea came to us after seeing Champion's advertisement back in '07. There are a lot of parahumans out in the world. More than we know. More than most people can even imagine. Not everyone is cut out to be in Just Cause, though. There are very strict and exacting guidelines for membership in the world's premier superhero team, and even with the guidance provided by the excellent instructors at the Hero Academy, a lot of would-be heroes still don't quite measure up. That doesn't mean their desire to do good is any less, but for whatever reason, be it psychological, parapower-based, or something else, they are unfit for Just Cause membership.

We took Champion's idea and ran with it, setting up teams around the country with PRA backing. It's analogous to minor-league sports teams. Almost anyone can be a Champion. All it takes is some paperwork and a demonstration of abilities at a local Champion franchise. The idea is you don't have to be a full-time superhero if you don't want to be, but you can be on call if your particular skill set is needed. On the other hand, if you have the desire and motivation to be a superhero, the Champions give you that opportunity. And if you really prove yourself, there's always the chance you might get called up to the major leagues.

With the expanding parahuman population, the Hero Academy has been cranking out larger and larger graduating classes, and we at the PRA thought it might be time to expand Just Cause again, something we hadn't done since 1998. We approached the big private teams—the New Guard, the Lucky Seven—and asked if they wanted to become part of the Just Cause organization. Frankly, they jumped at the chance to have the kind of resources available to them that Just Cause has had for years. Other than the minor restructuring required to bring them from the private to government sector, the teams can still operate as they always have. Additionally, we're expanding to a total of eight Just Cause teams around the country [San Francisco, Seattle, Denver, Dallas/Fort Worth, Chicago, New York City, Richmond, and Miami—CB], each staffed with a mixture of rookies and experienced heroes. Chicago and San Francisco are already up and running, and Richmond has been around for ten years already. New York is next.

Is Champion in Just Cause now? Or is he running a Champions franchise?

We don't actually know where he is. It's one of the many unsolved mysteries at the PRA. We spent a lot of resources trying to track him down and identify the man behind the mask, but at the end of the day we never did figure out who he was. For all we know, he could be a Champion. All he had to do was take off the mask and we wouldn't ever know who he was before.

But his powers are identifiable, right?

Yes, that's part of what we do at the PRA. By cataloguing abilities, we have a better chance of identifying parahuman criminals, who change their names and costumes as often as some people change their clothes. And for that matter, a lot of them don't even bother with the whole super identity thing. It's one thing to rob a bank as Asphalt, and another to do so as just some guy with a throwaway identity. But if we know he has the ability to armor himself in paving compound, it's easier to find him no matter what name he's using.

Is that a violation of his civil rights?

Is it a violation for the FBI to profile criminals? To maintain a database of their fingerprints and vital statistics? To share information with other law enforcement agencies? No, of course not. That's what we do at the PRA. We profile and share information so Just Cause and Champions teams can respond accordingly.

That's the attorney in you talking. The PRA also profiles parahumans who haven't broken any laws, right?

Yes, but that's because parahuman abilities are a unique resource in the world, and if we have the resources to match someone's power to a situation where it can save lives or property, we're going to do it. For example, when that coal mine collapsed last month in Utah, we were able to get parahumans to that location within eighteen hours. One of them had the ability to generate oxygen sufficient to keep a dozen people alive in close quarters. Another could reshape solid rock. A third could generate a powerful force field. The three of them worked in tandem to explore deep into the mine, much faster and safer than mining crews could. Sadly, when they reached the trapped miners, they had already died, but at least we were able to recover their bodies. If the PRA hadn't had the resources we do, those miners might never have been found.

Although the primary Just Cause team will still be headquartered in Denver, the world is most anticipating the return of Just Cause to New York City. Tell us about the two heroes you've picked to spearhead the new branch.

Just Cause New York will be led by two heroes that happen to be close personal friends of mine. Mustang Sally, who's been like a daughter to me over the years, will be running the show. I was briefly in Just Cause with her parents *[Pony Girl and Audio—CB]* before one retired and the other died in 1985. I've watched Salena grow from a precocious youngster with unbelievable speed, into a talented young heroine with the strongest desire to do good I've ever encountered, into a confident leader. She's only twenty-four, but she's accomplished more in that time than a lot of people who are two, three times her age. Quite simply, I would trust her with my life, the lives of my children. If I had to call on only one single person to save the world, she'd be on my speed-dial. She will be a brilliant leader for what is likely to become the most well-known team of heroes on the planet.

Backing her up as her second-in-command will be Jack Raymond, whom everyone in the world already knows as Crackerjack and the so-called Face of Just Cause. Jack is old-school, like I am. We came up to the team together back in the '80s. He's sharp as a tack and has a surprisingly refreshing perspective when it comes to solving problems. It helps that he's pretty much fearless, and believe me, in New York, Just Cause will be under a constant spotlight, with everyone analyzing and second-guessing their every move.

People are already second-guessing you, based upon the heroes who will be filling out the ranks of the team. You've opened the door to a lot of potential criticism from every political corner.

[laughs] Well, if we went with a politically-safe route when it came to staffing, we'd have a team of uniformly ineffective people. Look at how certain Senators and Congressmen are insisting their goal has to be to make President-Elect Obama a single term president. I fear the next four years are going to be plagued by inertia and confrontation. You can't please everyone, so I'm not trying to please anyone with my staff selections for Just Cause New York. Instead, I'm picking a mix of heroes I feel will make a complete, useful team able to respond to a variety of emergencies, whether natural disasters, man-made disasters, or things we haven't even anticipated yet.

Besides Sally and Jack, we have four veteran heroes coming over from Just Cause: Mastiff, Minerva, Ment, and Snowball. In addition to them, we've drawn from the ranks of recent Hero Academy graduates to bring aboard Snapdragon and Shillelagh. We have a parolee from Deep Six, called Failsafe, who was instrumental in helping to halt the escape attempt back in 2006. He's volunteered to serve his parole and beyond as a member of Just Cause. Detroit Steel is an independent hero whom I've had my eye on for a couple of years, and she finally accepted a position with us. Finally, rounding things out we have a Chinese superhero named Yunbao, which means Clouded Leopard. She's here essentially as a visiting dignitary. China literally has tens of thousands of parahumans in its population, and the Chinese government is very interested in how the PRA and Just Cause are working together to put a structure in place for parahuman issues.

I can see how that will upset certain political elements. What you haven't said is that you've got a team staffed with hot potatoes: an LGBTQ hero, a Muslim, a Chinese citizen, an ex-con, the son of a supervillain, and the notorious Crackerjack, a man whose face has graced the cover of every tabloid on the planet.

He's also been interviewed here four times, as I recall.

I believe diversity makes for stronger teams. Like for a professional sports league, it's important for children of varying ethnic, religious, and political backgrounds to see athletes that can set aside their differences and work together. Parahumans are even more diverse in their origins, and I wanted to be sure the most visible team of all will have heroes anyone can look up to.

And it helps that they can kick ass when needed.

One

"Parahuman proliferation is the arms race of the 21st Century. We must take steps to ensure that America is at the forefront of this challenge."
—Senator Christine Goodwin (R-NY)

January, 2009
New York City, NY

"Mustang Sally, checking in at Pier 11." The microphone button sewn against the collar of her bodysuit picked up Sally's voice and relayed it across the water back to Fort Justice in New York Harbor. "I'm going to patrol."

"Control, receiving you." The disembodied voice sounded in her ear. "We'll monitor you and inform you if you're needed."

"Copy that." Sally took her goggles off her forehead and shook out her hair. She was still getting used to her new short hairstyle after years of having long braids hanging down her back. She'd felt like she needed a look that was more grown-up given her new command position, and had spent an entire weekend flipping through webpage after webpage of hairstyles until she'd found one she thought she could live with.

Jason had given her his blessing, and she'd cried when almost two feet of her hair hit the floor. Once the stylist had finished giving her a layered cut that accentuated her natural waves, she had to admit that she looked pretty good. At least it was easier to manage and could all fit beneath her cowl so it didn't get windburned. She pulled the cowl up and over her head, tucking any flyaway locks beneath the edges. The goggles went back on over the cowl, connecting to tiny catches that would keep them from being ripped away due to wind friction. She wouldn't be running fast enough to need the breath mask to protect her lungs, but she wore it anyway because there was nothing worse than aspirating road grit at triple-digit speeds.

Her face fully protected from the wind, she waved at the onlookers, and then lit out. Her perceptions accelerated along with her speed, giving her plenty of time to avoid collisions. She zipped across the pier and turned right to follow FDR Drive along the East River. She'd checked the GPS map on her phone on the ferry, and she knew to count bridges. The fourth one would be the Queensboro, and taking a left there would bring her right to Central Park, which was where her mother had run when she was in Just Cause back in the Seventies. The Brooklyn and Manhattan Bridges flashed past, great titans sprawling across the icy waters. Sally kept well to the right of traffic, running along the breakdown lane as much as possible. It had been her experience that running too close to the speed of traffic tended to be a distraction for drivers as they actually had time to look at her. Going two or three times faster than the flow meant she was gone from most drivers' vision before they really registered what they'd seen. When there was no breakdown lane, she dipped down an exit ramp to run beneath the FDR viaduct, having to weave around ubiquitous construction sites.

She passed by a lovely park near the Williamsburg Bridge, which was a welcome relief from all the gray. It was too early in the season for any real greenery, but a few hardy crocuses were pushing their way up through the dirt. Horns honked and a police siren blared and she wondered if she should stop, but one of the things Juice had told her was that Just Cause wasn't supposed to respond to every minor infraction or incident. If local law enforcement needed parahuman assistance, there were avenues for them to request it, whether from local-level Champions or escalating to Just Cause if needed. "It's important that local police don't grow to resent you. We want them to be willing to call for help, and they can't do that if they feel like you're trying to replace them."

"But how will I know what to do to help, then?"

"You'll know in your gut. You always have, Sally. That's why we chose you."

The buildings went from brown stone to gray as Sally continued her trek northward. She skipped off of FDR to run along a bike path right alongside the river. "Sally, Control," said the voice in her ear.

"Go ahead, Control."

"We've got some unusual activity on social network monitoring. Your name has popped up tied to Central Park and we don't show that you're anywhere near there yet."

Sally skidded to a halt, startling several joggers. "What do you mean, *my name has popped up*?"

"We're seeing images tagged with you. It looks like someone has burned letters spelling out your name into the grass on the southern end of Central Park. We're seeing multiple mentions of it as well as pictures."

"I'm heading there to investigate it now, Control. Is the fire out?"

"We have no information on it at this time."

"Copy that." Sally launched into motion once again, blowing well past a hundred fifty until the buildings and cars blurred past. She spotted an exit ramp and turned down it to head inland, towards Central Park. She had to be very careful on the narrow and congested road, and there were a lot more pedestrians milling about. She zigged and zagged around them, outrunning the confused and typical-New-Yorker angry shouts in her wake. She realized she'd turned the wrong way up a one-way street but it didn't matter; her speed made the cars seemed like they were standing still.

She slipped between a bus and a panel truck and then she was crossing a plaza into Central Park. "Control, I'm at Central Park. Where's this fire?"

"Roughly a hundred yards from the southeast corner," said the voice in her ear.

Sally slowed her headlong rush and lowered her rebreather. The chill air made her skin prickle and sting. The trees that would be so lush and green by the spring were still mostly bare black and gray trunks with branches like skeletal fingers. She sniffed at the air and there was indeed a tang of smoke present, which she recognized as the burning of dry grass, a common enough scent in Colorado during fire season. She raised her tinted goggles and tried to pick smoke out against the cloudy sky, but with no success.

"Hey, Mustang Sally!" someone called. She looked to see a young man waving at her. "Somebody wrote your name on the ground."

She moved beside him in a flash. "Where?"

He jumped at her sudden appearance. "Whoa!"

"Sir, please."

"Oh, sorry. Right over there, behind those trees." He licked his lips. "You, uh, you seeing anyone?"

She smiled at him. "I'm married."

"Yeah, but is it working out?"

She didn't dignify his query with a response. Instead, she zipped past him, through the trees, to confront whoever had called her out.

A woman in a tight-fitting turquoise and black bodysuit similar to Sally's in cut and design stood there, arms crossed, looking impatient. She was several inches taller than Sally—no real feat there, given Sally was barely over five feet tall herself—but with a much more muscular build. She wore a blue helmet with a gold-tinted visor and a rudder emerging from the back. Her boots were much more stylized in design than Sally's high-tech utilitarian clunkers. Instead of matching the blue-and-black color scheme, the other woman's boots were orange and red with a flame design upon them that reminded Sally of hot rod paint jobs.

"About time you showed up," she sneered at Sally. "For a speedster, you're pretty slow upstairs."

Sally felt her ears burn. She'd faced down some of the world's most dangerous supervillains and not only lived to tell about it, but in many cases been triumphant. How could this unknown woman get to her with such a simple insult? She made herself shake it off. The snide statement demanded a response, and although Sally wasn't the wittiest conversationalist in the world, she could at least hold her own. "If you were in that much of a hurry, why didn't you just call? I had to wait for social media to catch up." She folded her own arms. "Who are you and what do you want?"

The woman smiled behind her visor. Sally didn't recognize her face. She realized she ought to have cameras built into her goggles so she didn't have to take time to use her phone to snap a picture. She could take a picture faster than anyone could move, but she invariably moved too fast and the camera would only ever show a blur. "I'm Afterburner," said the woman. "And I'm here to take you down, Mustang Sally."

Sally snorted. "Just like that? You show up out of the blue, set some grass on fire, and now you're going to . . . to fight me like some kind of stupid archenemy? Who writes your dialogue, George Lucas?"

5

"Who's that? I don't . . . oh." Sally got the distinct impression that the woman was speaking to someone else. And then in a flash of motion the woman was in front of her. Sally's accelerated perceptions kicked in a fraction of a second too late—a side effect of never dealing with anyone whose speed could approach her own—and the woman shoved her backwards. Sally stumbled and fell onto her ass, bruising her tail bone on the hard-packed dirt with its layer of dead grass. "I'm not afraid of you. You ain't jack shit. Get up, or are you gonna just let me kick your ass laying down?"

Sally sprang to her feet, her heart hammering behind her ribs. In her life she'd encountered only two other parahumans with what she'd categorize as extreme examples of enhanced speed. Carousel was an advanced android who'd been a member of the Lucky Seven team where Sally had trained before joining Just Cause. Johnny Go was a good friend who'd gone through the Hero Academy and now one of the trainers for Champions. Neither of them came close to approaching Sally's level of speed; they were like thoroughbred racing horses trying to compete against a Formula I car.

This woman, Afterburner, was dangerously fast. Maybe even as fast as Sally. She was also bigger, stronger, and knew how to fight by the way she carried herself. Smoke leaked from beneath her feet and Sally realized she had another, even more sinister power. She could ignite the ground where she stood. Hence the name, Sally thought. Sally hadn't ever trained in physical combat very hard; with her speed, standing and fighting an opponent was a poor use of her abilities.

Afterburner leaped and spun, her right foot arcing around in a devastating roundhouse kick. Flames trailed off her heel, making a whooshing noise. Sally just barely ducked out of the way as Afterburner's foot flashed through the air where Sally's head had been a moment before. Sally tried to remember all her basic combat training, which she'd had in her very first year at the Hero Academy. She hadn't paid attention then, trusting her speed to get her out of a dangerous situation.

She hadn't ever planned for this. She threw a punch the way she'd seen Jason do it when he sparred with other bricks.

Afterburner laughed, slapped aside Sally's ineffectual blow, and smashed her helmet against Sally's face. Sally's mouth and nose filled with blood. She staggered back, tears of pain blinding her. Her foot caught against something and she fell. Afterburner leaped into a forward tuck. She extended her right foot as she came up and around, lashing downward with an axe kick that could have broken any bone it struck. Sally rolled aside to avoid the strike and kicked at Afterburner's ankle. Afterburner turned her foot enough that Sally's kick only glanced off the edge. "That's more like it. Ain't no fun when they don't have any spirit."

She stomped down on Sally's leg but Sally's heavy boot absorbed the worst of the blow. Sally tried to fight back by grabbing at the woman's foot, but it was like grabbing a pan out of the oven without a hot pad. Sally yelped as she burned her fingers through her gloves. Blood ran down the side of her face and dribbled onto her logo.

Afterburner lunged and grabbed Sally's neck. "There's a new sheriff in town, bitch."

Sally felt her lungs burning and she struggled against the woman's grip. Afterburner lifted her off the ground. Sally tried to kick but she had no strength left as the life was being choked out of her. As a last-ditch effort, she let go of Afterburner's wrists, grabbed the woman's helmet, and twisted it hard to one side. The helmet turned faster than Afterburner's head did and the edge of the visor opening cracked hard across Afterburner's nose, breaking it. Afterburner dropped her and struggled with her helmet, cursing and spitting out blood.

Sally ran. She couldn't stand and trade punches with Afterburner; the woman fought like a martial artist, and Sally barely had basic brawling skills. Afterburner was after her in a flash and they raced across the park, a red streak pursued by a blue one. Sally's head cleared as she ran, but she had to keep spitting out blood so she wouldn't swallow it, and she couldn't breathe through her swollen nose so her breath mask was out of the question.

They raced through the trees, whipping up a storm of dry grass, dead leaves, and twigs in their wake. Sally realized not only was Afterburner a much better fighter, but the blue-garbed woman was keeping pace with her. Sally put her head down and poured on the speed. She'd broken the speed of sound once; she could outrun Afterburner. Everywhere her pursuer set a foot down, the ground was left smoldering, but Sally discovered she could turn and change directions much faster. She doubled back twice, forcing Afterburner to skid to a stop with a curse each time.

"I know, I know," Afterburner yelled at whoever was on the other end of her radio.

That gave Sally an idea. She headed across the gigantic meadow where she could really unleash the speed. With her attention no longer needed to keep her from smashing into a tree trunk, she called in to headquarters. "Control, Sally. I'm engaged with an unknown parahuman assailant," she gasped out between breaths. "Enhanced speed at my level. Scramble backup."

"Roger that, Sally," said the voice in her ear. "The *Dorothy* will be airborne in five minutes. ETA to your location in thirteen minutes, plus or minus two minutes."

Sally wasn't sure she'd last another five minutes against Afterburner. Her backup might arrive to find themselves claiming her body. "Sooner would be better, Control. Also, she's in radio communication with someone. Try to locate and track that signal."

"That may be difficult given your speed and altitude, but we'll work on it. You could shave five minutes off the response time if you came to the southern tip of Manhattan."

"Negative. Central Park is the safest place for this. Sally out." Being late winter, the park wasn't nearly as crowded as it might have been had the weather been warmer. She dashed across a bridge and around a rocky outcropping, trying to outmaneuver her pursuer.

"You won't get away like that," hissed Afterburner. She sounded winded to Sally. Perhaps she didn't have Sally's stamina for long sprints.

"I don't have to get away. I just have to outlast you." Sally grabbed hold of a sign pole and swung, letting her momentum carry her around it like a tether ball. Her feet flashed over a sliding Afterburner's head, just missing a double kick that might have decapitated her assailant, or broken every bone in Sally's legs, or both.

Afterburner rolled into a combat crouch to face Sally as Sally dropped down beside the sign pole, her sides heaving. Behind her visor, Afterburner's face was crimson and evaporating sweat rose off her body like steam in the chilly air. "That was dirty." Smoke curled upward from around her feet as the grass beneath them ignited.

"You want to call this off now, before one of us gets really hurt? Come on, I'll buy you a beer and you can tell me what I did to earn your wrath." Sally held out a hand. "What's your name?"

"Martina. What? I know, I know!"

"Who are you talking to? Sounds like they're being a real pain in your ass. Somebody putting you up to this?"

"Shut up, I got this."

9

Sally couldn't tell if Afterburner was talking to her or to whoever was on the other end of her radio. "Look, if you're in trouble, let me help you. You might have heard that me and my people are pretty good at this sort of thing."

"*I know!*" Afterburner charged at Sally.

"Shit." Sally found herself engaged before she had a chance to flee. She danced backward, ducking underneath Afterburner's punches and jumping to avoid her kicks. The flurry of limbs seemed to come at her from every direction. A hard roundhouse kick caught her hip and made her right leg go numb. Afterburner followed up with a hard punch straight to Sally's face. Blood splattered up Afterburner's hand from Sally's already-bruised nose, and she yelped from the pain. Her hands found her horseshoes where they were still clamped to her belt. Over the years she'd used them as brass knuckles when she needed a little more heft to her super-speedy punches, and if there was ever a moment where that was required, this was it.

Afterburner punched at her again and Sally dropped her chin so Afterburner's fist smashed against her forehead, breaking her goggles. Sally responded by driving the twin forks of the horseshoe clutched in her right hand hard into Afterburner's visor. The yellow-tinted faceplate cracked and the sharp plastic ends lacerated Afterburner's face.

She staggered back, shrieking incoherence. Sally knew she should have pressed the advantage while she had it, but her entire face hurt, and her nose and lips were swelling like an allergic reaction. Her vision was growing blurry but she didn't know whether it was because of swelling around her eyes or something worse. She'd suffered concussions before and knew she was high risk for them.

She hooked the horseshoes back on her belt and ran again, hoping she could outrun Afterburner. With her goggles destroyed, she couldn't get up much faster than two hundred or so before the stream of icy air against her tender face became too much to bear. She skirted the edge of the large lake. When she looked back over her shoulder, she didn't see any sign of Afterburner, and thought perhaps she'd escaped the mysterious speedster at last. But then she glanced back across the lake and got the shock of her life.

Afterburner was crossing straight over the surface of the water, racing toward Sally like a speed skater. Her feet kicked up steamy rooster tails of water vapor with every step.

"No. No way." That wasn't fair. Not only was Afterburner fast, setting fires with every step, and a superior hand-to-hand fighter, but she could run on water too? Physics said Sally should have been able to cross open water at her speeds without any problems, but she couldn't do it no matter how many times she tried. Deep down, she knew it was a psychological barrier, but that didn't change the fact that Sally couldn't run across water and Afterburner was racing towards her. Sally gathered up a handful of suitably flat rocks and hurled them at Afterburner, using her speed to accelerate the stones like bullets.

Afterburner stepped around the first couple of skipping stones but then one caught her in the knee and another followed immediately after, striking the top of her foot. Sally saw blood splatter from each wound. Afterburner yelped and lost her balance. She fell sideways, kicking up a tremendous wave as she plowed into the water. The water seemed to move like molasses in Sally's accelerated perceptions, and she saw Afterburner tumble into it in a jumble of twisting limbs. Sally didn't like the way Afterburner's head snapped back when it hit the water, and she slowed her racing senses to get a better feel for time passing. Seconds ticked away and still Afterburner didn't emerge from the water.

Sally realized that the other speedster wasn't going to come up. "Shit." She raced to unlace her tall boots. "Control. ETA to my location." Speaking hurt her face, she discovered, and so did wincing at the pain.

"Less than four minutes."

Sally shook her head. "Not fast enough. Tell them to prepare for a water rescue, and get some paramedics out here stat!" She yanked off her thick socks, cringing at the cold on her bare feet, and charged into the water.

She still couldn't run across the water, but years of trying had necessitated her becoming a good swimmer, and she struck out toward the area where she'd seen Afterburner go under. The icy water seeped into her uniform and made her hands and feet go numb instantly. At least the cold would help with the swelling in her face, although her swollen nose made it impossible for her to swim in any way but a dog paddle.

It was a speedy dog paddle, though, and she found Afterburner after only a few seconds. The waterlogged woman was a few feet below the surface, unmoving. Sally took a deep breath and dove down beneath Afterburner, moving her legs in a blur to push the woman back to the surface. Their heads broke water and Sally grabbed Afterburner beneath her arms and kicked backward, pushing for the shoreline.

She was so cold she barely felt her feet brush against the soft bottom, and a moment later she was dragging Afterburner up onto the sand at the water's edge. Both women choked, coughing up lake water. Sally's shivers seemed to take over her entire body. As the water drained from her ears, she heard the distant roar of the approaching *Dorothy*, loud enough to drown out the much closer howls of emergency vehicles. "Y-you all r-right?" she managed through chattering teeth.

Afterburner gagged and spit up a lungful of water onto the sand, so weak that she couldn't even raise her head. Steam rose from her feet as the heat they produced evaporated the lake water. Sally could feel the radiance from them and wondered if it would be too weird to use them to warm herself back up. "W-why?" asked Afterburner. "I t-tried to . . . You still s-saved me."

"I'm a hero. That's what we d-do." Her chattering teeth made her nose throb.

"What? No. I'm not—" Afterburner paused and her eyes narrowed. "What do you m-mean *no longer required*?" She started to say something else but Sally's perceptions accelerated to their maximum and for a moment she didn't understand why, but then she saw Afterburner's face tearing apart as slow-motion flames forced their way through her skin. Sally was fast, but she was exhausted and injured and the shock wave of the explosion caught her as she turned to flee and sent her tumbling along the sand of the lake front. When she rolled over to look back at Afterburner, she saw the woman's helmet split in half and nothing but ruin above her neck and below her wrists.

Feeling like she'd failed, Sally lay back and cried silent, painful tears as the *Dorothy* circled overhead, spilling colorful heroes from its bomb bay doors.

* * *

They gave Sally New York.

She'd known Just Cause was going to expand, because Juice had already talked to her and the other team members about it. She'd suspected she would be put in charge of one of the expansions, because the PRA needed experienced leaders for the new superhero teams across the country, and no matter how little confidence Sally felt she had in her own abilities, everyone else seemed to think she was darn good at being a superhero.

But New York? Come on, that was ridiculous. New York was the most important city in the country, maybe in the world. Just Cause hadn't had a presence there since 9/11, and now they were going back with a brand new team in a brand new facility, and Sally was Head Chef and Chief Bottle Washer.

It was ruining her beauty sleep.

Even though the official facility was called *Just Cause New York Headquarters*, everyone in the media referred to it as *Fort Justice*, which rolled off the tongue much easier. It was a refurbished oil platform, cleaned and rebuilt into a high-tech superhero headquarters and sitting well out in the middle of New York Bay. The first day on board, Sally and Jason had stood on the deck, bundled up against the chill wind of the Atlantic coast winter, and could just make out the Statue of Liberty to the north through the gray skies. Jason squeezed her hand and Sally began to think that maybe they would be okay after all.

Just as long as she didn't look down. She understood the reason for placing Fort Justice out in the water, well away from the skyline of Manhattan and the rest of the densely-populated East Coast. Like it or not, Just Cause was and always would be a strategic target for terrorists, parahuman criminals, and even foreign military powers. After losing more than half the team when their headquarters in World Trade Center 2 took the jet strike point blank in 2001, the organization had learned from its mistakes. Isolating the headquarters meant collateral damage in an attack would be minimal at worst. The facility wasn't entirely toothless either. Besides carrying a large complement of powerful parahumans, Sally knew the breakaway buildings at the corners of the top deck housed turrets of surface-to-air missiles and cannons.

The turrets made Sally think of explosives, which reminded her that someone hadn't wanted Just Cause to dig deeper into the mystery of Afterburner, and that had Sally pacing at super-speed through the Command

Center. She wished Jason was around, but knew he was doing important work down in the training center, working with the structural engineers, testing the limits of the reinforcements they'd built inside one of Fort Justice's legs, and interrupting it for personal reasons would be extremely unprofessional of her. She left the Command Center, probably to the relief of the crew trying to get everything up and running, and retreated into her office.

Her office. When had she ever needed an office before? She didn't even know what she was supposed to do in one. She had a big comfy chair, a sleek, modern-looking desk. There was a slender laptop folded shut on top of it and she knew she had a printer and scanner built into one of the drawers, in case she ever needed to print out pictures of cats she found on the internet, she supposed. One wall was dominated by a huge flatscreen television that had her aching to lock the door up tight and watch classic space operas until she could forget about the problems of the real world. Another had distressingly empty bookshelves, with only a hard-bound copy of the *Just Cause Rules and Regulations* manual, Matasuko Musashi's *The Origin of Parapowers*, and Grace Devereaux's definitive work on the team her grandfather had envisioned, *Just Cause: Sixty Years of Heroism*. Sally knew she should at least put up her copy of her own grandfather's book, *Dangerous: The Autobiography of Doctor Danger*. What else was she supposed to do with those shelves? She barely had time to read for pleasure, much less for work. Her office even had its own wet bar, in case she wanted to get started on her alcoholism, she supposed. She wondered if she could even get a cup of coffee. She had a feeling she was going to need to be freebasing caffeine if she was going to get a handle on weaving all the various strings it took to run a superhero team together into something resembling an actual tapestry.

"*Now buttle off and tell Baron Brunwald that Lord Clarence McDonald and his lovely assistant are here to view the tapestries,*" Sally uttered in a horrible impression of a Scottish brogue. Thinking of tapestries had put her in mind of the line from *Indiana Jones and the Last Crusade*, and she was thinking about running back down to hers and Jason's apartment to find her DVD and hide somewhere to watch it when a knock on her door startled her.

Sally's heart leaped into her throat. Had someone read her mind? Was there an emergency already? Maybe Fort Justice had sprung a leak and was heading for the bottom of the Bay. A million disastrous possibilities raced through her mind as she crossed the office to open the door. "Yes?"

She found herself face-to-face with a slender woman in a gray business suit, bearing a mass of wavy blonde hair that immediately made her miss her braids. Sally realized she was staring at the young woman's hair and made herself look into the woman's eyes instead. "Can I help you?"

The woman extended her hand and Sally shook it. "I'm Davey Spicoli, no relation to the Ridgemont High character. I'm your new assistant."

"I have an assistant?"

Davey smiled. "James Forsythe personally offered me the position. I was working at his law firm. He said this would be more of a challenge for me, and I do love a good challenge." She looked Sally up and down. "I'd say you're overdue for some help. What are the three things you need off your plate most right this second?"

"I, uh, I'm not even sure what's on my plate. I feel like, um, I'm a little lost, I guess." Sally almost felt like crying at the admission, which would have done nothing to improve her outlook on her new job.

Davey stepped past her into the office and shut the door. "You're from Arizona, aren't you?"

"Yes . . ."

Davey went to the wall thermostat and upped the temperature several degrees. Then she picked up the remote, turned on the flatscreen television, and selected a screensaver that showed a rocky desert landscape, loaded with mesquite trees and saguaro cacti. "This is your office. It needs to feel like it belongs to you. If you want to change anything about it, let me know and I'll make it happen."

The hot air blowing from the heat vents and the serene desert landscape had already done wonders to cut down on Sally's stress level. All she needed was a little soft music and it would almost feel like a place in which she could truly relax. "That's really great. I didn't even think about that."

"That's why I'm here. To think about the things you don't, and to try to have solutions to your problems before you even have them." Davey pulled a PDA from her jacket pocket. "Would you feel more comfortable having your calendar information in hard copy or sent to your phone and desktop computer?"

"Um, electronic is fine."

Davey made a note. "I've sent you all my contact information. You can text or call me anytime, day or night. I have quarters here on base, and I will match my own schedule to yours." She handed Sally a piece of paper. "These are my credentials and security clearance. I can pre-screen your emails for you, and I have access to your files. You can lock me out of any of them at any time if you need to."

"Wow. That's, um, that's great." Sally glanced at the paperwork Davey had handed her, realized she wouldn't know forged papers from legitimate, and decided Davey wouldn't have gotten this far purely on bullshit. She'd call Juice later just to make sure everything was on the up and up, but Davey exuded confidence, which was exactly what Sally needed. "So you said three things I need right now? I need to know where everyone on my team is and how soon they can all be here for a meeting. I need to put together a duty and training schedule. I need a cup of coffee, but I can get that myself." She paused, trying to remember her whirlwind tour of Fort Justice. "As soon as I remember where the cafeteria is."

Davey snorted. "This place is a maze. Some hospitals use colored stripes on the floors to help guide people through them. I'll see about getting something like that set up here. Coffee I can do right now. I'm going to get you your own brew station to put on your bar so you don't have to go looking when you really need your fix. A place like this runs on caffeine. I'll have a duty and training schedule lined up for you in an hour and a report on your personnel and a selection of meeting times then as well. Sound good?"

"It sounds amazing. Davey, are you a parahuman?"

Davey stopped by the door and smiled. "Nope. Just goddamn efficient."

"Yeah, you are. Thank you." Sally sat down in her chair, took a deep breath, and smiled.

Things were going to be okay.

* * *

Some time less than an hour later, but long enough that Sally finished the amazing cup of coffee Davey had sent up, Jason stopped by her office to report on the status of the Combat Simulation Chamber. Also, to deliver hugs and kisses to his wife, but that was something Sally intended to try to keep out of the view of coworkers, mindful of the discomfort it caused. A husband-wife duo, MetalBlade and Icebreaker, had been running the Just Cause Second Team in Richmond for years, and nobody ever brought up their marriage because they kept things professional in public. Sally intended to emulate that, no matter how good Jason looked when he was in his post-workout afterglow.

She allowed herself one lengthy, deep passionate kiss. Then another. Then she made herself push away before things went any further. "Save it for tonight, silly boy. I'm working right now."

Jason's lopsided grin and twinkling blue eyes nearly made Sally go back on her intentions. "Looks to me like you're watching TV and basking in a furnace."

"It's not a furnace. This is the kind of regular temperature people are supposed to live in, not that blizzard outside." This was old, familiar ground for the two of them. Despite growing up in Georgia, Jason had the kind of thick skin that made him immediately at home in subzero temperatures, whereas Sally began to complain as soon as the numbers on the thermometer dropped below the fifty-degree mark. "Did you know I have an assistant?"

"No. What's that like?"

"It's pretty awesome, actually. I think with her help, I might actually get a handle on this potential disaster." Sally perched on the edge of her desk, fussing with her abnormally short hair and wishing she had braids again. "So tell me about the CSC."

"It's tall. I mean, like, really tall. We can do a lot of high-rise training sessions in there. It'll be good for our fliers and climbers. Do we have any climbers?"

"Yunbao and Shillelagh. Neither of whom are here yet. Davey—that's my assistant—she's supposed to be tracking the rest of the team down for me."

Davey poked her head into the office. "And she's done. Got a minute, Sally?"

"Of course. Davey, this is my husband, Jason."

"Also known as Mastiff. Of course. I've read your file." Davey stuck out her hand and shook Jason's giant paw without the fear that most normal folks would have when touching someone who could toss cars around like toys. "Davey Spicoli. No relation to the Ridgemont High character."

"Uh, what?" Jason looked to Sally for help.

"It's a movie. Sean Penn was in it," said Sally. "Before he was an Academy Award guy. You found my missing personnel?"

"Yes. Minerva, Ment, Snowball, Snapdragon, and Failsafe are already on base. Shillelagh and Detroit Steel are coming in on the very next ferry. In fact, they should arrive in about fifteen minutes if you want to meet them. Yunbao apparently had some problems at the Embassy and she's flying in directly from Washington with Crackerjack. They're scheduled to arrive in forty-five minutes."

"What kind of problems?" asked Sally.

"I wasn't privy to the particulars. I can try to find out for you if it's important."

"No, I guess it's just normal political garbage. How dare we have a Chinese superhero here on American soil and all that. They're already screaming about it all over talk radio."

"I didn't know you listened to that stuff," said Jason.

"I don't, but it's hard to get away from it, and the media is always reporting on *this hater* and *that hater.*"

"It's a tough time to be a superhero." Jason rested his hand on Sally's shoulder and she leaned her cheek against it.

"I think it's what you make of it," said Davey. "James Forsythe tried to recruit me to work for him at the PRA and I said no, but I'd work for Just Cause. I might not be a parahuman, but that doesn't mean I can't be a super assistant to one."

"Aren't you an attorney?" asked Sally. "I mean, you're from his law firm, right?"

"Yeah, I never really got the hang of courtroom etiquette. I'm more effective working behind the scenes."

"The perfect assistant." Jason grinned.

"Now if you're going to go meet your new team members, you'd better go get ready. Sally, your overcoat is hanging in the closet, and I'll send up some hot chocolate. I sent you a list of suggested times for your initial team meeting. The soonest available is three hours from now. That work for you?"

Sally nodded, flabbergasted by Davey's efficiency.

Davey left the office again.

"She's like a force of nature, that one. You're lucky to have her."

"I'm lucky to have you, doofus."

"That too."

* * *

They met Shillelagh and Detroit Steel down at water level, where the ferry docked. The former was a Bostonian and recent graduate from the Hero Academy. When in costume, she wore a billowing crimson wig, but in reality her hair was short and black, but she moved with an unnatural grace. Sally knew Shillelagh had what equated to perfect balance and body control with the ability to run across anything that would support her weight, no matter how slender or wiggly. She stepped off the swaying ferry with her duffel bag slung over one shoulder and her shillelagh, a four-foot-long hardwood cudgel with a bulbous head and a sharp steel spike tip, resting across the other.

Detroit Steel's body was made of steel much in the same way as the principal of the Hero Academy John Stone's body was made of granite. Dreadlocks like coiled springs hung halfway down her back where they made a noise like cables crunching over each other. The cold didn't seem to bother her, and in fact she only wore a t-shirt and a pair of gym shorts. Sally was surprised the woman's bare feet didn't clank on the decking, but upon closer inspection, it looked like she had glued rubber pads onto her feet and likewise onto her palms and fingertips.

"I better not rust, workin' out here," said Detroit Steel, and Sally wasn't sure if she was joking or not.

Sally and Jason showed the newest recruits to their quarters, and Sally assigned a Command Center employee to give them a tour of the entire facility.

"Guess we better head topside to meet the *Dorothy.*" Jason checked the time on his phone. "Jack and, uh, the other noob ought to be here shortly."

"Her name's Yunbao," said Sally. "And you really ought to read up on her. Did you know she's Lionheart's daughter?"

"Lionheart? But she's Chinese."

"He went to China for a few years after leaving Just Cause. She looks a lot like him according to her pictures."

"Does she speak English?"

"Her file says she does." An icy wind swept across the upper deck of Fort Justice, making Sally consider whether she might run back downstairs to her quarters to put on yet one more layer before the *Dorothy* arrived bearing the last two errant members of the team.

Sally held her cranberry overcoat tightly about her, and the ends of her golden scarf flapped in the breeze. Jason stood beside her in what amounted to a sweatshirt and windbreaker, his cheeks and nose reddened in the cold, sniffling cheerfully as he squinted into the gray skies. Sally had placed herself strategically close to him so his bulk would block the worst of the wind. "There's the *Dorothy* now." Sally pointed at the approaching lights. "It'll be good to see Jack again. Feels like it's been weeks."

The VTOL jet circled around the platform once, and then set down on the pad with a gentle bump. Jack stepped out of the side door, all smiles and curly hair blowing in the downdraft. "Sally! Great to see you, kid." He hugged her.

"You too. Where's all your gear?" Jack was normally a walking arsenal, carrying a variety of tactical and special purpose equipment and weapons because, in his words, he liked to have choices.

"What, I got here without my luggage? I'm going to give the airline a piece of my mind." He chuckled. "No, it's shipping separately."

"How's Sondra?" Sondra was Desert Eagle, second-in-command of Just Cause back in Denver, and Sally's best friend in the whole world. She was also Jack's longtime girlfriend and more recently, his wife.

"Feathery." Jack laughed. "And I'm sure she's pining away for me already. I know I am for her."

"I promise that once I get my feet under me, I'll give you some time to head home. Oh, hello!" Sally tried not to stare at Yunbao as she stepped off the jet, wrapped in a parka and jeans and a large bag clutched in one clawed hand.

Sally had only ever seen pictures of Lionheart, who'd died at the same time as her father, before she was born, but seeing a true animalistic person up close for the first time was jarring. The young Chinese woman had skin covered with short, tawny fur that seemed to shimmer under the landing platform lights. She had the broad nose of a lion and her upper lip forked like a cat's, but her eyes were slanted and dark like a native Asian's. Her soft brown hair resembled a mane in texture but was pulled back into a ponytail. Her ears were pointed and sat higher on her head than a normal human's would. There was no sign of the black blotches that decorated her fur in the photos in her file, and Sally wondered if she painted them on with some kind of makeup.

Sally extended her hand. "Yunbao, I'm Mustang Sally. Welcome to Just Cause."

The cat-like woman shook her hand. Sally shivered at the sensation of claws lightly pricking against her skin. "I am pleased to be here."

"Come on, let's get in out of this wind before we all freeze," said Jack before Sally could suggest the same thing, and she looked at him in gratitude. Being invulnerable to harm extended to things like frostbite, and it was doubtful he was the least bit uncomfortable, but Jack was one of her closest friends and he knew her almost as well as Jason did.

The four heroes left the landing pad for the warmer corridors of Fort Justice. "Did you guys get to eat yet?" Sally asked.

"Nope, and yes, we'd love to," said Jack.

"Me, too," added Jason, who was always hungry.

"Well, we don't have a precognitive chef here on base . . ." Sally referred to the legendary house chef for Just Cause back in Denver. "But Chef Moroni is pretty darn good and knows her way around something called nouveau Italian."

"I'm going to die fat and happy from a pasta overdose." Jason rubbed his stomach.

"Why don't you guys take an hour to get settled in from your trip and whatnot?" said Sally. "We'll have a team dinner, followed by a meeting."

Jack winced. "You have to go and ruin a perfectly good meal with a meeting? It's my first day, Sally."

"We've got a lot of new faces and stuff to get through, and that's as good a time as any." Sally winked at him. "Besides, I know how much you love the meetings. Thrive on them, you will. Stronger, you will become."

"Whatever you say, Yoda." Jack chuckled. "Let's hope your first meeting here goes better than your first meeting in Denver."

Sally recalled how her own first day as an intern at Just Cause had culminated in a meeting interrupted by an emergency call-out. It had been a serious case of being thrown into the deep end of the pool with the hope that she could swim. She'd floundered and nearly drowned, but somehow she managed to stay afloat in the insane asylum that was being part of the world's greatest team of superheroes. "You realize that by putting it out there, you're just tempting fate, Jack. Now we'll get called out for sure."

Jack grinned. "Of course we will. We're Just Cause. That's the way it goes."

Two

"The very presence of so-called parahuman law-enforcement has been shown to increase the likelihood of parahuman attacks in the same geographic area. These are verifiable statistics, people."
—Ken Reichel, Top Flight Radio Network

January, 2009
New York City, NY

Sally coded the get-to-know-your-teammates meeting as *full dress*, which meant everyone was to show up in costume, or at least as much of a costume as they would normally wear in the field.

The notion of superheroes wearing costumes and utilizing code names was a practice that began during and after World War II. The first publicly known parahumans were a pair of commando squads in the U.S. Army that fought both in Europe and the Pacific theaters. Sally's grandmother was on one of those squads as the speedster Colt, who could outrace Army jeeps on foot. The Army did love their code names and every soldier involved in Projects Circus and Shetland was given a unique codename, reminiscent of their powers. The practice of parahumans using codenames continued after the war, partly to honor the traditions established by the first and partly to disguise identities.

The first two parahumans to wear costumes were the veterans Strongman and Flicker, both of whom had suffered grotesque scarring and mutilation in their final European mission. In order not to repulse the public when they began operating as superheroes in private life, they wore masks and special outfits that made them instantly recognizable, often enough to stop would-be criminals in their tracks.

Sally sat at the head of the conference room table and looked around the room at the colorfully-attired people staring back at her and felt a little sick to her stomach. She'd never much liked public speaking, but she knew she had to learn to get over it. Being a team leader meant she'd always be dealing with press conferences and inquiries and the like, so she'd better start with getting used to speaking to her teammates. And really, they weren't just teammates. She was their commanding officer.

She'd better start acting like it.

She cleared her throat. "Uh . . ." It wasn't a very auspicious start to her first meeting. She made the mistake of glancing at Jack, who had pasted an expression of rapt attention on his face, like a kindergartener at story time. He did that every time she had to speak in public, the jerk. She almost had to bite her tongue to keep from bursting into nervous giggles. Her gaze wandered over to Jason, who gave her an encouraging nod, which helped much more.

"Welcome to Just Cause New York. I'm Salena Tibbets, also known as Mustang Sally, and I'm in charge here." That was better, but it sounded a little too bossy. "I mean, uh, somebody's got to be, and I'm who they picked. This is my first command role, and I'm a little nervous, so if you all can bear with me I think we'll get through it."

Jason and Jack both started clapping, and the other heroes joined in as well, and Sally had to stand mute, waiting for the applause to die down. It felt like it took forever. "Anyway, I think we'll begin by introducing around the table. *I don't know half of you half as well as I should like, and I like less than half of you half as well as you deserve.*"

Her *Fellowship of the Ring* quote was met with vague confusion around most of the table except from Jack, who was as well-versed in movie lore as Sally. "I guess that makes me a fool of a Took," he said. He wore his standard tactical gear outfit, although the equipment webbing stretched across his torso was bare of even the smallest knife. Most SWAT officers would wear helmets and bulletproof vests and such, but Jack was immune to all kinds of harm, and his outfit was mostly utilitarian in design. "I'm Jack Raymond, also known as Crackerjack. You may possibly have seen me on television or in magazines." He had, in fact, been voted among *People* magazine's *Fifty Sexiest Stars* several times, a fact of which he was rather proud. "I've been in the superhero game longer than anyone else here. Almost twenty years, in fact. And because of that, they made the thoroughly amusing decision to make me second-in-command, a position which I'm sure I will use to embarrass the entire organization to great effect before I'm done." He grinned. "I also hate meetings."

"Thanks, Jack, I'll try not to have too many," said Sally. "Jason?"

Jason grinned, as usual. He still looked fantastic to Sally in his gray and brown form-fitting bodysuit. Unlike some modern heroes, his suit still incorporated a half-mask that allowed his blonde hair to flop around his face. The mask was his way of honoring those who had come before him, the heroes of the Fifties and Sixties, who had to hide their identities because it had been illegal to be a parahuman during that era. Sally liked to think things were more permissive in modern times, but then it seemed like there were always rumblings of a new Parahuman Registration and Identification Act or something of its ilk. How great of a step would it be to get there, what with the PRA already keeping tabs on parahumans across the country and even around the world? "I'm Jason Tibbets, also known as Mr. Mustang Sally, or Mastiff to my friends." He hadn't bothered to pull his mask up and over his ears, leaving it crumpled around his neck like a cowboy's bandana. "Super-strong, super-tough, and can eat more chicken wings than any three of you combined."

"Believe it," said Ment. "I've seen tigers tear apart entertainers with less gusto. Uh, no offense . . . Leopard Girl, is it?"

"None taken." Yunbao's voice was a surprising husky alto. "Clouded Leopard is how my name translates into English, but I prefer Yunbao. It is easier to say or shout in the heat of battle."

Detroit Steel rapped her knuckles on the table with a loud clink. "I heard that. My name's long enough that the bad guys will get away while you're saying it."

Sally cleared her throat. This was the way every Just Cause meeting had gone as long as she could remember. Tangents, distractions, and one harried leader, either Juice or after him Doublecharge, trying desperately to keep the wallowing ship of fools on course. "Ment, you're up."

Ment didn't so much wear a costume as rock a look. Dressed all in black from head to toe with skinny jeans and combat boots, a tight black t-shirt over his slender chest, wraparound sunglasses resting on top of his hair and a long lightweight overcoat, he looked like he'd stepped right out of *The Matrix*. He was the son of a former supervillain and had worked hard to overcome his family's reputation. "I'm Ment. Short for Mentat if you want to get technical, but nobody calls me that. Or Ryan Wheeler, either. Telepathy and related Jedi Mind Tricks."

Minerva didn't wait for Sally to point to her. When heading into battle, she wore a Roman centurion-style cuirass and helmet, and carried a spear. The rest of the time she wore a voluminous, hooded burgundy cloak. Sally hadn't ever seen her put on the armor and was of the opinion that it just sort of . . . *appeared.* "I'm Minerva, and that's my name, too. My abilities center around my senses, which are significantly improved over a normal human's, and paying attention to what they tell me." She clasped her hands on the table in front of her and looked to her left at Snowball.

Snowball, being barely three feet tall, had a special chair to accommodate her stature. It lowered so she could easily get into it and then raised so she could sit at a height to make interaction with her teammates that much easier. Her outfit of light blue and white fur trim looked like it might have been modeled after a nine-year-old figure skater's, although no child had curves like the little woman did. "Hi everyone. I'm Sara Gunnarsson, a.k.a. Snowball. I'm the opposite of Snapdragon, the Human Barbecue over here. He can cook the steaks, and I'll make sure the beers are ice cold." She made a swirling cloud of frost appear over one hand. "Don't call me a midget and we'll get along just fine. I'm bad-ass."

"I can vouch for that," said Snapdragon beside her. He was the son of Algerian immigrants and looked the part with a rust-colored burnoose over a tight red vest and loose-fitting trousers. A crimson turban was wound tightly around his head and hung beneath his chin as well. His dark beard was well-trimmed and he spoke with the slightest hint of a Chicago accent, reflecting his upbringing in the stomping grounds of the Lucky Seven team. He was one of the rookies, gangly and eager to prove himself. "We were training together earlier. We turned the CSC into a sauna. I think the technicians were pissed. Anyway, I'm Nabil Al-Ejel, but I know you guys will never remember that. My roommate at the Academy called me Nabi. I can shoot, you know, fire and stuff."

"Fire and stuff," repeated Jack. "Sally, I can't deal with all the high-level terminology you darn kids are spouting off. Get off my lawn!"

Sally snorted and ignored Jack. Apparently his meeting shenanigans hadn't dampened in the least from his time under Juice and Doublecharge as commanders. He could try anyone's patience, and that was one of the things Sally had to struggle with on a daily basis. "Go ahead, Aramis."

Aramis was a heavy-set Hispanic. Being a former supervillain named *Escudo* had made him into one of the oddest kind of notorious celebrities, up there with the athletes who got slapped on the wrist for their domestic violence and the actors who threw legendary hotel-room-destroying tantrums. He tried to stay out of the limelight as much as possible, but was a favorite target for anti-parahuman politicians. Neither did it help that he was a naturalized immigrant from south of the border. "I am Aramis Solano. Failsafe. I create force screens."

"Guess I'm next," said Detroit Steel. She tapped her metallic fingers on the conference room table again. "I'm Shawna Steele. Detroit Steel, and proud of it. You can call me Dee. Or Steel. Or just *Hey you* so long as I know you mean me. My family worked for car companies for years. I want to go back to Detroit and start a team there."

"That's an admirable goal," said Jack. "If there was ever a town that needed some real heroes, it's Detroit. I hate seeing a place like that go down the tubes."

"You and me both. Anyway, I'm strong and tough like Mastiff over there, and I'm also made of good old-fashioned American steel." Detroit Steel wore a leotard that looked like heavy black leather and metallic mesh. Sally could tell it was a purely functional outfit, designed to give her maximum mobility while holding up to the stresses of hand-to-hand combat and Shawna's own armored skin.

"I'm Eileen Macready." Shillelagh was perched upon her chair with her legs crossed. Her staff rested against her shoulder. "Shillelagh. I've got, like, super-balance and super-timing. Is that even a thing? Anyway, I've got it." She had on her sparkling red wig over her butch haircut, black tights, and a balloon-sleeved white pirate blouse with a green vest over it. Sally thought she looked like a leprechaun.

Sally turned to Yunbao, who sat closest to her at the table. The cat-faced young woman had painted spots across her fur with some kind of dye, giving her a much more traditional leopard pattern than the basic tawny gold that she'd inherited from her father Lionheart. "I am Li'ang Bao. You may call me Yunbao. I am pleased to be here to continue in the tradition of my father. I have trained in *hei hu quan*, a style of kung fu."

"So you're a ninja?" asked Ment.

"No. Ninjas are Japanese. And ridiculous." Yunbao smiled, showing her overlong canines.

"I guess that's everyone," said Sally. "We'll have our first training session tomorrow where you all will get to see each other's individual capabilities. There are a couple other people I need to introduce to all of you. My assistant is Davey. She's got a pretty good handle on things here. If you have any problems or questions, you can start with her."

Davey, who had been sitting quietly behind Sally, making notes on her tablet, stood to address the team. "I've read through all your files and I'm looking forward to working with all of you. I've got schedules set up for all of you on your—"

The conference room door burst open and a tall woman with ombréed hair rushed into the room. "Sorry to barge in, you guys." She glared up at the unlit warning lights on the walls. "Caitlin Leigh, Command Center supervisor. Apparently this headquarters still has some technical kinks to work out. There's a situation in Manhattan that needs your attention."

Sally looked at Jack, who shrugged in resignation. Every first meeting, it seemed, ended prematurely just like this. "Of course there is," said Sally. "Fill us in."

* * *

Following Leigh's briefing, Sally gave the group three minutes to retrieve whatever gear they needed and be on the launch pad, ready to depart. Of course, not everyone took *three minutes* literally. Just as she was about to find Jack and tear him a new one, he appeared at the door, his sniper rifle slung over his shoulder and his combat webbing full of grenades, magazines, knives, brass knuckles, and various and sundry dirty tricks. "Sorry, boss. Some of my stuff was still packed in boxes."

"Just don't let it happen again." As the *Dorothy* transported them toward Manhattan, Sally was grasping for any shred of self-confidence.

The Command Center woman didn't provide much information. An unknown group of parahumans had invaded a Manhattan high-rise, fighting their way through security and infiltrating the executive offices of a company called Syrinx Research Associates. Before they could make their escape, one of the security officers managed to call for help and the NYPD surrounded the building. The Chief of Police himself had called for help from Just Cause, which meant it was serious.

Sally told the Command Center to notify Surfboy and the Champions to be on alert in case any other emergencies cropped up needing parahuman intervention. It was unlikely but not unheard of for multiple situations to arise, especially if a group was trying to spread a hero organization thin in order to succeed at a specific goal.

"Four minutes to target," said the pilot over the cabin loudspeaker. Zach Hurley was a former Marine who'd flown combat missions in a Harrier in Iraq. His clipped, professional tones reminded Sally of her friend Ace, who'd flown the *Betty* for Just Cause when Sally was a fresh-faced rookie.

"All right, gear check," said Sally. "Everyone got throat mics and earbuds? Got your phones?"

It turned out that Yunbao and Detroit Steel hadn't yet been issued Just Cause phones yet, and Shillelagh had forgotten the wireless earbud and clip-on mic that allowed the heroes hands-free communication with each other on a closed frequency. "Sorry, that was stupid of me."

"We have spares." Jack handed her the appropriate gear while Sally rummaged through the stores on board the *Dorothy* to find temporary phones for the other two. She located them and passed them to Yunbao and Detroit Steel.

"I'm dividing us into three teams. I'll command Alpha Squad—Mastiff, Snapdragon, and Yunbao. Jack will head up Beta Squad with Snowball, Detroit Steel, and Shillelagh. Gamma Squad will be under Minerva's command with Ment and Failsafe. Alpha Squad, we go in through the front. Beta Squad will approach from the rear of the building. Gamma Squad, you're protecting civilians and rescuing anyone who's in trouble. If we need support, we'll call you in. Our primary mission is to incapacitate and capture the unknowns as quickly as possible. Do not let any civilians come to harm, even if it means you have to let one of the bad guys go. Someone will track him down." Sally paused. "Does anyone have questions?"

Jack opened his mouth to make one of his usual smart comments and Sally stared him down.

"We're dealing with unknown parahumans," said Sally. "Report whatever you can on the open frequency if it's safe to do so. The Command Center will be listening in and have access to the PRA database. Something you think might be unimportant could be the one thing that lets us identify one of the attackers and the best way to stop him or her."

"Thirty seconds," warned Hurley from the cockpit. "Civilian air traffic in the area. Media copters." The tone of his voice suggested exactly how little Hurley thought of the overeager reporters and pilots, desperate to be the first ones to catch something that could lead the exclusive report from the scene.

"Please don't shoot any of them down," said Sally. "No matter how much you might want to."

Jack chuckled. "You beat me to it, boss."

"Yes, ma'am. Stand by for descent."

"Open the bomb bay doors, Hurley, on my mark. Everyone be ready to deploy as soon as we touch down." Sally was trying to remember how Juice had called deployments when she'd been a rookie.

The glass and steel canyons of Manhattan rose around them as Hurley changed the pitch and angle of the variable jet nozzles to slow the *Dorothy*'s forward momentum. Sally saw the bright blue Just Cause logo on the jet's tail reflected in the mirror-bright windows of a building as the ship dropped down over an avenue. She wondered if they were going to break any windows. Property damage was never far from the mind of anyone in Just Cause, as it was drilled into them from the start that civilians tended to respond poorly to the massive collateral damage that came with super-powered combat, even if their lives were being saved in the process. And even though the government had a special fund set up to pay for damages, the House and Senate were forever chipping away at it, always wanting to put the money to use somewhere else.

"Everyone clear of the doors?" asked Sally. The belly doors were right behind the passenger seats, lined with striped yellow and black warning paint. "Mark, Hurley."

The doors split down the middle and opened downward, acting as shields from the heat and jet wash from the nozzles along the transport's hull. Sally looked down at the street, still a good hundred feet down but growing closer by the second. Dozens of police cars filled the streets, lights flashing, and officers either running toward the target building or working to clear civilians from the area. She also saw fire trucks and ambulances lined up just outside the emergency zone, ready to respond when called upon.

"Snapdragon, Snowball, Minerva, go," said Sally.

His cloak snapping behind him, Snapdragon leaped through the open doors. Curving wings of flame billowed around him in the characteristic shape that gave him his moniker. A giggling Snowball tumbled after him. She blasted forth an icy ramp, turning her fall into a roller coaster ride that Sally envied. No wonder Snowball laughed; for her, being a superhero was fun. Minerva grasped her spear in one hand and flew away, her own cloak spreading out like the magnificent wings of an owl.

"Five seconds to landing, everyone brace," said Hurley. The *Dorothy* hit the pavement, heavy-duty shock absorbers in her landing gear taking the brunt of the impact.

"Out, everyone!" Sally shouted to be heard over the roar of the jets.

She and the others dropped to the steaming asphalt. Failsafe produced a ring-shaped energy shield around the group, protecting them from the exhaust as they hurried out from beneath the nose of the jet. As soon as Hurley saw they were clear, he powered up the

Dorothy's engines and the transport jet rose, circling away as it gained altitude.

Sally watched the jet ascend. "Hurley, find a nearby rooftop and keep her on hot standby."

"Roger that."

Sally accelerated her perceptions to make a quick assessment of the area. She saw dozens of police officers with their weapons drawn, ducking behind their cars or firing at the building. Someone up on the third floor stood in front of a broken window, her fists clenched by her hips and her mouth wide open, emitting a scream powerful enough to distort the very air around her. A man two windows away was hurling a desk. Below them, a police car was splitting apart under the focused force of the woman's scream, and another one nearby had a large chunk of debris sticking out of its hood.

Sally spotted a NYPD command van. "Beta and Gamma squads, move into position. Alpha squad, follow me. Command Center, do you copy?"

"Affirmative, Sally."

"I've got two paras so far, wearing unmarked black jumpsuits. One brick, one blaster with a sonic scream." The police car the woman was screaming at exploded from her auditory onslaught. It flipped up and over, sending officers running for better cover. "A nasty one. Just Cause, prepare to move in." She looked at her squad. "Be right back, you guys."

She sprinted across the plaza to the command vehicle, covering the distance in about a second. To the officer manning the microphone, she would simply have appeared in front of him. He yelped in surprise and fumbled for his pistol, but Sally reached down, ejected the clip, popped out the bullet in the chamber, tucked the pistol back into his holster, and snapped the flap back over it all in the space between heartbeats. "Excuse me, sir. I'm one of the good guys. Just Cause checking in to help. Can you ask your men to fall back and stop shooting? I'd hate for one of my people to catch a stray bullet."

The officer gaped at her but managed to stammer out an affirmative.

"Thanks so much. We'll get this wrapped up as quick as possible. Thanks for your service!" Sally gave him her best dazzling smile and zipped away to rejoin her teammates.

A moment later, the repetitive pops and bangs of pistol and rifle fire slowed, and then stopped altogether. Sally took a deep breath.

It was fighting time.

Three

"New Yorkers suffered eight years ago when Just Cause was targeted by terrorists. I say, 'Thanks but no thanks' to their return, Mr. President."
—Senator Christine Goodwin (R, NY)

January, 2009
New York City, NY

"Alpha and Beta squads, move in. I say again, move in. Gamma Squad, assist in locating and retrieving the wounded. *Dorothy*, stand by." Sally's palms were sweating inside her gloves and she struggled to keep a tremor out of her voice.

"Beta Squad ready," said Jack over the comm frequency. "We've got media all around. Don't just beat the bad guys, try to look good doing it. We've got a golden opportunity here, guys."

"Take them down no matter what." Sally kept her voice firm. "Don't worry about how it looks."

"Gamma squad ready," said Minerva. "Good luck. Call us in if you need us."

Three of the jumpsuited criminals were conferring by the third floor windows, keeping the big strong guy between them and potential snipers. They couldn't possibly have missed seeing Just Cause's arrival, which meant they knew they had parahuman law enforcement coming after them.

Sally figured it wouldn't be right to disappoint them. "Mastiff, you think you can jump up to that window there? That guy's just begging to get hit."

Despite his super-strength, Jason sometimes had issues with utilizing it for jumping. He was better when he could stay close to the earth, lumbering along and taking on other grounded parahumans. He looked excited and strong to Sally, as if the chilly air was invigorating him. "Oh yeah, I got this. Been waiting for weeks to hit someone."

"Yunbao, can you climb the face of that building to get in through one of those broken windows?"

"Yes." Yunbao spread her fingers and toes, pushing out inch-long black claws with wicked-looking curves to them.

"Do it. We'll hit them from several different angles at once. Snapdragon, clear the way for Mastiff."

"Yes, boss." Snapdragon spread his flaming wings wide and rose high into the air to have a clear shot at the third floor.

Over her earbud, Sally heard Jack issuing similar orders and learned there were a couple of jumpsuited foes facing out the rear of the building as well. She wasn't worried about that side. Jack knew what he was doing. She watched Jason shuffle his feet into the starting position he wanted to, clenching his fists at his sides as he judged his distance and angle.

"Okay, Snapdragon, go!" Jason took a half dozen strides, trying to build up his speed as much as possible in that short distance, and then sprang up and forward, barreling toward the window like a human missile.

Yunbao charged toward the building in long leaps, using her hands and arms as much as her feet to propel her. Sally had heard a lot of graceful folks described as *catlike*, but for the first time, she could honestly say she knew what that really looked like. Yunbao bounced onto the roof of a patrol cruiser and used its light bar as a springboard. She scampered across the street and up a light pole, then ran along the beam holding a stoplight. It was springy enough to launch her halfway across the plaza where she slid down a bronze and glass modern art sculpture to reach the ground and run once more.

Snapdragon pressed his hands together and a globe of flame enveloped them in the moment before he unleashed his *dragon's breath* attack.

And just then, of course, everything went wrong.

The big brick guy spun around and hurled a chunk of concrete at Snapdragon just as a jet of bright flame emerged from his hands. The whirling concrete broke up Snapdragon's blast, spreading it into a mostly ineffective cloud. Snapdragon dodged a moment too late and the concrete crashed into his side, bouncing him back into the face of a building across the plaza. He dropped, barely still flying, but he looked shaken up and he winced in pain as he touched down to the ground.

Without having to worry about being roasted alive, the screaming woman had an easy shot at Jason —who couldn't dodge anything while he was airborne —and she took it. Even as Sally launched herself toward the building, she could see the concentric rings of auditory shock waves in the air. They enveloped Jason, pummeling him with their unseen force and slowing his headlong flight so he crashed into the floor below his target with blood droplets flying from his ears. His bulk smashed through the window and plate glass shards rained down to the street in his wake.

The third jumpsuited criminal stretched out flat and placed his hands on the outside of the building as Yunbao, climbing like her leopard namesake, reached for him with bared claws. The entire face of the building vibrated and rang like a bell, cracking and shattering dozens of glass panes. The tremors shook Yunbao loose and she fell almost thirty feet, twisting herself like a cat to try to get her feet beneath her.

Sally rushed into the building. All she knew was in the space of a single breath, her entire squad had been taken out. Who were these guys, and how had they stayed under the radar so long? Parahuman criminals didn't just appear out of the woodwork at random, especially when they were working as a team. There had to be records on these guys somewhere.

And then Sally ran across someone who could move nearly as fast as she could, and she was fortunate not to have been gutted like a fish by the barbed quills sprouting from the new combatant's arms. He slashed at her and she twisted and dodged through the lobby of the building on full defense. Unlike the criminals two floors above, the guy attacking Sally wore less of a jumpsuit and more of a wrestling-style singlet. The quills seemed to grow all over his body and she thought of him as Porcupine Man.

Super-speed abilities were rare in the world, even more so than psionic powers, and yet this was the second speedster Sally had fought in as many weeks. "Is there a factory churning you guys out or something?"

Porcupine Man's perceptions were apparently accelerated like hers, for he understood her despite her rapid speech. "The times, they are a-changin'." He spread his arms wide and flexed his chest in a peculiar way.

Sally dropped to the floor as several quills whisked over her head to embed themselves in the reception desk, quivering like arrows. A sharp, burning pain shot down her back and she knew one of them had grazed her. She hoped like hell they weren't tipped with poison. "That's a Bob Dylan lyric. My husband loves that song." She pulled her horseshoes from her belt.

"Maybe he can play it at your funeral." Porcupine Man shot more quills at Sally and she threw herself backwards over the reception desk to put something solid between her and her opponent. With his speed, she only had a moment to decide on her next action, and she froze when she saw a terrified woman huddled beneath the desk, eyes wide, a quill poking out of her bloodstained blouse.

Sally had no time to check to see if the woman was severely hurt. She couldn't stay hiding where she was and put the civilian in danger. Nor could she risk slowing herself down enough to offer any comfort. She heard the patter of Porcupine Man's approaching footsteps and forced herself to move. She ran, leaning forward to make herself a smaller target. The slice on her back burned like a paper cut with lemon juice in it. He skidded to a stop and Sally knew she had an advantage over him, being able to stop and start instantly.

She glanced back and saw him fire another quill at her from his chest. It had gone from a veritable barbed forest to a sparse stand in just a few moments. His quills didn't replace themselves very quickly. Maybe she could get him to use them up. She dove for the floor again, twisting herself around to land on her shoulder. The quill passed right over her face, close enough that she could see the wicked barbs on its tip. As she slid, she hurled one of her horseshoes at him. Normally, throwing away one's melee weapons was a poor choice, but Sally had spent thousands of hours at the targeting range, learning how to throw things effectively. When accelerated by her super-speed arms, the most innocent objects could become deadly projectiles.

Her horseshoes were hardly innocent.

The iron ring caught Porcupine Man on his sternum, hitting him hard enough to send him flying back into a wall, which cracked with his impact. He fell amid a pile of broken drywall and didn't move.

Sally ran back to the reception desk and slowed her perceptions enough that she could interact with the injured woman hiding there. "Miss, I'm Mustang Sally from Just Cause, and I'm going to get you out of here now, all right?"

The woman nodded, her eyes wide in terror. She took Sally's outstretched hand and let Sally pull her out from her hiding spot.

"Minerva, I'm coming out with a civilian. She needs medical attention. Update me on Alpha squad."

"Snapdragon and Yunbao are injured but able to return. I have no update on Mastiff," said Minerva promptly over Sally's earbud. "There are seven opponents. Crackerjack is down."

"Jack's down? How?" Sally glanced back to make sure Porcupine Man wasn't coming after her and the wounded receptionist.

"They have a psi. Ment has engaged him."

Sally shivered. Fighting psis was always a dicey proposition. The really talented ones could make heroes see things, convince them that they were fighting opponents when they were really fighting their friends. Some of them could even put people to sleep without touching them, like Ment could. Sally knew of one who could scramble a mind permanently, turning the victim into a hapless vegetable.

She heard the rustle of falling drywall and looked over her shoulder to see Porcupine Man climbing out of the debris. "Shit. Miss, right through those doors and we'll get you to safety. Failsafe? Get this woman out of here. I'm not done with the Human Hedgehog yet."

"*Sí*, Sally." The telltale glow of Failsafe's force shield appeared around the doorway.

Sally dashed across the reception area and raised her remaining horseshoe high to deliver a knockout blow. At least, that was her plan, but the spiny man had reserves of speed that let him dodge her fastest punch. He swiped at her, opening another painful wound in her forearm. She gasped and ran, trying to get some distance between them. He gave chase, and Sally led him into the stairwell where she was going to try a trick she'd practiced in training. Running up a stairwell at speed allowed her centrifugal force to push her against the walls until she was moving against them like a ball inside a pipe. She whirled upward, Porcupine Man in hot pursuit, astonishing her with his ability to keep up.

She pushed off the wall suddenly, diving across the width of the stairs for a dangerous moment where she wasn't touching anything. His spiky arms whistled just wide of her as she twisted herself horizontal and slipped between the railing bars. She let her momentum carry her all the way to the wall, where she crouched against it and then accelerated up the stairwell again. Her sudden move had put her right behind Porcupine Man, and before he could react, she clocked him across the back of his head with her horseshoe.

He stumbled and fell face first into a stair in an explosion of blood and tooth fragments. Sally came to an instantaneous stop, horseshoe raised, ready to drill him again if needed, but he lay unmoving, his chest hitching with ragged, irregular breaths. Out like the proverbial light. Sally hesitated, wondering what to do with him. She had zip tie restraints in her belt, but his quills would slice through them easily. There were other more pressing problems, however, and it was worth the risk to leave him alone for now while she handled the rest of the criminals. They would all get Deep Six sleeper sets when this was all through.

"This is Sally. The speedster's taken out for now."

"His name is Slash," said Minerva. "This group calls itself Syndicate S. I've heard their radio communication. His partners are Sunder, Sirene, Splatter, Salt, Shockwave, and Screen." Minerva paused. "Somebody must have spent a long time with a dictionary."

Sally hoped the Command Center could get them some useful information based upon those names. "How's Mastiff?"

"I haven't been able to check on him yet. I'm helping Ment against Screen."

Ment's psionic powers were fairly wild, but Minerva was able to help him focus those abilities, to tame them and bend them to his will. Without her quiet and solemn guidance, when he opened up his mind, it would be like explosions going off in everyone's minds around him.

"I understand. I'll check him myself." Sally dashed back down the stairwell, bypassing the third floor where the majority of Syndicate S seemed to be concentrated, and entering the second floor where Jason had crashed into the building.

She found her husband partially through an interior wall where he'd finally come to rest. Her first instinct was to scream for help—or cry or throw up or try to wake him up or drag him to safety. It was only through sheer force of will she did none of those things. Jason's face was white as a ghost's, but she wiped away plaster dust and his color was its normal rosy pink beneath. At least he was taking slow and regular breaths. Blood trickled from his ears and down his neck, staining the collar of his costume. Suddenly she couldn't find enough oxygen in the air, and the room seemed to spin around her. She yanked her cowl back off her face and bent down with her head between her knees, trying to get some blood back into her brain. Where was everyone on her team? Jack was out of it, right when she was desperate for his experience. Ditto for Jason, who despite his easygoing attitude still had two more years of field experience than Sally did.

She couldn't keep a shudder out of her voice. "Mustang Sally reporting in. Mastiff is down, unconscious, with s-severity of injuries unknown. He's on the second floor of the target building in a direct line from the entry hole in th-the windows."

Somewhere on the floor above, Sirene uttered another of her ear-bleeding shrieks. The feedback in Sally's earbud nearly blew out the tiny speaker. Someone gasped over the frequency, but Sally couldn't tell who it was.

"Shillelagh is down," said another voice that Sally thought was Snowball. "That bitch is going to pay." The diminutive hero flashed past the windows, riding a wave of ice like it was a surfboard. A steady stream of snowballs blasted from her outstretched hand. At first it might seem like a ridiculous, juvenile power, but Sally had been on the receiving end of one of those fusillades. It was like being attacked by a snowy machine gun. The snowballs impacted so hard and fast that you couldn't see, you couldn't breathe, your mouth and nose and ears filled with snow. You lost your balance and all sense of which way was up as the snow piled around you. People died in avalanches all the time in the mountains in Colorado, and suffering a rapid-fire attack from Snowball was similar.

"Hah! Got one." A cloud of white crystal particles enveloped Snowball. "Hey—" Her indignation turned into choking and gasping. The particles bit into Snowball's ice ramp and Sally realized she'd been attacked by the one Minerva had identified as Salt. A spray of pure sodium chloride didn't seem any more dangerous on the surface than snowballs might, but Sally knew that it was the perfect foil for her ice-powered teammate. Snowball tumbled out of sight and Sally clenched her fists. She couldn't have done anything to help her anyway.

She had never felt so helpless in her entire life.

"Who . . . who's left, Just Cause? Sound off."

"Minerva and Ment," said Minerva. "We're still fighting Screen. He's stronger than Ment but I'm making up the difference."

"Detroit Steel, I'm coming up the stairs right now. Where you at, Sally?"

"Second floor." Sally thought back to how she'd gotten to Jason. "Go left from the stairwell, corner office."

Failsafe checked in, still helping to remove civilians from the danger zone. "Keep at it," Sally told him. "Right now you're the only one protecting people."

"Snapdragon here. I'm bruised but still in the fight. I caught Snowball before she could hit the ground. She looks in a bad way. I don't know what's wrong with her."

"Get her to the paramedics and then come to me," said Sally. "We need to regroup."

"This is Yunbao. I am . . . slightly damaged, but still able to fight. I can see the criminals from my vantage point. They appear to be preparing to move."

"Get up here," said Sally. "No, wait. Go to Minerva and Ment. See if you can take out Screen while he's occupied with the two of them."

A shriek from overhead set Sally's teeth on edge and she clapped her hands over her ears. The ceiling shuddered and fell, depositing the massive Sunder on the floor only a few feet away from Jason and Sally. He laughed. "I wondered where that little puppy went. I was hoping he wanted to play tug-of-war with me." He picked up an office chair, weighing it like it was a baseball bat. "Maybe I'll play with you instead, girlie." He raised the chair. "Go fetch."

A steel hand intercepted Sunder's wrist, forcing him to drop the chair. "My girl ain't no dog," said Detroit Steel. "You want to dance, big boy? Let's go." And with that, she delivered a fist to his solar plexus that made Sally wince in sympathy.

Sunder gasped from the blow and turned a little green. His thick arms came up without much certainty behind the motion, and Sally realized that although he was super-strong, he wasn't much of a fighter.

Detroit Steel, on the other hand, had grown up on the streets of Detroit during the worst economic downturn in a century. She must have learned every dirty trick in the book, and come up with a few of her own, and she used three of them on Sunder in quick succession. She stepped inside his guard, trusting her metallic body to absorb any blows, and stomped down on the inside of one of his feet, hard enough to tear through his boot and crack the floor beneath him. When she drew her own foot back, it was streaked with blood. Sunder yelled and flailed at her without much success. Detroit Steel held up her arms vertically like a kickboxer, taking the blows on her forearms and deflecting them aside. Then she drove her knee upward, not into his groin like he might have expected, but into the adductor muscle on the inside of his thigh. He screamed and fell, his leg hanging limp. On his way down, Detroit Steel drove her metal elbow into the back of his head with a sound like a hammer hitting a rock. He hit the ground and didn't move. "And that's how we do it where I'm from, bitch. Sally, you doin' all right?"

Sally nodded. "Yeah. Let's take it back to them. Meet you up a floor."

Detroit Steel clenched her fists together to make a battering ram. "About damn time." She crouched and then leaped, barreling through the ceiling. Sally hesitated just a moment to make sure debris wasn't going to rain down upon her beloved Jason, but then sprinted back to the stairwell. She was in and up a flight and back out again in only a couple of seconds, but in that time she overheard Failsafe scream for help over her earbud. As she burst out of the stairwell, Salt was just turning away from the windows while Splatter was firing glob after glob of whatever-it-was at Snapdragon. He twisted through the air, struggling against the weight of the goop that built up all over him. Although he couldn't be hurt by his own flames, other burning materials could injure him, so he couldn't

51

try to burn off Splatter's muck. His flight grew uncontrolled and he smashed into the side of a SWAT van where he stuck like a bug on flypaper.

Detroit Steel charged at Salt, who gleefully blasted a cloud of sodium chloride at her. The salt had no effect upon the metallic woman, and she drove her shoulder into Salt and knocked her right out of the broken window. It was three stories up, and Sally didn't care. This Syndicate S, whoever they were, had decimated her team in a matter of seconds, and she was ready for some payback. She closed with Sirene, ducking beneath the brunt of the woman's shriek. As she closed, Sally grabbed a metal wastebasket from a ruined cubicle and held it over her head, directly in the line of Sirene's auditory blast. The force of the sound waves vibrated the can right out of Sally's hands, but before it did, it reflected a portion of them right back into Sirene's face. Her nose shattered and she flew backward, trailing droplets in a slow-motion arc.

"Ment!" Minerva screamed over the team frequency.

Detroit Steel took a half a step toward Splatter, stumbled, and fell as if she'd been shot with a tranquilizer dart. Her spring-like dreadlocks spread out like a net around her head as she pitched face-first through the hole Sunder had knocked in the floor earlier.

A furry form catapulted through the broken window right into Splatter's line of fire. He fired so many globs of his sticky material that Yunbao wound up glued to the floor by the window, looking like something that had risen out of a swamp instead of a tawny-furred felinoid.

Minerva rose in the window behind Yunbao, her spear raised to attack, tears tracking down her face. Sirene screamed in her direction and Minerva spun away, her cloak shredded in Sirene's shriek.

Sally felt a hand on her shoulder spin her around, barbs tearing through her costume, ripping at her flesh.

She found herself face to face with Slash. "Remember me, bitch? I'm the last thing you're going to—"

A black spot appeared on Slash's forehead, and the back half of his head exploded in a spray of crimson and gray.

Four

"Sure, Mustang Sally is great eye candy in her tight little red spandex, but what experience does she really have that's applicable toward leading the so-called 'Greatest Superhero Team in the World'?"
—Ken Reichel, Top Flight Radio Network

January, 2009
New York City, NY

At first, Sally thought Jack must have shaken off whatever Screen did to him to shoot Slash, but Jack was a fantastic shot and he didn't kill unless absolutely necessary. He would have known Sally could take care of herself and either shot to wound or taken on someone else. Sally's next thought was perhaps a police sniper had rejected the order to back off and taken an opportunity shot.

Someone in a red, white, and blue costume appeared from nowhere, ruffling Sally's hair with a sudden displacement of air. He was built like a Mixed Martial Arts fighter, full of lean, hard muscles, with a representation of the Liberty Bell on his chest. He glanced around, taking quick stock of the room, then teleported behind Splatter, grabbed his head in the crook of his elbow and twisted hard. Splatter's neck gave way with a sickening *pop* and he collapsed like a rag doll.

Sirene screamed, not just to cause harm with her voice, but from real terror. "*OH GOD, OH GOD!*" Every word from Sirene's mouth shattered windows and blew cubicle dividers like leaves in the wind.

Sally felt like screaming herself, but she ducked beneath the shrieking woman's panic blasts and got behind her to yell in her ear, "Surrender, Sirene. It's over."

"*PROTECT ME! YOU HAVE TO PROTECT ME!*" Sirene started to turn to look back at Sally.

A shadow appeared in the corner of Sally's eye, almost too far behind her to see, but it was moving fast, and she ducked out of reflex. It was a hammer, she realized, like a judge's gavel if it was made of titanium steel. As it passed over her head, she tried to stop its flight or at least deflect it, but it had been hurled with great strength, and its inertia was too great for her to alter its course in the slightest. Her only option was to try to move Sirene out of its path. She'd moved Juice out of the way of an explosion once, and it had nearly killed her. Sirene was much smaller than Sally's former team leader, but Sally had burning barbs in her back and arms from fighting Slash earlier, and the wounds protested as she battled the inertia of someone trapped at regular speed.

She didn't get Sirene quite out of the way, and the edge of the hurled gavel caught the woman high up on her cheekbone. Sally gasped and turned away as the mallet tore through bone and brain, bursting Sirene's eye and dragging a good chunk of her scalp away with it. Sally released her hold on Sirene and twisted to avoid the spray of bright arterial blood from the ragged gouge the hammer had left in its wake.

Sally dashed over to Jason's side. "Jason? Oh God, please wake up. Jason, we've got more trouble. Killers, Jason." She hesitated, wondering whether or not she would injure him more seriously in doing so, but then she trusted to his own parahuman metabolism and strength and reached down to slap his face a few times. "Come on, wake up. Please." She felt tears threatening to overwhelm her. How had everything gone so horribly wrong in so short of a time? She was going to be fired from her position leading Just Cause. She was sure of that. If she didn't get canned, she might just resign anyway. She had no business trying to lead a superhero team after things had gone this way on their very first call-out.

"Sally?" It was Minerva on the open frequency. She sounded subdued and upset. "You better get down here. New players on the field. What's going on up there?"

"Um . . ." Sally swallowed, trying to get the tremor out of her voice. "Jason and Detroit Steel are down and possibly injured. Yunbao is trapped, but I don't think she's hurt. Slash, Splatter, and Sirene are dead. Not by us." She emphasized that last sentence. "Sunder and Shockwave are unconscious. We need paramedics and sleeper sets up here right away."

"I'm already on it," said Minerva. "They're on their way up. The situation down here is . . . stable."

The way she said *stable* convinced Sally that there was more trouble on the horizon. "As soon as I have Sunder and Shockwave secured, I'll be down. How are our people? And what about the rest of Syndicate S?"

"Ment and Jack are still unconscious from Screen. Snowball and Failsafe are on their way to the hospital for what I think is severe, acute dehydration. Shillelagh has ruptured eardrums and possibly a concussion. Snapdragon is being treated here on the scene for minor injuries. I'm all right. Salt and Screen are dead, Salt from falling and Screen from one of these new people."

Sally went over to where Yunbao was crouched down in the window, held in place by Splatter's hardening slime. She was growling in the pit of her throat, but stopped when Sally approached. "Are you all right?"

"I am upset at myself for being so easily defeated." Yunbao sounded huskier than normal. "This material is disgusting, but I cannot break free."

"I'll get Minerva up here to look at it. She'll be able to figure out how we get you out of it."

Sally saw the stairwell door open and a group of SWAT officers emerged, escorting paramedics. She waved them over.

"Go talk to your police. I am not going anywhere." Yunbao's lips curled up into a feline smile. Or perhaps it was a snarl.

Either way, Sally smiled back at her. "It was a good joke." She turned to the SWAT officers. "Situation is secure up here. Did you bring up the sleeper sets?"

"Affirmative, ma'am." One officer kept his short rifle in hand, letting it point at the floor while he held up two of the Deep Six sleeper sets, the standard restraints for parahuman lawbreakers. They were bulky and fragile enough that Just Cause members didn't carry them on hand when entering combat, but they kept several on the transport jets, and every SWAT team had two in their possession. The sets were adjustable helmets that locked around a recipient's head and broadcast a coma-inducing signal in the wearer. They were effective on anyone who had human or near-human biology.

"You know how to install them?"

"We've been trained."

"Good. I need to get down to the ground. I'll coordinate with on-site command."

The SWAT officer nodded. "All right, let's get these paras secured and the heroes checked." He tugged on his shoulder radio. "Command, Flannery. We're going to need the coroner up here. We've got three for the body bags."

Sally shuddered. She was no stranger to death after a few years in the field. It was a given that when people had the ability to punch holes in solid steel, shoot lightning bolts, and punch as fast as the speed of sound, there would be casualties. Such knowledge didn't make it any easier to deal with.

The lobby was carpeted with a fine sheen of shattered glass and mounds of masonry where ceiling tiles and sections of wall had collapsed.

A handful of patriotically-attired parahumans surrounded by police. The cops weren't holding them at bay; if anything, they were looking upon them with admiration. Sally spotted Minerva and Snapdragon. The flamethrowing hero was also coated in the drying slime, but Minerva seemed to have discovered some method for stripping it away from him, like peeling shreds of latex away from a model. "What's going on?" Sally asked.

Minerva nodded toward the throng of police and the new costumed parahumans, resplendent in their patriotic colors. "Meet The Militia. Our . . . saviors." She grated out the last word as she threw away another stringy handful of the goop she'd pulled loose from Snapdragon. "The big guy there in the front, who's doing all the talking, he calls himself Patriot. He punched a hole through Screen's chest and then threw him across the street like a crumpled coffee cup."

"And they're supposed to be heroes?" Sally glared at them, already disliking them for their violent behavior and lethal tactics.

"I don't know what they're supposed to be." Minerva glanced overhead where media and police helicopters circled the area. "What I do know is that this is going to shake out badly for us."

"We'll see about that. I'm going to go talk to them."

"Be careful. They stink of pride."

"I'm no rose petal myself right now."

"Sally . . . your back. You're wounded." Snapdragon touched her arm. "You should get checked out."

"I will. This is more important." She looked back over her shoulder. "I'm a speedster. I heal fast." She could have crossed the space between her team and the newcomers in an instant, but she wanted them to see her coming. She wanted the patriotically-colored parahumans and the police around them to see she was angry as she approached.

The cops noticed Sally and melted aside to let her through until she stood in the middle of a semicircle of dark blue police uniforms, facing down the half-dozen new parahumans.

" . . . And here she is now," said the lantern-jawed Aryan who had the air of a well-practiced public speaker around him. "No thanks are necessary, Mustang Sally. We heroes of the Militia are glad to assist wherever we are needed."

And just like that, Sally realized *she* was the one on the hot seat. The muscle-bound man was built like Jason, if not quite as tall, and had a deep, resonant voice that carried well without amplification. His bodysuit was blue, with two vertical rows of white stars like a double-breasted cavalry jacket. His boots and gauntlets were red, and he had a matching cape. It gave him a very traditional, old-fashioned look. "Who are you?"

"Patriot at your service, Miss, and these are my fellow American heroes of the Militia. I know you have already met Liberty." The man who had the Liberty Bell emblem on his chest nodded. "And Liberty would be nothing without Justice." Justice nodded almost exactly the same way Liberty had. He wore a flowing black robe and held the heavy metal gavel in one hand. A yoke stretched across his shoulders and the back of his neck, modeled after the traditional Scales of Justice. "This is the Minuteman." Patriot indicated a man dressed like an American Revolutionary War soldier, right down to the black tricorner hat. "Second Amendment, who I believe may have directly saved your life." Second Amendment appeared to be the Militia's answer to Just Cause's Crackerjack. He wore a tight-fitting camouflage bodysuit, with tactical webbing all over it. Holsters spread down his chest and around his legs. They hung beneath his arms and stuck out of his boots. He even had two small ones strapped onto his helmet. Sally figured he had something like twenty pistols on his person, and that wasn't even counting the lengthy sniper rifle he held against his hip. "And last but not least, our lovely Maverick." Maverick was under-dressed for the weather, exposing far too much midriff, cleavage, and leg skin for Sally's liking. Her outfit followed a similar pattern to Patriot's, although without a cape. Unlike the others, her name gave no indication of her abilities.

"You're certainly a . . . patriotic bunch." Sally wished Jack had heard her. He'd have approved of the pun.

The joke appeared lost on Patriot. "Naturally. We are real Americans, real heroes." He said it like it was a slogan, like he'd been practicing. Sally suspected he probably had.

"Sally, this is the Command Center," said a voice in her ear. "We have no confirmed matches on any of the members of this Militia group. We need more information than just names and observed abilities."

"Where've you been keeping yourselves?" Sally asked, trying to be smooth about it. "I'm pretty well-traveled throughout the parahuman community, and I've never heard of any of you."

"The time was right for us to come forth," said Patriot. "There was a need, and we answered the call."

"Lucky for us it was today," said Sally.

Patriot grinned like he was a cover model. Sally could almost hear the *ding* of a sparkle reflecting off his teeth. "I'd say our timing was impeccable."

"Yeah, you were really on the ropes," added Liberty.

Sally refused to take that bait. She knew that her team had been beaten badly by Syndicate S, and the truth was if the Militia hadn't shown up, Just Cause might have suffered more than just injuries. "Nevertheless, I'm going to need you to leave. This is an active, federal crime scene, and we can't have you interfering with our investigation."

Patriot's nod was so small that Sally couldn't be sure if he'd even dipped his head at all. She wondered if she might have just scored a point. "Of course."

"We'll need to get statements from all of you, and because of your direct involvement, I'm requiring you to refrain from any superhero-type activities," said Sally.

"We're a private organization, kiddo," said Maverick in a *gosh-darn-looky-here* Midwestern accent. "Your rules don't apply to us."

Sally narrowed her eyes. What game was this? "But the rule of law still applies. At the very least, I have four deaths that are all directly attributed to you."

"I can produce any number of witnesses from among these fine members of the New York Police Department that can confirm we were acting to protect Just Cause," said Patriot. "Without our involvement, there might be a few more deaths in this incident. You should be thanking us."

"I think you're underestimating Just Cause, Patriot."

"And I think you're overestimating yourself, which I think is far more dangerous. Nevertheless, we will accede to your request." Patriot looked past Sally. She glanced back over her shoulder at super-speed to see what he'd seen, and to her dismay, it was a forest of microphones and cameras. The press had arrived on the scene.

Sally wished she had someone to tell her whether or not she had the authority to arrest Patriot and his people. She wanted to, but they might really have saved the lives of her teammates with their timely arrival. Then she hearkened back to something her grandmother used to say: *you can catch more flies with honey than with vinegar.* As a child, Sally hadn't ever understood what she would want with a bunch of flies, but it made perfect sense to her now. "Thank you for everything. I'd be honored if you'd come out to Fort Justice and let us thank you with dinner. How can we reach you?"

"You can't," said Patriot. "But we'll consider your offer. In the meantime, I suggest you look to your own people, and your prisoners." With a flapping of his cape, Patriot lifted up into the air, majestic and graceful, and cruised over toward the eager press corps. The rest of the Militia followed him on foot. Justice said nothing, but Liberty gave Sally a tight smile. Second Amendment's gear and weapons rattled as he stepped around Sally. Maverick said nothing, but Sally heard her snort of disdain as loud as if it had been a gunshot. The Minuteman sighed and kicked at the ground, as if a press conference was the last place he wanted to be, but then he, too, followed after Patriot, pouting full-force as if it were his parahuman ability.

Even the bulk of the police officers drifted after Patriot, like they hadn't heard enough from him yet. For a moment, Sally felt very much alone. Then burgundy fabric rustled beside her and she turned to see Minerva. "What a bunch of douches," said Minerva.

Sally gaped at her. It was the first time she'd ever seen Minerva express any kind of real dislike for someone. "Can't say as I disagree. They're their own biggest fans, that's for sure. How are you doing?"

"I'm upset." Minerva's voice returned to its usual calm once more. "Patriot is no hero. He's a murderer. They may claim extenuating circumstances, but I know he could have stopped Screen without killing him."

"I could have stopped him." Ment brushed off a worried-looking paramedic. "I was just about through his shields when someone distracted me."

"Someone distracted you . . . Another psi?"

"Maybe. It was like . . . you know how when you're taking a test or something and all of a sudden a tiny bug flies into your ear? It was like that. I lost the thread and then he blindsided me." Ment shrugged. "It doesn't really make sense if you're not a psi. It's like trying to explain colors to someone born blind."

"Looks like I missed the party." Jack was rubbing his nose and sniffling as he walked up to rejoin his comrades. "They just gave me a face full of ammonia capsules to wake me up. You guys made a real mess, and you two especially." He stared at Yunbao and Snapdragon, still coated with the mucousy glop that Splatter had shot at them. "So Captain Codpiece and His Amazing Color Guard showed up to save the day, huh? Wonder what flag-lined hole they came out of."

"I don't know," said Sally. "Juice is going to want to know about them. He's going to be pissed to find out two new groups of parahumans showed up on the same day and we don't have prior information on any of them."

"That we know of," said Snapdragon. "They could have changed their costumes, or disguised their powers somehow. They might be known."

"They smelled funny," said Minerva. "Unfamiliar. I can't place it."

"All right, this isn't the time or place to debrief," said Sally. "Let's get our two prisoners handled, check on our injured teammates, and find out if there's anything else we've got to do here." She glared in Patriot's direction. "I'm sure the Militia has the situation well in hand, and I'm not sure we're really needed any longer."

"Anybody else get a distinct hardcore right wing vibe from them?" asked Snapdragon. "Because I'm pretty sure I heard Maverick call me a sand nigger under her breath." Flames danced in his eyes. "I may have been imagining it."

"Patriotic colors and names doesn't necessarily mean they're affiliated with any political party," said Jack. "It could just be their thing. And Maverick could just be an uppity bitch."

"Who's an uppity bitch?" Detroit Steel clomped up to join the group. She was rubbing the back of her head. "I hope it's me."

"Are you all right?" Sally asked.

"I have the mother of all headaches," said Detroit Steel. "Somebody nailed me good."

"Probably Screen," said Ment.

"It was his final act," said Minerva. "That he chose to expend it upon you should honor you."

Detroit Steel looked sideways at Minerva. "I ain't sure if you're teasing me or not." She turned to Sally. "The paramedics are bringing your husband down now. You want to see him before they take him on to the hospital?"

"Yes, very much. Jack, can you oversee the prisoners? Minerva, check with the local authorities and see if there's anything else they need from Just Cause before we close up shop." Sally sighed. "We've got a lot of wounds to lick."

"I need a bath," said Yunbao.

Sally spotted four burly paramedics carrying Jason on a stretcher, and she was beside them in an instant. "Jason, baby? Are you all right?"

"What? Sally, I can't hear you," Jason shouted. "I can't hear anything."

"I'm pretty sure his eardrums are ruptured and he's suffered some inner ear damage," said one of the paramedics. "He's not able to regain his balance. That's why we're carrying him. Christ, he's heavy. What's he made of?"

"Sandwiches," said Sally. "Lots and lots of sandwiches. Pizza. Pasta. Burgers. F-fries. God, is he going to be all right?"

"I don't know yet," said the paramedic. "He's got to get checked out."

"I'll be fine, babe," Jason shouted. "Did we win? I think I crashed into a wall."

"We're fine. We did good." Sally squeezed his hand, biting back tears. Jason seemed jovial as ever, but his lack of hearing worried her to no end. What if he'd suffered some kind of permanent damage? No, she wouldn't accept that. Just Cause had Dr. Grace Devereaux from the Paris Institute of Parahuman Medicine on speed-dial. She would take care of any of them who were wounded beyond the means of conventional medicine to heal. Still, seeing Jason about to be loaded into the back of an ambulance was almost more than Sally could bear. She almost dropped everything to ride to the hospital with him, but she knew that as team leader, she couldn't shirk her other responsibilities. She'd have time to check on Jason—and the other wounded heroes as well—as soon as she finished with the immediate crime scene. "I love you."

Even if he couldn't hear her, he could still read her lips. "I love you too," he boomed. "I'll see you soon."

Sally's perceptions snapped into full acceleration for some reason and the world around her grated to a near stop, with everything moving in slow motion. Unexpected brightness in the corner of her vision made her look in that direction.

An expanse of flame was blossoming from the third floor of the building where several of the Syndicate S parahumans had died. What windows hadn't broken in the fight were spraying outward in clouds of sparkling shards, catching the light of the explosion and redirecting it. Pieces of a person in SWAT gear were flying out from one of the already-broken windows. Another explosion was spreading outward at the base of the building, where Salt had fallen, flinging uniformed officers away in grotesque poses. Further away, a similar explosion immolated Screen's corpse and threw an officer against a solid marble wall. The ambulance that had held the two unconscious Syndicate S prisoners was bursting at the seams, its rear end coming off the ground as flame blasted out of it in six directions. Sally saw Jack tumbling away, his gear flying off of him and his clothing coming apart in the force of the explosion. He wouldn't be hurt, but others would be.

Sally drew a deep, shuddering breath, and commenced running.

She wouldn't be able to save everyone, but she'd save as many as she could.

Five

"Seven police officers and four civilians were killed, and nineteen more people injured thanks to Just Cause's inability to properly secure the scene. I hate to think what might have happened had The Militia not shown up to prevent the situation from getting worse."
—Senator Christine Goodwin (R, NY)

January, 2009
New York City, NY

Sally couldn't stop reading and rereading the medical reports of her injured teammates. She had her office temperature cranked up nearly to eighty degrees, with pictures of Arizona's Painted Desert pasted across her flatscreens to try and soothe her with its stark beauty. Davey had brought her a steaming hazelnut mocha latte, mentioned that she'd be in the Command Center if Sally needed anything, and then left. For all her efficiency, Sally was glad that Davey had given her some space to deal with the outcome of her team's very first call-out.

She herself had already healed from the cuts Slash had inflicted upon her with his barbed quills. One of the benefits of being a speedster was being quick to heal.

Failsafe and Snowball had suffered the most harm in the conflict with Syndicate S, at the hands of Salt. The cloud of sodium particles he'd sprayed at them leached fluids out of their bodies at a frightening rate, and by the time the paramedics got to them they had both suffered severe dehydration, losing more than ten percent of their bodily fluids within minutes. They'd required emergency intravenous electrolyte replenishment and had to be fully submerged in water tanks to remove the excess salt from their skin. The prognosis was good, and neither one appeared to have suffered any lasting damage from their close call. As far as dangerous effects of parahuman abilities went, dehydration was at least fairly easy to treat, according to the physician who'd reported back to Sally. They were staying in the hospital for an additional twenty-four hours of monitoring, but the doctor anticipated Failsafe and Snowball could return to Fort Justice afterward, although they would have to be cleared by the team's own medical staff before they could resume active duties.

Snapdragon and Yunbao hadn't suffered any ill effects from their contact with Splatter's goop. As it had dried on the flight back to Fort Justice, it developed a shiny patina and then flaked away until the two heroes looked like they'd been sprayed with mica. Snapdragon got himself cleaned up without incident, but after Yunbao was unable to remove the material from her fur, Davey suggested calling in a professional dog groomer. Yunbao suffered the young woman's patient ministrations and despite the Chinese hero's poor attitude about the cleaning in general, she was so pleased with her appearance and fur texture afterward she inquired whether the woman could be hired to work on her regularly.

Detroit Steel, Ment and Minerva were uninjured, and of course Jack was fine. Jack would always be fine; that was the nature of his unique parahuman power.

All of which brought her to Shillelagh and Jason. They'd both suffered severe damage to their inner ears from Sirene's shrieks, with perforated eardrums and swelling in their ear canals that required surgical repair. Shillelagh's surgery was routine and went smoothly, but working on Jason proved exceptionally difficult for the surgical team, thanks to his body's innate toughness. There wasn't enough time for Dr. Devereaux to fly in from Paris to oversee the procedure herself, so she advised the team via closed-circuit television, and they had to use some tools likely never used in a surgical ward before, uniformly industrial in origin and tipped with tungsten carbide or even diamond. The doctors had to wear musician-style earplug monitors so they could hear over the roar of the air compressor that drove the drills, dremels, and saws they needed to work on Jason.

Sally asked bluntly whether her teammates would be able to hear again, and the doctor said most likely, but it was possible both Jason and Shillelagh had both suffered some permanent hearing loss. It could be corrected using hearing aids, but he wanted to prepare them for the worst possible case. Shillelagh's preternatural balance might have been adversely affected by Sirene, and it could mean the end of her effectiveness as a member of Just Cause. Jason's ability to hear wouldn't affect his muscular strength at all, but —and this is what really broke Sally's heart—he was a musician. Losing his hearing would be a devastating emotional blow. He'd already had to leave behind his long-time band when they moved to New York. What if he couldn't use music as an escape any longer, the way he had his entire life?

A knock on Sally's door startled her out of her black spiral of dismay and she looked up to see Juice filling the doorway with his bulky chest and shoulders, his head coming dangerously close to brushing the lintel. "Hello, Sally. Mind if I come in?"

For a long moment, Sally thought she was going to break down and cry, but the one overwhelming thought keeping her from doing so was it would pretty much confirm everyone's suspicions about her inability to run a superhero team. Nevertheless, she had to take a lengthy drink from her coffee before she felt confident enough to speak without her voice shaking. "Yes, please do. Can I get you something to drink?"

"Actually, whatever you're drinking smells damn delicious. May I have one myself?"

"Of course." Sally shot a quick instant message from her phone to Davey, asking for Juice's drink. Davey replied right away and asked if she should load it with anything like bourbon, whiskey, or cyanide. Sally almost laughed, and she realized how dire things had really gotten for her.

Juice sat down in a chair facing Sally's desk. "This is a switch from your first day in Denver. I was on the other side of the desk that day."

"Are you going to be our new intern?" Sally tried to find a shred of humor in her situation. "Please?"

Juice smiled. "Sorry, no. I wish I could, though. I hate being in an office all day. What I wouldn't give for a chance to buckle on my boots once again."

"It's not always all it's cracked up to be." Sally took a deep breath. She'd been planning for the possibility of what could be the next step, and she saw no reason to delay. "Are you here to ask for my resignation? Because if so, you can have it." She slid a letter across the desk that she'd typed up that morning. On one hand, it felt like she was giving up and admitting she was a failure. On the other, it felt like the sort of thing she was supposed to do as a leader. She'd been the one in command when everything went south against Syndicate S and in the aftermath. Whether her team was a success or failure, it rested upon her shoulders, and she was willing to accept the responsibility for it, no matter the consequences.

Juice didn't even glance down at the paper. "Throw that shit away. I didn't come here for that, and I don't plan to leave with it, either. Sally, I've seen you at your worst, and it's a damn sight better than a lot of people at their best. What happened yesterday was not your fault."

"Juice . . . a third of my team got sent to the hospital. Jason m-might have permanent hearing damage. We had to get rescued by a bunch of violent right-wingers. We don't even have a prisoner to show for it."

Davey entered the office with Juice's coffee. "I didn't doctor it up, but there's a full bar over there if you want to belt it with something."

"You doing all right, Davey?" asked Juice.

"Not bad for the first few days on the job. It's a little tame compared to trial preparation, but then, most things are."

Juice chuckled. "You make sure you take good care of Sally here. She needs someone like you."

"Everyone needs someone like me." Davey spun on her heel and left with a confident stride.

"She's really something," said Sally. "She's like a force of nature."

"That's an excellent way to describe her. Now, let's talk about yesterday. Are you familiar with Helmuth von Moltke?"

"Sounds German. Is he on Feuerkraft?" Sally referred to the German superhero team.

"No. He was a field marshal in the Nineteenth Century. You may have heard his most famous quote. *No plan of operations extends with any certainty beyond the first contact with the main hostile force.*"

"No battle plan survives contact with the enemy, right? I've heard that before."

"Right. He was a brilliant strategist and I suggest you should read his work. In fact . . ." Juice reached inside his coat and removed a well-thumbed hardcover book from a pocket. The binding looked as if it had been repaired and the edges of the fabric were frayed. "This is my personal copy of *Truppenführung*. Much of his most important work is contained in here. It's a good translation. I want you to have it." He nodded at Sally's empty bookshelves. "You'll want to read as much as you can about strategy, tactics, and leadership. Trust me, in your position, you can't ever afford to stop learning."

"But . . . but this is yours. I can't take it."

"No, it's yours now. Haven't you ever heard you're not supposed to lend a book? This is a gift, and one I think is probably overdue, and that's my fault." Juice set it on top of Sally's resignation letter. "Jack and I have had numerous arguments about military and leadership philosophies. He'll want to argue with you too once he sees you have this. He'll think I've corrupted you."

"Haven't you?"

"Not any more than he will. You'll want to listen to him, too. He's a canny commander in his own right. He's the perfect second-in-command who would never be successful at the head of the organization." Juice sipped his coffee. "My point in bringing up von Moltke is that your initial plan to take down Syndicate S didn't survive the first contact with them."

Sally leaned forward, put her elbows on the desk, and rested her chin on her hands. "I know. I can see that now. There were about a thousand things I could have done differently. Should have done differently." She sighed. "How did you do it? How did you keep from going crazy and second-guessing yourself all the time?"

"Who says I didn't second-guess myself all the time? I still do. That's the indication of a good leader. You should always be open to analysis of your decisions, whether by someone else or by yourself. Part of becoming a better leader is learning from your mistakes."

"Even when your mistakes get people hurt and killed? Civilians? Your family?"

"*Especially* those mistakes. Just don't let your second-guessing become all-consuming, because then you're too paralyzed to make any decisions at all. And then you're Congress."

Sally snickered. She knew Juice detested that august body of representatives.

"Sometime, when the dust has cleared from the hearings, we'll sit down and have a beer and I'll tell you about the Branch Davidians and how I nearly quit Just Cause because of it."

"That's required reading at the Hero Academy. Also, beer . . . yuck."

"You just haven't had a really good one yet. And there are several things that never made it into the official report."

"Now I'm all curious."

"Later, Sally."

"What hearings did you mean just now?"

Juice frowned. "There's a certain Senator making some very loud noises about an investigation into Just Cause and the PRA after yesterday's events. If she gets her way, and in the current political climate, I suspect she will, there's going to be a hearing of some kind."

"You mean, like, where we have to testify?"

"Yes, it'll be that kind of dog-and-pony show. Although as the head of the PRA, I think I'm much more likely to be on the hot seat. She has it in for me more than she does for you. In her eyes, you're just a way to get back at me."

"Senator Goodwin, of course."

"Naturally."

Senator Goodwin had formerly worked for Homeland Security during the Archmage fiasco, and when Juice and Sally and several others had disappeared for several months due to accidental time travel, she'd stepped in to take command of Just Cause. When Juice and Sally returned, she was advocating for a nuclear strike against the Archmage's stronghold. Juice had sent her packing after pulling some strings with President Bush, who was his friend, and Goodwin had never forgiven that.

"She's willing to take down the PRA just because she hates you?"

Juice grinned. "Some folks can't let a grudge go."

* * *

One of the primary tenets of the Just Cause charter was to protect civilian lives and property whenever possible. Sometimes, though, that was an impossibility. The government had a fund to absorb rebuilding costs that property insurance wouldn't cover, and any time money needed to come out of it, the way some Senators and Representatives screamed about it, one might think the money was coming directly out of their pockets, or being ripped from their skin. It was a boondoggle, many claimed. A government slush fund equivalent to bridges to nowhere and missile defense systems nobody wanted and didn't work anyway. Nevertheless, homeowners and business owners whose livelihoods were saved by the fund were always grateful, and Just Cause members did their best to apologize in person for the inconvenience caused.

When civilians were injured—or worse, killed— from exposure to parahuman abilities, things got much more complicated. The government insurance fund was designated solely for property reconstruction, but attorneys had figured out loopholes to dip into it for the payouts and settlements from the inevitable lawsuits filed by injured survivors or the loved ones of the deceased. For every hundred dollars paid to repair or rebuild a damaged property, almost a thousand dollars went to an out-of-court settlement. This fact was drilled into Just Cause members on a regular basis. Saving lives and preventing injuries to bystanders was the most important thing superheroes could do.

Even though Sally understood the economic cost, she had a great sense of the human cost as well. She'd asked Jack to go visit the families of the eleven dead civilians and police officers on behalf of Just Cause. She knew someday it would have to be her handling that unpleasant chore. The idea of walking up to someone's front door, in full costume, in full view of the neighbors and the press, to apologize for letting a loved one die . . . well, Sally would rather give a lengthy speech to a huge gallery of people, naked, with a full bladder.

Instead, she pulled Minerva and Detroit Steel from active duty and brought them to Manhattan where they could visit the injured civilians in the hospital. Again, they were in full costume, in full view of everyone, but it looked good to the general public. Media reports on the Syndicate S debacle had been uniformly less-than-flattering, and a lot of talking heads were second and third-guessing whether Sally was even qualified to lead. There had been calls for her resignation, of course. And calls for Juice's resignation. And a few politicians were loudly calling for the President's resignation for appointing Juice in the first place, conveniently forgetting that his position was a product of the previous administration.

All things being equal, Sally would much rather have been cuddling with Jason in their apartment and babying him as needed. The team physician had put him on what Jason called the Fifteen-Day Disabled List, meaning he had two weeks and a day before he would be re-evaluated for active duty again. It sounded suspiciously like something from sports, but Jason had said he was looking forward to catching up on the NFL playoffs anyway. The surgeon used grafts to repair Jason's and Shillelagh's tympanic membranes. They had to wear waterproof earplugs to keep the surgical sites dry while they healed. The good news, the doctor said, was inner ears tended to heal well if treated, although it might take some time.

Jason was worried about losing some portion of his hearing, saying everything sounded like it was coming to him through a busted Chevy speaker. The physician agreed with the analogy. "Try to keep your environment as quiet as possible," said the doctor. "The less your inner ear has to move around, the faster it will heal. That means no loud music or television. No training or weightlifting. No yelling." He looked over his glasses at Sally. "I trust you'll work at being quiet as well, Sally."

Sally nudged Jason. "I'll do all my screaming in my office, I promise."

They made love, carefully and tenderly—and quietly —that evening, and it helped Sally to forget the troubles of being a superhero team leader for a couple of hours.

Those troubles were back at the forefront of her mind as she stepped out of the Just Cause van with Minerva and Detroit Steel and looked up at the towering white edifices of New York Presbyterian, where all the injured bystanders had been taken.

"Look, Momma," said a little girl who was walking out of the main doors with her mother. "Superheroes! Can I meet them?"

"No, sweetie." Her mother tugged her away. "They're dangerous."

That was almost enough for Sally to turn around and get back in the van, but Minerva touched her elbow. "It's all right," she said, her voice soft enough that only Sally would hear it. "Watch."

The woman squired her daughter away at a brisk pace, heading for a subway kiosk. The little girl, who couldn't have been older than five or six, looked back and gave a shy wave. Sally waved back and the girl's face lit up like a ray of sunshine through the clouds.

"Not everybody hates us," said Detroit Steel. "We're just like cops. When they need us, they're glad to see us. Otherwise, they'd just as soon we ain't around."

"Maybe we can change that," said Sally, and then she thought about what she'd said. "Yeah. We should really work on that." She dashed off a text to Davey, asking her to put together some kind of marketing focus group to work on improving Just Cause's image.

Ok, replied Davey, who never bothered with punctuation in a text unless she needed more than one sentence to convey her thought, which was unlikely.

"You guys ready?" Sally asked, more to convince herself than question them.

"Yes," said Minerva.

"Hell, yeah," added Detroit Steel.

They entered the hospital.

Receptionists, patients, and other visitors stared in open-mouthed wonder at Detroit Steel's carefully brushed and polished skin, at Minerva's gleaming breastplate and helmet, at Sally's sunshine-yellow boots and proud horse's head logo on her chest. Camera phones and tablets were raised. Soon the Internet would be flooded with new images and videos of the three heroines. Sally led the others up to the reception desk. "Hi," she said as brightly as she could manage. "I'm Mustang Sally, this is Minerva, and this is Detroit Steel. We're from Just Cause and we'd like to visit the patients who were injured in the Syndicate S attacks."

"O-of course, ma'am." The receptionist stared at the three superheroes, wide-eyed. "Let me just notify the director that you're here."

"That's fine," said Sally. "And while we're here, we'd be happy to stop by the children's ward to say hello to the kids." In Denver, she and Jason often visited the local children's hospitals and disadvantaged youth centers. Jason especially loved children and Sally was dreading the inevitable conversation about when she would like to become a mother herself. She did want kids . . . someday . . . but not before she'd gotten in a good, long fill of being a superhero first. Her grandmother's career had been cut short with the birth of her mother. At least her mother had spent many years on Just Cause before finally getting pregnant with Sally. Sally hoped to follow that family-planning path herself. Maybe she'd start thinking about it seriously in her mid-thirties. Maybe.

They took their time getting up to the ward. They signed a lot of autographs, posed for pictures, and shook a lot of hands. Despite the obvious adulation, especially from the younger patients and visitors, Sally caught a lot of dark glances from some people. Not everyone saw her and her teammates as heroes, and she was pretty sure they were all disciples of the talk-radio maestro Ken Reichel, who made no bones about his dislike of the parahuman community. His show seemed to be on multiple channels, repeated multiple times per day, so someone could always find his preacher's voice belting out of a radio, espousing hate and disseminating disinformation, half-truths, and outright lies. She even heard the man's voice coming from a couple hospital rooms and people clustered around them tended to glare more at her and her friends.

Eventually, they made it to the ward, and Sally and the others spent a lot of time talking with the injured victims, or to their families if the victims were unable to converse. They sat with them, asked questions, listened to the answers. Sally tried very hard to show genuine interest in the victims, because none of them would have been in the hospital if not for her and her team. Well, that wasn't entirely true, and she knew it, but the guilt complex kept rearing its ugly head. And it didn't help that every once in a while, she overheard someone nearby bitching about *those goddamn parahumans* and how *they think they're so much better*. The hatred and fear never seemed very far away, and the political factions in the government were becoming more and more polarized by the day.

Then Sally met the woman she'd personally rescued from Slash in the building lobby, and she forgot about the political games for a few minutes. The woman's face lit up with a brilliant smile as Sally paused by her door and knocked. "May I come in?"

"Yes! Please do!" The woman winced as she raised her hand. Sally saw that she had bandages wrapped around her chest beneath her hospital robe.

"Does it hurt?" Sally nodded toward the wound.

"Only when I breathe." The woman smiled again. "The doctor said the quill went between my ribs and pierced my lung. They had to put a tube in me to keep it from collapsing. I don't really understand it very well."

Sally sat down beside her. "It sounds pretty complicated. That porcupine guy nailed me a couple of times too, but he only caught me in the back. It's healing up, so I think it'll be all right for you too." She wanted to give the woman as much hope as she can. "What's your name?"

"Lisa."

"Hi, Lisa. I'm Salena, but everyone calls me Sally."

"Thank you for coming to help me, Sally. You and your superhero friends. I know there are people who don't like you very much, but I might have died if you hadn't been there." She squeezed Sally's hand. "I'm in your debt."

Sally swallowed a sudden lump in her throat. "I don't collect debts like that, Lisa. Saving you is my job, and I'm glad to do it."

"Well, thank you anyway."

Sally smiled. There was nothing quite like being appreciated for doing one's job.

* * *

Evening found Sally loitering in her office, dressed down in tights and one of Jason's hoodies that hung off her spare frame like a tent. She had a glass of iced tea sitting on a coaster on her desk and was watching the droplets of condensation trickle down the sides. Jason was down in their apartment, sacked out on a combination of painkillers, and even though Sally was looking forward to spending the night beside her husband again, she wasn't quite ready to call her day done.

Maybe she should take up drinking, she thought wryly as she lifted up the tea and watched the sparkles reflect off the ice cubes within it. This was the kind of thing leaders did, right? They reflected on their decisions, bad or good, and drank scotch. Or bourbon. Or whiskey. Jack would probably know for sure. He'd been working in the Command Center all day, trying to dig up any kind of information on Syndicate S or The Militia. He hadn't come to Sally with anything yet, which meant he was still looking.

Davey knocked on the office door. It was open, of course. Juice had always had an open-door policy when he ran Just Cause, and Sally wanted to emulate that as much as she could. "Come in, Davey."

"I'm about to turn in for the night. Do you need anything else?"

Sally didn't look at her assistant. "Davey . . . Am I doing as poorly as I think I am?"

"How do you mean?"

"Everything's already falling apart and it's been less than a week. Things never seemed to be like this in Just Cause in Denver. Even the Second Team doesn't run from one calamity to another. Is this the way it's going to be here?"

"I have no idea." Davey tapped a pen against her lips as if punctuating her thoughts. "But I don't think you're doing a poor job at all. You are, as they say, the best woman for the job. You've had a rough couple of days for sure, but that doesn't mean it's going to be like this all the time. How many times a year do you really get called out for emergencies? Eight or ten times, maybe? Even if it was fifty call-outs, one a week, it would still be less than a New York firefighter gets."

"I never thought about it like that." She sipped her tea. It was weak, but that was all right because she was tired and needed to get some sleep.

"You're not fighting a war on the front lines here, Sally. You're specialized law enforcement. You're going to get called out for special emergencies. That kind of thing doesn't happen every day. Or every week, according to all the statistics I've seen. It was just bad timing that Syndicate S turned up the day they did."

"I guess so."

"If it had been a couple of weeks later, you and your team would have had some training under your belts, and you'd know the actual strengths and weaknesses of your team much better than you do now. You'd probably have mopped the floor with Syndicate S."

Sally smiled. "That wouldn't have left anything for The Militia to do."

"And next time, they could be the ones needing help from Just Cause. These things have a tendency to iron themselves out over time. I think you should be a little less hard on yourself."

Sally looked over at Davey, who had her nose buried in her phone. "And you should unplug and call it a night yourself, Davey."

"I will, but a report just came in that you're going to want to see."

"What's that?"

"Your dead parahuman friend Afterburner. Martina, she called herself."

"She wasn't my friend. She was trying to kill me."

"She's been identified."

Sally sat up. "I need to see that report right away."

Six

"*I don't want someone walking down a public street with a nuclear bomb or a vial full of VX nerve gas, and neither do I want someone with parahuman powers on that street. In my eyes, a weapon of mass destruction is a weapon of mass destruction, no matter whether it's nuclear, chemical, or paragene.*"
—Ken Reichel, Top Flight Radio Network

January, 2009
New York City, NY

Morning came for Sally far too early, as it always did. Jason joked that she wasn't faster than anyone else, she just slept more and was more rested than everyone else in the world. Why in the world had she set her alarm for the ungodly hour of six o'clock? She wasn't on monitor duty or . . .

Then her brain got itself up to speed and she remembered that they'd gotten a break in the Afterburner investigation late the night before. Afterburner's death had been no accident; she had some kind of explosive embedded inside her, according to the final report by the medical examiner, and Sally presumed whoever was monitoring her detonated the device instead of letting the woman surrender to Sally. The way the Syndicate S members exploded was too similar for it to be a coincidence. In her tossing and turning as she tried to fall asleep the night before, an idea occurred to her.

Syndicate S had been well-prepared to fight Just Cause. Afterburner had called out Sally publicly, challenging her to a fight.

Someone was testing Just Cause, and they were covering their tracks by killing those they sent up against Sally and her teammates. "I don't like being used," Sally growled into her bowl of yogurt and oatmeal later that morning, stabbing a piece of peach with a vengeance.

"Me neither." Jack sat across from her with a plate piled high with eggs and bacon. "Except in the bedroom. Then I'll tolerate it."

Sally eyed his breakfast. "I'm willing to bet you're not invulnerable to high cholesterol, Jack."

He chewed on a piece of bacon. "For this, I'll risk it."

"Here . . ." Sally snagged a piece at super-speed before Jack could react. "This is me, saving your life." She took a bite and let the salty, fatty goodness coat her mouth.

"Hey!" Jack slid his plate out of her reach. "You want bacon, there's plenty more."

"This is all I wanted. What's on your agenda today?"

"Well, you're the boss. You tell me."

"Everyone should be back up for active duty starting today, except Shillelagh and Jason. I'd like you to run a training session. Nothing huge or formal. Just put everyone through their paces. Get them some time working together. We need to be more of a team."

"And by having me run the training, you're not going to be involved?" Jack ate another piece of bacon. "Isn't that opposite of what you're trying to accomplish?"

"I have a reason. We got a break in the Afterburner case last night. A positive identification. I'm going to take Minerva and we're going to go check out her last known address, and see what kind of stuff we can dig up on her." Sally considered stealing another piece of bacon, but her common sense won out at last and she ate some more yogurt.

"You know I like that investigation stuff. Maybe you should run the training."

"I'll run the next one. I need Minerva for her sensory capabilities, and I'm the one Afterburner came after in the first place. I need to know why."

"You think she's tied to Syndicate S."

"Yes, I do. Prisoners and corpses exploding to avoid being captured, questioned, or autopsied on two separate occasions? What are the odds?"

"*Never tell me the odds.*" Jack did his best Han Solo.

"*I've got a bad feeling about this.* I don't like that Afterburner didn't show any indication of parahuman genes in her remains. It reminds me of Guatemala."

"Thanks. I hate being reminded of Guatemala."

"Still, if someone has rebuilt that technology, we need to find it and shut it down."

"No argument from me there." Jack dumped ketchup all over his eggs, thoroughly ruining them in Sally's eyes. "As long as there are parahumans and people who aren't parahumans, some have-nots are going to do everything they can to become haves."

Sally drank her coffee. "And if they can't, they're going to do their best to stop us."

Jack nodded. "We're the new Jim Crow. Gays getting married isn't anything compared to the parahuman next door."

"You're a long-time PR guy. How do we improve our public image?"

"Save kittens from trees? Rescue toddlers from wells? It doesn't matter what good we do. Good deeds don't make the twenty-four-hour news networks. The talking heads have to have something to scream about. If we rescued a bunch of nuns and orphans from a bus about to plunge off the George Washington Bridge, somebody would be yelling that we let X, Y, and Z happen on our watch while we were performing that rescue. If we'd been handling X, Y, and Z, we'd be at fault for letting the nuns and orphans fall to their deaths."

"That's a terribly cheerful thought to start the day. So what do we do?"

"We keep on doing what we're supposed to do. Muddle through and hope that in the end when our balances are tallied, we've done more good than failed to halt bad."

"Very poetic, Jack."

Jack belched, wafting bacon across the table. "Good luck with your investigation today. Keep me in the loop?"

"Count on it." Sally finished her coffee. "Try not to kill any of the new recruits in the CSC today."

Jack snapped his fingers. "Aw, Mom, you never let me have any fun."

* * *

Jason was awake when Sally returned to the apartment to change into something more subtle than her crimson and gold costume. "Hey," he said, his voice barely above a whisper. He had his earplugs sitting on the bedside table and was idly picking at his guitar with it unplugged.

"Hey, babycakes. How are your ears feeling?" Sally made sure to keep her voice down, knowing that loud noises would hurt him as well as inhibit his healing.

"They hurt." Jason grimaced. "But I can hear just a little bit better today. I can't hear my guitar, though."

Sally went over to him and kissed his cheek and then put her arms around his shoulders and rested her head against the side of his neck. "It's not plugged in, sweetie."

"No, I mean I can't hear it at all. Can you hear this?" He strummed the strings in a chord that Sally was pretty sure was an A major. He'd been trying to teach her a bit about how to play the guitar, but Sally was about as tone-deaf as they came. She tried to learn, and could even play *Mary Had a Little Lamb* without having to read the music, but that was the extent of it.

"Yes."

"I can't hear it at all. What if I can't hear music anymore? That bitch took away my hearing. Took away my music." Jason sniffled a little and Sally realized his pain ran much deeper than just his ears.

"Baby . . . you can hear my voice today. You couldn't hardly hear anything when you first got out of the hospital. You're going to be fine. The doctor said permanent hearing loss is rare with perforated eardrums. Surgery went well for both you and Shillelagh. It's just going to take time. Not everybody heals as fast as I do."

Jason pouted. "It's not fair."

"No, of course it isn't fair. Nothing about this is fair. We should have waltzed in there and demolished Syndicate S before they even knew what hit them. I think we were set up to fail."

"What do you mean?"

"You read the reports, right?"

"Uh . . . I've been a little preoccupied."

Sally bit back an angry retort. She reminded herself that being super-strong and super-tough meant Jason wasn't used to being injured, even slightly. He was scared and worried and feeling helpless, which Sally knew was the worst feeling in the world, especially for someone who had the mindset of a hero. "They exploded. Every last one of them. Just like Afterburner did. Someone sent her to test me, and when they got what they wanted, they killed her. Just threw her away like she was a broken tool. Syndicate S blew up the same way. I hate to say this, but they might have been victims as much as we were. Someone wanted to test Just Cause, and I think they used Syndicate S to do it."

Jason's eyes widened. "That's messed up."

"But I have good news." Sally pulled off her hoodie. "We have a lead on Afterburner's true identity." She skinned out of her yoga pants and ruffled her hair. "And I have better news than that."

"Yeah?" Jason found a bit of his old grin.

Sally unhooked her bra and threw it aside. "I don't have to leave just yet."

* * *

The unmarked black sedan slid through the streets of Brooklyn as snowflakes swirled down from the pewter sky. Sally snuggled her overcoat a little tighter around her and wished she'd put on one more layer. Beside her in the back seat, Minerva looked completely out of character in a tan overcoat with her black curls down and flowing around her shoulders instead of being pinned up underneath a helmet, but she did have her eyes closed and was probably listening to the variations of the tires rubbing across the pavement, Sally thought. She reread the dossier handed to her by Davey just before the two young women boarded the ferry back to the mainland. It was as much information as the Command Center could retrieve on one Martina Hladky, whose roommate had reported her missing the day before and who Sally thought might very well have been the woman underneath Afterburner's helmet. She hadn't gotten a lot of time to look at the super-villain's face, but when Sally's perceptions were accelerated, she didn't need a lot of time.

When Sally had first joined Just Cause, there was a psi on the team named Glimmer. He spent some time with Sally, constructing some mental architecture in her mind to allow her to act as a psionic video camera. His constructions remained in place even years later, and with Ment's help, Sally was able to transfer her half-remembered images and sounds of Afterburner to

Minerva. Even though Sally herself didn't have the enhanced senses Minerva had, the raw data was still there for Minerva to analyze. Minerva could look at pictures or video, listen to a voice mail, and be able to tell with a high probability of accuracy whether or not a potential suspect was a match for Afterburner.

Just thinking about it made Sally's head hurt.

"I think they're related," Minerva said to Sally as the car turned a corner, kicking up slush against a bus going the opposite direction.

"What is?"

"Syndicate S and Afterburner. I've been reviewing the scents of the explosive residue used in both cases. It's very similar, even allowing for differences in the biochemistry of the carriers."

"I'm not sure whether or not to be grossed out or not," said Sally. "You can smell everyone's funk mixed with the explosives?"

Minerva cracked open an eye to look at Sally. "I can smell everyone all the time."

"Oh." Sally realized what that must mean. "Oh. Geez. I'm sorry. I bet we all stink."

"I don't find scents unpleasant. They're interesting. Although some are better than others."

Sally avoided asking whether she was one of the good ones, because she didn't want to put Minerva in the position of maybe having to lie about it. Nevertheless, she would take a long, hot shower when she got home and scrub everything, just in case. She read through the sparse dossier on Martina Hladky once more instead, hoping she had missed some critical piece of information the first five times she'd examined it. The Command Center hadn't been able to pull up much more than school and work history. They were notoriously behind the times when it came to monitoring social media. It occurred to Sally that social media should be a priority for Just Cause. The reason she had even known about Afterburner in the first place was because someone had Tweeted pictures of Mustang Sally's name burned into the side of a hill by the would-be super-villain. *Have the Command Center assign a full-time dedicated social media monitoring team. Make sure they're young!* Sally texted to Davey.

Ok.

"Ladies, we're here," said the driver, checking his address against the GPS and the number on the building beside the street.

"Find a place to park and wait for us. We'll call you when we're finished," said Sally. She and Minerva slipped out of the car and crossed the street in typical New York fashion, trotting in front of traffic and waving off the angry horns. "I feel like we're two detectives from *Law and Order*."

"All right, but you have to be Jerry Orbach."

"Ewww. I want to be Benjamin Bratt."

"*Well . . . you can't.*"

"*Serenity.* You should know better than to try to stump me with a Captain Tightpants quote." Sally checked the names beside the buzzers. "I don't see a Hladky here at all. Half of these don't even have names. How are we supposed to find anyone?"

Minerva pushed a button and waited.

"Yes?" came an annoyed voice after a few seconds.

"It's the police, ma'am. We're looking for Martina Hladky's apartment."

"Three-oh-seven," said the voice.

"Thank you."

"How did you know?" Sally asked, feeling stupid as soon as she'd asked it, because of course Minerva knew. That was what she did.

"That button has seen twenty times as much traffic as all the others. It's almost worn smooth from so many fingers. I figured it was the super's apartment, or at least the neighborhood busybody."

Minerva smiled. "Jerry Orbach would have something witty to say here."

Sally pushed the button for 307. "I wonder if anybody's home. Why did you say we were the police instead of Just Cause?"

"*Police* would get better results. Not everyone knows about Just Cause. Or cares to help."

A sleepy voice came over the intercom. "Yes?"

"Just . . . uh, police, ma'am," said Sally. "We're looking for Martina Hladky. Do you know her?"

"Y-yes. She's my roommate. Did you find her?"

Sally looked at Minerva, who said nothing. "May we come up and speak with you?"

"Yes please. The, uh, the elevator's busted. You'll have to walk up." The buzzer sounded and the door lock clicked open. Sally pulled it open, welcoming the warm air from the building interior despite the mixed smells of different meals cooking.

Minerva pulled her overcoat a bit tighter around herself and wrinkled her nose in dismay. "Try not to touch anything."

They climbed the stairs that stank of urine and mildew, the dirty walls stained with who-knows-what. It looked like the building was sweating onto itself. Naked, yellowed light bulbs sat haphazardly on fixtures that poked out of the walls, each one a mute testament to a graveyard of long-dead moths and flies on the floor beneath them.. The air was thick and moist, and the combination of food smells from two dozen different cultures mixed into a miasma that might have even put Jason off his food. Sally's perceptions accelerated of their own accord and she turned to look where she thought she'd seen movement out of the corner of her eye, but when she turned, there was nothing. Roaches, she thought. Or spiders. Or rats. "Jesus," she muttered. "How has this building not been condemned?"

"I have no idea."

They reached Room 307. The door was decorated with cheerful Christmas-themed wrapping paper, although someone had torn a large swath from it. Sally reached her gloved hand up to the door and knocked with soft authority. "Miss? We're here."

"She's coming," Minerva said right away.

A moment later the door opened to reveal a short, top-heavy young woman with her hair caught up in a ponytail and glasses perched upon the end of her upturned nose. She had on pajama bottoms and a hotel-monogrammed bathrobe over a black t-shirt advertising some band of which Sally had never heard. "You the cops?" she asked around a mouthful of peppermint gum.

Sally held up her Just Cause badge, something she rarely got the opportunity to do. "Miss, I'm Salena Tibbets and this is Minerva. We're from Just Cause."

The young woman squinted at them. "So you're superheroes, not cops? You're that Mustang Sally girl, right? I thought you were taller."

Sally shrugged. "Everyone does. We're helping out the police with the investigation into your roommate. May we come in?"

"Yeah, sure." She pushed her glasses up her nose and stepped aside to let the two heroes into the apartment. "Can I, uh, get you anything?"

"No," said Sally. "We're just here to ask some questions and look around if you give us permission." The apartment was sparsely furnished, suggesting the inhabitants weren't rolling in money, and it was less a home than a place to keep from having to sleep on the street. The only picture on the wall was an amateurish painting of a bowl of fruit that looked like it might have come with the apartment. No dishes were piled up in the sink, but the uncovered trash can was full of microwave entree wrappers and take-out containers. The couch was threadbare and didn't match the two office chairs beside it. A stack of martial arts magazines covered the coffee table on one corner and a pile of envelopes that looked like bills dominated the other. The pink cat-shaped clock perched on the kitchen counter was the only thing giving any kind of personality to the dwelling.

"What's your name?" Minerva asked.

"Destiny. Really," said the young woman, clearly used to explaining herself. "I know it sounds like a stage name. And I'm even a dancer. But yeah. Do you want to sit down?" Destiny indicated the couch.

Sally sat, but Minerva wandered around the main room of the apartment, moving slowly with her hands slightly outstretched as if she were feeling the air. "Martina Hladky is your roommate?"

Destiny sat on one of the office chairs and drew one knee up to her chest. "She's been my roommate for a couple years. We met through an online roommate finder, but we get along real well. When I'm on late shifts at the club, she's quiet when she's here. She keeps up on her half the chores and bills. She, uh, makes real good latkes. I can't cook at all."

"Why did you report her missing?" asked Sally.

"I haven't seen her in like two weeks. Sometimes she'd take off for a few days for a job or a fight. She's an MMA fighter. I saw her fight once and she won. I guess she's pretty good. She makes enough at it to pay her share of the rent, anyway. She works odd jobs to make ends meet when she's not fighting. But she's never been gone this long before. And she missed making her half of the rent, which is a first in all the time we've been living together. I checked her Facebook. No posts. No texts either. I'm just worried that something, you know, happened to her."

"Does she have any enemies that you know of?" asked Minerva. "Anyone who would want to hurt her? Anyone who had some kind of hold over her?"

Destiny shrugged. "I don't think so, unless someone who she beat in the ring had a bone to pick with her. I don't think she's a dirty fighter, but I'm not an expert in it. She hasn't had a boyfriend for almost a year. Said it would distract her from training. Last time we talked, she said she was onto something that could pay off real big. She wouldn't say what. I thought maybe she'd gotten into a Pay-Per-View event, or landed a manager to get her some better fight cards."

Sally leaned forward. "Destiny, do you have any current pictures of Martina?"

"Just on Facebook." Destiny picked up a laptop that was leaning on the side of the couch and opened it. She tapped some keys and then turned the computer around so Sally and Minerva could see. "That's her. And, uh, me." She sniffled. "She's dead, isn't she? Th-that's why you're here. You needed to be sure before you told me."

Sally only needed one look at the picture to be sure Martina and Afterburner was one and the same person. "I'm so sorry, Destiny. I'm afraid she's dead."

Destiny lowered her head and wiped her eyes. "I knew it. I've had a terrible feeling about it for the past week. How did she die?"

Sally glanced up at Minerva. "It was quick. She didn't suffer."

"We believe she was murdered," said Minerva. "Which is why we're here. If you can give us any more information about her that might help, please do. Anything you can think of might be the clue we need. May I look at her room?"

Destiny nodded. "Yeah. It's d-down the hall on the left. Oh, God. Who would murder Tina? She wasn't out to do anybody any wrong. She just wanted to make a good life for herself."

"We're trying to find that out," said Sally. She watched Minerva drift down the hall, tracing her fingers along the wall, reading its secrets. "Can you tell me more about the big job she told you about?"

"I told you all I know already. She was excited about it. She didn't post about it or anything."

"Was she ever involved in anything illegal?"

"I don't think so. Maybe some fights for cash under the table. Does that count?"

"I doubt it. Gambling, maybe? Did she owe anyone a large amount of money?"

"I don't know. God, I'm no help at all. Excuse me." Destiny went to the kitchen, pulled a paper towel off the dispenser, and blew her nose.

"Did she have parahuman abilities? Did she ever display any in front of you?"

"Not as far as I know. Is that why you're here instead of regular cops? Was she a para?"

"We're still investigating that. Who else might know more about her?"

"Probably the people down at the gym where she trained. It's, uh, Title something."

"Title Boxing Club," said Minerva as she came out from Martina's room.

"That's it," said Destiny.

"One last question and we'll be on our way, Destiny," said Sally. "Did Martina have any family that we need to notify of her death?"

Destiny sniffled again. "Not as far as I know. At least, she n-never talked about anyone if she did." She took a shuddering breath. "What am I supposed to do?"

Minerva crouched down beside Destiny and looked up into her eyes. "You live on. You remember the good times with your friend. You tell others about her so her story becomes part of their lives too. In this way, she lives beyond her mortal self."

Destiny looked down at Minerva. "I d-don't know why, but that makes me feel better."

Minerva took her hand. "I will remember her."

Wonder filled Destiny's eyes. "I believe you."

Sally set a business card on the coffee table. "If you think of anything else that might be helpful to us, call that number anytime, day or night."

"I will."

Sally and Minerva headed to the door. Destiny followed after them like a lost puppy. Sally felt terrible about delivering bad news, even though she knew it had needed to be done. When she'd lost her friend Shannon Tokugawa during the Archmage crisis, she'd been the one to deliver the news to Shannon's family, and that had been immeasurably difficult. She hoped it wouldn't ever get easier, because that would mean she'd have to do it often enough to become jaded and inured to it.

"Hey," said Destiny as Sally opened the door. "You're going to find whoever did this to Tina, right? I mean, that's what you guys do, right?"

"Yes, it is," said Minerva.

"She didn't deserve to die. She was a good person," said Destiny. "Punish them for it."

"Don't worry," said Sally. "We intend to."

Seven

"Parahuman crime is the lowest it's been since 2001. Why do we suddenly need all these additional hero groups? Are we supposed to just let them sit in their high castles, lording it over us? That's not my America, and it shouldn't be yours either."
—Senator Christine Goodwin (R-NY)

January, 2009
New York City, NY

Title Boxing Club was as much of a relic as anything could be in the Twenty-First Century. It didn't have a Twitter account, or a Facebook page. It didn't even have a website. The only way the Command Center could even find an address for the place was by searching the New York City phone book. Sure, it was an online phone book, but even that was only a transcription of the paper version.

"Phone book," grumbled Sally. "What's next? Smoke signals and the Pony Express?"

"I thought that was you." Minerva's lips curved into a gentle smile.

"What was?"

"The Pony Express."

"What? Oh!" Sally laughed at the unexpected joke. Minerva wasn't as humorless as Just Cause Denver commander Doublecharge, but her jokes were few and far between. And when she did deliver them, it was with the timing of a professional headlining comedienne. "I can't believe nobody has ever called me that before."

"Their loss, then." The snow had picked up and it swirled beneath the orange cones of the streetlights as their driver navigated his way to the borough known as Spanish Harlem. When he'd plugged the address for the boxing club into the car's GPS, he actually paused as if he were about to suggest it was no place for two nice young ladies before remembering he was shuttling around two superheroes who could probably take very good care of themselves.

"What did you find out in Martina's room?"

"She was desperate for money. The whole room stank of fear sweat and nervous tension."

"How does fear equate to financial desperation?"

"The pattern of footprints on the carpet suggested she was pacing a lot. She had a pile of receipts on her bedside table with the totals circled, and impressions on a notepad showed the same numbers written down there. There was a list of fight schedules with dollar amounts notated beside each."

"Okay, Sherlock Holmes. I should know better than to question your methods."

"You should always question. It keeps us honest and focused. I could smell other people's blood in the room, which is to be expected with a career fighter. I also caught hints of gun oil and cocaine."

"Ahhh," said Sally. "That's interesting. Good people don't generally get mixed up in both those things together. You think she was dealing?"

"No. I saw no indication of large amounts of drugs or weapons passing through her apartment."

"So it wasn't her, but somebody she knew. Someone in her circle."

"That is likely."

"Maybe they can point us in the right direction at the Boxing Club."

"It is possible."

"Whatever the gig was, they gave her parahuman powers. That's scary. First was that reactor down in Guatemala. Then Champion with his nanotech. Now someone else is giving out powers. It's like a new arms race."

"We don't know if bestowed parahuman abilities can be passed on through reproduction. Let me tell you something I've learned over the years. Parahumans have a distinctive odor note in their sweat. I can detect it, but it's not something I could tell anyone else how to detect."

"You can smell parahumans?"

"That is what I just said. I have never found a parahuman who did not exude that scent. I presume what I am smelling is the parahuman gene."

"Are there non-parahumans who smell that way?"

"Yes. I presume they are unpowered carriers of the gene. My own parents were carriers but neither has ever exhibited the slightest parahuman ability. When I searched Martina's room, I didn't detect any hint of that odor in her bed, or her clothing. As far as I can tell, she wasn't a latent carrier."

"I wonder if Syndicate S is tied to the same origin as Martina." Sally drummed her fingers on the armrest at a rapid tattoo. "With them getting all blown up like she did. Maybe someone gave them their powers too. Did you smell the parahuman gene on any of them?"

"I'm sorry, I was a little busy at the time." Minerva bowed her head in dismay. "It's very faint. I have to be actively searching for it or I won't notice."

"It's all right. You weren't the only one too busy to think properly."

Both women sat in silence for a minute, each alone with her thoughts.

"I believe we have arrived," said Minerva.

Title Boxing Club looked like it might have been a small grocery store in a former life. The old brick building had windows facing the street with iron bars protecting them. Light streamed out from some of the windows, while others had been painted over. Condensation had frozen on the glass, making it impossible to see any details inside the building. The roof was arched like a barn's. The front door was propped open, presumably to let some cold evening air inside.

Sally directed the driver to find a place to park and wait for them. "Don't let anyone steal your hubcaps," she said, only halfway kidding.

Minerva sniffed the winter air as they crossed the street. "Mmmm . . ."

"What is it?" Sally asked.

"Cuban sandwiches. Now I'm hungry."

"You would have to say that. I am too. We'll eat after this. Come on, let's go be detectives some more."

"Dun-dun." Minerva aped the *Law & Order* musical punch that had become a staple of pop culture.

Walking into Title Boxing Club was a lot like walking into a sauna. Despite the open door, the air was thick and moist and warm enough to immediately make Sally unbutton her coat. It smelled like the locker room at headquarters did. Portable heaters and fans were plugged into extension cords from the walls. Several training stations stood at the ready, including a rack made from welded steel tubing that supported multiple heavy bags speed bags. Sally had tried using those, but found them slow and boring and prone to exploding under her flurries of high speed punches. A couple of boxers were working them, their fists taped up and towels resting across their necks. One guy was working out on one of the four weight machines, but all the treadmills were unoccupied. There were three raised boxing rings against one wall, only one of which was in use. Two young black men circled each other warily, red gloves on their hands and matching pads around their faces and heads as a man with a Puerto Rican accent yelled at them to quit being such pussies and hit each other.

Sally stopped dead in her tracks when she heard the trainer. She knew that voice.

"What is it?" Minerva asked.

"I know him. The trainer."

"How?"

"From Champion's organization."

"Interesting."

A young woman, maybe Sally's age, gave her speed bag one last pummel and turned to see Sally and Minerva standing by the door. She had strong, well-developed arms and shoulders that reminded Sally of her friend Desert Eagle back in Denver. The young woman looked over toward the trainer. "Hey, Hector."

"What?" The trainer glanced toward her, then spotted Sally and Minerva. "Huh." He looked back at the two boys in the ring. "If all you guys are gonna do is dance, maybe you need to join a repertory. 'Cept last I heard, they ain't takin' pussies either." He grabbed a towel, slung it across his shoulders, and crossed the gym toward Sally and Minerva. "Help you ladies? We're about to close."

"Hello, Hector," said Sally. "You probably don't remember me, but I remember you."

He narrowed his eyes. He was a muscular man beneath his sleeveless t-shirt and workout pants. He had shaved his head since the last time Sally had seen him, in the old Champions headquarters with the blood of a dead Nazi supervillain splattered across his fist. Tattoos covered both his arms and his neck. At about five and half feet tall, he reminded Sally of a junkyard bulldog, ready to rip out the throat of a trespasser. "You're right. This ain't about a paternity thing, is it? Because if it is, you got the wrong guy."

"Nothing like that. You once tried to hit me with a table leg." Sally smiled.

Hector kept his cool despite her provocative statement. She knew he was a parahuman who could transform his body into metal, like Detroit Steel except he could switch back and forth between nickel and flesh and blood. He'd been a trainer for the Champions before an undercover Sally discovered the true reason for the organization. He'd practiced a tough-love kind of training, like a drill sergeant in a lot of ways. And since he'd been training parahumans, he must have known Sally wasn't exaggerating. "You gonna have to be more specific. I hit a lot of people in my time."

"I bet if you had a . . . *nickel* for every time you did that, you'd be a rich man. I looked different back then. Taller. Brunette." She lowered her voice. "I took the heat off you."

"Juggler!" He referred to the alias Sally was using at the time. "What you doin' here, *chica*?"

"Well, I wasn't looking for you, so you can relax. You been working here long, Hector?"

"Couple years, maybe. Not a lot of places will hire an ex-con, so I got to take what I can get."

"Seems like your kind of place. And it's Sally. Mustang Sally. This is Minerva."

Hector's eyes widened. "No shit. I didn't recognize you out of your costumes."

"That's the general idea," said Sally. "You have time to answer some questions about someone who used to train here?"

"For you? Yeah." Hector had killed the man called Champion when the terrible truth about him came to light. Sally covered for him, claiming she delivered the killing blow to let Hector walk free. He pursed his lips and let loose with a cab-hailing whistle that rebounded off the walls and cut through the drone of the fans and heaters. "Yo. Closing time. Lonnie, Javon, get your dancing asses out of here. Next time you're here, if you ain't gonna throw some punches, I'm gonna let you play with me for a few rounds."

The two young men who'd been training in the ring muttered apologies. The man who'd been pounding weights picked up his bag. "Later, Hector."

"Night, Wallis. Shaw, you good?"

The woman who'd been hitting the bag shrugged into her jacket. She looked at Sally and Minerva with a mixture of curiosity and contempt. Sally thought she was probably estimating their toughness and wondering why two young ladies had come to visit Hector at closing time, and drawing conclusions forthwith. "Yeah. See you Thursday."

The last four patrons shuffled out the gym's door and Hector pulled it shut, and then lowered an iron grill over it. "We ain't got much here to steal. But every once in a while some punk ass decides to take a look around." He looked back over his shoulder at Sally. "You still trainin' or you give that shit up when you went back to being a superhero?"

"I never wasn't a superhero, Hector. And I never stop training."

"Good." He went over to the wall where numerous pairs of gloves hung from hooks. He selected a set and tossed it to her. "We can spar while we talk. Unless you gonna pussy out."

Sally took off her coat and her business jacket. "Sure, why not?" She proceeded to remove her blouse as well, thankful that she'd worn a sports bra for the comfort instead of something more fancy with hooks and underwires. Hector looked at her taut torso with the appreciation of someone looking at fine art, but she didn't get the sense he was ogling her. "How's your little girl, Hector?"

"Getting bigger every day. I don't get to see her too often except at a distance. Her mom don't like me much, that *puta*."

"Can't imagine why." Sally took a head protector from a cubby and strapped it over her head. They didn't do much boxing in Just Cause, but they'd learned some rudiments of it in the Hero Academy. She kicked off her shoes and pulled the gloves over her fists. They stank of old sweat and maybe even a little blood, but Sally tried to put it into perspective. The reek of the gym had to be making Minerva's stomach twist up in knots. Her teammate pulled up a stool beside the edge of the center boxing ring and leaned against the edge of the raised platform, ready to observe whatever show Sally was going to put on.

Sally slipped between the ropes and bounced on the ring's floor, testing its springiness and the traction with her bare feet. "Come on, old man. I'm getting bored in here."

Hector climbed into the ring himself, wearing gloves but no head protector. "Who you callin' old?" He'd thrown away his tank top to show off his chiseled physique and collection of jailhouse tattoos. Jason was much larger than Hector, and covered with slabs of muscle, but he had a thin veneer of fat over them that gave him a big of a soft, cuddly look that Sally absolutely adored. Hector was hard to the core, like the metal he could transform into.

Speaking of which . . . "Well, come on, Nickel. If we're going to spar, I'm not going to do it against a *crunchy.*" Sally hated using that word, a pejorative for the non-powered favored by certain members of the parahuman community, but Hector would understand.

He obliged her by changing. His skin took on a silvery-white luster. His tattoos vanished beneath the metal of his body. "Let's see if you learned anythin' in your castle out in the harbor, *chica.*"

The two of them circled each other in the ring. Hector didn't hold back. He pulled no punches as he launched combo after combo at Sally. She didn't need much super-speed to avoid them, but she used it enough to avoid taking any blows. There was no way she was going to let Hector nail her with one of his metallic fists. It would be like getting hit with a crowbar, and Sally had enough concussions in her history that one more could end her career, especially if it came from something as foolish as being careless in a boxing ring.

By the same stretch, she managed to get numerous blows upon Hector's head and body, but even her strongest blows had no effect on his metal flesh. He even started to take cheap shots, the sort of thing that would get him barred from the ring for life. Things like trying to stomp upon Sally's bare feet, punching at her throat and the back of her head. She wasn't offended by him cheating. In Hector's world, there were no rules except to survive and to win however one could. His simple take-no-prisoners philosophy was as refreshing to Sally as a cool drink on a hot day. She took a few cheap shots of her own, reminding him that even though they were nickel like the rest of him, he still had testicles. It didn't hurt him, but when she nailed them, he nodded like she'd scored a good point against him.

At last, they separated. Sally's sports bra and the top of her pants were soaked with sweat. Her hair was matted down with it beneath the head guard. Her arms were sore from throwing so many punches and her knuckles felt swollen inside the gloves. In spite of it all, she couldn't remember the last time she'd enjoyed a simple sparring session so much. "You ready to surrender?"

He snorted and bumped her gloves with his own. "We'll call it a draw. You're faster than I remember."

"And you're as hard-headed as ever. Do you remember a fighter named Martina Hladky?"

"Sure. She ain't been around for a while." Hector's tattoos reappeared as he transformed his metal back to flesh. He picked up a towel and slung it over his neck.

"She's dead, Hector. I'm sorry." It was easier to deliver the news to him than it would be to a civilian family, but it still made her clench her jaw until her teeth ached.

Hector kicked a folding chair beside the ring hard enough to warp it when it hit the wall. "Motherfucker!" Another chair went flying into a portable heater, shattering both into unrecognizable bits. Minerva floated away from the ring in the direction of a fire extinguisher. Dissatisfied with his limited destruction, Hector grabbed the scoring table and swung it into the side of the ring until it broke in half, and then he beat the broken pieces into splinters against the floor.

Sally waited until his tantrum wound down, knowing everyone dealt with grief in their own way.

Hector swung a table leg—that old favorite of his—against a training dummy shaped like a boxer's torso over and over until it, too, fell apart. Left with nothing but his hands, he beat the training dummy until it was covered with splatters of blood from his split knuckles. At last, he sank down in front of it, defeated, his head hanging forward, his bloody hands dangling at his sides. "Goddamn. Oh, goddamn it."

Sally grabbed the first aid kit beside the ring that had by some miracle avoided Hector's destructive temper. She removed gauze and tape and knelt down beside Hector. "Hector . . . I'm sorry. I'm really sorry."

He turned his shaved head toward her, glaring from beneath his lowered brows. "What the fuck do you know about it, *puta*?"

"I'm going to pretend like I didn't just hear you call me that, Hector, because I know you didn't really mean it." Sally took one of his hands in hers, knowing that she could dodge any punches he would throw in her direction if his temper flared up again. He let her tape gauze over his split knuckles and watched as she wound the tape around his palm to secure it. "Was she special to you?"

"All the kids who come here are special to me. They don't judge me for my past. Martina was the real deal. She wasn't just a boxer. She fought MMA, and she was fucking good at it." He held up his other hand so Sally could wrap it as well. "Lots of kids come in here with big dreams. Most of them ain't shit, though. But it gives them something to do instead of smash and grab, or selling drugs, or killing each other." He looked up at Sally. "Martina? She could fight, man. If anyone was gonna make it out of this shithole into the big time, it was gonna be her."

In fact, Sally had fought Martina, and knew the young woman had skills. "Was she involved in anything . . . shady? Drugs? Or guns?"

Hector's eyes flashed furious and Sally scooted back just out of his range. "No, and you ain't got to assume that just because she was a poor fucker like the rest of us in this part of town."

"I'm not assuming anything." Sally crossed her arms, not backing away from Hector any further. "When we searched her apartment, we found some evidence that suggested if she wasn't involved in it directly, she was involved with people who were."

Hector climbed to his feet, walked to an undamaged table, and retrieved a pair of water bottles from it. He threw one at Sally and upended the other over his head. "I might not be the smartest motherfucker in the world, but I can see something's going on, *chica*. Why you the one here askin' questions? You're a goddamn superhero. You're bigger than all this." He waved the empty bottle around the gym for emphasis.

Sally took a drink from her own water. "How long since you saw her here?"

"Probably three weeks. She was here training. Left with some guy in a suit. Looked too fucking nice for this town." He grimaced. "Didn't even change her clothes. I know she worked some side jobs. Figured she might have gotten in with one of the families."

"Families?" As soon as Sally said it, she winced, knowing she'd sounded just like a rube from the sticks.

"Gangs. Families. The Mafia. Whatever. They're always looking for someone who ain't afraid to use their fists to make a point. Because it ain't always about who's gonna bust a cap in who. I done some freelance for . . . well, for someone."

"Was Martina a parahuman? Did she have powers?"

"No." His answer was emphatic. Sally doubted that Hector had the same kind of ability to sense parahuman powers that Minerva had, but he was plenty canny, and she knew he was the sort of person from whom one couldn't keep secrets for long.

"Hector, when she was killed, she had powers. Super-speed. Flame powers."

Hector squinted at her as if trying to decide if she was making fun of him. "Bullshit."

"She was trying to kill me. She was winning, Hector. If I hadn't gotten lucky, she might have taken me out."

He took a step toward her. "So you killed her."

"No! She made a mistake. I got in a lucky shot, and she surrendered to me. Then someone set off a bomb they'd put inside her. Like that group a couple of days ago. You might have seen it on the news. Someone gave her powers and then killed her before I could bring her in."

"You ain't shitting me. Oh, fuck. Goddammit. She was a good kid. Ah, *dios mio* . . ." Hector swiped at his eyes as if accusing them of betraying him.

"You said she left without changing," Minerva said from where she was floating above the destruction Hector had wrought. "Did she leave a bag?"

"She has—*had* a locker. Anythin' she brought is probably still in there. You're welcome to it."

"Which one?" Sally asked.

"Top row, fourth from the left," said Minerva.

Hector looked surprised. "How'd you know that?"

"She can smell it. Spooky how she does that."

Minerva only nodded.

Sally looked at the locker in question. A padlock dangled from it. "Minerva?"

"I can probably pick it," she said, "but I've never done that before."

Hector stalked across the floor, his steps growing heavy as his body became nickel again. Without any preface or fanfare, he grabbed hold of the padlock and twisted his wrist. The metal loop snapped with a ringing sound like a coin bouncing off a plate. "All yours."

"You missed your calling. You should have been a locksmith." Sally slid the broken lock out of the latch.

"I done my share of B and E. Did six months upstate for it a few years back. Should have been more fucking careful."

"Crime doesn't pay." Sally opened the locker to reveal a crumpled blue duffel bag with some civilian clothing in it.

"Bullshit it don't. I made more bustin' heads and legs than I ever made trainin' dancers how to do it here." Hector looked over her shoulder in curiosity.

Sally handed the bag to Minerva. "But here, nobody's looking to arrest you. Also, I'm glad I found you. I was worried about you when you disappeared after . . . Champion."

Hector grimaced, the lights making odd reflections in his metallic countenance. "Yeah, well, I didn't think it would be smart to hang around. People talk."

"Nobody has."

"Still."

Minerva went through the bag methodically, carefully sniffing everything inside it, caressing it.

Hector watched her in disbelief as she inhaled deeply of a blouse. "What's she doin'?"

"Detective work," said Sally.

Minerva held something up in her fingertips. "This is interesting."

"What is it?" Sally asked. She leaned in closer and saw that Minerva was holding a white plastic chess piece—a pawn.

"It's a business card," said Minerva.

"How do you know that?"

"There's printing on the base. I can feel it." She turned it upside down.

Sally saw the words *Chessboard Industries*, and a phone number.

"What's that?" Hector asked.

"It's a start," said Sally. "Minerva, is there anything else we need from this bag?"

"No."

"Hector, do you mind if we take this with us?"

"I ain't gonna stop you. But you promise me one thing, *chica*."

"What's that?"

He slapped his fist into his other hand, making his entire metallic body ring with the impact. "You find the ones who killed Martina, you fuck them up good for me."

"You're not the first person who's asked me to do that today." Sally smiled. "I plan to."

Eight

"*Thanks to parahumans running around uncontrolled, anyone could do anything they wanted and use the so-called 'mind-control' defense in court. 'It wasn't me, I wasn't myself.' You know how you stop that from happening? You make using any parahuman ability illegal. All of them. And you detain parahumans to make sure it doesn't happen.*"

—Ken Reichel, First Choice Radio Network.

January 2009
New York City, NY

When Sally finally returned home, Jason was playing *Madden '09* in the eternal hope of making his beloved Atlanta Falcons win the Super Bowl. She and Minerva had been late getting back to Fort Justice, so much so that the Command Center had to dispatch a speedboat to collect them, as it was well after ferry hours. The ride back was bumpy and cold and Sally couldn't decide whether she was seasick or frozen or both.

Minerva advised her to get some sleep, which Sally promptly ignored. Instead, she mixed some hot chocolate and coffee together in the commissary to make something that wasn't quite as good as either separately, but seemed suitable to fill Sally's need for both caffeine and chocolate. She brought her drink back to hers and Jason's apartment, kicked off her shoes and threw her clothes on the floor as per normal —she promised herself she'd pick them up later; she was trying hard to absorb her husband's neatness tendencies—and pulled on her warmest thermal pajamas. After adding her fleece bathrobe, two pairs of socks, fuzzy bunny slippers, and her favorite *Mustang Sally*-logo knit cap that a fan had made for her, she started to feel warmth leaking back into her extremities again. She sipped her *café au chocolat* and fired up her computer to commence digging into Chessboard Industries.

"What are you doing, babe?" Jason came up behind Sally and put his giant hands upon her shoulders.

Sally reached up and clasped his fingers in hers and rested her cheek against the back of his hand. She'd lost track of time. Her drink had cooled to a barely tolerable lukewarm temperature, and her eyes were starting to cross from navigating website after website. "Trying to find my way through a maze of corporate triple-speak. Here, look at this." She clicked on the tab of Chessboard's home page. It was an expensive-looking site, with animated menus and a slick user interface. It had a chess theme, using 3D animated pieces as icons, while their logo was a quarter of a chessboard done up in black and white, with the rook, knight, bishop, and queen behind a row of four pawns.

Jason looked. "Fancy, if a bit dry. What do they do?"

"Defense contractor." Sally pointed at the corporate philosophy line, right below the company logo and beside a picture of the CEO, a woman who looked like she could eat a bucketful of iron filings and spit out nails. "*Keeping Your Enemies in Check.* Yeah, that's not a company looking to earn record war profits."

"Are we at war? Did I miss something during the fourth quarter? Besides an extra point, that is . . ." Jason nuzzled Sally's neck.

"Stop it. I'm working."

"So am I. I miss you. Restricted duty sucks balls."

Sally grimaced. "Gross."

"Sorry. But you know how it is. You've had your noggin beat up enough."

"And speaking of head injuries, you want to tell me what happened here?" He brushed her cheek and she winced. It was sore, and now that she'd noticed it, it felt a little swollen.

"Oh, uh, I was . . . boxing."

Jason chuckled. "Sure you were."

"I was! You can ask Minerva. We went to a boxing club in Brooklyn and I went a round with a guy."

"I hope he got the worse end of it. I get bent out of shape when my wife is tussling with another man."

"He's an old friend. Guy I ran into during my time in Champion's org."

"He's a parahuman?"

"Yeah, and a complete asshole to boot."

Jason laughed outright and winced at the noise in his ears. "Now I know for sure you got nailed in the head. Your brains are all rattled up."

Sally pushed Jason's hands off her shoulders. She didn't want to be angry with him, because he was just teasing in his laidback, good-natured sort of way, but she was also bound and determined to figure out what had happened with Syndicate S and Martina, and she was pretty sure Chessboard Industries was the missing connection, somehow. She'd been digging through some of the bids Chessboard had posted for government contracts and appropriations and lobbying history until every page of scanned black and white reports felt like it was printed with tiny daggers jabbing into her eyes.

Two words leaped out at her on one page, though, which indicated she was maybe digging in the right direction after all. "*Touchstone Technology.* They're calling it a copyrighted process to create parahumans. It appears they actually hold patents on it. Those guys, The Militia? Well, I guess you heard us talk about them. You were unconscious by the time they showed up."

"Ugh. Don't remind me."

"They own The Militia. At least, they own the process that created them. The idea is instead of some of the wild mismatches that come up with random parahuman powers in the population, like you, me, and everyone we know, they can select ideal candidates and imbue them with abilities."

"That doesn't sound like the biggest can of worms ever. Didn't we just leave this party in Guatemala?"

"I can't find out anything about the process. Obviously. It's a corporate secret. But they're angling to become the exclusive provider of strategic parahuman operatives for the U.S. Government."

"That's illegal, last time I checked. *Strategic* means *military*, doesn't it?" Jason rubbed his chin in thought.

"Yeah. And you're right. But there are people in the government trying to change that. Like a certain Senator here in New York."

"Isn't she the one Doublecharge knocked on her ass with one punch?"

"After Juice shut her down. Yep."

"Heh. I've seen some clips of her online. I kind of thought she hated parahumans."

"I think she does, but you can hate a tool and still need it." Sally clicked onto the page that described—in extremely general terms—the so-called Touchstone Technology to endow selected candidates with parahuman abilities. "We found a connection to Chessboard Industries in Martina's personal effects. If they used their Touchstone Technology on her—"

Red LEDs built into their apartment lighting illuminated, bathing the entire room in crimson. Alarms started hooting throughout the base simultaneously. Something drastic had happened, serious enough to warrant emergency response from Just Cause.

Sally was at the intercom even before the Command Center could make an announcement. "This is Sally. What's going on?"

"Sally, we've received reports there's been an assassination attempt on Senator Goodwin at a fundraiser just a few minutes ago."

A million thoughts raced through Sally's head, most of them unproductive snark toward the woman who clearly detested Just Cause and all it stood for, but she pushed those aside. "Is the Senator all right?"

"We have no information at this time, but The Militia is already on the scene, and you asked to be notified if they made subsequent appearances."

Sally grimaced. How was it that Patriot's team had beaten them to responding to an assassination attempt? The answer came to her right away. They were already there in some capacity. Maybe Goodwin had hired them to make her look better. Image was everything for politicians. Or maybe she had them for bodyguards. If that was the case, they sucked at their jobs. Still, Sally couldn't let the sponsored team grab all the headlines. She was rapidly learning that image was everything for superhero teams too, and with an attempt on the life of a U.S. Senator, it was important for Just Cause to be part of the emergency response, even if said Senator was trying to shut down Just Cause. Maybe if they made all the right moves, Goodwin would soften her stance. "Give me basewide 'com."

The speakers built into the walls crackled as the Command Center transferred full intercom privileges to Sally. "Um . . ." She winced as she heard her uncertainty blare through the speakers. "This is Sally. I need all team members cleared for active duty to report to the flight deck in five minutes for immediate departure. Flight crew, prepare the *Dorothy*. Sally out."

She turned to Jason. He looked miserable. "One lousy day. They couldn't wait one lousy day? I'm supposed to be cleared tomorrow morning."

"Sorry, baby." Sally stripped out of her pajamas and into a fresh costume. She picked up her grandmother's horseshoes and hung them from the loops on her belt, ready at a moment's notice to be called into play if someone needed some pummeling. "Mind the store for me till I get back?"

"Sure, what else am I going to do?" He sat on the edge of the bed, dejected.

Sally jumped into his lap and kissed him as passionately as she could for a few brief seconds. "You wait right here. When I get back, I'm going to put you on active duty until neither of us can keep our eyes open."

Jason's sulky demeanor vanished as quickly as it had come upon him. "Well, that sounds like a fine way to get back into the swing of things."

"This'll be an easy call-out. We're not going to fight supervillains. We're just making an appearance and if we're lucky, catching an assassin before The Militia kills him a lot."

"I hope you're right." He straightened Sally's goggles for her. "I love you."

"I love you too, baby. See you soon."

* * *

The *Dorothy* held a lot fewer heroes than the first time Just Cause New York had been called out on an emergency. Jason and Shillelagh were still out on medical restriction; Failsafe was on monitor duty and Sally determined the emergency wasn't severe enough to warrant pulling him from that position. Jack was on a boat between Manhattan and Fort Justice. Sally contacted him to let him know about the situation. He offered to turn around and join them, but Sally said no, she'd call him and Failsafe in if they were needed and otherwise to enjoy the rest of his evening off.

Ment sat with Minerva, his sunglasses perched on top of his head despite it being late in the evening. Yunbao had spent the day dyeing spots back into her fur and now she looked much more like the leopard of her namesake. Snapdragon amused himself by making a marble-sized fireball dance through his fingers. Not to be outdone, Snowball was swirling a frost fountain around her fingertips. Detroit Steel looked like she'd buffed out her skin and she shone like the chrome on a bumper with just the slightest hint of baby oil, which she said she wiped on to inhibit rust. Sally hadn't ever really thought about the work it must take to keep a metallic body clean and looking good, and had already developed a great respect for the woman from Detroit.

Sally had her eyes glued to CNN as they reported on the developing story of the attempted assassination. As per usual, the reporters were filling every available second with the sounds of their voices and saying very little of substance. What they did know was Senator Goodwin was speaking at a fundraiser dinner about her proposed act to consider parahumans as strategic resources and place them under control of the military instead of civilian or regulatory agencies. The new team called The Militia was present, perhaps acting as security or as special guests. Someone took a shot at the Senator from outside the building, possibly using a sniper rifle or similar type weapon. The Senator was hit and had been rushed to the nearest hospital under guard of Militia members Liberty and Justice. Patriot was coordinating the search for the sniper in the surrounding neighborhood.

"One minute to destination," said the pilot.

Sally turned off the news. "All right, let's see if we can give a better accounting for ourselves than we did a few days ago. If you find the sniper, you do what you can to protect him—or her—from The Militia, because I want our perpetrator taken alive if at all possible. Everyone stays in teams of two. Ment and Minerva. Steel and Yunbao. Snapdragon and Snowball. I'll coordinate." She paused. "I'll probably have to deal with Patriot. I can't tell you how much I'm looking forward to that."

"You'll be fine, girl," said Detroit Steel. "Put that asshole in his place."

"Landing now," said the pilot. "Stand by."

The *Dorothy* swung around the hotel and touched down neatly in the middle of the circle drive. Jet exhaust made snow flash into steam as the regular door opened to dispatch the team. It wasn't a combat emergency, so they didn't need to use the bomb bay doors, which was just fine with Sally, who'd always felt like she was falling into pit trap every time she went through them.

Civilians and law enforcement gaped as the jet disgorged its passengers and then covered their ears as its engines ramped up and it went airborne again. Sally and the others approached the knot of emergency workers gathered by the front of the hotel.

Patriot was there off to one side, surrounded by police officers and members of the press as he shouted into a walkie talkie, directing other Militia heroes in their search. He looked up as Sally approached and lowered his radio, anger spreading across his lantern-jawed face. "You."

"Us." She gave him her sweetest smile. "We're here to help."

"Well, you can hop back into your jet and go back to your little island. We've got this situation under control here and don't need government interference."

"A U.S. Senator is shot and you don't need government interference? Seems to me you could use a little more of exactly that, for all the good you did by being here." Sally pointed at him, in her mind drawing a circle around him with a line through it. "Now, what information do you have, or are you unwilling to share it for the greater good?" She made sure to speak loudly enough that the reporters nearby would be able to hear it. She had her team's reputation to repair.

"Is Crackerjack with you? I don't see him." Patriot looked around like he was trying to locate the source of a bad smell.

"No, he's off-duty tonight. Where did the shot come from, and where's the rest of your team? I'd hate for one of my people to make a mistake in thinking one of them is the shooter."

"Across the highway, eight floors up." Minerva squinted up at the distant building. "That's the best angle, and I see a hole in the window consistent with a bullet."

"My team is already in that building." Patriot's voice dripped with disdain. "Awfully convenient that Jack isn't with you. He's our primary suspect in this shooting."

The bottom dropped out of Sally's world, and her plans to embarrass and humiliate The Militia evaporated as Patriot's words sank into her mind. "J-Jack? You can't be serious."

Minerva immediately took charge. "All teams spread out, look for a shooter. Watch out for civilian law enforcement and Militia members. Snapdragon and Snowball, work from the top down. Detroit Steel and Yunbao from the ground up. Ment and I will case the area to look for residual traces."

The other six heroes dispersed, leaving Sally alone to face Patriot. Get a hold of yourself, she screamed in her mind. This is not how a superhero team leader acts. "I find that difficult to believe. Especially knowing that Jack is back at Fort Justice right now."

"We have evidence. Security video of him entering the building."

Minerva must have overheard him, even from across the street, and she flew back to rejoin Sally, her cloak fluttering in the wintry evening air. "I'd like to see that video."

"As would I." Sally fought to keep a tremor out of her voice. "Because I don't believe it."

"Believe what you want. Evidence is evidence, and we're looking for a murderer."

"Is the Senator dead?" Minerva raised an eyebrow.

"No . . . Not as far as we know," said Patriot.

"Last I checked, murder requires a death. Now I want to see that video." Sally felt like grabbing Patriot and shaking him, even though he was close to Jason's size. She tried to choose her words carefully, knowing she was in full view of the press and civilians.

"Fine." Patriot snapped his fingers and pointed in the direction of a nondescript guy in a suit. That guy came forward with a laptop in hand and passed it to Patriot.

"Who's this? A Chessboard Industries employee?" Sally was careful to speak slowly enough so Patriot couldn't miss her mentioning Chessboard.

If her dropping of the company's name startled Patriot, he didn't show it. "He's an assistant to the Militia." He opened the laptop and tapped some keys to light up the screen. After a moment, a few seconds of security video played, showing someone Sally had to admit looked a whole lot like Jack entering the building across the way, with a large duffel bag that might very well contain a disassembled sniper rifle.

"Play it again." Sally knew she was stalling for time. She needed to see it again. It had looked so much like Jack that she'd have assumed it was him if nobody had said. She found herself calculating travel times. Had he already been on the boat when the assassination attempt had occurred? Could he have crossed Manhattan quickly enough to cover his tracks if he'd really been the one to do it? And on the heels of that, she realized she was looking at Jack as a suspect. How dare she? And how dare Patriot make her doubt one of her closest friends?

"There, you see?" Patriot sounded triumphant. "Bring me Jack Raymond. Now."

"That's not Jack." Minerva pointed to details on the screen that only she could see. "That man's legs are too long. He moves with an entirely different rhythm in his steps. He carries his head differently. And Jack carries his bag in his left hand, not his right."

Sally could have kissed Minerva for that observation right there. She didn't see the fine details Minerva did, but then, that was right in Minerva's wheelhouse of parapowers. "And even if it was, Patriot, you are a civilian and we don't answer to you. You have a problem with it? File a report with my boss, James Forsythe." She managed a smile. "There's a link on the main page of the PRA.gov website."

Patriot clenched his fists and Sally's perceptions went into overdrive. She knew he was super-strong and wasn't about to let him get the drop on her. Nevertheless, he let no further physical response show. "You think you've got all the answers, don't you? Well let me tell you something. There's a change blowing in the wind, and you and your team of barely-heroes are going to get swept away like dust." He made a brushing motion with his palms. "Dust."

"My team isn't going around like a SWAT team with too much testosterone, killing people. You're not judge and jury, Patriot, despite having Liberty and Justice on your team. Just because no charges were filed against you and your group for your actions last week doesn't mean that I condone them." Sally was used to confronting men much larger than her; she'd even married one of them. She wasn't going to back down from Patriot, especially in front of the cameras. "You make just one mistake, and I will not hesitate to take you and yours down. And you better believe my so-called *barely heroes* will destroy you and your goon squad." She put her hands on her hips. "I'm sure Deep Six would be happy to find accommodations for all of you."

Patriot opened his mouth to bellow a reply but his radio crackled. "Patriot, we found the weapon!"

Patriot glared at Sally and raised the radio to his lips. "Say again, S.A."

"We found the weapon. It's an FN Special Police Rifle. It's been recently fired. I recognize the custom modifications to it. Looks like the one used by Crackerjack on numerous occasions."

"Roger. Secure it and bring it in." Patriot raised his voice to be sure that everyone in the press would hear him. "Second Amendment knows his firearms. You may say that our suspect isn't Jack Raymond, but a lot of evidence is pointing to him anyway. It would be best if he turn himself in until this is cleared up."

"We'll be taking that weapon." Sally stepped up, trying to throw her weight around despite her size. "I'm not leaving it in your hands."

"So your people can make it disappear? I don't think so." Patriot laughed. "It will go to the Secret Service, as they will be very interested in finding out who took a shot at a U.S. Senator."

Sally glanced at Minerva, who gave back a barely-perceptible nod so fast that nobody would see it clearly except her. "That's acceptable. I'm sure they'll find that someone is trying to frame Jack."

"Where is Raymond now?" Patriot's voice was the growl of a dog denied a tasty treat.

"He's on base." Sally had to assume that was the truth. Anything else meant Jack was not where he was supposed to be, which would in turn beg the question of *why*. "Why, are you going to come get him?"

"If the Feds ask for The Militia's help, we are ready, willing, and able to retrieve Jack Raymond, no matter where he might be hiding. Or who might be protecting him." Patriot folded his arms and frowned down at Sally.

Sally sincerely hoped that there wouldn't be a head-to-head showdown with The Militia in the future. In the brief encounters with them she'd had, she could tell they were far more paramilitary in their training than were the members of Just Cause, and they didn't have any compunctions about using lethal force to achieve their goals. Whatever the eventual outcome, a Militia-versus-Just Cause fight would be a bloodbath, and Sally would end up putting some of her friends in the ground, if she herself wasn't counted among the casualties. She suspected she'd rubbed Patriot the wrong way enough that he would go out of his way to seek her out in a battle.

"Whatever." She injected as much acid as she could into that single word, turned her back to Patriot and walked away, trying to show just how little she thought of him and his team of so-called heroes. "JCNY, it's Sally. Report in."

"Sally, it's Snowball. Me and Snapdragon have been circling this building and we haven't seen a goddamn thing except some of those Militia assholes."

"Gotcha. No activity on the roof?"

"Negative," said Snapdragon.

"Detroit Steel here. We had a run-in with them too. Second Amendment and that Maverick bitch didn't want to let us in to check out the shooter's nest."

Sally grimaced. "You didn't get into it with them, did you?"

"No. I politely pointed out that they were interfering with an official investigation and I could arrest them for obstruction. They suggested we kiss their asses. Yunbao reminded them that she's a Chinese citizen and her embassy would be very disappointed if she were attacked. They offered more profanity but let us by. I'm summarizing here, by the way."

"I'm sure you are." Sally knew Detroit Steel wouldn't hesitate to unleash a torrent of profanity so profound it would raise blisters and peel paint. "Any evidence?"

"No. The shooter cleaned up his mess before he left. I'm betting the rifle Second Amendment found is wiped clean too."

"Jack would never leave his weapon behind." Minerva came up beside Sally. "He'd look on it as unprofessional. Even if it was damaged or useless, he'd still bring it with him rather than leave it where someone could find it and accidentally be hurt by it."

"I agree with that." Sally started to flip her braids, then remembered she didn't have them anymore. Old habits died hard. "I don't know a lot about snipers, but I think in general they'd rather not leave any potentially damning evidence behind. It's odd that the shooter left his gun."

"Maybe we were supposed to find it." Ment rejoined them. "Or someone was, anyway. Listen, I scanned that entire building. Ain't nobody in it but our people and The Militia. And a few cops down on the first floor. Whoever was in there is long gone."

"All right, I'm declaring our job here done for now," said Sally. "This needs to be back in the hands of local law enforcement. I'll let them know we're leaving for now, but to contact us if they need any assistance of any kind."

"Yeah, make sure those Militia sons of bitches know it too. This town ain't big enough for the both of us," said Detroit Steel. "They can go back to their plantations or wherever the hell they came from."

Sally looked around and spotted the police unit commander, giving orders to a veritable platoon of uniformed and plainclothes officers. He looked harried, with locks of his hair standing up wildly as if he'd been dragging his fingers through it. Sally knew exactly how he felt. She crossed the plaza toward him. "Command Center, come in."

"Command Center, go ahead, Sally."

"Is Jack back on base yet?"

"Yes he is."

"Tell him when we get back, I want to see him." She told herself it was only to debrief him on the incident. It was to make sure everyone was on the same page with what had happened to Senator Goodwin.

Not because he was a suspect.

Nine

"The Senator is improving daily and is grateful to the private organization The Militia for stepping in to help protect her from further harm. She urges Jack Raymond to turn himself in to the authorities."

—Statement from the office of Senator Christine Goodwin (R-NY)

January, 2009
New York City, NY

Jack was already in Sally's office when she came down from the top deck. Just a few minutes out in the chill Atlantic winds with snow blowing around Fort Justice had frozen her almost to the bone and she'd stopped to get a hot chocolate.

"Well, here we are." Sally sat at her desk.

Jack nodded. "I've been following the news. Apparently I shot a U.S. Senator tonight. Is that right?"

"I don't believe you did for a second. You know I'd trust you to the ends of the earth and a good deal beyond. You wouldn't go that far off the reservation."

Jack shrugged. "Goodwin is a terrible person, and she hates us with a fundamentalist's passion. Having her go away would be a good thing for Just Cause."

"Would it? I'd think turning her into a martyr would do more harm than good for us in the long run."

"Well, yes, there's that. It would be better if she just kind of disappeared from the public view of her own accord. Like if she lost an election or had a scandal come out that ruined her reputation. She could get a job on Fox News or something. They hate us too, don't they?"

"Seems like everyone hates us these days. We're a drain on public resources. We're an economic black hole. We increase insurance rates and the risk to anyone in our vicinity."

"Don't forget that you're a poor role model for young girls and that we eat babies to maintain our powers. Well, maybe not that last one."

Sally smiled. As long as she'd known him, Jack had a way to get to the root of what was bothering Sally, bring it to light, and then make fun of it so it didn't seem quite so bad. "So now that we've established that shooting Senator Goodwin is a bad idea for us politically, can you tell me where you were exactly at 9:50 this evening so we can discount you as a suspect?"

"I was in a cab on my way back to the docks. I spent the afternoon in intimate congress with a lovely woman at the Park 79 hotel on the Upper West Side."

"Does Sondra know?"

Jack snorted. "She was in town today to make a presentation to a United Nations committee on the development of rule structures for government-run superteams. We had a few hours to kill before her flight back to Denver. Made the most of it."

Sondra and Jack had the kind of easygoing relationship that Sally envied, where they could be apart for days or weeks at a time, with their love strong enough to keep them going during the dry times. Sally hoped hers and Jason's marriage would be as strong. "And she didn't come in to see me at all?"

"I told her you'd be mad. She said she'd call you later on and set up a time the two of you could go fly someplace warm together." Jack nodded at Sally's half-empty cup of hot chocolate. "I've gathered that you're utterly miserable here."

Sally sighed. "If it's not the damn parahuman population, it's the weather. Or the political situation."

Jack shrugged. "*Have you been outside lately? Do you know how weird it is out there? We've taken our own head count. There seem to be six million completely miserable assholes living in the tri-state area.*"

"*Ghostbusters 2.* The first one was better."

"Park 79 can verify I was registered there under the name Joel Hodgson. Room service can verify I ordered and paid for dinner for two around seven P.M., and tipped the waiter more handsomely than he deserved. Sondra can verify that I'm still a fantastic lover after all these years."

Sally rolled her eyes. "And the cab company will verify you were in the cab at the time of the shooting. That's fine. I never believed it was you anyway, but it would be good to have evidence to support it."

Minerva and Davey entered Sally's office. Minerva had changed from her duty uniform to jeans and a sweatshirt. Without the large cloak fluttering around her, Minerva looked much less imposing. In fact, she was only an inch taller than Sally. She appeared as calm as ever, waiting patiently for Sally to finish her conversation with Jack before intruding. Davey, on the other hand, looked annoyed and Sally hoped she wasn't the one making Davey look that way. "What is it, Davey?"

"Well, we've got a problem."

"Just one?" Jack beamed. "Oh, good. I can handle them when they come singly."

"A little less brevity would be appreciated, Jack. You're part of this problem." Davey glared at him.

"Ah. Then I guess I'm not part of the solution."

"What's the matter?" Sally asked.

"Tell them what you told me, Minerva," said Davey.

Minerva turned to Sally. "I caught a whiff of Second Amendment when he turned that rifle over to the Secret Service. I'm certain he was the one who fired it."

"What?" Sally's hand flew to her mouth in surprise. "He's the shooter? Are you sure?"

"As much as I can be about anything."

"Why would he shoot at Senator Goodwin. She's the one who wants us gone and teams like The Militia in our place."

"Wait a second." Jack snapped his fingers. "I was looking at the video footage leading up to the shooting. I'm positive Second Amendment was there." He looked over at Sally's large flatscreen television. "May I?"

Sally stepped aside from her desk, letting Jack have access to her workstation. He sat down, working on the keyboard and the mouse until he got the video file from the server and opened it. Sure enough, all the members of The Militia were present, sitting behind Senator Goodwin as she presented her pitch to those in attendance at the function. Second Amendment was clearly visible in his spot between Patriot and Maverick. The shot struck Goodwin, the video feed swung crazily for a moment as someone bumped the camera, and then it ended.

"Rewind that and play it again in slow motion." Minerva moved to stand directly in front of the screen.

Jack obliged and they watched the seconds leading up to the shooting once more. "Are you sure that's Second Amendment sitting there?"

"No, but I'm not sure it isn't, either. If it's not him, it's an excellent copy. I'm more interested in the reactions of everyone on the stage."

"How do you mean?" Sally looked at them but didn't see anything amiss.

"Fast forward through the five minutes before the shooting, Jack. Look at the Senator specifically."

Jack played with the controls and five minutes of footage played out over a few seconds. Goodwin swayed back and forth, shifting weight between her feet regularly, making her look like a metronome. She gestured with her hands, emphasizing certain aspects of her speech, occasionally tossing her head so her chin-length auburn hair would flip back out of her face. But then, in the last minute before she was shot, she stopped moving. She grasped the edges of the podium and leaned against it, planting herself firmly in place. Jack's eyes widened. "Son of a bitch! She knew it was coming. She's holding still so she can take the shot safely."

He played it again at fast speed and then slowed it back down to normal time. Sure enough, Goodwin froze in place for the last seconds of her speech before the bullet hit her. Sally saw the hole appear high on her right shoulder. "Not that there's a good place to get shot, but isn't that a better place than most?"

Jack nodded. "It's away from major arteries and bones. She'll be in physical therapy for a while, and she might suffer some range of motion and strength issues for the rest of her life, but no, that's not generally a fatal place to be shot, especially if the bullet passed right through."

"There's no way to tell if it did." Sally pointed at the screen. "Justice is right behind her. I don't know for sure, but I'd bet he's bulletproof. He's big and strong like Jason."

"He doesn't react like he's been shot. He may not have felt it." Minerva stepped back to view the footage from another angle.

"The goal wasn't to kill Goodwin, but to wound her. And she was in collusion with whoever pulled the trigger, whether it was Second Amendment or someone else. But why?" Sally looked at the others for help.

"And that's where we have a problem." Davey twirled her pen through her fingers. "We have all the evidence on the scene pointing to Jack as the triggerman. Yes, a lot of it is circumstantial, and we have evidence we can present to the contrary. Sorry, I was listening to your conversation with him. But the press has gotten hold of it, and they're running with Jack as the prime suspect. The internet is exploding about it." She turned to Jack. "Congratulations, you're officially wanted for attempted murder of a U.S. Senator."

Jack, for perhaps the first time since Sally had met him, had nothing to say. He opened his mouth but nothing came forth.

"What? No! We have to do something. What do we do? We can't just . . . just let them come and take him." Sally reached up to twist her fingers in her braids, forgetting once again that she'd cut them off. "This is all a set-up. Goodwin hates us. Everybody knows it. She's . . ."

"Willing to let herself get shot just to make us look bad?" said Jack. "You're reaching, Sally."

"Am I? In just over a week, Just Cause's reputation has been shot completely to shit. We got beat by Syndicate S. We got saved by Goodwin's pet superheroes. And now she gets shot by someone who looks just like you, Jack, and you're now the prime suspect. I'd say this is all part of a bigger plan."

Davey nodded. "It's a good working theory. Senator Goodwin is trying to get legislation passed to shut down the PRA and put all parahumans under the direct control of the Pentagon. That means they finally get the supersoldiers they've been wanting for years."

"And Chessboard Industries steps in to provide them." The acid in Sally's voice was making her feel nauseous. "So what do we do?"

"I'm half tempted to go clear my name myself." Jack rubbed his chin. "If Second Amendment took that shot, I can wring a confession out of him. All I need is some time and a room with a locked door. And maybe some pliers."

"Jack!" Sally gasped.

"I'm kidding." He grinned at her. "I can do it without the room."

Minerva shook her head. "You can't leave. Anything you do on your own will look like you've gone rogue. Regardless of the actual circumstances, we can't risk being ordered to bring you down."

Jack's smile disappeared. "You wouldn't find it quite as easy as that."

"Yes, we would." Minerva didn't expand upon her simple declaration, but Sally shivered a little. She'd seen Minerva put Jack back together cell by cell after he'd been grievously wounded by a magical weapon a few years ago. Sally didn't doubt Minerva could use that knowledge to bypass his invulnerability.

Davey glanced out of the windows and clicked her tongue in irritation at what she saw. "We have press helicopters circling our base, just outside of the no-fly zone. And we're fielding several calls every minute from the media. I have a standing order that we are investigating the situation and have no further comment at this time. That will hold the press in the short term, but you know that sooner or later someone will get their hooks into an employee here and then it will crack open."

"And it's only a matter of time until we're ordered to turn you over by the PRA." Minerva looked at Jack. "You need to surrender yourself to the authorities. Let us bring you in. We can do so safely, without involving The Militia. By turning yourself in, it looks like you're anxious to help, and that makes everyone in Just Cause look better, especially when we prove you weren't involved in the shooting in any way."

Sally paced. "That brings up another issue. Do we disclose what we do know?"

Jack shook his head. "No, you've got to keep some cards in your hand. Besides, there's no way anyone could corroborate Minerva's theory about Second Amendment."

"A psi could. How about Ment? Or a neutral third party?" Sally looked at Davey for confirmation.

Davey made a chopping-off motion with one hand. "No way that would fly in a court of law. Trying to get telepathic evidence introduced in court is like running an insanity defense. It just doesn't work. I mean, like, ever."

Jack looked back at the flatscreen again. "And on top of all that, we've got an unknown player in this game. If Second Amendment pulled the trigger, who was that sitting beside Patriot?"

Sally felt like slapping her forehead. She couldn't believe she'd missed that. "There aren't many who can duplicate someone's appearance. Minerva could do it to someone else, but I think that's a fairly unique ability."

"Indeed. Until we discover someone else who can."

"Then there's illusion powers, like Mosaic from the Second Team has. And self-duplication. And morphing. Any of those are possibilities." Jack looked grim.

"And if it's someone associated with The Militia, that means they won't be in the PRA database yet." Sally sighed. "I'll check it anyway, because you never know." She looked down at Jack, still sitting in her chair, and put her hand over his. "Are you okay with turning yourself in?"

"Am I okay with it? No. Will I do it?" Jack wouldn't meet her gaze. "Yes."

Sally turned to Davey. "Issue a statement. Tell them we're eager to help get to the bottom of the attempted assassination of Senator Goodwin. Tell them we hope she will recover fully. And tell them . . ." She took a deep breath. "Tell them we're bringing in Jack."

* * *

Juice called Sally just as she was boarding the *Dorothy*. Jack had agreed to let Sally and Minerva bring him in, and Detroit Steel offered to come along, in her words, "in case those Militia fuckers are around." Juice listened patiently while Sally debriefed him at her typical scattered high-speed verbosity. When she was finished, he said he was glad Jack had decided to turn himself in. He didn't believe Jack was at fault, and hoped they would be able to prove his innocence fairly quickly, but it was a relief that he hadn't had to order Just Cause to turn him over to the authorities. Sally asked in a low voice if he would have, and he said yes, absolutely without question.

It was a different world, Sally knew, where her former team leader and the man who said he'd always thought of her as his third daughter could order her to detain one of her best friends.

The flight across the bay was short and uneventful. Davey had made arrangements with the U.S. Marshals to meet Just Cause at the Downtown Manhattan Heliport, which was the only place the *Dorothy* could safely land in a non-emergency setting. Sally looked out of the windows at the orange lights of FDR Drive, their individual glows diffusing out into the light snowfall. Titanic office buildings rose out of the coppery morass of the streets, replacing orange with harsh fluorescent white, only to vanish into the low clouds hanging over Manhattan. If she hadn't been about to deliver Jack to the Feds, Sally would have found it a beautiful sight, especially if she didn't ever have to get out of the *Dorothy* into the cold weather.

Flashing red and blue lights at the edge of the concrete pier of the helipad suggested the Marshals had already arrived. Jack looked down at them as the *Dorothy* came around on her final approach. "There's still time to back out of this. If you pop open the bomb bay doors right now, I might even miss the water entirely when I jump." He grinned. "Even I can disappear in New York City."

Sally smiled. "I suppose you have safe houses all over the island. Caches of weapons and gold, right?"

"Oh, indubitably." Jack chuckled.

Sally leaned over to hug him. "I wish I could let you go. Nobody'd believe you overpowered all three of us, though. And it wouldn't look good for your innocence. This is still the best way to go."

"I know. Just trying to brighten your evening. You look like someone stepped on your favorite puppy."

"You're one of my favorite puppies. And I hate this."

"You and me both, kiddo. Don't worry. There's enough evidence to exonerate me, and once we've done that, we can really get to work proving it was Second Amendment."

"Twenty seconds to landing," warned the pilot.

Sally felt her heart jump into her throat. She did her best to swallow it down. "Well, here we go."

"*Suck in the guts, guys. We're the Ghostbusters.*"

"You just won't let the sequel go, will you?"

"I'm a slave to my passions."

Flames spread out across the helipad where the *Dorothy* touched down as the jet exhaust bounced off the concrete pad, flash-melting the accumulated ice into steam and surrounding the jet for a moment with brilliant, billowing clouds. "Never let it be said we don't make an entrance." Jack zipped up his parka.

Sally had made sure he didn't have any weapons on him before they boarded the jet. "Not even one. No holdout pistols, no hidden knife blades or garrotes, and there better not be anything stuck up your ass either."

"Uh, I need a minute in the bathroom then. Kidding!" he added upon seeing the look of horror upon Sally's face.

Sally had her cranberry overcoat on over her costume. Minerva kept her cloak wrapped around her. Detroit Steel didn't seem to be bothered by the cold, and only had on a pair of jeans and a sky-blue t-shirt with the Just Cause logo upon it.

"Yo, I got a bad feeling about this." Detroit Steel peeked through the fog at the flashing lights. "Why are there so many cops out there?"

Sally shrugged. "This is a high-traffic public helipad. They need to make sure no civilians get in the way."

"Or hurt in the crossfire," muttered Jack.

Sally wished she hadn't heard it. "All right, let's do this by the numbers. Minerva, you see anything out there that suggests we're going to have some problems?"

Minerva gazed out into the darkness for several long seconds. Each tick of the clock felt like there were days or weeks between them to Sally. "No. There are a lot of uniformed NYPD officers as well as the U.S. Marshals. I don't see any obvious parahumans, and no tactical or military gear on the pier. If there are forces gathered in the terminal, I can't see them. Likewise, there are a couple of boats holding station beyond the lights, but they are unmarked and I can't tell if they are police or something else."

"We'll assume they are." Jack studied his fingernails, careful not to meet anyone's eyes. "I would."

Sally stood. "All right, enough stalling. Let's go. Remember, Jack, you're cooperating with the investigation. We'll work on providing the Feds with evidence to corroborate your alibi."

Jack smiled. "They'll find it pretty tough going, working me over with the phone book and rubber pipe."

"What's a phone book?" asked Minerva.

"What's a—seriously, you're not *that* young!" protested Jack.

Sally chuckled. Minerva was in rare form.

"They'll ask me some questions, try to get me to admit to something without arresting me. They won't want to arrest me because then I can lawyer up and they won't be able to question me anymore. They won't have anything concrete to pin on me and without a confession, they'll hang onto me for a few hours and then they'll have to let me go, at which point I'm going to take a couple of days off to go spend with my wife, because I'm sure I'll be inconsolable." Jack winked at Sally.

Sally pulled the lever that unlocked the *Dorothy*'s side door and swung it open into the darkness. Frigid wind blew into the jet's interior, pockmarking everything with snowflakes and giving Sally goosebumps on her goosebumps. She pulled her hat down lower over her ears and jammed her hands into her overcoat pockets. "What a lovely night. We couldn't do this in, say, a nice, warm police station?"

The four heroes walked across the concrete pad, which was dry as a bone close to the *Dorothy*, but coated with a thin sheen of ice the further away from the jet they got. A handful of uniformed police officers were waiting by the terminal, as well as four plainclothes who wore off-the-rack suits and overcoats that seemed to be the standard uniform of federal law enforcement. One of them ordered the police officers to stay back and then they approached the heroes, meeting them some dozen yards away from the terminal.

"Good evening," said the tall, blonde woman with the severe haircut and a square jaw. "I'm Marshal Ann Haeckel. These are agents from my field office."

The cold nearly took away Sally's breath, but she stepped forward and shook the Marshal's hand. "Salena Tibbets of Just Cause, Marshal. This is Minerva Kostakis. Shawna Steele, and Jack Raymond. I believe you needed to speak with him?"

"Yes, we do. Thank you for bringing him. Mr. Raymond, will you step forward, please?"

A chill not borne by the wind raced down Sally's spine as she saw one of the Marshals remove a set of handcuffs from inside his coat. "Wait . . ."

Jack pushed past Sally, his teeth clenched and his jawline standing out in sharp relief from the lights on the terminal. "Am I free to go?" Despite his question, he already had his hands together in front of him.

Sally tensed up, feeling herself about to snap into high-speed, but Minerva placed a calming hand on her arm. "Wait, this isn't right. You're just supposed to question him!"

"Mr. Raymond, you are under arrest for the attempted murder of a United States Senator. Place your hands behind your head, please." Marshal Haeckel spoke clearly, with the full weight of the authority vested in her by the United States Government.

Detroit Steel whispered in Sally's ear. "Don't say anything else. I'm watchin' them. They're lookin' for any excuse to bring us all in."

Marshal Haeckel stepped behind Jack, pulled his arms down across his back, and snapped handcuffs around them. She proceeded to tell him his rights and then asked if he understood them as she had explained them.

"Yes I do."

"Having these rights in mind, do you wish to talk to us now?"

"No." Jack flashed a tight smile at Sally. He'd been arrested before, she knew, but not for many years. He had a strong anti-authority streak in him, which could cause him all kinds of grief in an arrest scenario, but he also had a sharp sense of self-preservation, and he knew when to keep his mouth shut.

One of the younger Marshals nodded his head toward Sally, Minerva, and Detroit Steel. "What about the others? Do we book them as accomplices?"

She shook her head. "No. You three are free to go. Let's get out of this damn wind." She turned Jack around to face the terminal and she and the other Marshals walked toward it.

Jack had his head held high, angry but proud.

Sally felt like she'd just been served up another big piece of failure pie. "We'll get this cleared up. We've got evidence to clear him. He didn't do it!"

"Hush, girl." Detroit Steel placed a chilly, hard hand upon Sally's shoulder. "That ain't helpin'."

Without another word, Sally spun on her heel and stalked back toward the *Dorothy*.

Ten

"Raymond was at one point an enemy combatant. He was working for the so-called Archmage, leading his armies. He attacked U.S. troops on U.S. soil and instead of answering for it, he was cleared by none other than James Forsythe, director of the PRA. I ask you, my friends, is that justice? Or is that just a charade?"

        —Ken Reichel, First Choice Radio Network

January, 2009
New York City, NY

Sally stayed up well past midnight, working on getting the evidence together to exonerate Jack. Some overeager prosecutor, determined to make a name for him or herself, had jumped the gun on filing charges. She inquired about bailing out Jack, but he'd been listed as a likely flight risk and the judge denied him bail altogether. Jack's lawyer, hand-selected by Juice, was filing documents as fast as she could, but the federal prosecutor was looking to force a speedy trial and conviction before popular opinion swung in Jack's favor. Right now in the government's eyes, he was a traitor, and trying to change the minds of those in charge was like trying to stop an out-of-control oil tanker from crashing into the New

Jersey shoreline. Yes, Sally had helped to stop that exact event from happening a couple years before, but it was still a tangible enemy, something she could put her hands on and try to defeat. Fighting against politics and the media was a lot like trying to wrestle a giant amoeba covered in grease.

The way things had been piling up on Sally, she wouldn't have been the least bit surprised to discover Jason in the arms of another woman when she finally gave in and went to lie down with him, but he was sprawled alone across the bed, snoring gently. Sally pulled on her warmest flannels and climbed in beside him, careful not to wake him. Her last thought before passing out was that she probably smelled like jet exhaust and should have showered before bed.

She surprised herself awake at a few minutes before seven. Jason was already up, a pot of coffee with cream and sugar in it sitting on the desk beside him as he read the news on his favorite website. Sally stuck her feet into her slippers and padded over to him and put her arms around his shoulders. "Hey, babe. I was going to let you sleep in. Looks here like you had a really rough evening." He pointed at a picture someone had snapped of her, Minerva, and Detroit Steel on the pier from the night before. Sally's face was twisted up in anger as she shouted after the Marshals escorting Jack away.

Sally bowed her head. "I screwed up, Jase, and I'm not even sure how. They were only going to talk to Jack and they ended up arresting him. By the time we got back here to headquarters, charges had been filed against him. They really think he did it. They think he shot Goodwin."

Jason snorted. "If Jack had shot her, she'd be D.R.T."

"D.R.T.?"

"Dead Right There. Jack doesn't miss."

Sally sniffed at Jason's coffee pot. "Can I have some or is it all spoken for?"

He slid her mug forward. She was so tired that she hadn't even noticed it sitting on the desk already. "It's my kind of coffee, so it's your kind of coffee."

"At least it's not that tar that Sondra likes." Sally poured some out from Jason's pot. He tended not to bother with mugs and generally drank straight from the pot. She tasted it, decided it was sweet enough for her to manage, and rested her chin on his massive shoulder. "I miss Sondra."

Jason sighed. "I miss everyone back in Denver. I miss the band. I miss that burger joint we used to go to all the time. I miss Lazzarino's. Best peach pie that wasn't made by my grandma."

"Maybe we can go back soon. Or maybe we can find a good place for pie here. I hear there are one or two good places to eat in Manhattan."

"Maybe." Jason sounded doubtful.

"Is there any news on Jack?"

"Just that he's been arrested and being held at an undisclosed facility."

"They don't want us busting him out." Sally wished she could do exactly that.

"How hard could it be, really? They do it in movies all the time."

Sally kissed his cheek. "They do lots of things in movies all the time that they don't do in real life, babycakes. Like win."

Jason kissed her back. "You're not losing. You're triumph-challenged."

Sally snorted. "That's almost funny."

"Here, maybe this'll cheer you up. Goodwin was released from the hospital this morning. She's already made a statement to the press."

"You have a funny idea of cheering me up." Sally finished her cup of coffee and realized that in spite of everything, she was hungry. "Want breakfast?"

Jason grinned. "Does a baby go *goo*?"

Sally winced. "Please, no talk about babies right now. That's something I can't even handle on top of everything else."

"I'm not—aw, y'all know what I mean." Jason emphasized his southern drawl. "My momma's anxious to see her first grandbaby."

"You've got brothers," said Sally.

"Yeah, and they're both a couple of tools."

"Makes it all the more likely that they'll touch off the first baby, right?"

"Now who's being funny?"

"I'm sure I don't know. Come on, let's go eat."

"Three of my favorite little words."

"I love you."

"That's another three."

* * *

Senator Christine Goodwin was nothing if not efficient. Sally thought it was almost as if being shot had sharpened her focus, like tightening the beam of a spotlight that shone squarely upon Juice, the Parahuman Resources Agency, and Just Cause. Less than a day after her release from the hospital she announced her intent to open an investigation into what she called *extreme, perhaps criminal negligence* in the operation of the PRA. Sally thought it was just another load of political bullshit until Juice called her the very next day and ordered her to pack a bag and fly to Washington.

"What happened? Do I want to know?" Sally asked.

"I don't know how she managed it, but Goodwin has convened the Permanent Subcommittee on Investigations to hold a hearing on the PRA."

"Wait, you're being investigated by the government?"

"*We* are being investigated by a Senate sub-committee. They will determine if we have been negligent in the operation of the PRA and Just Cause and if so, determine what will be the course of action." Juice sounded almost sick with the idea.

"Negligent? That's insane."

"That's the way things work here on Capitol Hill. I don't know how long the hearings will last. Possibly a week, depending upon how long Goodwin wants to drag things out."

"She's running the investigation?" Sally felt her own stomach start churning.

"She's the committee chair."

"We're screwed."

"Perhaps, perhaps not." Juice put on his courtroom voice. "I do know a few legal tricks and when I might apply them, but they'll only work as long as Goodwin permits it. She can grandstand for a while, but eventually the press is going to start needling at her for it, and she's smart enough to know that'll backfire upon her."

"Is this because of Jack? Or because of me?"

"Sally, this is because of things that happened years ago. It's a politically convenient time for Goodwin."

"What's her game? She's planning something."

"I know, and I'm not sure what her endgame is yet."

"Listen, boss, I didn't have a chance to talk to you about what we've learned in our investigations so far. I was going to write a report, but it's been one thing after another and it just kind of . . . slipped my mind. I'm sorry." Sally felt her cheeks grow hot, embarrassed to be admitting her failure to her superior.

"Leave it. Don't tell me now, before the hearing. If I'm on the hot seat and they ask me about that stuff, I can honestly tell them I don't know. But believe me, afterward I want to hear all about it."

"Okay. What do I do here? Jack's unavailable and I guess I have to come to Washington."

"Put someone else in command. You know your team best."

Sally considered for a moment. "Minerva, I guess. She's who I'd pick to replace Jack if . . . if he wasn't able to continue in his current role."

"I think that's an excellent decision."

"About time I made one."

"Sally, believe me, everyone makes mistakes in command roles. And you'll give yourself ulcers and high blood pressure second-guessing yourself. Whatever else happens, when you make a decision, own it. Stand by it, whether it was a spur-of-the-moment or one after careful consideration. Good leaders learn from their mistakes, and I wouldn't have picked you to run New York if I didn't think you were capable of it."

"Thanks for that vote of confidence, boss." Sally meant it. It felt good to be told she was doing all right, especially by someone who was so important to her.

"One more thing. Pack your costume."

Sally had been planning to anyway; her costume was like her phone—she never left home without it, because one never knew when one would need to be a superhero, and Sally would destroy any other pair of shoes within minutes doing what she did at high speed. But still, it was an unusual request given that she'd most likely be spending her time sitting on a hard wooden chair in an uncomfortable business suit, trying not to fidget or fall asleep while Senators droned on and on behind their podiums. "Why, are you expecting trouble?"

"Sally, I'm always expecting trouble."

* * *

The Dirksen Senate Office Building looked to Sally like every other piece of government architecture in Washington. It was white, with columns, and row upon row of darkened windows behind which all manner of nefarious business was probably being conducted. She'd spent the night at Juice's house, enjoying some time with his family, although his oldest daughter Quinn was in California, attending UCLA. Juice and his wife Chantelle often laughed about how she could only have gotten farther away from them if she'd left the continental United States. Their younger daughter Yvette was midway through her junior year of high school and was devoted to theater in the way that Sally was devoted to being a superhero. Neither of Juice's daughters exhibited the slightest bit of parahuman abilities, something which he confessed to Sally made him grateful. "This is a terrible business, some days. I'm just glad that they can be insulated from it, at least as much as possible."

"That's why you're a good dad," said Sally.

Now, standing in front of the imposing edifice of the Dirksen building, Sally wished she had her dad available to hold her hand. Juice probably wouldn't have minded if she'd grabbed his; he'd been a father to her in a lot of ways. But someone would see, and then the internet would blow up again. Being accused publicly of having an affair would be the least of her issues. A gentle snow fell, dusting the black tree branches and dead grass with its powdered-sugar quality, but melted as soon as it touched the sidewalks or cars. Juice and Sally got out of the car he'd chartered and crossed the broad sidewalk to the imposing columns framing the main entrance. Doublecharge and MetalBlade, respectively in command of Just Cause Denver and Just Cause Richmond, were waiting for them. Like Juice, MetalBlade was a tall black man, with the faintest hint of gray starting to creep into his close-cut hair. Both men wore navy blue suits with muted ties. Doublecharge wore a conservatively-cut business suit—even more conservative than Sally's—but Sally was surprised to see she also wore her black half-mask. Her hair, normally free-flowing and frizzy with the electricity she generated, was pulled back into a tight bun.

"Keith, Stacey." Juice shook their hands. "Good to see you. I only wish it was under better circumstances."

"Likewise," said Keith. "Nothing I like better than kangaroo court being conducted by The Man."

Juice snorted. "She's got enough balls, at any rate."

Stacey grimaced. "Gross. Hi, Sally. Good to see you. How's New York?"

Sally matched Stacey's grimace. "You've read my reports. You tell me."

Stacey smiled, something she rarely did. "You're doing a good job up there. You're a credit to Just Cause."

"We'll see how the Senators feel about that," said Sally. "Why are you wearing your mask?"

"I want them to remember that in the past, parahumans were persecuted solely for their existence, and those heroes who chose to help out society had to do so under cover of masks." Stacey sounded grim but full of pride.

Juice smiled. "That's an honorable sentiment. I hope they see it that way."

Stacey looked away toward the entrance of the building. "Fuck 'em."

The four heroes checked the posted schedule of events, found the meeting room in which they were going to be, and walked through the building. Sally felt dwarfed between the others. Even Stacey was several inches taller than her. The high ceiling of the main lobby didn't help either, which Sally knew was by design. *This is the Government-with-a-capital-G*, it said. *You are like the buzzing of flies to it.* Then she smiled. That last one sounded suspiciously like another *Ghostbusters 2* quote.

A security guard stopped them before they entered the meeting room. "You have to remove your mask."

"Here we go . . ." Keith muttered under his breath.

"My identity is public record. According to the Crowley Act, I am permitted to wear a mask at any public or private function, so long as I provide clear identification. I am Doublecharge, commander of Just Cause Denver." Stacey held up her official badge to the security guard, sparks dancing in her eyes, daring him to challenge her further. "Will that be all?"

The guard backed down. "Y-yes, ma'am." He stepped aside to let them into the meeting room.

Sally felt like giggling, but clamped down on her tongue. She'd been on the receiving end of Doublecharge's wrath before and didn't wish it upon anyone, but she was glad for once it wasn't directed her way. Maybe she'd wear her mask and goggles too the next day if the hearing continued on that long. She was also connected to the Crowley Act; her grandfather, known to the world as Dr. Danger, had written and sponsored it way back in 1969.

The hearing was open to the press and public, which Sally had expected. Senator Goodwin was desperate for as much public attention as she could get in her crusade, and it showed by the number of media personnel jammed into the observation gallery and the forest of cameras spread across the back of the room. The Senators of the committee were clustered together behind their desk, conversing. Goodwin seemed to be at the center of the group, basking in the attention, flaunting her shoulder sling. She nodded toward the four heroes as they entered the room to a soundtrack of clicking cameras and the drone of reporters muttering into their recorders.

Juice directed Sally, Stacey, and Keith to sit at the table behind him, while he took the sole spot at the center of the room, facing the semicircular table where the Senators would sit. A pair of stenographers bookended the Senatorial table. The wood-paneled walls gave a false sense of cheery intimacy, lit by warm yellow lights on the wall fixtures, but the blue carpet on the floor looked to Sally like it belonged in a skeevy hotel.

The Senators took their seats at Goodwin's direction. She patted her hair with the hand that wasn't in the sling to make sure it wasn't out of place, and then adjusted her glasses and leaned forward to speak into her microphone. "We'll go ahead and get started now. This hearing is to open the investigation into allegations of gross misconduct of the Parahuman Resources Agency and its attendant superhero teams, known collectively as Just Cause. For the record, I am Senator Christine Goodwin, representing New York. I'll ask the other Senators present to introduce themselves and then I'll begin my opening statement."

The Senators went down the line of the table and announced their names and the states they represented. Alaska. New Hampshire. Kansas. Missouri. Louisiana. Two from Wisconsin. Arizona. North Dakota. Texas. Delaware. Sally recognized McCain from Arizona, who'd lost to the President only a few short weeks before, but didn't know who any of the rest of them were except for Goodwin. She leaned over to whisper to Keith. "Do we have any allies up there?"

"I can't be too sure. Maybe Johnson from Kansas, or Golino from Wisconsin."

"I don't know anything about them. I'm really bad at politics." Sally tried to read the Senators' faces.

"You better start improving. Once you get up to the level of running a superhero team, it's all about greasing the right wheels." Keith smiled at her.

Goodwin took a sip of water, glanced down at her notes, and then leaned once more into her microphone. The overhead spotlights gave her normally pale skin an odd jaundiced color and turned her auburn bob into a shiny copper helmet. "Parahumans have been plaguing this country now for more than seven decades, and time and time again, the question has come up in regards to what to do with them. Despite what some activists would have us believe, the problem of parahumans is not a civil rights issue. Parahumans are not enjoined from participating in elections or owning property. Their movements or individual rights are not restricted in any way by law, and in fact they are protected in the same ways that racial minorities and religious groups are. Discriminating against a parahuman strictly upon the basis of his or her abilities is and has been illegal since the passage of the Crowley Act of 1969.

"The problem of parahumans is twofold. The first is one of public safety, and the second is of the disposition of parahumans as strategic assets, and this hearing is to examine the Parahuman Resources Agency and to determine whether its director, James Forsythe, is guilty of gross misconduct in the administration of the agency." A slight, satisfied smirk crossed Goodwin's lips as she continued.

"As Senators, our jobs are not only to serve our constituents, but to ensure their safety as well. Unregulated parahumans make that aspect of our jobs nearly impossible to maintain. How can we protect citizens from individuals who can cause death and destruction on catastrophic scales? How do we ensure that those parahumans are regulated and controlled? The creation of the Parahuman Resources Agency was intended to address this, but how effective has it been?

"In the short time that the PRA has been operating under Director Forsythe, there has been a tremendous spike in the appearance of new parahumans and the inevitable conflicts when people who can toss buses around like toys or blast flame have disagreements. The PRA's solution for this spike in the parahuman population has been to build training centers and to encourage parahumans to join the ranks of the Champions. Those parahumans are under no obligation to do any such thing, and according to statistics I've seen, fewer than twenty percent of all known American parahumans are involved with the Champions. Where are these other independents? They are walking the streets, unfettered by rules governing them, unafraid of legal retribution. It's been said that only a parahuman can halt another parahuman, but in the immortal words of the Roman poet Juvenal, *quis custodiet ipsos custodes*? Who watches the watchmen? Clearly, the Parahuman Resources Agency is not fulfilling that aspect of its charter, and that responsibility falls squarely on the shoulders of Director Forsythe."

Juice shifted in his chair and Sally could tell he was working hard to keep from interrupting.

"The problem as I see it is parahumans have been considered law enforcement ever since the end of World War Two. You have parahumans with abilities comparable to military weaponry, or even worse, working with the limited oversight and training that comes from substandard programs like the Hero Academy, which is little more than a glorified high school, and one that scores on the low end of average when it comes to standardized testing."

Sally recalled the stupid little fill-in-the-bubble tests they had to do every year and how not one of the Hero Academy students had ever taken them seriously. Why should they? They were going to be superheroes. Even the instructors had said they were a waste of time, but a requirement by the state. Now she wished she'd given them a little more consideration.

"Parahumans need to receive the kind of intensive, duty-specific training that can only come from a military setting. If they're going to have the kind of firepower one would expect from a military regiment, they need the training to match it. This means that parahumans need to be removed from the private sector and be given over to military control under the Joint Chiefs of Staff, who can then dispatch them where they are most needed. That may be within the confines of the United States to deal with specific threats, or beyond our borders, depending upon what is required."

An audible gasp came from some of the onlookers. It had been against the law for parahumans to be in the military since the end of World War II. The rationale for such a decision was that America would bolster its strategic resources using its nuclear armaments, which were much easier to control and direct than a fighting force of wildly divergent and often incompatible parapowers. Goodwin had just laid out her intent to strip that law from the books, and furthermore, she was recommending parahumans should and would be drafted into the military. To Sally, it sounded very much like free will might not be an option, which suggested Goodwin was intending to remove as many civil rights as she could from the parahuman population.

"And finally, it is the understanding of this committee that the biggest question mark surrounding parahumans is how random the acquisition of powers seems to be. Despite genetic markers that would seem to indicate parahuman abilities, the truth is this is only sometimes the case. There have been numerous examples of individuals who do not possess genetic indicators exhibiting parahuman powers, such as the former member of the Lucky Seven known as Stratocaster, the members of the faith-based team Divine Right, and the newest American heroes known as The Militia. Often times, the genetic indicators never manifest any kind of abilities, suggesting that an as-yet-unknown factor is in play, or perhaps the manifestation of parapowers is truly random. In the past four years, hospitals and morgues recorded nearly one thousand cases of individuals who were seriously or fatally injured in an attempt to trigger the manifestation of their powers. This plague cannot continue. When undeserving people gain powers, such as the criminals incarcerated in Deep Six, or those who are still at large, such as Destroyer, it means we are always fighting a defensive battle. There needs to be a means by which specific, exemplary individuals can be granted parahuman powers, regardless of their genetic predilection, who can receive top-level, specialized training. The United States Marines refer to themselves as *the few, the proud.* Only the finest, most suitable candidates are selected to become Marines, and they are the ones who receive the training. I propose an immediate investigation into the feasibility of endowing selected individuals with parahuman abilities."

Super-soldiers, Sally realized with a sickening twist in her gut. Goodwin wanted her own toy superpowered army, picked from her list of *suitable candidates.*

Sally suspected pretty much everyone in Just Cause would be crossed off that list.

Eleven

*"I urge the Senate and House to pass the Goodwin Act
for the good of the country, to protect our citizens from
parahuman violence."*
— Senator Christine Goodwin (R-NY)

January, 2009
Washington, D.C.

Senator Goodwin listened while the Senator from
Texas, the other leader of the committee, made his
opening remarks, which were generally of the can't-
we-all-just-get-along variety with a healthy smattering
of Jesus-loves-us and hate-the-sin-love-the-sinner. Sally
hated when religion entered the discussion. She hadn't
ever been to church except a few times with her
grandmother when she was much younger. It was
boring and nonsensical, and she had much preferred to
spend her Sunday mornings watching *Doctor Who*
reruns on the public television station. When people
tried to shoehorn religion into areas of life where it
clearly didn't belong, like politics or school or science,
it made her want to grind her teeth into dull nubs.

At last the Texas Senator wound down with a
thinly-veiled insult, pointing out how glad he was to

have some of the lovely young ladies from Just Cause in the audience that day to protect the committee from harm. Sally and Keith had to each put a hand on Stacey's legs or she'd have come flying out of her seat, shooting electrical death from both hands at the patronizing asshole.

Senator Goodwin took the floor once more. "The committee calls James Forsythe, also known as Juice, the director of the Parahuman Resources Agency, as its first witness. Sergeant-at-arms, will you please swear in the witness?"

A uniformed officer came forward with a Bible and asked Juice if he swore to tell the truth, the whole truth, and nothing but the truth. Juice stood, raised his right hand and said he did.

Goodwin gave him a nasty smile. "Thank you, Director Forsythe. Welcome."

"Thank you, Senator." Sally couldn't see Juice's face, but it sounded like he had an equally nasty smile. "How's the arm?"

"I—what?" Goodwin looked down at her arm, still wrapped in its sling. "It's sore. I will be in physical therapy for quite some time, thanks to your former teammate Jack Raymond."

Juice cleared his throat. "I'm sorry, Senator. I was under the impression that he had not been convicted of a crime. Am I mistaken?"

"No."

Keith chuckled under his breath. "Already got her on the defensive."

"Good. I'd hate to think you suspended due process over a shaky case built upon some sketchy circumstantial evidence." Juice was going full-on attorney, which Sally had seen him do a few times in Just Cause, and it was truly a thing of beauty to behold.

"Director Forsythe, if we could return to the investigation of this committee?" The Senator from

Texas was an oily-voiced balding man with freckles and the smile of a pedophile. Sally didn't know if pedophiles smiled like Senator Deakins did, but she knew if she'd seen that smile coming from the recesses of a van, she'd run the other way as fast as she could.

"Of course. Go ahead, Senator." And just like that, he had the upper hand, and the media would see it that way as well. He was the one giving permission for the investigation to continue, not the one under investigation himself.

Goodwin cleared her throat. "We've questioned your judgment and decision-making ability, and I'd like to bring to the committee's attention some of your previously questionable actions as commander of Just Cause before we get to the root of whether your decisions as PRA director are similarly imperiled."

Juice folded his arms as if to say *bring it on.*

"Let's start with the Siege in Waco, in 1993, Director. I'm sure you recall it. It was your first major call-out as the leader of Just Cause. The incident resulted in the deaths of seventy-six civilians, including twenty-two children. Certainly a black spot on your record. Why don't you give us all a summary of what happened that day?" Goodwin leaned back in her chair, her face an expression of rapt attention.

Juice sighed and his shoulders slumped a little—only enough for Sally to see because she was sitting right behind him. Whenever Just Cause was involved in a major incident, it always resulted in upheavals of policy, changing the way the heroes were required to respond to a crisis situation. Destroyer's assault on Tornado's funeral in 1985 had left several heroes dead, including Sally's father, and the eventual result was that no more than two Just Cause members could attend any public function except in extreme circumstances. Sally and Jason had to pull every string they could just to get their friends and family to attend their wedding, and even so, a great number of heroes had attended in plainclothes, undercover, acting as security. Had any villain taken it upon himself to attack the Tibbets-Thompson wedding, he'd have found himself facing the largest unified force of heroes ever assembled since Juice had brought all the teams together in 2004 to assault Isotope's parahuman-creating reactor in Guatemala.

Sally realized she was far away in her thoughts and pulled herself back to the present, trying to focus upon Juice's narrative. "What we didn't know at the time was that the Branch Davidians had two parahumans in their midst. One was a young psionic with the ability to permanently scramble a mind until the victim was for all intents and purposes forever trapped in a vegetative state. That woman took to calling herself Brainstorm and eventually was incarcerated in Deep Six to serve consecutive life sentences for her crimes. The other died in the compound, but not before igniting multiple fires with his powers. Multiple witnesses reported seeing him cast the flames out of his eyes."

"And all this was in response to the Just Cause assault upon the compound, which you ordered?" asked Senator Deakins.

"Point of correction, Senator. I commanded the operation. The assault was ordered by Attorney General Reno and approved by President Clinton. I worked in conjunction with the FBI commander on-scene. We had reports that children were being abused and beaten inside the compound. We couldn't stand by and let that happen. I ordered my team to participate in a full assault, knowing they might come under heavy, sustained fire from the church members inside the compound."

Senator Paulsen of North Dakota was a tall man with a head of tight white curls and a nose like a beak that bobbed when he spoke. "And so you and your team of so-called heroes barged blindly into a fortified compound, not knowing what opposition you would face inside? Not knowing if the Davidians might use their own children as human shields? That's horrible, Director."

"We were operating on the best information we had at the time/ Not all the agencies were sharing it as openly as they might have. Everyone wanted to be the hero of the hour, it seemed, but in the end we wound up counting the bodies together instead."

Goodwin looked vindicated. "A testament to your failure as a leader. To your poor judgment."

"With all due respect, Senator . . ." Juice's voice flowed as smoothly as lava down a mountainside. "They were religious extremists. They were brainwashed by their leader, and terrified of the power he held over them with his own parahumans. I'm not sure anyone could have resolved that situation without a lot of dead bodies on one or both sides."

"So you say," said Senator Golino from Wisconsin, "but you can't really know, can you?" She fixed her large eyes upon Juice with the kind of penetrative gaze principals used when interrogating students.

"No, of course not. But then, it takes a special kind of zealotry to murder your own children, as the Davidians did. Do you have children, Senator? My daughters were just babies in 1993. I couldn't, and still can't comprehend what kind of person would stoop so low as to put a gun to a baby's head and pull the trigger."

"Are you glad they're dead?" asked the kindly-looking Senator Johnson from Kansas.

"No, Senator. I'm never glad someone is dead. My mission has always been to save as many lives as possible. I still lose sleep over Waco, and I probably always will. It didn't turn out as I, or most people would have liked, but I stand by the decisions I made that day. If I'm guilty of any failure, it was not to storm the compound faster in the hopes of saving more lives."

Goodwin cleared her throat. "Interesting that you mention saving lives. Because I'd like to move ahead a decade to discuss how you caused the Northeast Blackout of 2003, which resulted in civilian deaths both in the United States and Canada. This was due to your negligence and poor judgment in having Just Cause engage a parahuman criminal in an Ohio power station."

Juice clasped his hands together on top of the table. Sally could see his knuckles were pale from squeezing his fingers. It was hard enough for her being a passive observer, watching her friend getting flayed alive by the committee. She couldn't imagine what it must have been like for him in the hot seat, and she was afraid it wouldn't be long before she was forced to find out for herself. "What you're not mentioning here, Senator, is that the parahuman criminal was a domestic terrorist named Gigawatt, and he was threatening to shut down the northeastern power grid if his demands were not met."

"One man? How could one man accomplish all that?" said John Hodak, the junior Senator from Louisiana. "Surely there are safeguards in place to prevent such a thing."

"There are, but Gigawatt was a professional familiar with the industry and how to exploit loopholes in it. He chose to utilize his knowledge to try to blackmail the United States. The President made it very clear that America would not negotiate with terrorists. Just Cause was sent in to take down Gigawatt before he could follow through on his threat."

"And you failed," said Goodwin.

"Actually, no. We succeeded. My team arrived and entered the facility. We engaged Gigawatt, successfully drawing him away from the generators before he could cause harm to them with his powers. My second-in-command, Doublecharge, was instrumental in keeping the flow of power uninterrupted as the rest of us battled, then contained, and finally subdued Gigawatt. What we couldn't know was that the very act of rendering him unconscious awakened a previously unknown ability of his, a wide-area power surge. It overloaded local power lines which in turn cascaded into the failure of regional grids. Unfortunately, it also stopped Gigawatt's heart, and we were unable to revive him. He could possibly have utilized his abilities to assist in repairing the grid had he still been alive. The power station had been evacuated and the system failed before we could safely bring any knowledgeable personnel back into the control room."

Senator Rand of Alaska, who had the thick neck and broad shoulders of a man who'd spent thirty years working in oilfields before going into politics, leaned into the questioning for the first time. "But why were you fighting, uh, Gigawatt at all? Isn't it in your charter not to engage criminals where civilians or property could come to harm?"

"That is our preference, yes, but it doesn't always work out that way." Sally couldn't see it but she heard the smile in Juice's voice. "Criminals aren't very cooperative in that regard."

"So why not acquiesce to his demands for the moment and then hit him when he went to take a leak or something?" asked Rand.

Juice clasped his hands upon the table in front of him. "When the President of the United States gives you a direct order, it's not a good idea to leave it open to too much interpretation."

The hearing dragged on and on until Sally felt like her head was exploding. Goodwin brought up the time that Juice called all hero teams in the country together to perform a secret mission in Central America. Sally knew the intimate details of that event, but only because she'd been directly involved in it. It was an act of questionable legality, given that American parahumans had entered Guatemala and openly battled Guatemalan citizens. This was a dicey part of Juice's defense, because almost everything about the Guatemalan Action was labeled top secret and the hearing was still open to the public and the media. The last thing anyone needed to learn was that there had been a reactor churning out new parahumans that were then being telepathically controlled into becoming an army of super-soldiers. Parahuman creation was the new brass ring of strategic weaponry, and the process that had been in use in Guatemala was fatal in more than ninety percent of cases. It wasn't hard to imagine another country recovering that technology and decimating large chunks of its population just to create its own strategic parahuman reserve.

During that particular question-and-answer period, Juice was forced to refuse to answer question after question due to security restrictions, and it looked bad. Goodwin kept pressing the issue, asking the same questions with different phrasing sometimes three or four times. Juice kept refusing to answer and to most viewers, it would have looked like he'd become a completely hostile witness.

Deakins waggled his finger at Juice. "We can legally compel you to answer. We have the authority to do so."

"I'm sorry, Senator. That information is classified at the highest level, and I am not at liberty to discuss it in full view of the press and uncleared civilians. If you wish to clear the chambers, I will answer your questions, but only in front of witnesses whose security clearances have been fully vetted."

Goodwin raised her voice. "No, that's all right." Sally wasn't surprised. The last thing Goodwin wanted was for her moment in the spotlight to end, and she'd do anything to keep the press there, making Juice look bad and making herself look better. She went on to bring up the failures of Just Cause to successfully deal with the Archmage in 2005 before numerous civilians were conscripted into forming the base of his magical armies. "It was the first time in hundreds of years that a foreign power successfully commenced an invasion of United States sovereign territory."

Senator Paulsen cleared his throat, sounding embarrassed. "I'd just like to interject here. Hundreds of North Dakotans were involved in the Archmage fiasco, and in the end, it took Just Cause to bring him down."

Goodwin glared down the table at him. "Be that as it may, Juice and some members of his team vanished for several weeks, allowing the Archmage to increase his foothold on U.S. soil. In the Army, that's called going A.W.O.L., Director."

It was Sally's turn to be politely restrained by Keith and Stacey. Sally, Juice, and several others had been catapulted back in time due to a miscast spell, and it had taken the help of Nikola Tesla and a whole lot of luck to get themselves back to their present. Their return had been the first time any of them had met Christine Goodwin, who was at the time a ranking official in the Department of Homeland Security, and had taken over the administration of Just Cause in Juice's absence. She had actually proposed a plan to use a nuclear device to take down the Archmage, which would have ultimately caused far more death and destruction than anything Just Cause might have managed. As it was, Sally managed to get inside the Archmage's defenses and take him down permanently, and here this woman hiding behind her Senatorial rank was willing to toss all that aside in order to score a few more cheap shots against Juice.

At last, the committee called a recess and announced they would resume questioning in two hours. Sally figured the break would allow the Senators plenty of time to drink martinis at lunch, and she couldn't blame them for that. She felt like she could use a drink herself. She refrained from mentioning it to Juice, Stacey, and Keith, though. That would have seemed unprofessional to her. But when Stacey growled something out about wishing she had a cocktail, Sally agreed with unabashed enthusiasm. She was tempted to get a ninety-minute head start on the lynch mob before they called her up to answer for herself. She figured at her best cruising speed, she could make it to Chicago. All she needed to do was throw on her boots and go. But if she did that, she may as well have kept on running forever, because she'd lose everything that was important to her.

So instead of fleeing, Sally joined Juice, Keith, and Stacey in a nearby bistro where they had overpriced coffee and scones, and discussed what they might expect from the second half of the day's Senatorial whippings.

"They really did a number on you, Jim." Keith dunked his scone into his coffee to make it more palatable. "You have any ass left after that chewing Goodwin gave you?"

"I'm sitting on something." Juice signaled the tattooed waitress that he'd like some more coffee. "She's certainly got an axe to grind with us."

"You stopped her from nuking the Archmage, James." Stacey removed her mask when they left the Dirksen Senate building, less as a statement and more so she could enjoy the time with her fellow soldiers without anything between them. "Nukes, James, on American soil."

"I know," said Juice. "It still scares me to know how close we got to losing that one. If we hadn't gotten Sally to infiltrate, I don't know that we could have stopped him. I bet he could have shut down a nuke."

"I wouldn't take that bet," said Keith. "Even if you win, you still lose. Know what I mean?"

"At least you got your licks in on Goodwin, Stacey," said Sally.

Stacey smiled at the memory of the time she hauled off and knocked Christine Goodwin unconscious with a single punch. A psi named Switchboard had intervened on Stacey's behalf, muddling Goodwin's memories so she wouldn't remember being punched. "I should have hit her harder." Sparks jumped between Stacey's eyes. "And more."

"Yeah, not a real solution either," said Juice.

"No, but it would have felt amazing."

The heroes laughed, making some of the hipster writers pecking away on their laptops look up from their hack poems and novels in frustration.

"We're going to get screwed, aren't we?" asked Sally. "Goodwin's got our backs against the wall."

"Not necessarily." Juice spread some butter across his scone. "We know what she wants, for starters, and that gives us some leverage. She wants me gone. And then she wants the PRA shut down."

"And don't forget she wants to weaponize all parahumans," said Keith. "We'll all make lovely soldiers for the New World Order."

"Isotope controlled his supersoldiers with his telepath," said Stacey. "You think Goodwin's plan would result in a similar control structure? Because I can tell you now, there are a lot of parahumans who wouldn't want to have anything to do with it."

"I doubt they'd have much choice," said Juice. "They'd become fugitives. Hunted. It would be like the roundup of the Jews by the Nazis."

"You think they'd put people to death?" asked Sally.

"Why not? If they can't control us, what's their only other option?" asked Juice.

Nobody answered him.

* * *

The committee reconvened, and Goodwin wasted no time in her ongoing crucifixion. "Director Forsythe, I'd like to change direction and talk about the people you've placed in leadership roles in the various Just Cause teams. My reason for this is to show that your choices have been flawed from the start and that it continues your pattern of poor decision making."

"Of course, Senator." Sally couldn't believe how calm Juice could be when Goodwin was labeling him incompetent and then throwing it in his face.

"Let's begin with Keith Jordan, also known as MetalBlade, who I see is sitting right behind you."

"I did not promote Mr. Jordan," said Juice. "Although I endorsed him for the leadership role of the Second Team. That decision ultimately came from Mr. Lane Devereaux, who was managing Just Cause in 1995 when the Second Team was created. I think you'll find that the Second Team has an impeccable record in the past fourteen years."

"It's true, the team has been exceptional," said Senator Harrison of New Hampshire, who was so short that he made Sally feel gangly and disconnected from her feet.

"Now then, you did promote Stacey Martin, known as Doublecharge, to her current position as leader of Just Cause, did you not?" asked Goodwin.

"I did."

"And under her watchful eyes, we've seen a mass breakout from Deep Six, allowing the world's most dangerous parahuman criminals to reach freedom."

"Just Cause halted the escape attempt—"

Goodwin interrupted Juice. "Not before civilians were killed both here in the United States and in Germany. Multiple fatalities including foreign parahumans and prisoners, and the worst of the lot, Misrule, is still unaccounted for."

Juice rose his voice, letting his sonorous baritone carry through the chamber. "The escapees' plane went down in the Mediterranean Ocean. There's no indication Misrule survived, and we searched for days, with help from a Canadian water-based parahuman named Triton and the Greek Coast Guard as well."

"But he could have survived," said Senator Rand. "He had regenerative abilities, didn't he? Couldn't he have just relied upon them until he reached safety?"

"That's not how they work—" said Juice.

Goodwin raised her voice to a calculated shout, aiming to be a most-watched video clip. "It's risky for you to assume that Misrule, who was for years at the top of Interpol's Most Wanted list, died in something as mundane as a plane crash. He could be out there right now, planning revenge. He was going to use nerve gas on major population centers! He was going to ally with Islamic terrorists!"

"And you were going to nuke North Dakota!" Juice finally started to lose his cool. "How dare you, Senator." Sally felt the tension rise throughout the chamber.

"You're out of order, Director!"

"This whole investigation is out of order." Juice jumped to his feet. He looked like a volcano on the verge of blowing its top. She could almost see the heat waves rising off the top of his head. "It's a farce, being perpetrated by a Senator who is letting her personal feelings interfere with her professional position."

Deakins stood as well. "Sit down, Director. I'm warning you. I will have you removed from these chambers."

Juice snarled back, "I'll save you the trouble. This is a waste of my time, and of taxpayers' money. Shame on you, Senator."

Sally glanced at Stacey. She'd pulled her mask back up over her face again and stood beside Juice in a show of solidarity. A moment later, Keith joined them, drawing iron out of the surrounding environment to wrap himself in his black, medieval-style armor. Sally pulled up her own cowl. "Shit." Were they about to fight their way out of the Senatorial chambers? That would be a good way to get them all thrown into Federal pound-me-in-the-ass prison.

"Director Forsythe, you are in contempt of these proceedings!" Goodwin shouted over the rising murmurs of astonishment from the onlookers. "Sergeant-at-arms, take the Director into custody."

The uniformed officer looked terrified at the prospect of trying to arrest a man who was a good foot taller and hundred pounds heavier than he was, but Juice stood his ground without attempting to flee.

"James, what are you doing?" Sparks crackled around Stacey's fingertips.

"Go. All of you. I'm buying you what time I can." Juice raised his voice. "Parahumans are not the problem here, Senator. It's people like you wanting to criminalize them just for their existence."

Stacey took Keith's and Sally's arms. The electricity in her hands made Sally's fingertips tingle. "Let's go, before they decide to haul us off as well."

"But what about Juice?" Sally hesitated as Juice raised his hands, wrists together, toward the approaching Sergeant-at-arms, showing his willingness to be arrested.

Keith took her arm. "He's buying us time, like he said. Don't waste it." The three heroes hurried out of the Dirksen building into the cold, pursued by the press, eager to catch something worthy of a front page or website headline or lead-in on the evening news. Their car was out front and they got in just ahead of the throng of shouting reporters, snapping pictures and hurling questions like bullets.

"What do we do now?" Sally watched out the back window as the car pulled away, leaving the press behind in impotent rage.

Stacey's quiet anger was as scary as Juice's shouting. "Go home. Call in all your people. Batten down the hatches. Things are going to get very ugly now."

Sally shuddered. "You make it sound like you're expecting a mob with torches and pitchforks."

A spark bounced back and forth between Stacey's eyes. "That's not a bad analogy. Between Goodwin waging a constant battle in the media against parahumans and that son of a bitch Reichel stirring up a shitstorm with his rabid fanbase, we'll be lucky if they don't start rounding up all parahumans as a threat to American security."

Sally shivered. The sun had already set and darkness was spreading across the city.

And across the nation.

Twelve

"Director Forsythe's history of obstructionist actions has come back to bite him. One can only hope that the President will consider the Goodwin Act now that Forsythe can't play pick-up basketball with him any longer."
—Ken Reichel, First Choice Radio Network

February, 2009
New York City, NY

They gave Juice's job to someone else.

His name was Michael Sapo, and until he was appointed to fill Juice's position as Director of the Parahuman Resources Agency, he'd been a fairly low-level bureaucrat in Homeland Security. It appeared he'd been selected as the new director, because he had worked with Christine Goodwin during her own Homeland Security tenure. Nepotism was as alive and well as ever in the government.

Sapo's very first act as Director was to order an immediate re-evaluation of all Just Cause members and team administrators. During that time, Just Cause was enjoined from acting in any official capacity except in the case of dire emergencies, which would require a direct order from the Director to proceed.

"Grounded!" Sally felt like throwing her coffee cup across the room, except that wouldn't have solved anything beyond breaking her favorite Happy Puppies cup and ruining coffee that was perfectly doctored. "I can't believe it."

Davey took away Sally's cup and set it upon her desk. "It's bullshit. But it's also policy. We're stuck for the time being. Might as well make the most of it. What do you need me to do?"

Sally clenched her fist. She refused to take this new development in stride. "Team meeting. Whoever's here. Ten minutes."

Davey nodded. "On it." She left Sally's office.

"She's good" Jason sprawled on one of the guest chairs, his eyes shut as he fingered chords on an imaginary guitar. "You think she has any experience managing bands?"

"I wouldn't be surprised. She seems very worldly to me. Are you thinking about starting a new group?"

Jason shrugged. "Depends on my hearing. It'll be awhile before I can play at the kind of, um, volume to which I am accustomed."

Sally zipped across the room in a flash to kiss the top of his head and ruffle his hair in a playful way. "Baby, you're not always going to be able to keep stuff at *eleven*."

"They can take my volume knob when they pry it away from my cold, dead hand. What are we going to do about this PRA thing? It feels like we're getting hosed at every turn."

"We are. This is an orchestrated effort to shut down Just Cause. I can feel it in my bones."

"Speaking of which, you could use a sandwich. You're looking a little on the skinny side, babe."

"You're just saying that because you remember me when I went undercover into the Champions."

Jason shrugged. "It was a good look for you."

Davey poked her head into the office. "Everyone's in the conference room."

"Thanks, Davey. We'll be there directly. I want you to make sure all monitoring in there is disabled for the duration of the meeting. It's going to be a lot of ears-only secret superhero club stuff."

"I'll make that happen. You want me there or you want me to steer clear? If I don't know what you're talking about, I can't tell anyone if I'm coerced."

"No, I need you there."

"Got it." Davey vanished again.

Sally tugged on Jason's hand. She might as well have been trying to pull a mountain, but he allowed himself to come up and out of the chair. "Come on, you big galoot. I need to go make like General Patton."

Jason grinned. "I think there's a helmet downstairs in the CSC."

Except for Jack's notable absence, the entire Just Cause New York team was waiting in the conference room when Sally and Jason entered. Nobody was in costume. Why would they bother? They'd all received the same notification that Sally had. They were grounded. At least everyone had been returned to active duty, such as it was. Sally stepped up to Shillelagh. "How are you feeling?"

The Bostonian shrugged. "I can walk without falling over. That's a positive."

"Something we should all strive to achieve. Thanks for coming, everyone. I wanted to go over our latest directive from the PRA and give you some directives of my own." She glanced at Davey, who gave her a thumbs-up. "This meeting is not being monitored. Anything said in this room stays here."

"Ohhh, secrets. How exciting!" Ment shrugged. "Jack would have said something like that."

Sally nodded. "He would, and we need to remember that he is where he is right now because of a lie, and we need to shine the, uh, the light of truth on it. Look, I know that sounds stupid, but it is what it is. There is a concerted effort going on to shut us down, maybe permanently, and we need to figure out what's going on and why."

Minerva crossed her legs, hovering in the air beside Ment. "What do you suggest? More investigation?"

Sally nodded. "More of everything. Now that everyone is medically cleared, we need to accelerate our training schedule. The only way we're going to be able to deal with some of the problems we're going to face is to be comfortable working with each other. Effective immediately, we're running two training sessions per day. Two hours in the morning and two in the afternoon. I'm suspending all monitor center duties. I've always thought monitor duty was a waste of time when we have a staff on hand already who can pick up a phone to notify us of a situation."

Detroit Steel smacked a fist into her palm with a dull ringing sound. "Good call. We ain't doin' anybody any good sitting in there, anyway."

"Training every day, twice a day?" Snowball grimaced. "You're going to tire us right the fuck out, you know."

Sally shook her head. "I'm going to make you stronger. We're on the cusp of a war, and we have to be ready for it."

"What do you mean, a war?" Snapdragon made a tiny flame dance across his palm.

"This has all happened before." Sally walked around the room, recognizing that she could think better when she was in motion. "In 1953. My grandparents—and Minerva's grandmother too, actually—were part of American Justice when Senator McCarthy blacklisted them. For the next sixteen years, it was illegal to be a parahuman. If you went out in public and used your powers, you were subject to arrest . . . or worse, depending upon where in the country you were. That was where Just Cause began, out of the ashes of the American Justice team. They had to stay ahead of the law and sometimes the military, even while they were fighting to protect the very people who hated them."

"Sounds like *The A-Team*," said Detroit Steel.

Sally nodded. "Yeah, but with fewer mohawks. That was back in the Fifties and Sixties. Things are different now. If we have to go underground again, we're going to have a lot harder time of it. There's surveillance everywhere. Everyone has a cell phone. If we're still going to be superheroes in a police state, we're going to have to work a lot harder than ever to stay fit, and there will be times we have to fight for our very freedom or survival against cops or soldiers. We'll be branded as terrorists. Hunted."

Snapdragon's sigh carried the weight of many years of discrimination. As the son of ethnic Algerian immigrants and a practicing Muslim, he was well-acquainted with the branding to which Sally referred. "And yet, we cannot treat them as our enemies, if they see us as such. They will never change their perceptions of us so long as we do anything to reinforce them."

"Fuck 'em." Snowball patted Snapdragon's knee.

Sally cleared her throat. "Anyway, that's why we're upping our training schedule. I don't want anything to happen to any of you again. Not after we got our asses handed to us by Syndicate S."

"Speaking of them, and more specifically, The Militia, did you hear what that bastard Patriot said?" asked Shillelagh.

Sally nodded. Almost immediately after the announcement that Just Cause would be temporarily suspending operations, Patriot announced that he and The Militia would be on call in the event that they were needed to help *quell an emergency*—his term, Sally had noted, suggested that they were fans of permanent, often fatal solutions—but would stay out of the public view so as to avoid discomforting the civilian population. "We're going to steal a page from their playbook, and we're going to do them one better. Just Cause is enjoined from acting in an official capacity. Therefore, I'm telling you I can't and won't stop any of you from acting in an *unofficial* capacity. I don't need or want to know about it if you do, and expect you to avoid getting caught. Unfortunately, Shawna, Yunbao, that's going to make it difficult for the two of you to leave headquarters. If you decide to, though, you're free to leave."

Detroit Steel nodded. "I can paint myself if I have to. It's itchy, but it's better than nothing."

Yunbao quivered with restrained discomfort. "I once shaved off my fur. It is an . . . unpleasant feeling. It is also odd for others to see. I do not look as a proper human without it any more than I do with it."

Sally admired the Chinese woman's fur. "I think you look beautiful as you are."

"Me too." Shillelagh winked. "Rawr."

"We'll figure it out if you want to leave the base." Sally returned to her desk to find her coffee cup undamaged where Davey had saved it. "In the meantime, everyone needs to prepare. At some point we're going to have to jump, and jump quickly. I don't know what direction it will be, so we better be ready."

"What are you going to do about the PRA?" Ment wrapped his hand around Minerva's.

"I don't know I've got some ideas about that, but I need to bounce them off of someone who's got more experience dealing with fascists than I do."

"Who would that be?" asked Snapdragon.

"Jack," said Sally.

* * *

The Metropolitan Correctional Center was something Sally hadn't experienced before: a prison in a high-rise.

She stepped out of the car and looked up at the massive cement tower. In all her experience as a superhero, she'd never actually been inside of a prison before. She was nervous—not because she was particularly afraid of the inmates, but because she was worried about making some kind of mistake that would hurt Just Cause's reputation further, or Jack's chances at his charges being dismissed. She'd considered approaching the prison in disguise, as she was enough of a celebrity to attract undue attention, but Jason had quelled that idea as soon as he'd seen her looking at a wig.

"You're kidding, right?"

"What if someone recognizes me?"

"What if they do? This is New York, babe. There are famous people all over the place and these jaded residents couldn't care less. Just be yourself. Your professional . . . beautiful . . . competent . . . sexy self."

His final kiss had left her lips tingling and she ran her tongue across them once as if she could draw strength from the memory. She went to the main entrance and checked in with the front desk. The civilians behind the thick, bulletproof glass took her information and confirmed it with the appointment she'd had Davey set before she left. Somewhere behind the glass, in a back office, she could hear the ranting, preachy tones of Ken Reichel blasting from someone's radio, and it set her teeth on edge.

"Ms. Thompson?" A tall, white-haired man with broad shoulders and an ill-fitting navy blue suit came up to her.

"It's Tibbets now, actually. Warden?"

The man smiled and brushed a hand through his thinning, short haircut and Sally saw him try to suck in his gut as he bent down to shake her hand. At least his gaze didn't linger upon her. She'd dressed in her least-flattering business suit. The inside of the prison was cold enough that she didn't feel the need to remove her overcoat or hat, at least until they told her to. "Warden Roberts. I was told we were expecting you today."

"Jack's not caused any problems, has he?"

Warden Roberts led her through a security door into a corridor. "No, not at all. He's been very much a model prisoner. We've kept him away from general population. Everyone wants to see how invulnerable he really is, and we'd just as soon not let things come to that point."

"I can understand that."

They stopped at another security door. "I'm afraid you'll need to be searched before we proceed into the visiting wing. I have two female officers here to assist with that. I'll wait beyond the checkpoint." The door opened to reveal two burly female officers who wouldn't have looked out of place on the defensive line of an NFL team. Either one of them could have broken her in half had they put their minds to it, and despite his strength and toughness, Jason might have had his hands full in a scrap with either of them. She surrendered her phone, badge, and turned out all her pockets. One of the women took and thoroughly searched her coat while the other patted her down from head to toe, making her glad she hadn't worn the wig after all. Sally made herself hold still while the woman checked inside the bands of her underwear and bra.

Satisfied that Sally wasn't smuggling any contraband, the guards returned her coat to her and announced she was cleared to proceed. The Warden rejoined her and took her to a small antechamber beside the visiting area where she had to fill out a ream of paperwork. If they were intending to delay her, they were going to be disappointed. She used her super-speed powers to zip through it in a few seconds and before the Warden quite realized what had happened, she handed him the stack of signed forms. "I'm sure you'll find everything in order, Warden."

The Warden paged through the papers. Did he seem like he was stalling? Sally couldn't tell. Perhaps he was just being thorough. She forced herself to sit quietly, putting on a show of patience. She needed to speak to Jack, but she would have to play by their rules. At last the Warden set down the stack on the desk. "It appears you are correct." He waved at the security camera in the room. "We'll bring him in after we get you settled. Please leave your coat and hat in here."

Sally followed the Warden to the visiting room. She thought it might be a booth with a glass partition where she and Jack would have to speak to each other through a telephone, but instead they brought her to a small room with a table and chairs bolted to the floor. An iron ring was attached to the table in front of one chair. Condensation made the gray walls damp, and the room felt like it was barely warmer than it had been outdoors. Sally shivered and wished she could have kept her coat on, and sat in the chair facing the door.

"You can embrace him," said the Warden. "But you will be subject to another search after this visit if there is any physical contact between the two of you at all. You may not give him anything, nor accept anything from him. If you have documents he needs, turn them in to me and I will deliver them. He has not given us anything to give to you. Your visit will be monitored both on camera and by a guard in person, and it can be terminated at any time for any reason. If you violate any laws during your visit, you will be detained and subject to criminal proceedings."

"I understand."

A guard knocked on the door. The Warden turned to look. "He's here. You have thirty minutes."

Sally bit back an acerbic reply, knowing it wouldn't help Jack at all.

The door opened and two guards escorted Jack into the visiting room. He looked haggard, with a few days' growth of steel-gray beard on his cheeks and chin. The circles under his eyes suggested he hadn't slept much in his incarceration. He was dressed in a khaki jumpsuit. A chain ran between his ankles while another from his wrists looped on a belt around his waist. He smiled at Sally, his eyes sparkling with their usual amusement. The guards sat him in the chair facing Sally. They undid one of his handcuffs, fed the chain between them through the loop in the table, and then cuffed him once more. One guard then left the visiting room while the other stood by the door, hands on his hips, watching the two heroes.

Sally decided she didn't care if they searched her again, and wrapped her arms around Jack for a few seconds, taking comfort in his nearness even though he couldn't return the embrace. At last, after too short a time, she took her seat once more. "You look terrible."

"Really? And here I put on my best outfit just for you." Jack's eyes crinkled up around the edges. "I take it you're not here to say *Jack, there's been a terrible mistake and I'm bringing you home*?"

"Jack, there *has* been a terrible mistake, and I'm going to do everything I can to get you out of here. The D.A. has no case. As soon as a judge gets to look at the evidence, your case will be tossed."

"That's going to make sleeping a lot easier. This place isn't very conducive to rest. At least I'm having all kinds of time to think about the important things in life."

"Come to any conclusions?"

"I don't think the *Star Wars* prequels were as bad as people like to say. I don't understand why people keep giving money to Tyler Perry to make movies. And I'm damn sure I didn't shoot Senator Christine Goodwin."

Sally smiled. "I'm sure about that too. Besides not sleeping, how are things here?"

"The food is shit, but you can't beat the entertainment. And despite what they said in *Office Space*, there's next to no ass-pounding going on in Federal pound-me-in-the-ass prison. Also, I miss Sondra."

"Has she been out to visit you?" Sally winced when she said it. What if Sondra hadn't been? How would that make Jack feel.

He smiled. "Yeah, once. I hear they're still pulling pinfeathers out of the ventilation system." He cleared his throat and raised his voice slightly. "Which would have been unnecessary if I hadn't been deemed a flight risk."

"Easy, Jack. We'll get you out of here and make sure your record is cleared and all that." Sally.

"So enough about me, kiddo. What brings you out of your castle down here to muck about with us lowly peasant folk?"

Sally sighed. "I needed to talk to someone and I can't talk to Juice because he's under arrest for contempt of Congress and the Capitol Police won't let me see him. I can't talk to the new director because he's a dickhead. You're the closest friend I've got, and I need advice."

"Good on him for getting under their skin." Jack rattled his chains. "It appears I'm not going anywhere. I am, as they say, a captive audience."

"I don't know where to start."

"I'd suggest the beginning."

Over the next fifteen minutes, Sally outlined everything she'd learned in her investigation of the death of Martina Hladky, how she felt it tied into Chessboard and into Senator Goodwin and The Militia. "I just feel like it's all tied together somehow, but I can't figure out how. I can't see the bigger picture."

Jack leaned forward over the table enough to scratch his stubble with one chained hand. "Times like this, the thing to do is to start by studying your enemy."

"You mean Goodwin?"

"Everything seems to tie back to her in some way. She's the one at the forefront of trying to shut down Just Cause. She's the one who called and ran the Senate investigation that now has Juice without a job and facing contempt charges. And she's the one who got herself shot by someone who conveniently looked like me. You tell me someone else is higher up on the food chain and I'm going to call bullshit unless I see some real proof."

"No, you're right. It has to be her."

"So why is she so invested in taking us down?"

"Well, she hates us."

"No." Jack leaned back. "That's the easy way out, Sally. You're better than that."

Sally sighed. She knew this was what she needed, but Jack was going to make it difficult. A learning experience. Building character. Sally thought if she built any more goddamn character, she was going to need a clone to handle the overflow. Something about that flippant thought stuck in her mind, and she made a point of filing it for future reference. "Okay, so it's something more than her hating us. We . . . embarrassed her back in 2004. She was trying to use nuclear weapons against The Archmage. Never mind that he was powerful enough that he probably could have stopped them, or redirected them, or turned them into something even worse and sent them back against us. Juice shut her down by going over her head all the way to the top."

"President Bush. They're still good friends, you know. Bush never had anyone else in mind to run the PRA besides Juice."

"It can't just be politics. Goodwin's a Republican too."

"But now Juice is friends with Obama, and the Grand Ole Party doesn't take too kindly to folks crossing the lines like that."

"Juice wasn't ever on their side . . . was he? I mean, I don't have time for politics."

Jack clicked his tongue in irritation. "You'd better make time. You're in a political position, Sally. You have to learn how to play the game."

"Okay, I can learn anything. What are the rules?"

"Nothing happens in Washington if it doesn't make money for someone. It takes money to grease the wheels, and nobody even bothers to get out of bed if there isn't an angle in it. If it's not money, it's power over someone else, which usually means someone owes someone else a favor."

"So Goodwin is doing this because it's getting her something valuable. Power. Money."

"Politicians turn their coats faster than we change our clothes sometimes. One minute they're full of desperate hate for someone, and the next they're all buddy-buddy. It's all in the angle."

"I get it. We need to find out what her angle is."

"I don't think I'll be much help for the next couple of weeks. I hear they're trying to get a judge lined up to hear the D.A.'s case, but . . . yeah, they're not hurrying as much as they could be. I don't suppose you want to bust me out of here?" Jack winked.

Sally gasped, but the guard by the door just snorted. He'd probably heard that kind of statement a thousand times before. "Uh, no. I mean, I would, but I'm already in enough hot water without that kind of trouble."

"No worries, kiddo. You know I jest."

"So I uncover Goodwin's angle. Then what?"

Jack smiled. It wasn't a smile of amusement so much as it was the smile of a sniper about to pull a trigger. "Then you exploit it to get what you want. And that's how you play the game."

A knock sounded on the door and the guard by it cleared his throat. "I'm sorry, Ma'am. Your time's up."

Sally stood and squeezed Jack's hands for a moment. "Thank you. You have no idea how much I needed this."

Jack's smile was much softer. "Probably not as much as I did. Go get 'em, kiddo. Give 'em hell."

Thirteen

"The random aspect of parahuman abilities is one of the most disturbing factors. What if we could control who came into those powers? You can be sure it would be people of high moral caliber, people who would be responsible and judicious in the use of those powers, people we could trust."

—Senator Christine Goodwin (R-NY)

February, 2009
New York City, NY

Sally set her large flatscreens to display images from the Painted Desert in Arizona, one of the most beautiful and serene places she'd ever seen. She had Jason bring a coffee brewing station up from the commissary, and set up a table full of every kind of salty, sweet, high-calorie, zero-nutrient snack she could find in headquarters, and then supplemented them with brain-boosting foods like berries, salmon, and granola. Thus fortified, she sent out a text to all her teammates that anyone who felt like doing some major headache-inducing brainwork over the next several hours was welcome to join her, but she wouldn't hold it against anyone who begged off.

She was happy Jason decided to join her in the office, but suspected he'd spend most of the time playing quiet games on his laptop. That was okay, though. The brainwork wasn't really his forte, and she was glad to have his company. Davey joined in right away, kicking off her shoes the second she walked into the office and wrapping her hair up into a bun. Minerva and Ment swung by as well. Ment shrugged at Sally. "There's nothing good on TV."

Yunbao entered the room. "I do not know how much help I can be, but I will do what I can."

Detroit Steel was right behind her. "I can't stand those weight machines any longer. I need to use these muscles—" She tapped her head with a clinking sound. "—instead of these muscles." She flexed her arms, making her biceps bulge out like silvery cantaloupes.

Failsafe wandered over to the table to check out the snack spread, selected some items for his plate, and then sat down with his back against the Painted Desert. "I'll help."

"Shillelagh, reporting for duty." The slender redhead as she walked into the office. "Crowded in here, hey?" She hopped up onto the still-mostly-empty bookshelves and stretched out atop them. "At least we haven't been open long enough for it to be dusty up here. Someone want to toss me a plate?"

Jason stretched up to hand her some snacks and a cup of coffee.

Eventually, even Snapdragon and Snowball happened into the office, looking a little embarrassed at the realization they were last.

Sally recognized the way they came in, trying very hard not to be obvious about the fact that they were sleeping together. She wondered if she and Jason had been as poor at covering it up when they were trying to, and how anybody could have possibly thought otherwise. She smiled to herself. Juice and Doublecharge had both said on separate occasions that they didn't have a problem with internal team relationships, so long as they didn't interfere with superhero duties in the field. "Okay, since we're all turning this into a hipster beach party, everyone take a laptop and some snacks and claim your space. We're going to put together a complete dossier on Christine Goodwin. I want to know everything about her. We understand her, and that will help us to understand what she really wants and why she's trying to destroy Just Cause."

Ment picked a pretzel stick off his plate and contemplated it. "You have a strategy in mind, Boss? Or you just want us each to flounder in our own way?"

Sally found that being called *Boss* gave her a thrill she'd never really felt before. Ment hadn't delivered it with cynicism, or sarcasm. It was a title of honestly-earned respect, and somehow it had been exactly the thing Sally needed to hear. "No. Well, not exactly. Research is a pretty organic thing, and there's no way to tell what paths you might uncover and choose to follow. You won't know how deep the rabbit hole goes until you dive into it."

"Red pill. Got it." Ment grinned at Sally, and she grinned back, not even realizing she'd made a *Matrix* reference until he'd thrown it back at her.

"Davey, dig into the proposed Goodwin Act. I know it's probably a couple of hundred pages, but see if you can summarize it for us."

"On it." Davey slipped on her earbuds and a moment later it was like she wasn't even in the room with them.

"Minerva, Ment, see what you can find out about Goodwin's career before she became a Senator. Go as far back as you can. See what kind of indicators you can find early on that might suggest what she's doing now. Jason, sweetie, find what you can about her current work as a Senator. Aramis, you do the same."

Jason wiped crumbs from his mouth. "Yeah, got it."

Failsafe gave her a thumbs-up.

"Shawna, known associates. Eileen, dig into her private life." Detroit Steel and Shillelagh nodded and got to work. "Sara, Nabi, I want you to get as much as you can on The Militia and anything you can find out about Syndicate S. See if you can track them back to their origins and identities if possible." Snowball and Snapdragon made themselves comfortable against a wall with a bag of pretzels between them. "Yunbao . . ."

"Yes?"

"Come over here and work with me. We're going to examine Chessboard Industries more in-depth. I know that they have a Chinese division, and you can help me with that part of it."

Yunbao picked her way across the floor, careful not to gouge anyone with her toe claws, and sat herself down right on Sally's desk with her furry legs crossed and a laptop resting across her knees.

"All right, everyone. Two hours and then we'll recap what we've learned. Take breaks when you need them. Plenty of snacks and caffeine if you want them. If you need to walk away for a while, go ahead. I know this stuff can be tough. Believe me, I'm less patient than any five of you combined." That generated some chuckles around the room before Just Cause New York got busy with a far-less-glamorous type of heroism.

* * *

Of course, Davey put together a professional presentation despite such a short time to prepare, using a white board to highlight the salient points. "The proposed Goodwin Act is intended to supplant and update the existing laws governing the rights and disposition of American parahumans. It is a sweeping, wide-reaching law that would reach into nearly every aspect of life for those who are in possession either of the Musashi Genetic Structure, exhibit powers or abilities without the presence of that genetic structure, or otherwise exhibit powers or abilities attributed to forces not yet defined."

Snapdragon sipped at his coffee. "That last one is scary. If they don't define what is a parapower, they could define anything as a parapower and then apply this law to them. You could be really good at, say, chess, and someone could accuse you of having a power. And how do you prove you don't have it for something like that?"

"How do you prove you're not a witch?" Sally wished Jack was there, for he'd have made a timely *Monty Python and the Holy Grail* joke for her. "This is a legalized witch-hunt, plain and simple. Please continue, Davey."

"The first part of the Act deals with the reorganization of the Parahuman Resources Agency into the United States Parahuman Reserve. It would become associated with the United States Armed Forces, and would be led by an appointed General, who would then become part of the Joint Chiefs. The USPR would follow standard military protocols and chain of command."

Ment sighed. "So much for Juice getting his job back."

"I'm not sure what it would take at this point for him to get his job back at all. Exoneration, maybe? A presidential pardon?" Sally looked at Davey for help.

"He hasn't done anything wrong," said Jason.

"He's in contempt of the Senate," said Sally. "That's pretty serious, as far as I know."

Davey waited patiently for the extraneous conversation to die down and then resumed her explanation. "The second part of the Act deals with the registration of existing and future parahumans. All known parahumans would be required to register with the USPR. Failure to do so would be a Federal felony with varying penalties. The USPR would create a comprehensive database of American parahumans. All medical personnel would be required to administer a Musashi test to anyone needing medical treatment who hasn't already been listed or cleared in the USPR database. All newborn babies would likewise be tested, as well as anyone legally immigrating to the United States or visiting for a period of longer than two weeks."

"Jesus, they're not fucking around, are they? No more secrets." Snowball made frost appear on her soda bottle.

"You know what that's gonna mean? Black market doctors. You want to keep your genes a secret? Best be willin' to pay for it." Detroit Steel shook her head.

"I wonder if they'd make home births illegal." Shillelagh brushed her fingers through her short black hair. "Or if there could be a religious exemption. I could see that becoming a sticky issue."

Davey made a note of Shillelagh's question on her white board. "There are further penalties listed for medical professionals failing to administer a Musashi test during the course of treatment. Essentially, if you're sick enough to go to the doctor, you're going to get a genetic test, unless you're already on the list. The third part of the Act is very lengthy and deals with defining the individual rights of parahumans and when the government can suspend those rights in a time of need. It's very, very dry reading, let me tell you."

"Take a few days off," said Sally. "Seriously, what else are you going to do with us being shut down and all?"

Davey grinned like a shark. "Prepare for when we are not shut down and all. Essentially what this part of the Act says is that parahumans are considered strategic resources and can be drafted by the USPR at any time for any purpose. Basically, if you have a parahuman ability and the government needs you to use it on their behalf for something, you can expect to get notified. Failure to do so is equivalent to refusing to report during a draft. Once the USPR has drafted you to fulfill its need, it can release you outright once the job is completed, or at its discretion it can retain you indefinitely."

Failsafe shook his head. "Shit, I'd rather go back to the Six if it came to that. I been a conscript in an army once. Never again, *amigos*."

Sally nodded. "What's really worrisome is that indefinite retention. They're detaining prisoners in Guantanamo indefinitely, without charges. This sounds just like that. You think parahuman soldiers will be any better off than prisoners?"

Jason scrunched up his face in thought. "Well . . . no, I guess not. They're not going to have any civil rights in that kind of situation."

"Welcome to the New World Order." Snapdragon looked miserable. "You know how many times my family and I have been questioned because my parents are Algerian? For a while, it seemed like we were getting pulled in for questioning every couple of weeks. I wear a turban. I have a beard. Therefore, I must be a terrorist." He snorted. "We're a family of florists. Got a wedding or a funeral happening? That's where we come in. We're no danger to anyone unless they're allergic to pollen."

Davey circled the letters *USPR* on her white board. "The USPR will have authority to dispatch parahuman operatives *wherever they are needed.* With the USPR becoming the sole commanding entity over American parahumans, this suggests that all existing superhero teams will be disbanded and the members absorbed into USPR operations."

"Something we can't say no to." Minerva spoke softly, but her voice carried enough concern that she might as well have been shouting from the top of a mountain. "If this is signed into law, the most important part of being a parahuman is no longer valid."

"What's that, babe?" Ment squeezed her hand.

"Being a human." Minerva cracked a rare smile.

Sally looked at Davey's white board, trying to absorb all that information. "Davey, does it say specifically that the USPR cannot send parahumans out of the country?"

"It does not."

Sally sighed. She'd figured as much. "Ladies and gentlemen, we're looking at becoming the new supersoldiers for the United States if the Goodwin Act passes. Does anyone not think this will lead to parahuman troops fighting on foreign soil?"

Nobody replied except Snowball muttering under her breath about how she'd give Goodwin an icy fucking enema. Snapdragon clasped her hand and tried to calm her down.

"This is the kind of thing my grandfather fought against his entire career." Sally paced some more. "Senator McCarthy closed down American Justice back in the Fifties. My grandfather spent fifteen years trying to get the laws changed and it wasn't until '69 that he succeeded. We can do what we're doing as heroes because of what he accomplished back then. I'm not about to let that legacy get swept away. We have to do whatever we can to stop the Goodwin Act from becoming law, and it starts with getting to her. So what do we know about her?"

Ment stood and addressed the group. Christine Goodwin entered public service in 2002, after obtaining a Master's Degree in Political Science from Columbia University. She grew up in upstate New York and spent her formative years involved in clubs like the Young Republicans at her high school. Upon completing her degree, she applied for and was accepted into the Department of Homeland Security. She received numerous commendations for her work and over two years was given greater and greater responsibilities, culminating in the role that caused her to cross paths with Just Cause. "That was 2004. You and Juice were stuck back in the Nineteenth Century, and Jack was in thrall to the Archmage then."

"The day she came to us at the Hero Academy, she had so much presence she seemed like she must have been ten feet tall." Minerva shut her eyes so she could better recall the events. "Principal Stone called the senior class together and she was there to address us. She informed us that our country needed us and that she was drafting us to replace the missing members of Just Cause."

Snowball snorted. "We actually never officially graduated. I mean, they gave us the diplomas and everything later, but we were all inducted into Just Cause that same afternoon."

"Twenty-four hours later, we were on the front lines." Ment's jaw tightened as he remembered the disastrous battle. "And it was ugly. Not a one of us really knew what we were doing. Doublecharge did her best to keep us from the worst of it. But we were still fighting civilians the Archmage had recruited and turned, and those damn magical creatures he kept calling up."

Jason shook his head. "We were lucky not to be overrun. All of us were hurt, exhausted. I hate to admit it, but when Goodwin proposed nuking the Archmage's castle, I was all for it. Anything to put an end to the war."

Sally squeezed his hand. They'd talked some about the battles that had gone on during the seven weeks she had been trapped in the past, but Jason clearly didn't like talking about it. He always got a hollow look in his eyes that dampened his otherwise perpetual twinkle. She hated seeing him like that, and made a point not to bring it up to him. "What was Goodwin like during that time?"

Minerva opened her eyes again. "She was like a force of nature. It seemed like every time we were flagging in our resolve, she was there to pump us up and exhort us to keep going. She had a team of strategists doing their best to utilize us effectively, and I saw her fire two of them on the spot when they gave some bad directives that lost us an entire armor division to the dragons."

"Those fucking dragons." Snowball's viciousness seemed far too powerful for someone so tiny. "I still have nightmares about them coming in low over the fields and setting everything on fire."

"After that whole fiasco was resolved, she received several rapid promotions in Homeland Security until she was maybe fourth in line to be the director." Jason's eye twinkle returned. "See? I can research too, Boss."

Sally kissed his cheek. "Good job, Jase."

"I'm only just getting started. She got married to a guy at a public relations firm in 2006. Kept her name. Shortly after her wedding, she announced her intent to run for the Senate in her home state of New York. She won, despite stiff competition from the Democratic incumbent. She's been a loud voice in the Senate since then, and the rumors are that she might make a presidential run in 2012 or 2016."

Shillelagh shuddered. "God, that's terrifying. I'd be out of this country so fast, all that would be left behind would be smoking footprints." She stretched and ran her fingers through her short pixie haircut. "Guys, we haven't found out jack shit about Syndicate S. The only mentions online are surrounding our ass-kicking by them."

Failsafe looked up. "The Militia has their own website. They are very patriotic. And they have some very strong opinions about politics and taxes and things. They hate the President and he's barely had time to do anything yet. Bunch of *pendejos.*"

Sally nodded. She didn't dispute his assessment in the least. "Besides that attitude, is there any more information about them? Have we met all of them?"

"They each have a profile page. There is nobody else listed. They were all volunteers that received their powers from Chessboard Industries. They see themselves as the first of a new breed of parahumans.

And yeah, they're all dickheads." Shillelagh grinned down from her vantage point atop the bookshelves.

Sally snorted. "That's nothing we didn't already know. So here's Chessboard coming up again. They have something they call Touchstone Technology. It's listed as patent pending, so they don't have any other information on it. Whatever it is, it's how they're imbuing people with powers. I don't think it's like the Guatemalan reactor. That had something like a three percent success rate, which meant a whole lot of people missing, presumed dead. When you're turned into ash, there's nothing to identify you."

Yunbao scratched at her cheek. "They would have to waste a lot of the people whose philosophy they need if that was the case. It would be inefficient."

Sally nodded. "Yeah. Whatever Touchstone Technology is, it's reliable."

"That plays right into Goodwin's hands," said Snapdragon. "If someone can give powers to their ideal candidates, they could just sterilize the rest of us so we don't breed more random powers into the general population. They could make actual parahumans an extinct species."

Sally frowned. She hated when people took the philosophy that parahumans were a different race than so-called mundanes . . . or *crunchies*, the favorite derogatory term adopted by the powerhouse heroes like her husband. Weren't they all human beings? She wondered if Neanderthals had felt the same way about Cro-Magnons.

Detroit Steel looked up from her laptop. "Hey, I got something. Goodwin's husband? His P.R. firm had Chessboard Industries as a client. He don't work there any more, though. Now he's a lobbyist. For Chessboard. Ain't that some shit?"

Shillelagh pointed at her in excitement. "And Chessboard donated to Goodwin's campaign!"

Sally stood. "That's it. That's the connection. Jack was right. It's about the money." She paced back and forth, faster than necessary, ticking off the points on her fingers. "If Goodwin gets her Act passed into law, Chessboard becomes the go-to contractor to provide parahumans to the military. That's a huge government contract. Goodwin's husband gets rich from it, and she reaps the benefits of that. There's her campaign fund for her presidential bid, right there." She looked across the room at her team, seeing their faces fall as they realized the kind of stakes they were facing. "Parahumans are the next arms race, and she's already got her hand deep in that till."

Jason sat up. "We have to stop her."

Sally nodded. "We're going to."

Fourteen

"Parahumans are plain and simple the most dangerous threat to the American way of life. You're worried about gay marriage? Listen, friends, gay marriage is peanuts compared to these unregulated mass murderers roaming our streets and skies. If our new President fails to sign the Goodwin Act into law, I fear for your safety, listeners."
> —Ken Reichel, First Choice Radio Network

February 2009
New York City, NY

Sally's phone buzzed her awake at the ungodly hour of four o'clock. Her perceptions leaped into high gear and the phone was in her hands before her eyes could manage to focus. She knocked her head with one hand a couple of times, trying to shake herself awake. After what felt like an eternity, her eyes caught up with the rest of her and she could read the text message on her phone. It was from Davey. What the heck was she doing up at four in the morning?

Ur boots are finished & clean inside & out by ur door.

Sally blinked and read the message again. That wasn't right. Davey was brusque in her texts, but always took time to use full words and never abbreviations. And what was this about Sally's boots? She hadn't told Davey to do anything with them, and besides, that wasn't even Davey's responsibility. Just Cause had its own costumier that handled outfit cleaning, maintenance, and tailoring.

Then Sally snapped her fingers. Davey was sending her a message inside of a message. She would have known that the incongruities would have stood out to Sally like a beacon. She glanced over at Jason, still snoring with those cute, delicate snorts that belonged on someone much tinier. She was careful not to wake him when she slipped from the bed. The apartment was chilly, and the walls were cold to the touch. Sally grimaced. She expected that despite the refurbishments to the oil platform, it would still probably be a frozen chunk of metal all winter long. She already had socks on but pulled on her fuzzy slippers and wrapped her flannel bathrobe around her. She caught a glimpse of herself in the bathroom mirror and declared herself Queen Cowlick of Bedheadlandia.

Nobody was in the corridor outside her apartment. Headquarters was still on its nighttime lighting and would be for another hour or so. Despite the dim hall, Sally's freshly-polished boots sat gleaming outside her door like golden beacons. She retrieved them and went to sit down on the couch to examine them. Davey's message had said *clean inside*, so Sally stuck her hand into each boot, reaching all the way down to the toe. The second one had a folded piece of paper right at the toe. She glanced around the room. If Davey was sending a paper message, it was because she wanted to communicate outside of official channels, which meant off the record, which meant something was up and not in a good way.

There wasn't supposed to be any kind of surveillance inside the heroes' quarters, but Sally guessed that someone might have installed some anyway, *just in case.* She picked up the copy of *Truppenführung* that Juice had given her, slipped the folded note into the pages, and retreated into the bathroom. She turned on the shower full blast at its hottest without bothering to turn on the fan and waited. The bathroom filled with steam in a couple of minutes, fogging over the mirror and, she hoped, the lenses of any hidden cameras. She didn't realize just how much Davey's text had rattled her until she started to unfold the paper, hunching over it to hide it from any overhead view. She was being terribly paranoid, wasn't she? But then, she had a United States Senator on her enemies list, and she was pretty sure she'd rather face Destroyer any day than Christine Goodwin. And then, reading the note, she knew she'd been right to be paranoid.

Word came down overnight from Sapo that you and your team are to remain on base due to security concerns. Someone in the Command Center monitored the meeting in your office last night and sent details to Sapo. No idea who yet, but HQ is no longer secure. I have a few people I trust. Waiting in workout room to meet with you. Dress for aerobics.

Sally read the note twice to make sure she hadn't missed anything important, and then soaked it in the sink, shredded it, and flushed it. She went back to the bedroom long enough to put on something resembling a workout outfit and to brush her lips across Jason's forehead softly enough not to wake him. Then she went down to the workout room where she found Davey contorted into a yoga pose that looked incredibly painful and difficult, but the tall blonde had no problems unfolding herself when Sally entered the room.

"About time you got down here."

"Aerobics, huh?"

Davey raised a remote. "Yeah, I figure you'll want to start with some stretches first." She punched buttons and a throbbing techno beat emerged from the speakers around the room, loud enough to remind Sally of some of the concerts she had attended with Jason. The music should drown out any conversation between the two women, so long as they kept close enough not to have to yell over it.

"What's going on?"

"You've got to get your team off this base, and soon. Someone snitched on you to Sapo and the immediate instructions were to keep you on base. They think you're a threat to Senator Goodwin."

"We are a threat. But not to her personally. To her career and freedom to continue her jihad against us."

"Once Sapo reviews the transcript of our little pow-wow last night, he may decide to arrest us all on conspiracy charges." Davey shifted to a different position and Sally did her best to match it.

"Okay, how much time do we have? Hours?"

"If that. The sooner we clear out, the better."

A plan was already forming in Sally's mind, but it was going to require some perfect timing and a lot of luck. "Who can we trust in the Command Center?"

"Caitlin Leigh is there today. I'd trust her, but she's the only one I'm sure about. I've had to be careful about what I'm looking up. Our internet use and cell phone communications are monitored."

"All right. We're going to get out of here. All of us, in less than two hours. Here's what I need . . ."

* * *

"Good morning." Sally faced her team on the floor of the Combat Simulation Chamber. It was a reinforced vertical tube inside one of the legs that supported the upper decks of Fort Justice. It held a quantity of the nanobots developed for Just Cause training sessions. Given time and raw materials, they could build any kind of setting in which the team could train. Sally hadn't established a particular setting, so the walls and floor of the CSC were unadorned, and the only lighting came from the metal halide floodlights built into the ceiling behind heavy shielding. At her orders, the team had dressed out for their training in their full costumes. "Everyone eaten? Had coffee?"

Everyone nodded. They all looked sleepy. They'd awakened to Sally informing them of a seven A.M. mandatory training. Jason yawned. "I don't think bad guys get up this early."

"Oh, trust me. Sometimes they never sleep at all." Sally smiled at him and then glanced up at the CSC technicians in the booth, there to monitor and record the training. She let her eyes wander in the direction of the emergency exit, high up on the inside of the reinforced hull. It was a sea-level exit, accessible by ladder for anyone who couldn't fly. It made Sally a little nervous to know that she was a good hundred feet below the surface where she was standing, but she trusted the construction of the CSC to hold together. The engineers had lots of experience designing facilities to resist the various energies and impacts generated by parahuman training, and she tried not to think about the fact that it had probably been built by the lowest bidder.

"What's the plan for today, Boss?" Shillelagh shook out her red wig and pulled it on over her hair.

"Standard two-on-two drills. Minimal power levels only, Snowball."

"Yeah, yeah." The tiny woman rolled her eyes.

"Ment, sit out for a moment and check my architecture." Sally tried to sound as casual as she could. She didn't want to come right out and say *read my mind*, because that would be a dead giveaway to anyone monitoring them. But years ago, a psi named Glimmer had built some psionic constructs in Sally's mind to assist with information storage and retention when she was performing reconnaissance. Later on, Ment had helped to refine and improve that architecture. Sally hoped he would get the message.

Sure enough, his voice popped up in her mind. *What's up?*

Trouble. Sally recapped what she knew already. Conversing via telepathy was odd because as much as she tried to use words and sentences, much of the communication came in the sense of images, concepts, and feelings. *Can you bring the others into the loop?*

Not without some of them giving it away.

Minerva, then.

That was easy; Ment and Minerva had been together nearly as long as Jason and Sally had, and the two of them knew each other's minds as well as their own.

I'm here, said Minerva in Sally's mind. She communed with Ment and Sally for a moment, gathering their knowledge about the risk to the team. *What do you need us to do?*

Sally told them, and then returned her attention to the rest of the team. "Okay, let's get to work. By the numbers, everyone. Make it look good."

Two-on-two drills were intended to focus on working with a partner to take out multiple opponents. The drills usually went in a round-robin format, with pairs of heroes fighting against other pairs until the CSC monitor determined a victor based upon a variety of designated results. Sally enjoyed them a lot more than some other training scenarios because she got to partner up with a variety of teammates and work out various methods to take down power archetypes. She and the others watched as Snowball and Yunbao took on Shillelagh and Snapdragon, with mixed results. Shillelagh's preternatural balance and grace kept Snowball from getting enough ice around her to encase her, whereas Yunbao was a better hand-to-hand fighter than the Bostonian and managed to get her into a joint lock that the CSC monitors declared a victory. Snapdragon's flaming wings illuminated the entire hollow column of the CSC, and heat washed across Sally's face as he fired his lowest-power flame stream at Snowball. She countered with a jet of frost particles that flashed into steam, and used the ensuing vapor cloud to slide beneath Snapdragon and douse his wings with snowballs.

Failsafe and Detroit Steel held their own against Sally and Jason. Sally couldn't break through Failsafe's force field to get to him, and when he snapped it around her instead, she was stuck. Detroit Steel and Jason traded blow after blow, pounding upon one another hard enough to shake the walls. Jason looked like he was enjoying himself more than he had in months—it had been awhile since he had anyone he could really cut loose upon, and Detroit Steel was a competent fighter to boot. At last she caught him with a pair of uppercuts that staggered him to his knees.

Sally watched the others until she was satisfied with their work. "Good. Do it again. Same partners."

That phrase was what Ment and Minerva had been waiting to hear. Nothing overt happened but Ment grinned and turned to Sally. "They're out." Boosted by Minerva's powers, he'd telepathically induced sleep in the CSC personnel in the monitor booth. While training began again, Sally ran up to the booth, pulled up the recording of the previous fifteen minutes of training, and set it up to replay. It wouldn't be perfect, but might be enough to give them a head start. Anyone up in the Command Center would see the heroes training, and unless they'd been watching from the very beginning, might not realize they were seeing a loop.

A few seconds later, Sally returned to the training floor. "Everyone stop. We're all in big trouble, and we need to get out of here. You all have five minutes to get into civilian clothes. Pack your costumes. If you have any cash, bring it. Leave your phones, badges, and credit cards behind. Go!"

To her team's credit, they all moved with professional purpose. Sally ran to the locker room and was back on the training floor in less than thirty seconds in her civvies. The others hurried and rejoined her in minutes. "How much cash do we have as a group?"

Everyone put what they had forward. It wasn't much; superheroes didn't have much need to carry cash with them, especially in headquarters where their needs were all provided. They had between them only fifty-eight dollars until Failsafe shuffled forward and put a hundred and twenty-two dollars into the pile. "Never got the hang of credit cards."

"Good for you, and good for us." Sally paired everyone up and gave every team twenty-five dollars. Jason and Detroit Steel. Shillelagh and Snowball. Ment and Snapdragon. Failsafe and Minerva. Yunbao with Sally. "Okay, up the ladder to the exit."

Failsafe looked at Snowball. "We got this." He formed his energy shield into a rimmed bowl shape and had everyone step onto it. It was oddly slippery, like standing on a greasy waterbed. Snowball reached over the side and began building up an ice column beneath it. The bowl rose along the side of the CSC walls like a chilly elevator.

Jason squeezed Sally's hand in his giant paw. "You want to tell us what's going on, babe?"

"Not just yet. Once we're clear from here." In the event that something happened and they didn't get away cleanly, it would be easier for the others since they had no prior knowledge. "Open that hatch, would you, sweetie?"

Jason grinned and wrenched the wheel holding the hatch fast, forcing it to spin past encrusted sea salt and rust. A freezing wind blew into the CSC as soon as he swung open the hatch. They emerged onto a railed grate that ringed the outside of the support hull. The bottom of Fort Justice loomed a hundred feet over them like some titanic alien mothership hovering over the choppy seas. Sally heard the sound of an engine and a boat swung around the swell of the hull, bobbing like a cork. Behind the glass, Davey gritted her teeth as she fought the water. "All aboard," she yelled over the noise of the wind and waves and engine. "Hurry up. I don't know how long Leigh can keep us hidden from the Command Center."

The heroes made their way onto the boat. Shillelagh and Yunbao leaped across the intervening distance between the dock and the pitching boat, one trusting in her grace and balance and the other to her canine muscles and claws to keep hold. Minerva touched Ment, allowing him to fly like she did, and the two of them crossed to the deck. Jason used his powerful muscles to spring ahead like he'd been launched from a catapult. He almost jumped too far and it was only through the combined efforts of the others that he didn't pitch forward into the icy water. Detroit Steel let Jason catch her to keep from harming the boat with her metallic feet. Snapdragon lifted Sally easily and flew her across, and Failsafe grabbed hold of Snowball and rode behind her on her ice stream.

As soon as the last of them was aboard, Davey spun the wheel and pushed the throttle forward. "Christ, you guys weigh a lot. If you can fly, do it so we don't capsize."

Half of the heroes let themselves hover over the deck instead of resting upon it. "Where'd you get the boat?" Sally looked in dismay at the small fishing vessel.

"It's my dad's, so don't break anything. He couldn't believe I wanted to take it out in weather like this. If I'd been anyone else, he'd have told me to fuck off." She grunted as the boat hit a particularly large swell and water slopped onto the aft deck. "But he trusts me."

"I hope he still does afterward," said Sally.

Snowball had one of her hands locked around the rail to keep from being pitched into the choppy sea. "What's going on, Boss?"

Sally raised her voice so everyone could hear her. "Someone in the Command Center ratted us out to Director Sapo. I don't know who, and it doesn't matter right now. The important thing is he issued a directive to Headquarters that we were to be kept on base while they followed up on threats made to a certain Senator."

"We were going to be under house arrest?" Failsafe used his force field to try to stabilize the boat.

"Ostensibly, but I think the Director wanted to keep it on the down-low. I imagine that if he followed up with Senator Goodwin, she'd tell him she was in real danger from us, and he might have sent in troops to actually detain us."

"So we're on the lam now? Jack'll be sorry as shit that he's missing out on this." Snowball looked green from the rocking boat.

Detroit Steel braced herself against the sides of the boat, doing her best to keep her weight central. "What are we supposed to do? We ain't gonna get very far on twenty-five bucks."

Sally could see Detroit Steel was terrified at being out on the water in the way she held her breath every time the boat topped a swell. "It's New York City. Anyone can disappear here for a day. I'm going to give you all an address to meet at, but otherwise I don't want you anywhere near each other except in pairs. Remember, two of you working together will be five times as safe as each of you on your own."

Detroit Steel's laugh was brief and cynical. "Not to be a bother or nothin', but I kind of stand out. And so does the Leopard over here."

"I've got that handled. Planned ahead. You can handle being painted, can't you, Shawna?" Davey held up a can of spray paint from a shopping bag on the back of the driver's seat.

Detroit Steel shrugged. "Done it before."

"As for you, Yunbao, I got you this." Davey reached into her bag again and withdrew a knit balaclava that had a face printed upon it.

Sally thought it might have been Justin Bieber, but she immediately understood the benefit. "Put that on, pull up your hood, and anyone just glancing casually at you will only see a face. They won't see your fur unless they look really close. Smart, Davey."

"That's why you pay me. Which reminds me, I'll probably need to use you for a job reference after today."

"Anything. You're a lifesaver."

"Don't thank me until I get us to a pier."

Sally turned to Ment. "I need you to put an address into everyone's mind so they won't forget it. Can you do that?"

"Yeah." He winced as salt water sprayed across his face. "Give it to me."

Sally gave him the address of the Title Boxing Club. She figured it was a good neutral location that the Feds wouldn't be likely to discover. She'd make a point of arriving early enough to prepare Hector to have a bunch of undercover superheroes descend upon his place. "I'm having Ment give each of you an address. I want you to meet me there tonight at eleven o'clock. Don't be late. If you don't show, I'm going to assume you got pinched, and I'll do what I can to get you out, but it might be awhile." Sally hardened her voice. "And depending on what happens in the next couple of days, it might be a really long while. So don't get caught. Keep with your partners. Be careful."

"But what are we going to do?" asked Shillelagh.

Sally gave her a humorless smile in return. "Counterattack."

Fifteen

"I don't need parahuman powers to know what's right and what's wrong, and I don't need a parahuman to enforce it for me."
                                        —Senator Christine Goodwin (R-NY)

February, 2009
New York City, NY

The bitter cold seeped through Sally's layers like they were nothing as she and Yunbao walked the streets of New York City, hunched over against the wind and prying eyes of civilians. At least with her trademark braids gone, Sally thought she might be less recognizable. People expected to see her in crimson and gold, not a cranberry overcoat and knit cap.

Yunbao didn't complain about the weather, or Sally's apparent lack of plan, instead following her across the avenues, a loyal soldier. New Yorkers being what they were, nobody bothered to look into Yunbao's face for more than a moment, and no questions about her odd face were blurted out at them. After a solid hour of seemingly aimless wandering, even Yunbao seemed like she was ready to start complaining. "It is very cold. I do not believe I have ever seen cold like this before."

"It doesn't get cold in China?"

"Yes, of course it does. It is just . . . I wish there were a warm fire and hot tea to drink beside it."

Sally spotted a familiar logo among all the storefronts. "How about coffee? My treat. I've got twenty-five bucks burning a hole in my pocket."

Yunbao made a grumbling growl behind the misshapen face of her balaclava. "Coffee is unpleasant, but perhaps they will have tea."

"I'm more hopeful they'll have a phone we can use. I need to call Hector and let him know we're coming in tonight. Also, I'm starving, and a scone sounds just about perfect."

"What is a scone?"

Sally thought about it. "Like a biscuit, but less disappointing. Come on, let's go eat and caffeinate and figure out our next move."

Once inside the coffee house, Sally had Yunbao sit at a table with her back to the rest of the cafe so her face wouldn't be so visible. Sally ordered coffee for herself, two scones, and some hot water and teabags for Yunbao. Yunbao looked at the small paper envelopes and shook her head sadly.

"Sorry, it's what they have." Sally had to raise her voice to be heard over the constant whine and hiss of the espresso machine. She sipped her coffee. It was too bitter and over-roasted, but the scone was fluffy and had a delicious orange crème frosting that reminded her of Phoenix in the spring.

Yunbao sniffed at her own scone. "This is . . . unusual. I thought it would be sweeter. It is good, though. I would have one again."

"What's your favorite food? I mean, at home?"

"*Gongbao ji ding*. You would call it kung pao chicken. Extra spicy."

"I love that. We'll have to go get some after we solve this mystery."

"What is our next move?"

"Need to find a pay phone and get hold of Hector. Then find a place to lay low for several hours. I'm thinking the public library. We could probably get onto one of their computers and spend some time doing more research."

Yunbao finished her scone and licked her fingers free of crumbs with a raspy feline tongue that Sally found fascinating.

"Can I ask you a personal question, Yunbao?"

"Yes."

"What was it like growing up in China, being so obviously different?"

Yunbao looked down at her furred hands with the short, razor-sharp claws at the fingertips. "Being different is not what made my childhood difficult. China has many parahumans, especially in Hong Kong. People who did not know me personally found my likeness appealing. Several times, I was asked to appear in movies, but it would have gone against my mother's wishes and so I refused. People who knew of my father thought less of me."

"How old were you when he died? I'm sorry if it brings up painful memories. I never had the chance to meet him. He died the same day as my father, at Destroyer's hands." Sally clenched her teeth. She'd had multiple opportunities to avenge her father's death and had never once taken that final step.

"I was four. I remember how he used to train with me. He taught me my first stances. My first kicks. And when he grew tired of forms and repetition, he would chase me all around the school, up the walls, across the ceiling beams. When he caught me, he would tickle me." Yunbao bowed her head, her hood falling forward to completely obscure her face. "I loved him very much."

Sally reached out and took Yunbao's hands. "I'm so sorry. I envy you the time you got with him, though."

"It was difficult, being the child of a *bak gwei*. A white American. Hong Kong has always looked at them with distrust. I was guilty by blood."

"Guilty of what?"

"Whatever the neighbors accused me of." Yunbao shrugged. "They did not like me. Or my mother. Or the school. It is well my father taught me the rudiments of fighting before his death. I had to use them many times growing up."

"I'm sorry about that."

"Why do you apologize for that which is not your fault?" Yunbao raised her balaclava up to uncover her face. Her fur was matted and damp.

Sally felt bad. She hadn't realized how uncomfortable wearing that hat must have been for her teammate. "I don't know. I just don't like knowing that someone was mistreated, even when I had nothing to do with it. I say I'm sorry because I'm sorry you had to go through it. I wish you hadn't."

"It made me a stronger person. What does not kill you makes you stronger."

"I should be stronger than Jason, then, based upon the sheer number of times someone's tried to kill me." Sally smiled into her coffee. Somehow all those threats of bodily harm she'd faced seemed far away when she was stuck with a foe she couldn't easily fight. At least when one was battling against Destroyer, or an army of brainwashed Guatemalan soldiers, one knew where one stood. Fighting in the political arena felt more like trying to cross a swimming pool filled with rubber cement.

"You are stronger than he. I can see that when I look at you. Director Juice made a good choice when he promoted you to lead us."

Sally sighed. "People keep telling me that. And here we are, drinking bad coffee and bad tea in a hipster's paradise." She looked out across the sea of ironic beards and black-framed glasses and her eye fell upon a headline of an article someone was reading on his laptop. *Shots Fired at Champions Training Facility; No Injuries Reported.*

"What is it, Sally?" Yunbao stared at her with her slanted cat's eyes.

"Things are getting worse out there for us. For . . . what did people call Lionheart?"

"*Bak gwei.*"

"Yeah. It's like parahumans are *bak gwei.* And everyone hates us. If only we could . . ." An insane notion had popped into Sally's head and before she realized it, she had stood up from the table.

Yunbao stood as well, pulling her balaclava back down. "We could what?"

"I just had a really *wild* idea. And if I can use a cliché, it's so crazy it just might work."

* * *

Sally and Yunbao hid themselves as far away as they could from the rest of the patrons in the branch of the New York Public Library while they could still get access to one of the free computers available. Sally found a website that would allow her to create an anonymous email account without having verify it with other information. "It's for spammers, hackers, and anybody who doesn't want to be tracked."

"Like us." Yunbao removed her balaclava again and sat with her back to the rest of the floor just to be safe.

"Yeah. I've got a friend who is totally into this stuff. I'm hoping she can help us. I don't know how long we're going to have to be off the grid, but if it's more than a day or two, we're going to need access to funds and communications."

"Are we going to rob a bank? Like in the movies?"

"What? No, silly! We're the good guys, even though we're temporarily not exactly at our best." Sally paused, considering. "Although, to be honest, I've always kind of wanted to be in a heist. You know, like in *Ocean's Eleven*. Nothing where anybody gets hurt. They just seem like so much . . . fun. Ah, here we go."

Sally's new email account was live, with a user name of *Bakgwei1985*. She thought that would be hard for anyone to link back to her for the time she planned to use it. There were many people she could have sent a message to: Juice; Doublecharge; her mother. In the end, though, there was only one logical person for her to reach out to, and that was a woman named Vanitha Bhat, who had a unique parahuman ability she'd used to help Sally solve a murder and prevent a related worldwide catastrophe.

It had been a good month for Just Cause back then.

She emailed Vanitha at an address she'd committed to memory a long time ago, threw in enough private information that nobody else could possibly have known short of an extensive telepathic mind probe, and awaited a response.

A new chat window opened right away with a hideous icon resembling the goddess Kali tucked up in the corner. Vanitha must have already been online. Of course she was, Sally thought. When was she not?

What's up, Sally?

I'm in trouble and need your help, Vanitha.

I wondered if I might hear from you. The feds are looking for you and your team. You've gone from heroes to fugitives in less than a month. I think that's got to be some kind of record.

Ha ha. Sally grimaced. *We're still the good guys, I promise. Need your help stopping the bad guys, though.*

What do you need?

Sally had already given it a lot of thought, and knew that ultimately she only needed one thing to make the rest of it all fall into place. *I need an untraceable account linked to a debit card and funds in it.*

How much money are we talking here?

That was a harder question. How much money would ten heroes need to stay underground? It all depended on how long they were stuck. Sally was determined it wouldn't be very long, but she was also determined to have enough money for the group to fulfill its needs, which might be varied and rapidly-changing over the next few days. *Ten thousand dollars*, Sally typed, not quite believing she'd been so bold.

Not a problem. I can provide you whatever funds you require, within reason, at a dollar-for-dollar fee.

"Geez, we should have gone to a loan shark instead. At least they charge less than a hundred percent interest."

"What is a loan shark?" Yunbao asked.

"Nothing. It's a stupid idea. Vanitha is much more trustworthy, and won't send anyone around to break our legs."

"I thought she was your friend. Why is she charging you so much?"

"This is her business. If she doesn't have a vested personal interest in something, she's got to eat. Oh, man. There's a Thai place just up the road from her flat. I'm hungry again. I could run to Boston right now for it." Sally turned back to the keyboard. *I can accept those terms. It will take me some work to handle it through the JCNY budget. I don't have access right now.*

Of course. I trust you. The account is set up now as an online-only source. The funds are not tied to any bank.

How do I access it?

Go get a library card. ;-)

Mystified, Sally trotted down to the main floor, filled out the application on the touchscreen terminal, and waited. For a brief moment, Vanitha's Kali avatar filled the screen in all her terrifying glory: blue skin, multiple arms clutching bloody severed heads, lolling tongue. Then the screen returned to normal, telling her that her card was ready at the circulation desk. She went over to the desk. The librarian on duty, a slender young man with an aquiline nose and gauges in his ears looked up from his terminal. "Can I help you?"

"Yeah, the screen said for me to come over here to pick up my card."

"Name?"

"Judy Gordon." Sally had used her grandmother's maiden name. She hoped it wasn't something that would give her away, but then she needed it to be something she would remember in case the question ever came up.

The man selected a card from the desk, swiped it through a reader and then handed it to Sally. "There you go, Ms. Gordon. Thanks for patronizing the New York Library." He said the last automatically, dragging it out into a single long syllable.

"Thanks." Sally rejoined Yunbao at the terminal.

"Success?"

"I think so." Sally typed into the terminal. *This is a debit card? How does that work?*

I hacked into the card reader system and crosslinked code from some banking software that I had lying around.

"I'll just bet you had it lying around." Sally knew a lot of Vanitha's paying work tended toward the legally murky areas.

When your card was swiped, the reader deposited a debit card code upon it. Boom. Instant money card, no banks involved. Nothing to tie it back to you.

You're a lifesaver, Vanitha.

I know.

Just one more thing and then I'll leave you alone.

Until the next time you need something.

Sally sighed. Sometimes Vanitha's mercenary tendencies were a little overbearing. *Yes, until then.*

What do you need? I can always add it to your tab.

Senator Christine Goodwin, typed Sally. *Where might she be this evening?*

* * *

"This is a bad idea." Yunbao and Sally were hunched down under some snowy bushes, peeking out beneath the black brambles at the mansion that was the ancestral home of the Goodwin family.

"Youshould say *I have a bad feeling about this.*"

"I do have a bad feeling about this. So should you. This is madness. Suicide."

"I'm not planning to die tonight. So can we try to have a little more optimism here?"

She and Yunbao had spent the afternoon putting their debit card to good use. They had a bag full of pre-paid cell phones that they would distribute to the other Just Cause New York fugitives when they rejoined them later in the evening. Out in the Hamptons, where Senator Goodwin lived, it had been snowing steadily but lightly all day, and there were two or three inches of fluffy snow covering everything, making it very difficult to hide in the darkness. Instead of a sensible black sky with sufficient local light pollution to block out the stars, the low-hanging clouds reflected the orange and white city lights back downward, making the sky look like the smoke hanging over a nighttime forest fire in the Colorado mountains.

"I do not understand what you intend to accomplish by confronting the Senator. She is unlikely to change her mind."

"I have to try, Yunbao. If there's any way I can defuse this before Just Cause has to fight against law enforcement, or soldiers . . . Nobody wants that."

"Perhaps you have not seen the security that I have."

Sally sighed. "Yes, I've seen it." U.S. Senators didn't generally have security protection unless there had been a specific threat. Apparently, having Just Cause New York on the loose qualified as a specific threat.

Sally had seen two United States Capitol Police cars parked outside the entrance to the Goodwin mansion's grounds, and counted at least four plainclothes security guards outside the large house itself. None of them were carrying overt weapons, but Sally didn't doubt for a moment they were all well-armed and had significant backup ready.

"And you are still committed to getting inside?"

"Yes. The good news is I don't see any of The Militia out there. I wish I knew where they were, though." Sally shivered as the cold seeped in through her coat. She'd spent so much time lurking in the bushes that she was half afraid she'd ruined her favorite winter coat, but it would be a small price to pay if it meant she could resolve the situation with her team without getting into any combat. "I can get past the guards."

"What about me? What can I do?"

"Just keep your eyes open. If you see the cops get jumpy, leave without me and get to Title Boxing Club to meet the others."

Yunbao looked offended. As darkness had fallen, she'd dispensed with her balaclava altogether. Snowflakes caught on her facial fur, making her look like she'd been frosted like a cake. "I will not leave you behind."

"That's an order, Yunbao."

Yunbao smiled, showing a mouthful of sharp teeth. "I do not believe the chain of command applies when we are fugitives. I will look out for you, and if you are in trouble, I will come get you."

"I can outrun anyone. I'll be fine."

"And I will make sure of it. I can outfight anyone."

"If you say so."

"I do. Be careful."

"You too." Sally clasped Yunbao's hand in hers. The Chinese woman's fingertips were naked of fur, like a cat's, with claws nestled in the tips. Beneath the soft fur was warm flesh and blood, and it was an odd discrepancy where Sally felt like she was stroking a pet, and yet the woman before her was as much a human beneath her fur as Sally was. "Watch my coat. It'll only slow me down."

She stripped off her cranberry overcoat, leaving herself lithe and unencumbered in the all-black stealth version of her costume. She pulled on her gloves and then raised her cowl up over her head. It wouldn't help against the cold, but would break up the shape of her face and make it easier for her to blend into shadows.

"The gate is shut."

"I'm not going through the gate." Sally rolled out from beneath the bush, let her perceptions accelerate until the world slowed down to a crawl, and ran down the slope toward the mansion.

Sixteen

"A paroled bank robber, a foreign national from a country hostile to America, a promoter of the homosexual agenda, the son of a supervillain, all led by someone who's skating by on the reputation of her ancestors. Is this who you want protecting you, friends? Or do you want real, true patriots, who will faithfully defend the Constitution from threats both foreign and domestic?"
—Ken Reichel, First Choice Radio Network

February, 2009
New York City, NY

Sally had spent many hours of her training time working on jumping. Her super-speed allowed her to cover long distances without touching the ground. She avoided it when she could, because even under the best of circumstances, she felt safer with her feet on the ground, where she could change directions instantly or stop on a dime if needed. When she was flying through the air in a long jump, anything could go wrong. At times, though, it was the perfect maneuver, and she was counting on it to get her over the fence and onto mansion grounds successfully without being spotted.

She lengthened her strides, picking up her pace until she was moving well over two hundred miles per hour. She'd spotted a car parked across the street, perhaps belonging to a neighbor of Goodwin's, that was parked at exactly the angle she required. Still moving at high speed, she planted one foot on the car's front bumper, scampered up the hood, mindful of the possibility of ice below the dusting of snow, and used the windshield to launch herself high into the darkness. The wrought-iron fence, with its spear-point top edge, was on her almost before she was ready, and she hadn't jumped high enough to clear it, but she hadn't expected to, either. As it rushed in upon her, she twisted her body in midair and grabbed hold of two of the bars. She pulled herself up and over, letting her momentum do most of the work. The world spun around her for a moment as she flipped head over heels before coming down in a crouch amid a grove of barren trees on one side of the estate. She couldn't help grinning; she was sure nobody had seen her fly over the fence like a wingless bird of prey, but she kind of wished someone had, because it had probably looked very cool. She knew she'd kicked up a blast of snow when she landed and pressed herself against a tree trunk, waiting to see if any of the security came in her direction to investigate.

After a couple of minutes of inactivity from the guards, Sally felt confident her landing hadn't been seen, and she proceeded toward the house. Leaving footprints in the fresh snow couldn't be helped, and she didn't have a good alternative. If she accelerated to a run and jumped across the open space, she was just as likely to be seen when she landed amid her cloud of snow anyway. At least with feet on the ground, she had options. And if she moved fast enough, she thought, her slipstream might disturb the snow enough to obliterate any footprints she'd left behind. She zipped from tree to tree like a human pinball, covering the distances between them in fractions of seconds and pausing between each jaunt to make sure nobody had seen her. Most of the guards seemed more interested in their phones than in their jobs. After all, it was snowing, they were out in the Hamptons where undesirables tended to get deflected by local law enforcement before ever making it into the neighborhoods to bother the aristocracy, and they were behind a secure fence. It never occurred to any of them to look up, and that was why Sally pulled herself up into a tree beside the large Goodwin house, ran lightly along a branch thick enough to support her weight, and sprang across several feet of open space to land on a third-floor balcony.

Light streamed out from the glass doors. Sally ducked behind the patio table on the broad balcony, for she'd seen Christine Goodwin in the room beyond, seated at a desk and working on a computer. Dressed for comfort instead of public life, the Senator was wearing thick flannel pajamas and a robe that made Sally envious at how warm it must have been. She'd pulled her red hair back into a sloppy ponytail and had on large glasses. Her arm was still caught up in a sling but she was managing to type one-handed with impressive effectiveness. Sally had risked her life and freedom to come and see this woman. What would the Senator do if Sally said the wrong things? Could she do to Just Cause Denver and Richmond what she'd already done to New York? Would she dismantle the entire organization? Sally suspected she would.

The door wasn't locked, which Sally took as a positive sign. If it had been and she'd been forced to knock, it would have completely changed the conversation from the outset. Indeed, the Senator could have refused to open the door at all and instead called security. Instead, Sally slipped through the door and shut it behind her just as the Senator looked up from her work, shock registering across her porcelain face.

Sally kept her hands in plain sight. "Senator, it's me. Mustang Sally. I came to talk."

Christine Goodwin produced a pistol from the recesses of her desk and leveled it at Sally. "You have one minute before I pull this trigger or call for help."

Sally was taken aback by the presence of the pistol. If she accelerated her perceptions to maximum, she could avoid being shot by dodging as soon as she saw the muzzle flash. It would be risky at such short range, but she'd practiced dodging bullets before. She was going to have to play things carefully. "Senator, I'm not here to hurt you. If that had been my intent, you'd never have seen me coming."

"You'd have had someone take another shot at me from a distance, I suppose," said Goodwin. "Fifty seconds. You're wasting your time."

"Jack didn't shoot you. Nobody in Just Cause did. And we are not your enemy. We're the good guys, and we're trying to help."

Goodwin didn't look the least bit moved by Sally's entreaty. "Forty seconds."

"I came here to ask you to stop your crusade against us. You're hampering our ability to do our jobs. There are people out there—innocent civilians—who need help, and we're the ones best-suited to do that."

"But you're not the only ones who can. That was proved when you got your asses kicked in that high-rise and The Militia had to bail you out." Goodwin smiled. "Let's call it twenty seconds left. I'm a very good shot, by the way. I grew up hunting with my father upstate."

Sally realized Goodwin wasn't going to be impressed by pleas. She respected power. "You know how fast I am, Senator? I broke the speed of sound earlier this year. Only one other human has ever gone that fast without needing a vehicle. I can disassemble that pistol before you can pull the trigger, and I can be out of this house before your security guards take five steps in this direction. Now are we going to keep having this pissing match or can we talk like civilized people for a few minutes?"

Goodwin kept the pistol leveled at Sally. Sally met her gaze. The seconds ticked by. Then Goodwin laughed, sudden, like a gunshot. She tucked the pistol back into its spot beneath her desk and rested her hand atop the blotter. "You showed a lot of nerve, coming in here the way you did. It was brave. Foolish, but brave. I can respect that, Tibbets."

"Why do you hate us?" Sally lowered her hands but stayed where she was, not wanting to approach Goodwin and risk further antagonizing the Senator. "All we ever wanted to do was to help people."

"It's nothing personal. I dislike all parahumans."

"Nothing personal?" Sally snorted. "Senator, don't lie to me."

Goodwin smiled. "Perhaps it's a little personal. Honestly, I should probably thank your friend Forsythe. If it hadn't been for his interference, I might have made a rash decision that would have cost me the future I've planned."

"So you had him thrown in prison."

"I'm not the one who blew up in a committee hearing. He's not good at playing the game in Washington. He's too simple, too noble. Boy Scouts aren't successful in politics. You have to be willing to slog through lakes of shit and when someone hands you a spoon, you better start eating, because it's all you're getting." Goodwin pushed her chair back from the desk. "Something to drink? I have an outstanding '90 Pinot noir that'll change your life."

"No thank you."

"Your loss." Goodwin took a bottle from the bar in her office and splashed some dark wine into a glass and swirled it around, sniffing the bouquet with unrestrained admiration. "You could stand to pick up some skills beyond the basic superhero set, Tibbets. I don't have high hopes that you'll have much of a career left in your chosen field."

"You're talking about the Goodwin Act. It'll never pass." Sally put her hands on her hips.

"Perhaps it will, perhaps it won't. But that's not the point. The point is it's now front and center in the media. Every news channel is full of pundits more than willing to talk parahuman rights to death. The more they talk about it, the more it becomes part of the American cultural *zeitgeist*. That will make it a campaign issue in 2010, 2012, 2016. The right candidates will be able to use that as a foundation for their platforms."

"So you don't care if it passes?"

Goodwin sipped at her wine and smiled. "An outstanding vintage. You really don't know what you're missing. Of course I care if it passes. I put my name on it. I can't exactly support mandatory sterilization of all parahumans, even if it's in my perfect America. You people with your polluted genes and your powers think you're the next stage of human evolution. You think you're better than the rest of us. You're just tools, nothing more. By shutting down your precious little superhero team and putting you under the control of the Joint Chiefs, I'm putting tools in the hands of the right tool users."

"You can't do that, Senator Goodwin. You can't militarize American parahumans. It's been against the law since World War II. You're going to touch off a new arms race."

Goodwin brought her wine glass back to her desk. "No, I'm going to bring us back to the forefront. You don't think other countries are militarizing their parahuman population? Talk to your ridiculous Chinese cat-girl. Ask her what's going on in her homeland. You don't think radical Islam is training parahuman terrorists right now to strike against us? You don't think North Korea is recruiting them and decimating their population as they try to artificially create new parahumans? The playing field doesn't just need to be leveled. It needs to be tilted in America's favor. This is how we do it."

"By stripping basic human rights away from parahumans and turning them into super-soldiers to fight wars for you. That'll never fly." Sally crossed her arms. She was itching to grab hold of Goodwin to shake some sense into her, but if she started shaking the Senator, she suspected that she wouldn't stop until the woman's head snapped off.

"*Parahuman* means *resembling human*. You know what it doesn't mean?" Goodwin finished her wine. "*Human*. You're tools, nothing more. And I won't stop until you and those like you are secured where you belong. Firmly in my hands." She set her wine glass down atop her desk. "You could come out in support of my legislation. You're well-respected among your people. It would tilt things in my favor. I could ensure you a position of command in the new arrangement."

"Better to rule in Hell than to serve in Heaven?" Sally said through clenched teeth.

"If you like. The offer is open."

"I'd sooner throw myself off a building."

Goodwin pushed her glasses up her nose. "The balcony is right behind you. It might be high enough to kill you, if you landed badly. You're welcome to leave by the front door, though."

Sally pointed at her. "I'm going to stop you."

"You're just a twig in the river, Tibbets. You can't stop anything. The current is going to sweep you away."

Sally went to the office door and paused by it, looking over her shoulder at the Senator. "I said I wasn't your enemy, Senator, but that doesn't mean I won't become it."

Goodwin chuckled. "You don't have the balls."

"Keep on underestimating me, Goodwin. See how well that's gone for every other opponent I've faced over the years."

Whatever snide remark Goodwin might have said fell upon an empty room, for Sally launched herself into speed and left by the front door, leaving pictures swaying and papers swirling in her wake as she sped off into the night.

* * *

Sally and Yunbao stood in the blowing snow, looking at the nearby warmth of the Title Boxing Club with longing. The outside lights were off, and the OPEN sign was dark, but the club's interior was still lit, and Sally could see people moving around inside it, obscured by condensation on the windows. Her team was there.

Sally handed two bags to Yunbao. One held all the burner cell phones they'd purchased, and the other was crammed full of fast food burgers and fries. "Hope nobody's a vegetarian," Sally had said when they purchased them.

"Is this even food?" Yunbao sniffed at the bag.

"It resembles it. Go on in. Pass out the phones and the food. I'll be in momentarily. I need to make a phone call first."

"I see. Be careful."

"I will." Sally watched as the woman crossed the street with her lithe, feline grace and entered the boxing club. She shivered as the wind picked up, blowing tiny ice crystals into her face. She turned away from it and punched out a text to a number she'd memorized. It was well past working hours in New York, but the recipient of her text was two time zones to the west.

It's Sally. I need Director Sapo's home number.

She waited. After a few minutes, a reply text came from Doublecharge with a phone number and an admonition for Sally to be careful. Sally sent a smiley face in reply and typed in Sapo's number.

The phone rang three times and just as Sally was about to hang up, thinking she was getting forwarded to voice mail, a female voice picked up. "Hello?"

"This is Mustang Sally. I need to speak to Director Sapo. It's urgent." Sally drummed her fingers in a rapid tattoo on her sleeve as she heard the sound of a phone being passed to someone else.

A deep voice came on the line. "Michael Sapo. Mustang Sally?"

"Yes, Director, it's me. I need to speak to you."

"Where are you? Tell me and we'll bring you in."

"I haven't done anything wrong, Director. I haven't broken any laws."

"You're absent without leave. I've issued orders that you and your team are to be arrested on sight."

"Director, we're still the same heroes. We're still working for the greater good. That hasn't changed, and won't change, whether we do it with the endorsement of the PRA or covertly." Sally heard frantic sounds and whispering in the background. She was fairly certain that Sapo was trying to set up a phone trace with his wife or mistress or whoever had answered the phone as the go-between with the PRA. Let them trace it. They might figure out the neighborhood based upon the location of the cell towers, but Sally had disabled the GPS locators on the burner phones as soon as she'd purchased them, and trying to find a dozen people in New York City was going to require more manpower than Sapo could bring to bear in hours, let alone the few minutes Sally would be on the phone with him.

"Sally, please. Just tell me where you are."

"Can you guarantee my safety? Can you guarantee the safety of my team?"

"What do you mean, guarantee your safety? Who's after you besides us?"

"You're a longtime associate of Senator Goodwin, Director. I'm sure you've been given orders that you are not to repeat to anyone else about our disposition."

"Listen, Sally, in spite of what you might think, we're on your side. We don't want to hurt you. We just need to clear a few things up."

"Yes, that's why I called. I need clarification on our duties." Sally pressed her lips close to the microphone.

"How do you mean? You're relieved of your duties."

"So you've appointed an emergency team of Champions to replace us?"

"No, I—"

Sally smiled into the darkness. "Director, you can't relieve us without appointing our replacements. I've read the charter governing Just Cause. If you relieve us without replacing us, you're violating your own duties. So if you haven't been appointing our replacements, we're still on duty."

"I'll appoint Champions in the morning."

"That's fine, Director, but until then, I need clarification on our duties as heroes. Are we supposed to sit around waiting for trouble to start and then respond? Or are we supposed to actively prevent it?"

"I . . . I don't understand."

"Director, I know you're not an idiot. Are we a deterrent or a response force? Do we wait for the planes to hit the buildings and then respond, or do we stop them if we can?"

"Stop them, of course!"

"Thank you, Director."

"But—"

Sally disconnected the call. Give a man enough rope and eventually he'll hang himself, she thought. She checked to make sure the call had recorded properly with the app she'd used. In New York, it was legal for one party to record a phone conversation, and Sally had made full use of that knowledge. She saved the sound file and sent it to the anonymous email address she'd created earlier in the day. That was one more piece of evidence she could use to exonerate the members of her team when the time came.

She only hoped that time would come, because she didn't know how long any of them could cope with being federal fugitives.

Seventeen

"As of this morning, the FBI has issued arrest warrants for the former members of Just Cause New York, and Director Sapo of the PRA has appointed an interim team to provide coverage in the event of parahuman issues. I urge all New Yorkers to be vigilant and report to your local law enforcement if you encounter any former Just Cause members."
— Senator Christine Goodwin (R-NY)

February, 2009
New York City, NY

Sally heard the sound of metal smashing together well before she walked into Title Boxing Club. It sounded like manufacturing gone amok in a factory, or trains crashing together. Upon entering, she saw Detroit Steel and Hector sparring with each other while the others munched on their burgers and fries, watching the bout, offering advice and catcalling. Detroit Steel had a fierce grin on her face that didn't fade in the least when Hector delivered a solid right cross to her chin. She responded with a vicious uppercut of her own and followed it up with an elbow to his cheek that sent him spinning to the mat.

"Whooo, I bet he feels that one in the morning." Jason crammed an entire burger into his mouth.

"I ain't feelin' nothin'. I could do this all night, dreadlocks." Hector bounced up to his feet, fists at the ready, and waded back into Detroit Steel's guard.

"What was that? You tryin' to tickle me, Nickelback?"

Jason winced. "That was cold, Shawna."

Sally crossed the club floor in a heartbeat to stand beside Jason. She put her arms around him and he swept her off her feet, finishing with a passionate kiss. "I missed you too."

"You brought phones! You brought food! I married the best woman in the world!"

Sally smiled at him. "I know, silly boy." She looked up at Detroit Steel and Hector, circling one another in the ring, trading jabs back and forth. "Hey, you two, knock it off, would you?"

Hector and Detroit Steel clasped hands, warriors offering one another their respect. "You got skills, yo."

"You're not so bad yourself."

Sally stepped away from Jason. "Bring it in, guys. We need to go over some things." The rest of the heroes closed in to form an oval with Sally at one end. "Okay, first things first. You all should know I spoke to Director Sapo tonight. He's going to burn us. By morning, if we haven't surrendered to the authorities, we will probably be federal fugitives. We're in direct violation of our orders and our duties will be rescinded and a team of Champions will be put in place to act in our stead." She paused, waiting to see if anyone had anything to say about that. Instead, everyone stared back at her, expectant and impatient for the next part. "So, uh, if anyone wants to leave and turn themselves in, nobody will stop you, and nobody will judge you for it."

"Shit, I will," said Hector into the silence. "Ain't got no respect for a quitter."

"Quiet, Hector. This is grownup conversation."

"Oh, right, right." He smiled.

"Anyone want to leave?" asked Sally.

Nobody moved.

"We're all together in this," said Snapdragon. "Win or lose."

"All right. Here's where we stand. I have some evidence that will cause a real problem for Senator Goodwin, and more that will get her stooge Sapo into a lot of hot water. Goodwin is tied to Chessboard Industries, and that's one part of the puzzle. Now what we need to find is evidence tying Chessboard to Martina Hladky and to Syndicate S. I'm positive that they're behind them. We already know Chessboard created The Militia using their Touchstone Technology. If we can prove they bestowed powers upon Hladky and Syndicate S, we've got them, and that means we've got Goodwin by the balls."

Jason snorted. "I can't believe you actually said that, babe."

"I hate that bitch." Sally let venom drip from every syllable. "If I accomplish nothing else before losing my job and getting sent to Deep Six, it'll be ruining her career for what she's done."

"So what the fuck's the plan?" Snowball affected a 1920s gangster voice, "You want we should maybe ventilate her?"

The others laughed, and Sally smiled. "No, we're not murderers. We're heroes. We're the good guys. Even when we're on the run. Don't forget that, anyone. We still need to act right, you understand?" Everyone nodded. "We're going to do worse to her, anyway. We'll get her crucified in the press. For a politician, that's a fate worse than death."

"Hold it." Minerva floated into the air. "Something's not right."

Sally froze. She'd learned to trust Minerva's instincts without fail. "What is it?"

Minerva left her spot in the circle, floated into the air, and moved around the outside edge of the group, her fingertips spread out and her head canted at a peculiar angle. "Something . . ."

"We ain't got time for this," said Failsafe.

Minerva stopped above him and looked down at him with an imperious gaze. "You're good. You almost fooled me. You're wearing his clothes. You took on the look of his body. But you're sweating, and you smell like *you*."

Failsafe reached his hand inside his jacket.

Sally took a step toward him but Ment was faster, acting at the speed of thought.

Failsafe's eyes rolled up in his head and he collapsed onto the floor.

"He's asleep," said Ment. "He'll be out for hours."

As they stared, Failsafe's facial features flowed like claymation, rearranging themselves into the unfamiliar face of a hawk-nosed Caucasian man. "Who is he?" asked Shillelagh. "Where's Aramis?"

Sally looked over at Ment. "Read his mind. We don't have time for interrogation."

Ment looked up at her. "We can't use anything we learn this way in court. You know, for our defense."

"I don't care. He was spying on us. He must have Failsafe held prisoner somewhere. And he knows what we're up to. We need to know what we're up against and how bad off we are."

Ment raised his sunglasses up to the top of his head and stretched a hand out to Minerva. "Need your help here, Min."

Minerva touched down to the ground as soft as if she were a feather and took Ment's hand. She would help him focus his raw abilities into the fine control he needed for something as tricky as mind reading. Sally hadn't spent a lot of time talking with psionicists about how their powers worked, but as she understood it, the difficult part of mind-reading was separating one's own thoughts from the thoughts of one's target.

Ment squatted down beside the unconscious stranger, placed his fingertips on the man's forehead, and shut his eyes. "His name is . . . John Bennett. And . . . John Q. Public."

"Like that guy who used to be in American Justice," said Snowball. "He got shot and killed in a robbery."

"He is with The Militia," said Ment. "He can change his face. He has been . . . many people."

"Was he disguised as Jack?" asked Sally. "Did he shoot the Senator?"

"No," said Ment. "He was . . . Second Amendment."

"That probably means Second Amendment took that shot," said Snapdragon. "He's probably a good enough shot to graze without permanent injury. It makes sense."

"It doesn't make jack shit for sense." Detroit Steel nudged the unconscious stranger with her foot. "Why would they shoot at her? She's on their side."

"It's the appearance of the thing. They cooked it up between them. It got Jack out of the picture, and probably led to getting Juice out too. And now look at us. Trust me, Goodwin is a devious bitch, and she planned all this. This is how she's taking down Just Cause." Sally felt like hitting something. Or some one. Preferably with the title of Senator. "Does he know where Failsafe is now, Ment? Is he . . . is he all right?" She couldn't bring herself to say dead, even though it wouldn't have surprised her in the least, given The Militia's propensity for solving their problems with mortal permanency.

"They have him. He's . . . locked up."

"In jail?" asked Shillelagh.

"No . . . Chessboard." Ment broke contact with John Q. Public. Sweat poured off his face, drenching his hair, and his hands shook like a junkie in withdrawal. "We have to go. He sent a text message when we were all here. The cops are coming."

Jason looked out the front windows. "Don't see them yet. Where are we going to go? How long was this guy Failsafe?"

"My brother has a garage in East Harlem. Ain't no cop gonna connect you there," said Hector. "Meet up there. I'll let him know we're comin'."

"We? Hector, this isn't your fight." Sally touched Hector's arm.

"Fuck that." Hector spat at John Q. Public's unconscious body on the floor. The well-aimed spittle struck right on the man's forehead. "This asshole made it my fight. Maybe I ain't good enough to be in Just Cause, but I know what's right."

Sally nodded. "All right, you're in. I trust you, Hector. Give Ment the address and he'll deposit it into our minds. And then everyone bug out. Partner up. Same as before for now. Hector . . ."

"It's cool, I got it." Hector was already at a power box on the wall. He yanked down the lever, plunging the inside of the boxing club into darkness.

"Two hours. I don't know how long we'll have to run. If the heat's on you, stay away from the rest of the group." Sally stretched up to kiss Jason, enjoying his arms around her for a few precious seconds. "Good luck, you guys. I'll see you soon."

The heroes fled into the night.

* * *

"Champion HQ," said the young woman on the other end of the phone. "How can I help you?"

Sally glanced around to make sure nobody was watching her. "Hi, this is the Juggler. I need to speak to Surfboy right away."

"Um, he's off-duty right now. Can I help you?"

"Look me up in your system. And then put me through to him." After Surfboy had been given authority over the Champions, with the full support of Just Cause and the PRA, Sally had put a note in the file for the fictional identity she'd once used to infiltrate the Champions, before they were a legitimate organization. That note would get her through any red tape to Champions leadership. *If contacted by this person, notify Surfboy right away.*

A couple of minutes passed and then Surfboy's sleepy voice picked up. "H'lo?"

"It's Juggler, Surfboy. You understand? Juggler?"

"Yeah, what's up, S—"

"*Juggler.* Nobody else, get it?"

Surfboy hadn't always been the brightest student when he was in Sally's class back at the Hero Academy, but he had a few years of experience running the main Champions branch, and that meant he wasn't dumb as a box of hair, as Sally's grandma used to say. "Juggler. Right, got it. What's up?"

"We need to meet. To discuss Champions business. It's really important."

"Where?"

"Times Square. You get there. I'll find you."

"I'll be there in fifteen minutes."

"See you soon." Sally disconnected and trotted toward her destination, rapidly for a normal person but not so fast she'd attract attention as a parahuman. It was already past midnight, and snowing, and she slipped from shadow to shadow as best she could. Even at the late hour, cars still lined the streets approaching Times Square, and Sally turned up her collar and tried to be invisible as she hurried along the sidewalks under the glare of the huge lights and brightly-colored signs.

She stationed herself near the Planet Hollywood, one of Surfboy's favorite restaurants, while Yunbao hid in the shadows of a nearby side street. With his ability to fly quickly, but at no altitude exceeding six feet, he would cover the distance from Champions HQ to Times Square in minutes. When Sally spotted him, he wasn't flying in the traditional sense, but positioned like a skier, floating only inches above the ground, sliding along like a human hovercraft. It looked odd, but she reasoned it probably wasn't the weirdest thing a typical New Yorker had seen in the middle of the night in Times Square. She caught his eye and waved, and he slid over beside her.

"Hey. You're in a whole lot of trouble. I could get arrested just for talking to you like this."

"And yet you're here anyway. Thanks for coming, Stefan." Sally squeezed his gloved hand with hers.

"I owe you so much, Sally. How could I not come to help you after you helped me find my way back from the darkness? What do you need? Name it, and it's yours." When Sally had been undercover with the Champions, Stefan had been played psychologically by a master of the art, turned into the very picture of an evil second-in-command. It was only through some canny psychology of her own that Sally had managed to convince him of the truth.

"Tell me . . . is Man of the Cloth still hanging around with you guys?"

"Yeah. He's not really active, though. Mostly he's doing outsource costume design and repair. Making damn good money with it, too. He's thinking about starting his own line. He's got fashionistas calling almost daily." Man of the Cloth was a fifty-year-old guy who had powers over fabric, which was one of the strangest things Sally had ever seen. He'd been the costumier for the Champions when they first came on the scene, and since then had kept himself busy doing the same kind of work for both the Champions and Just Cause.

"I need him to make some specific designs, and I need a group of Champions to wear them."

"Like I said, whatever you need, it's yours. I'm your Huckleberry until the bitter end."

"I'll be in touch."

* * *

On one hand, Sally should have been surprised at the coincidence that Hector's brother's garage was the site of one of the first murders attributed to Harlan Washington on the day he went on his initial rampage as Destroyer. On the other, she thought, coincidences seemed to surround parahumans like a second skin. "That little fucker killed our uncle." Hector's brother Carlos lit one cigarette from the stub of another. "The cops said it was just a random killing from the Blackout, but we knew better. Everyone knew that kid hung around here all the time. He was here that day, and didn't nobody see our uncle after he left."

"I'm sorry about that." After running for a couple of hours and consuming one twelve-ounce energy drink, Sally felt like her heart might kick apart her ribs and go on a rampage of its own. Anything to keep herself going. She knew she'd be able to rest soon, but not until they either resolved the situation they were in, or they got arrested. The longer she and the others stayed on the run, the more preferable that solution might start to seem. Exhaustion would take its toll. "I have plenty of history with him myself."

Other members of Just Cause New York trickled into the garage, arriving singly or in pairs. Every time someone slipped into the door, Sally's perceptions leaped into overdrive as she prepared to fight, but every time it was one of her friends instead. At last, her team was regrouped amid the barrels of oil, greasy tools, and half-torn-down automobiles.

Sally looked around at her ragtag group of fellow fugitives. "Anybody run into any trouble out there?"

Nobody had.

"Good. I've been thinking it over, and the only way we can clear our names is to come up with proof that we've been right all along, and release it publicly. This game is played out on the field of public media, and it's time we put them to work for us. Popular outcry will go a long way towards insulating us from what Goodwin is trying to accomplish."

"So what do we do? She's a Senator. She's basically untouchable." Jason looked up from a bench-mounted supercharger that he was examining with interest.

Sally clasped her hands behind her back. She'd spent hours thinking up a plan. "Exposed corruption is the bane of every public figure. All we have to do is prove Chessboard is behind Syndicate S, Martina Hladky, and we've got a ready-made conspiracy that works in our favor."

"So what do we need?" asked Ment.

"*Off the top of my head, I'd say you're looking at a Boeski, a Jim Brown, a Miss Daisy, two Jethros, and a Leon Spinks, not to mention the biggest Ella Fitzgerald ever.*" Sally smiled at her team.

"Hey, isn't that from a movie?" asked Detroit Steel.

Snowball grinned. "We're going to do a heist? Fuck yeah, I've always wanted to do that."

"How are we going to pull off a heist?" Shillelagh was perched on a floor lamp that looked far too flimsy to support her. "Last I checked, the only one of us who's ever been on the wrong side of the law before was Failsafe, and he's their prisoner."

"We can do it. I've made some arrangements and purchased some items that will help." Sally held up a couple of bags bearing the names of some all-night outlets.

"We're all exhausted." Snapdragon yawned. "I'm not sure I would trust us to sit through one heist movie, never mind actually do one."

Sally nodded. "I know. I'm wiped out too, but we've got to do this tomorrow."

"You mean later today. It's been tomorrow for a couple of hours already." Jason grinned at her.

"Yes, later today. We can all nap on the way there." Sally knew her artificial buzz wouldn't last much longer with her metabolic rate. Her best bet was to catch a good solid hour or two of shuteye.

"Where's *there*?" asked Detroit Steel.

"Yonkers."

Silence filled the garage for a minute.

"That is the strangest name for a town I have ever heard," Yunbao said at last.

Eighteen

"The time has come for all right-thinking Americans to take a stand. Are you for parahumans, like the namby-pamby liberals who don't see that the crimes committed by these monsters are because there is no control system in place? Or do you believe in the freedom of Americans not to be terrorized by near-humans?"
—Ken Reichel, First Choice Radio Network

February, 2009
Yonkers, NY

Chessboard Industries was located on a large estate to the southwest of Yonkers, with both road and sea access. The facility itself was a large, sprawling building sheathed in tinted glass, with multiple wings spreading outward from a large central annex that looked like a cylinder cut off at an angle. Despite the clouds and steady lake-effect snowfall, the building managed to find enough stray sunlight to gleam.

Just Cause New York was arriving in three separate vehicles, all provided by Hector's brother from the vehicles in his shop. Hector himself was driving a large windowless work van, with ladders on a roof rack fading paint, and rust spots. Detroit Steel and Yunbao rode with him in it, hidden from view among the tools in the back. Jason drove a burgundy SUV with Snapdragon riding shotgun. Both of them wore off-the-rack suits and ties. A large black sample case shared the back seat with Snowball, who would hide in it as soon as they arrived. She hadn't been happy with the idea, but as a little person, she stood out and the whole point of their infiltration was to avoid standing out as much as possible. The notion of waiting in the van with Detroit Steel and Yunbao as backup was off the table as far as Snowball had been concerned. "Fine, they can carry me in. I'm not sitting on my thumbs in the van waiting for shit to fall apart. No offense."

"None is taken." Yunbao looked at her own thumbs with a bemused expression as if trying to decipher the intricacies of English idioms.

Sally, Shillelagh, Minerva, and Ment were in a nondescript sedan. Shillelagh had insisted upon driving, as she was the only one who'd grown up behind the wheel in Boston. Sally had only been too glad to relinquish those duties to someone else. Jason had tried to teach her to drive, but they'd determined she was hopeless behind the wheel, and more of a danger to herself and others than if she were to run to a destination on her own two feet instead.

Slush splattered against the bottom of the floorboards as the car hit a deep puddle when Shillelagh turned into the entrance of the Chessboard Industries facility. She grunted as the car's rear end slid a little. Sally already had her hand on the door handle, ready to leap out and run for her life. She'd always thought of cars as deathtraps, and watching Shillelagh weave through traffic on the way to Yonkers hadn't changed her opinion in the least. Shillelagh somehow kept the car from slipping, flipping, and exploding as she drove up the gentle slope to the parking lot.

Sally brushed at her costume lab coat, wishing it looked a little more like something she wore every day and less like something she'd picked up in a costume boutique. Underneath it, she wore regular clothing, and under that was her skintight costume. The others were similarly-attired, although Ment had nearly balked at replacing his standard black overcoat with the thin white lab coat. It had taken Minerva a few minutes of speaking in her calming tones to convince him. Sally didn't think she'd have been able to do it at all, even if she'd given him a direct order. It was most crucial for Ment to look like he belonged out of all of them. Without him and his psionic abilities, their heist probably wouldn't get past the front door.

Shillelagh parked the car. She'd left her long red wig behind, but the way she flipped her head made Sally know that she missed it. She knew how the gymnast felt; she still missed her own lengthy tresses. She'd even thought about wearing a wig sometimes, just so she'd have some long hair to flip around and twist her fingers in while she was thinking. "All right, guys, let's do this." She pulled out her phone and sent a text to Jason.

We're here. Going in now.

They crossed the lot quickly, heads lowered against the blowing snow. Maintenance crews were pushing shovels and spreading salt along the sidewalks as they reached the main building. The main entrance had side-by-side rotating doors, like at one of the hotels Jason and Sally had stayed at during their cross-country honeymoon trip. They pushed through and found themselves in a large circular lobby that was open all the way to the angled glass roof several stories above. It felt like a museum to Sally, the way sound echoed off the walls. Stairwells and elevators led to the upper floors at each wing leading from the main lobby. Models of some of the technology developed by Chessboard researchers, like missiles and drones, hung from cables overhead. Various multimedia displays were set up around the perimeter of the lobby, along with signs and more models.

Sally looked up at the models overhead. "Looks like they're doing very well for themselves. I guess defense is big business."

"Well, look at all the wars we keep getting in." Shillelagh ran her fingers through her short black hair. "It's a growth industry."

"There's the reception desk for the offices." Minerva nodded toward one of the security stations in front of each wing. "We'll need badges. We may need keycards."

Ment nodded. "I'm on it. Just back me up, okay?"

The four heroes headed up to the desk to the offices. It was staffed by a pair of receptionists, male and female, in sweater vests with badges clipped to them. A burly security guard with a sidearm under a flap, radio, and metal detector wand stood beside the security gate. The male receptionist was talking into his headset and typing something into his workstation, so the woman smiled up at Ment and the others. "Welcome to Chessboard Industries. How can I help you?"

Minerva slipped her hand into Ment's. Sally kicked up her perceptions a notch, making sure she didn't miss any important cues of something about to go awry. Ment put on his best, nerdiest grin. "Hi! We're from Mento Research Group, here for our scheduled proposal meeting. You'll find us on your list."

The woman's eyes glazed over and she lowered her head to look at her screen. "Ah yes, here you are. I see all of you on my list. From Mento Research Group. You have a scheduled proposal meeting."

"You have our badges? And do we need keycards?" Sweat trickled down Ment's temples. Sally saw a muscle in his jaw twitching and she knew he was straining to rewrite the receptionist's mind in real time without damaging her or raising any suspicions. Sally had seen him put an entire building of people to sleep with Minerva's help, but that was as simple as throwing a switch. He'd once described real-time mind-control as akin to doing a complete oil change in a car racing down the highway without spilling a drop or alerting the driver.

"Yes, I have your badges right here." The receptionist slid four *VISITOR* passes across the top of her desk. "Keycards are for employees only. You shouldn't need them."

Ment took the passes and distributed them to the others. "Thank you. You won't really remember us except vaguely."

"No, probably not," agreed the woman.

"Nor you." Ment looked toward the male receptionist. "You never saw us."

He looked up at Ment for a moment. "No, I never saw you."

"What the—" The security guard reached for the flap of his holster.

Ment locked gazes with him and the guard froze. "You're thinking about something else." Ment's teeth were clenched tight and his hair was growing damp from the sweat leaching out of his scalp. "It's more important than we are. You'll forget us in a couple of minutes. Wave us through."

The guard nodded, his brow furrowed in deep thought, and stepped aside so they could pass through the gate.

Sally felt like racing all the way but instead, she walked with a slow, purposeful gait. Something that wouldn't raise any suspicions at all. As she passed by the guard, she accelerated her perceptions to maximum, located a keycard on his lanyard, filched it, and tucked it into her lab coat pocket, all without breaking her stride or giving any indication that she'd done anything untoward. Shillelagh, Ment, and Minerva followed after her. Ment was swaying on his feet and Shillelagh casually moved beside him to where she could support him on one side while Minerva did on the other, and the four of them walked to the elevators that way until they were safely inside one. "You see any cameras?"

Minerva floated into the air, sniffing and listening. "No. No monitoring equipment in here at all. We're safe for the moment."

Ment collapsed against the side of the elevator, leaving a sweaty streak on the cool metal from his fevered head. "Oh my God, I hope I don't have to do that again anytime soon."

"I've got you." Minerva took Ment's head in her hands and brushed her lips against his. "You're strong. You'll be fine in no time at all."

Sally sent another text. *We're in.*

Shillelagh shed her lab coat, to reveal her stream-lined, skintight costume. She sprang towards the roof of the elevator, locking her feet against the sides in a split that reminded Sally of late-night movies starring Jean-Claude Van Damme. "I'll have this hatch open in a sec."

"Keep the badge and coat with you." Sally handed them up to Shillelagh. "You never know when you'll run into a dead end and have to get back out amongst the rabble again."

"This whole place is full of rabble. I can feel it." Shillelagh rolled up the coat into a tight tube and slid it into a pouch on one of her hips. Then she popped open the roof door. The smell of industrial lubricant filled the elevator. "See you guys at the top. I'll try to temporarily disconnect cameras on your route if I can. Be careful." She wrapped her fingers around the edge of the hatch and flipped herself over the lip onto the elevator roof. A moment later she shut the hatch just as the elevator came to a halt at the highest floor it would allow them to go without keycard access.

"We've got to get a card." Minerva bent down to look in the slot beside the keypad.

Sally held up the one she'd taken from the security guard. "I figured a guard would have access to anywhere in the building. But there might be a record of his card being used when we swipe it here. There are cameras all over the place in this building. That means a central security office. We're on the short-term clock as soon as I swipe this."

Ment wiped sweat from his face. The blotchy spots on his otherwise pale cheeks made him look like he was suffering from a fever. "Do it. There's no way I can do anything useful for awhile."

Sally swiped the card and a touchscreen next to the elevator door activated, showing the upper floors for which the elevator had no physical buttons. "You want to make a guess, Minerva?"

"Executives generally prefer the top floor, I believe." Minerva selected the highest number on the list. The elevator lurched into motion once more.

Sally's phone buzzed with an incoming text. *We're in. Waiting for info on target.*

That meant Jason, Snapdragon, and Snowball were downstairs in the lobby, with the two fellows pretending to be sales reps while Snowball cozied up inside the large case Jason was carrying. It had been a struggle, but Sally convinced Jason to let Minerva perform a quick haircut on him to eliminate his trademark shagginess. When she finished, he looked like he'd just emerged from a high-priced salon. He looked at himself in the side mirror of the van right before they left Hector's brother's garage. "You ever give up superheroing, you've got a promising second career as a stylist."

"You look good, babycakes." Sally touched his cheek.

"I look like a damn stockbroker. Soon as this is done, I'm growing it back out. I hate this."

"Just so you know, I do too. I like my rough-and-tumble man."

Snowball had made a gagging sound.

Sally didn't think Snowball would be laughing much now, crammed into that sample case. She only hoped they could find out where Failsafe was being held quickly, so Jason's squad could free him.

The elevator doors opened into the top floor of the executive wing of Chessboard. The roof and left side of the corridor was entirely glass, and curved enough that snow only built up along the edges of the panes. Sally could almost see all the way out to the Hudson River even with the lake-effect snow coming down. The right side of the hall had several doors which led to offices or conference rooms, but the hall ended with a small lobby and another reception desk. The woman at the desk was staring at them in open-mouthed shock. Sally launched herself down the hall in a flash and yanked the cord out of the back of the receptionist's phone before she could call for help.

"What are you doing?" The receptionist started to stand up, but before she could complete the motion, her eyes shut and she put her head down on the desk, asleep.

"Stick a fork in me. I'm done." Ment staggered up the hall with Minerva supporting him. "You girls go on. I'll hold them off here."

Sally looked at him, wondering what he could possibly manage. "How?"

Ment stripped off his lab coat and moved the sleeping receptionist into the nook beneath the desk, slipping her headset around his ears and putting on a pair of thick black-framed glasses. Once he sat in the receptionist's chair and folded his hands on top of it, Sally had to admit that he did look kind of like he belonged there.

"Shillelagh, did you cut out the video feed up here?" Minerva seemed to be speaking to nobody in particular.

"Yes, but I'll have to reconnect it in a moment." A disembodied voice came from somewhere in the ventilation shaft running just beneath the keystone brace of the curved overhead glass. "Cramped in here."

Sally looked down at her phone. There was a new text from Surfboy. *Incoming*. Sally smiled just as alarms started hooting throughout the Chessboard facility. A calm, authoritative female voice echoed over the public address system. "Ladies and gentlemen. We are locking down the building due to an exterior security concern. You are in no danger, but we ask that you remain inside until we have secured the area. Thank you."

Sally looked out toward the parking lot. She spotted a splash of red and a swatch of brown amid the snow and pointed. "Look, Just Cause is here. No wonder they're upset."

"Just Cause?" Minerva frowned and squinted. "That's Johnny Go wearing your costume with a really bad wig. And Bombshell is dressed like Jason." She snorted. "Toxic is wearing mine. That's Surfboy pretending to be Snapdragon." She looked at Sally. "Your doing?"

"Yeah, I asked Surfboy for the distraction. He was totally into it."

"That's good thinking."

"They're under strict instructions not to engage anybody with parahuman powers. I'm afraid the rest of The Militia is here somewhere. Otherwise, they can torment Chessboard security forces as much as they see fit. It'll be several minutes before anyone realizes that's not really Just Cause." Sally turned to look at the office beyond the reception desk. "Come on, let's go find that evidence."

If Sally's office was designed to make her feel comfortable and at home, with the big overstuffed chairs, the wooden desk, and the large flatscreens showing images of her favorite desertscapes, Zoe Oswalt's office felt as cold and antiseptic as a preoperative surgery suite. Everything was glass and brushed aluminum and stainless steel from the huge leaded crystal desk to the cushionless chairs of sparse silvery curves. There were no human touches in the room, not even a picture of Oswalt's family on her desk. Nothing in there would serve as a distraction to the woman who ran Chessboard with an iron fist.

Minerva nodded, looking around. "I hate her already."

"You any good with hacking computers?"

"I . . . dabble."

"Well get on over here. I picked up a few pointers from a friend of mine." Sally slipped a USB drive from her pocket. "But I need you to help me crack the password. Take a look at the keyboard and see if you can figure it out. If we can't do it, we've got to take the entire hard drive out and hope for the best."

"Move aside, please." Minerva sat down in Oswalt's chair and faced the open laptop on the desktop. She let her hands hover just above the keyboard, bent forward, sniffed, and stuck her tongue out like a snake tasting the air. Sally felt like pacing, screaming, pounding on the glass wall. Any moment, their lead could evaporate and they'd have Security bearing down upon them. She turned to watch as Surfboy's Champions raced around the parking lot while security guards chased them to no effect. Then the security troops moved aside like a wave breaking.

The Militia burst forth.

Patriot flew low and fast, closing in on Bombshell in her Mastiff outfit. Liberty flickered in and out like he was in a strobe light, pursuing Johnny Go as he ran. Second Amendment raised his pistols, firing at a twisting Surfboy. The Minuteman fired his fireballs like a human Gatling gun, strafing them at Toxic, who surrounded herself with a chemical cloud that extinguished them as they reached her. Sally didn't see Justice or Maverick anywhere, but that didn't mean they weren't in the area. She clenched her fist and beat it against the thick glass in frustration. "Come on, Stefan, get out of there. Get your people out. You're not supposed to engage them."

An unmarked van screeched to a halt at the bottom of the parking lot. The side door flew open and heroes in yellow and red tumbled out of it like performers out of a clown car in the circus. Sally recognized the small man she knew as Particulate, transforming himself into a cloud and swarming around Second Amendment to distract him. The man called Shouty Ed bellowed at Patriot loud enough to crack windows in half the cars in the parking lot, making the leader of The Militia grab his ears in pain. Several other Champions Sally didn't immediately recognize joined in, using their abilities to distract, protect, and generally be difficult. "God, I hope none of them get killed."

"Sally . . ." Minerva sounded pleased with herself.

Sally turned around to see Minerva type something on the keyboard. "Did you get it?"

"Yes, we're in." Minerva floated away from the chair to make room for Sally.

"It's a good thing there's only one of you." Sally slipped into the seat. "Not quite enough hands to rule the world."

"Oh, I don't know. I can see a way to do it." Sally looked up at Minerva, feeling a twinge of creeping horror, but the girl was smiling. "Ruling the world sounds like a real pain in the ass to me. Like running a daycare full of obnoxious toddlers."

"Thanks . . . I think." Sally wasn't quite sure whether to be insulted or pleased. Instead, she slid the USB drive into a slot and started copying the contents of Oswalt's hard drive. According to the computer, transferring all the files would take just over seven minutes, which felt like an eternity to Sally. "How are the Champions looking out there? Please tell me they've left and nobody's hurt."

"They're fleeing. I see some injuries, but no fatalities. Patriot has hold of Surfboy and is questioning him. I can't see Patriot's lips, but Surfboy is saying they were just running a drill. Patriot doesn't appear to believe him. He's yelling in Surfboy's face. Oh. Something has changed."

Sally looked up from where she was browsing through files, looking for evidence. "What changed?"

"They have let Surfboy go. The Militia is hurrying back toward this building."

"Shit. You think they're onto us?"

"It's likely."

"Ment, we're going to have company. Do what you can to hold them off. We may have to fight our way out."

"Great," muttered the psionicist from the receptionist's desk.

"Shillelagh, you still here?"

The Bostonian's voice came from an overhead vent. "Yes. Very comfortable up here. Loads of space."

"Four minutes left on this file transfer and then you can leave. Oh, shit, I found it!"

"Found what?" Minerva asked.

"The Touchstone folder." Sally accelerated her perceptions and started flipping through files, reading reports, scanning pictures. There were videos saved as well, but she didn't want to take the extra time to watch them, as she'd have to do so in real time, and time was a commodity they didn't have enough of already. "God. It's here. It's all here."

"You found the evidence we can use? What is it?" Minerva leaned down over Sally's shoulder to look at the monitor.

"They're coming, you guys," called Ment. "I can sense them in the elevator now."

"Is it The Militia?" Sally asked.

"I can't tell. It's a packed car, though. I don't know that I can take them all down."

"Go help him. I'll be right behind you as soon as this file transfer is done." Sally checked the time remaining. Eighty seconds. It felt like an eternity. "I've still got to find Failsafe."

With a bang, the overhead vent burst open and Sally glanced up to see Shillelagh's worried face peering down at her. "Anything I can do to help?"

"Yeah. When I toss this thumbdrive up to you, don't lose it. I'm trusting you to get out of here. Meet us back where we started." The computer window showing the file transfer progress closed and Sally yanked out the drive and tossed it overhead.

Shillelagh snagged it at the zenith of its arc. "Got it!"

"Go!" Sally turned away from Shillelagh just as the elevator doors at the end of the hall opened up.

Several security guards spilled out, collapsing into psionically-induced sleep after one or two steps. The last two stepped over their unconscious comrades with their weapons drawn. "Hold it right there!"

Minerva flicked something down the hall at one of the security guards as Sally raced past her. In one smooth motion she engaged the safety on the guard's pistol, and then released the clip. She turned to the other but saw him reeling from a blow of some kind, so she settled for relieving him of his weapon altogether and tossing it up the hall. She finished up by taking the guards' own tasers and zapping each one into unconsciousness. By the time Minerva had closed the distance, Sally had already zip-tied the guards' wrists and ankles and used their belts to tie their chests together in a pose that looked like long-lost lovers entwined in each others' arms.

"Very nice." Minerva tested the restraints and nodded with approval.

"What'd you use on that guy?"

Minerva held up a chamois bag and shook a couple of ceramic marbles out of it. "These are a little more discreet than my spear, and don't show up on a metal detector."

"Clever. I need another minute on that computer to try to find Failsafe."

"You've got it."

Sally ran back up the hall but skidded to a halt beside the receptionist's desk. Ment was slumped in the chair, his arms dangling at his sides, a trickle of blood running from one nostril. She checked his pulse and was grateful to feel it fluttering beneath her fingers, although it wasn't as strong as she would have liked. "Minerva! Ment's hurt or something. You better come check on him."

Minerva glanced back over her shoulder. Sally knew she could probably diagnose him better than most doctors, at a distance, just from her advanced sensory perceptions. "He'll be fine. He strained himself. He needs rest and electrolytes and protein."

"We'll stop for Gatorade and peanuts on our way home. It's scary to see, though." She went back to the computer and began to flip through files at super-speed. She found a reference to Failsafe in a report showing a scheduled implantation of a CMCD that would take place in—Sally checked the time—less than an hour. Said procedure was to take place in Lab 4 on Sublevel 2. A CMCD was a *Cortical Monitoring and Correctional Device* . . .

. . . Also known as a *Cortex Bomb.*

"Got it!" Sally sent Jason a text with Failsafe's location. "That's our evidence. Let's get our people and get out of here before—"

Patriot crashed through the glass into Oswalt's office, and Liberty teleported into the hallway right beside Ment's barely conscious form.

Nineteen

"Parapowered combats do tremendous amounts of property damage, costing taxpayers hundreds of millions of dollars annually. Only through properly controlled parahumans can we eliminate this expense."
—Senator Christine Goodwin (R-NY)

February, 2009
Yonkers, NY

"Mustang Sally!" Patriot shouted with grim satisfaction. "You are under arrest! Stand down or I will use lethal force!"

"Take them." Sally sped out of the office in a fraction of a second, driving a hard punch into the side of Liberty's face just the way Hector had shown her. He was reaching for her friend's head, perhaps to snap his neck. Halfway through her blow, Liberty teleported away and it was only through a tremendous force of effort that Sally deflected her own punch aside enough not to land it upon Ment's lolling head. Liberty reappeared several feet away, his eyes rolling back in his head. A fierce smile crossed Sally's face. She'd beaten the speed of his thoughts. His teleport defense had been nothing more than a reflex. She wished Hector or Jason or Detroit Steel had seen her deliver that strike. They would have appreciated her one-punch knockout in the way that few others would have.

Patriot flung aside Oswalt's desk, not caring about the damage he inflicted upon the office as it shattered several panes of glass on its way to the parking lot below. "Liberty! You were warned, Sally! I'm going to tear you apart like the crunchy you are."

Sally knew she could dodge Patriot all day long, as slow as he was compared to her. Almost anyone on the ball could have done the same, though; he tended to telegraph his moves ahead of time, like a professional wrestler. She needed to get him away from Ment, though, and that meant letting him get very close to her so he'd pursue her. She dodged his thunderous blows at the last possible moment, feeling the wind of his massive fists passing by her face. If even one of those connected with her, she wouldn't have to worry about future head injuries ever again.

She wouldn't have to worry about anything.

Patriot's increasing frustration with his inability to hit Sally spread across his face like a sunburn, his skin going first red and then purple with fury. He howled in inarticulate rage, failing to notice Minerva where she floated near the curved glass ceiling. She reached down from her position, touching Patriot's shoulder with two fingers. His arm dropped like all the bones had fallen out of it. He yelped in surprise and Minerva shut down his other arm in the same way. "You whore, I don't need my arms to—"

Minerva touched the side of his neck and his eyes bulged out as he struggled to draw a breath. "I don't appreciate being called names." Minerva spoke in a soft, dangerous voice. "I could kill you by just touching you. I could stop your heart. I could give you a stroke. Or I could kill you slowly. I could give you cancer, or make your immune system attack your organs, or make your cells shed all their water. But I'll settle for knocking you out after I tell you this. My friends are off-limits. You stay away from us, Patriot, and you'll live." With that, she touched another spot on his neck. He gasped with a frantic inhalation, and then his eyes closed and he collapsed. "I do believe I hate that man."

Sally gaped in frank astonishment. "God, Minerva, would you . . . can you really do all those things?"

Minerva looked down at her. "I rebuilt Jack on a cellular level. I physically transformed your body into a completely new appearance and back. Yes, I can do all those things." The danger in her voice softened as she looked toward Ment. "But I choose not to, because that's not what the good guys do."

"You'd be a scary bad guy. I'm really glad you're on my side."

"I'm glad you're on mine. You have no idea how dangerous and powerful you really are. The things you can do at the speed you can do them . . . they give me the screaming meemies. I don't even know what a meemie is, but it's something my grandmother used to say and it feels like an apt description."

"My grandma said that too. Must have been a generational thing. Can you carry Ment?"

"Yes, I can transport him." Minerva could somehow transfer her flight abilities into people who touched her, making her into a human helicopter.

"Patriot is The Militia's only flier. Take Ment and go. Get yourselves to safety. I'm going to head down to Sublevel 2 and help rescue Failsafe."

"Are you sure you don't want me to stay and help? You know I'm an asset in battle."

"Yes, I know. But we can't bring Ment down to the basement with us, and it's not safe to leave him here. Bug out, Minerva. We'll regroup later."

"Be careful, Sally. I mean it, really careful. We're playing with dangerous stuff here. The kind of stuff that gets you encased in concrete and dumped in the river."

"I know. Go take care of Ment. We'll regroup soon. I have a plan."

"You going to let anyone else in on it?" Minerva floated over to Ment and touched him, a gentle caress to tousle his hair. Still unconscious, he drifted up into the air beside Minerva. She clasped his hand.

"No. The less you all know, the easier time you'll have of it if you get pinched. This may be a war for all of us, but I'm going to end it."

Minerva pulled Ment behind her like she was towing a kite and went out through the glass that Patriot had shattered with his entrance.

Sally turned away from them, knowing she had to focus on herself and getting the rest of her team out. "All of us. Even Failsafe." And with that, she made the building blur around her as she eschewed the elevator in favor of the much faster stairs to the Sublevels. Her stolen security card unlocked doors, and by the time they started to close themselves, she was long past them.

She heard the sounds of pitched parahuman battle before she rounded the last corner in the underground labyrinth beneath Chessboard to find Jason, Snapdragon, and Snowball fighting for their lives and the fate of Failsafe, who was strapped to a gurney and unconscious, oblivious to the battle going on around him. Jason was engaged with Justice in a rousing bout of fisticuffs that had already done massive damage to the laboratory around them, given the number of fist-sized holes in the cement walls and shattered granite tabletops. The way Jason was grinning suggested he was thoroughly enjoying himself, but his swollen eye and bloodied nose and knuckles meant he wasn't necessarily winning. Snapdragon didn't have enough room in the lab to really unfurl his trademark flame wings, so he stayed on the floor, alternating shots at Minuteman, who ran around the room firing back at Snapdragon and Snowball, who was likewise sniping at him. Second Amendment was encased in ice up to his neck like some kind of modern art. His lips were blue and his teeth chattered. Maverick was trying to escort an older woman in an expensive business suit out of the lab along with a half-dozen security guards when Sally happened upon them.

Sally felt Maverick's psionic attack hit the shields which a long-deceased teammate of hers had built in her mind long ago. "What the gosh darn heck?" Maverick clearly expected Sally to cooperate and collapse into unconsciousness.

Sally, for her own part, was done with psionicists and their unfair, unstoppable abilities, and she gave Maverick a really *fast* punch in the mouth, careful not to slice open her knuckles on the woman's carefully-whitened teeth. Maverick's lips mashed against those teeth and split apart, sending a fine mist of blood droplets in all directions. The Militia woman made a terrible gobbling sound as she gagged on her own blood. She hunched over, shrieking at the ruin of her face until Sally followed up her initial blow with another to the temple and Maverick lapsed into unconsciousness. Sally whirled to face Zoe Oswalt and froze as she saw what the woman was actually doing.

Zoe's hands were glowing with a speckled energy of all colors and none, and watching it for more than a moment was enough to give Sally the rumblings of an incipient migraine. The CEO of Chessboard Industries was a parahuman, she realized, and an unknown one at that. Oswalt grabbed hold of the two nearest security guards to her, and they screamed as her energized hands touched them. "Protect me."

One of the guards yelped as his skin began to run like melting ice cream. Sally froze, uncertain what to do. The other guard began sweating, but far more fluid than anyone could perspire quickly soaked through his clothing and ran off his hands to puddle around his feet.

"Protect me, damn you, or you're fired!" Oswalt grabbed another guard with her odd hands and he roared like a trapped beast as his muscles swelled through his clothing in the kind of show that would have made Hollywood special effects guys salivate.

"You!" Sally realized what Oswalt was doing. "There's no such thing as *Touchstone Technology*, is there? It's you. It's been you all along. You're creating these people!"

"Aren't you the smart one?" Oswalt lunged for another guard and he screamed as his body became engulfed in flame. He fell to the floor where his fire mixed with the sweating guard's fluids to fill the hallway with steam.

Sally stared at Oswalt's hands and wondered what would happen if they touched her. Would her powers change? Or vanish? Or would they have no effect upon her if she was already a parahuman? Either way, she wasn't excited about finding out firsthand. The newly-muscled guard staggered toward Sally, roaring like a horror movie monster. The problem with his newfound strength seemed to be that his muscles didn't stop growing after Oswalt had released her grip on him. He took two steps and his clothes and shoes burst apart, looking like the world's greatest bodybuilder. Purple and blue veins stood out on his flesh, throbbing under terrific pressure. Another step and he collapsed, unable to control his still-swelling muscles. Sally hesitated, not knowing how she could help him.

Something like thick mud wrapped around her legs and held her fast, and it was crawling up her sides in a parody of intimate familiarity. Sally realized it was the melted ice-cream man, and he was somehow reshaping his body around hers as if to imprison her. Oswalt was getting away, escorted by the sweating man and one other guard who hadn't run away in fear. Behind Sally, the battle with the remaining members of The Militia continued, and it seemed like they'd reached a stalemate.

Sally knew she had to do something to tip the scales. "You look just like ice cream," Sally said to the fluidic man wrapping around her. "I bet I can churn you." She started twitching her muscles the best that she could. Ripples appeared on the man's head and chest. She accelerated her vibrations and patterned spikes chased each other across the man's melting skin, like he had become a non-Newtonian fluid. He screamed and flowed away, some of his parts only connected by thin streams of mucousy glop.

Oswalt and her sweaty guard reached the elevator. Sally sped up the hall after them, giving the swelling man a wide berth. The sounds he made as he tried to draw breath against the giant muscles encapsulating his chest would haunt her for weeks to come. Oswalt's power to bestow parahuman abilities on others apparently had some drawbacks that could be as fatal as the Nazi parahuman-creating reactor that Sally and Just Cause had destroyed in her very first outing with the team. The elevator doors slammed shut just as Sally reached them. She beat a useless fist against the door. "Dammit!" Torn between pursuing Oswalt and helping her team, Sally knew there was no real choice in the matter.

She returned to the lab, torn to shambles and burning in places from the fight within it. Snowball was icing a burn along one of her arms while trying to maintain a hemispherical shield of ice around her and the unconscious Failsafe. Snapdragon and Minuteman traded fireballs back and forth, neither doing much to harm the other, while Jason and Justice each looked like they'd gone fifteen rounds in a title bout for Heavyweight Champion of the World. Second Amendment looked to have passed out at last from the cold of his icy entombment.

Sally dashed across the lab between fireballs, which felt to her like passing between floating balloons of flame, and stopped beside Snowball. "Hey, are you all right?"

Snowball grimaced. "I zigged when I should have zagged and that speedy fucker lit me right up. I'm supposed to be too goddamn small for people to hit."

"We're getting out of here. But first I need you to help me mop things up in here. You help Jason with Justice and I'll help Nabi with Minuteman."

"What should I do? Justice is too tough for me to bludgeon him with an ice ram, and I can't penetrate his skin with an icicle." Snowball's tough-as-nails exterior melted away and Sally could see the indecision tearing her apart.

"Make him lose his balance. Jason can do the rest."

Snowball nodded, and then smiled as she realized there was something she could do after all. She raised her undamaged arm and cast forth an icy ribbon. It wound its way across the floor until it found Justice's feet and then encased them. Sure enough, he took a step and slipped, arms pinwheeling for balance. Jason didn't disappoint. He grabbed the flailing Justice by the back of his neck and drove his knee upward into the Militia Man's face. Justice flew up and back, blood streaming from a shattered nose, and crashed against the wall, cracking the cement where he struck and then sliding down into a heap. Snowball crowed with success. "Goddamn, that showed him!"

Jason gave her a thumbs-up, although one of his eyes was swollen shut and the other was spinning in his head.

Sally watched Minuteman's moves for a few seconds. He was so wrapped up in trying to blast the Ay-rab, she figured, that he hadn't yet realized he was the only one still up and fighting. He was all offense, the way he fought, and gave no thought to protecting himself beyond trusting his speed to be his salvation.

That wouldn't work against Sally.

She grabbed the stainless steel pole attached to Failsafe's gurney that would normally support IV bottles and removed it from its holder. Then she crossed the lab floor, stepping over shattered glass and questionable chemical spills, until she reached the sweet spot distance between her hands and the back of Minuteman's head. "Say goodnight, Gracie." She gripped the pole tight in both hands and swung for the fences.

The crack of metal against bone was almost as satisfying as the sight of Minuteman tumbling forward, ass-over-teakettle, to fetch up against the wall like a rag doll. Sally ran over to stare down at him and grinned like a fool. "*Young man . . . you got knocked the fuck out.*" She looked up at Jason and giggled. "I always wanted to say that to someone." Then she sobered as she saw how badly he'd been beaten. "Oh, God, Jase. Your face."

"Yeah, but you should see the other guy." He tried to grin through his swollen and split lips.

"We're getting you back home and then checked out. I don't care how tough you are, mister. You look like Officer John McLane on a bad day." Sally looked at Snapdragon and Snowball. "You guys fit to travel? We're getting out of here."

Snapdragon nodded, sparks flashing in his eyes. "I'm done with this place. Want me to torch it?"

For a moment, Sally almost said *yes*. It would have felt good to give in to petty revenge, but they had to remember that they were the good guys, and good guys didn't do that kind of thing. They'd trashed the lab already as part of the rescue of Failsafe, and she was willing to file that under *incidental damage*. Likewise, The Militia had tried to stop them from rescuing someone who had been kidnapped and unlawfully held prisoner, and would have been subjected to an illegal and unethical surgical procedure had Just Cause not intervened. Sally felt like she was on fairly sturdy legal ground, but anything else would reflect poorly in the eyes of the inevitable grand jury or senate hearing or whatever would be her fate. "No, we're bailing out of here right now." She glanced at Failsafe, still unconscious from whatever anesthetic he'd been dosed with. She was about to ask Jason to carry him, but her husband was swaying on his feet and Sally wasn't sure he could carry the unconscious hero without accidentally dropping him. "Jase, keep Aramis on the gurney for right now. Can you push it for me?"

"Sure, babe. What are you going to do?"

"They'll be waiting for us upstairs. I'm going to clear you guys a path through the lobby. Take the elevator up and when you reach the main floor, head straight out the front doors and don't stop for anything." Sally grabbed her phone and sent a text to Hector. *We're coming out. Come get us.*

Sally wanted to kiss Jason on the lips, but she was afraid they'd burst apart from even the slightest pressure. Instead, she brushed her fingertips across the back of his hand, careful not to touch his swollen and bruised knuckles. "Love you, babe. See you upstairs. As for you two?" She looked at Snapdragon and Snowball. "As soon as you have clear sky above you, clear out. There may be pursuit. Stay together and stay safe."

"Where should we regroup? Back at the garage?" Snapdragon took Snowball's hand, making a quick puff of steam rise into the air as his heat met her frost.

"No. Back at Fort Justice. We need to stop running after this. We have to show the world that we're not criminals."

"How are we going to do that?" Snowball looked up at her.

Sally smiled. "We're going to expose the *real* ones. Go big or go home." She accelerated her perceptions to maximum and the world ground to a halt around her.

She ran for the stairs.

* * *

There were no more civilians in the Chessboard Industries main lobby. The only people left in it were either corporate security types, wearing dark suits with earbuds and throat mics and carrying pistols, and a smattering of local law enforcement officers wearing their riot gear. Sally took a quick count as she emerged from the stairwell at speed, targeting fifteen separate threats in the space between heartbeats. She wouldn't have time to disarm all of them before they started shooting, but if she was smart about the order she took them, she could minimize the shots they could take. When she was moving around at speed, she could still catch a bullet, but if the angle was right, it would be more like having a rock thrown at her than being shot. It would hurt, and maybe break the skin, but wouldn't do the kind of damage one wold expect when being shot.

The bigger danger was running right into a bullet that she didn't see coming. Every bullet was an armor-piercing, explosive-tipped nightmare with a closing speed approaching twenty-two hundred feet per second. Jason was bulletproof, even against the high-powered ammunition carried by SWAT teams, but Snapdragon and Snowball were just as fragile as Sally, and Failsafe's shield wouldn't work as long as he was unconscious. Sally already had a plan in mind for them, and she had a lot to do, so she got to work.

The six Chessboard security guys were the easiest to deal with, as none of them had anything worse than a pistol, and Sally could disarm pistols all day long without breaking a sweat. She ran from suit to suit, ejecting cartridges and unfired bullets and collecting them in an office trash can she appropriated from the reception desk. As she disarmed each man, she also undid his belt and fly and yanked his pants down to his knees. They would be falling all over themselves in no time.

The police officers were tougher to deal with, because they were far more professional and already were starting to point their guns, trying to track the blur racing through their midst. Of the nine officers in the lobby, six of them had enough foresight to wear their riot helmets. Sally removed each man's helmet in turn, turned it around, and strapped it back onto his head facing the wrong way. It wouldn't hurt any of them but for the sudden squishing of their noses, and it would buy her teammates several seconds while the men struggled to free their heads.

She heard the telltale thunder-growl of a weapon being fired in her accelerated perceptions, spotted the muzzle flash out of the corner of her eye, and slid toward the man on her knees to avoid any onrushing bullets. When she reached him, she yanked out his taser and shot him in the neck with it. His slow-motion twitches would have been funny if Sally had any spare moments to laugh. As he started to collapse, she released the clips on his armor vest and equipment harness, letting him fall right out of it. She took a moment to read the labels on his grenades and found he had one each of tear gas, smoke, and flash-bang. She left the other two on the harness and liberated the smoke grenade, yanking out its pin. It grew warm in her hand as she raced across the lobby to set it down between the other two unhelmeted officers and the elevator door.

The elevator made a sonorous gonging, announcing its arrival on the lobby floor, and Sally knew she had to step up her pace. She disarmed one of the remaining officers, used his holdout knife to slit down the sides of his shirt, and then pulled the flap up over his head and tied it.

The last officer swung his assault rifle around toward the elevator doors, spitting flames and bullets faster than Sally could run. The elevator opened and a massive piston of ice pushed outward, chipping away as bullets struck it. Thankful that Snowball had thought ahead in terms of defense, Sally proceeded to disarm the last officer, stripping away all his equipment and ammunition so fast that to anyone else it would have looked like he exploded.

The mass of ice parted like curtains drawing aside and the others emerged, Jason pushing Failsafe's gurney with Snowball escorting in front and Snapdragon above. Sally slowed herself down enough that she could interact with them. "Hurry, you guys. We've only got a couple of minutes at most before backup arrives."

Snapdragon's eyes widened as he saw something behind Sally. "Look out!"

Sally's perceptions accelerated to full and she whirled to see a van's rear end just starting to push through the floor-to-ceiling windows of the entrance. Cracks spread out like they were being mapped by busy spiders, and fragments of safety glass sparkled in the lights like stars. Sally threw herself to the floor as the wave of shards washed over her. Belatedly, a glowing field formed itself around her. She looked toward the gurney and saw Failsafe's eyes were open, albeit just barely. He had one shaking hand raised and a similarly-colored energy field limned it. Better late than never, thought Sally.

The van's rear doors flew open and Detroit Steel leaped out. "Hurry it up. All the cops in the world are on their way."

Sally pointed toward the sky. "Snowball, Snapdragon, go. Don't wait for us."

"But—" began Snowball.

"That's an order, Sara. Be safe."

"Yes, boss. Good luck." Snowball and Snapdragon hurried through the broken window pane and took to the skies, one surfing a wave of ice toward the Hudson river, the other spreading arching floral wings of flame. Fort Justice would be a straight shot south for them if they managed to avoid any interception efforts.

"Damn, son, you look like you got chewed up and spit out." Detroit Steel glanced at Jason as she lifted Failsafe off the gurney.

"Yeah, but you should see the other guy. I said it before, but I'm a little tired to think of new jokes."

"Yo, less jokin', more gettin' your asses in the van!" Hector banged his hand on the dashboard from the driver's seat. "I'm on the motherfuckin' clock here."

Sally stripped out of her shredded clothes, dropped them on the floor, and jumped into the van in her crimson bodysuit. "Get us out of here, Hector."

Hector hammered the accelerator to the floorboards and left a trail of burned rubber all the way across the carefully-plowed apron in front of Chessboard Industries, barreling straight toward a pair of police cars that were racing up the drive and blocking their way out. "Shit! Hang on!" He spun the wheel hard and the van dove into a snow-covered field, half-steering and half-sliding down the embankment until it hit the sidewalk at the bottom with a jolt. "Goddamn, I didn't think that would work."

The van took off, heading south toward Manhattan as howling police interceptors closed in on them.

Twenty

"I've just learned that the fugitives formerly known as Just Cause have attacked and severely damaged an American corporate headquarters under false pretenses. The only way to deal with these criminals has to be termination with extreme sanction. You can't let these so-called heroes run loose anymore, my friends."
—Ken Reichel, First Choice Radio Network

February, 2009
Yonkers, NY

"What's your plan, Hector?" Sally looked out the back windows of the van at the flashing lights in pursuit. The roads were slick with slush and snow, and she was terrified, hating being in cars at the best of times. She counted at least six pursuing vehicles with more joining every couple of blocks, it seemed. It would only be a matter of time before the police drew the net tight around them.

"Plan? I thought you was the brains of this sorry outfit, *malabarista*." Hector gunned the throttle and the van shot through an intersection against the light, narrowly missing getting broadsided by a delivery truck.

Sally gasped as one of the interceptors fishtailed into the truck and spun around the icy intersection like a top. "We're not making any friends in the police department today. We've got to get out of traffic before someone gets killed."

Hector whooped as the van sideswiped a cab. "*Hijo de puta!* Goddamn two lane road . . ."

"Do not go south, go west," said Yunbao.

"Manhattan's south, *gatita.*"

"There is a railroad that leads all the way there, even across the river."

"A railroad?"

Detroit Steel grabbed the back of a seat to keep from being flung against the van's side door as Hector swerved through traffic. "No, she's right. There'll be a service road. No traffic."

"That's good thinking." Sally felt like a popcorn kernel in hot oil the way she was bouncing around.

"I have done my research." Yunbao held up her phone. "Unblocked internet is wonderful."

Three more police cars joined in the chase, and Sally heard the sound of a helicopter even over the roar of the van's engine. "We're not going to lose them. They've got eyes in the sky."

Jason touched Sally's shoulder. "Babe, maybe you should run on your own. You could be back at the pier in a minute or two. Let us draw off the heat."

"No, I'm not leaving anyone behind. Never again, Jase." An idea occurred to her. "But I might be able to slow down the pursuit. Look around for a tire iron or crowbar, would you? Even a big wrench would work."

Jason rummaged through the stuff in the racks along the walls of the van until he came up with something that Sally thought might be a pipe wrench. "How about this?" He looked like he was trying to grin at her through his swollen lips.

"Perfect." She hefted the wrench in her hands, testing its weight. "Hector? Keep going. Head for the tracks, like Yunbao said. Hopefully we can get through."

"You got it." Horns blared as Hector ran another red light. The sounds of collisions followed in their wake.

"Shawna, get the side door for me." Sally pulled her cowl, goggles, and breathing mask up over her face.

Detroit Steel slid open the door, flooding the interior of the van with icy wind and splattering everyone with slush from the front wheels. Sally jumped out and was already pumping her legs as she touched the ground.

She hated running in wet conditions almost as much as she hated running in the cold. Even though she could start and stop on a dime with her speed, she still risked slipping on a wet or icy patch of asphalt, and there was no word for the kind of road rash she'd suffer if she wiped out at a couple hundred miles per hour. The ugly weather conditions made her mad, and she cultivated that flame of anger, knowing she'd need the strength it would lend her.

She made a quick u-turn, perceptions up to maximum, and ran backward through an extreme slow-motion world. She came up beside the first pursuing police car on the passenger side, raised the wrench, and smashed it into the window. It was like watching ice crystals floating on the water as she used the wrench to move the glass pieces out of the way, careful to knock them back so they wouldn't hit the officer in the face. He was just starting to turn to look at Sally, his face twisted into a rictus of concentration.

Sally leaned in across the seat, stretching out her hand as far as she could reach, and shut off the car's ignition. Then she slipped the keys into one of her belt pouches and pushed herself clear of the cruiser. She figured she'd be on the hook for the busted window, but at least she would be able to return the keys once everything was done. It was the small things that mattered. She repeated the process with four more cruisers and then rejoined the van as Hector pointed it toward a chain-link fence.

She yanked open the side door, jumped inside, shut the door, and had herself braced just as the van crashed through the fence, starring the windshield in several places and ripping off both side mirrors with a shower of sparks. The van's rear end swung wide and threatened to roll sideways down a slope, but Hector somehow managed to keep the wheels pointed at the ground. They bounced down the gentle hill, spraying snow in all directions and crashing through a low hedge. The railroad tracks were lined by gray and black slushy snow.

"I hope there ain't nothin' buried out there, because we're gonna hit it if it is." The van seemed like it would shake itself to pieces as it bumped and banged across the service road, which might only see a motor grader once a year to smooth it out. Tools and racks bounced loose, threatening to injure the van's more delicate occupants, namely Sally and Yunbao. "How many cops still back there?"

Sally tried to peek through the windows but the van's violent swinging kept her from getting more than a momentary glance. At her perception speed, though, that was all she needed. "Three cars, Hector."

"I ain't gonna lose them followin' a railroad. There's not a lot of places to get off."

"Just keep going." Sally needed her phone, but was afraid it would be jarred out of her grip even with her faster reaction time. If only there were some way to stabilize the van to keep it running smoothly. Then it occurred to her. "Aramis? You feeling up to doing some work?"

The heavyset Hispanic man groaned. "I feel like *mierda*, Sally. What'd they shoot me up with?"

"No idea, but if we hadn't stopped them, they'd have put a miniature bomb inside your skull."

"Then I'm glad you did. What do you need me to do?"

She tried to figure out how to explain what she was visualizing. "You ever been surfing?"

"Nah. I'd rather sit in the pool, drinking margaritas."

"Oh, me too!" Jason waved his hand in agreement.

"Count me in." Detroit Steel had her feet braced against the floorboards and her hands pushing dents into the roof.

"Not helpful, guys. What I'm trying to ask is if you can make your force field into a bubble underneath the van?" Sally had to use her accelerated reflexes to brace herself as the van bounced over something tall.

"Like a cushion? Yeah, that's easy."

"Can you shape it like a wedge, and put the van on the downhill slope, so the bubble is pushing the van forward and supporting it at the same time? The way I'm picturing it, it would be just like surfing a wave." Sally tried to gesture with her hands but Hector hit something solid and she flew into the air, nearly crashing against the roof.

"I . . . think I get what you're sayin'. You got to open the back doors so I can see what I'm doing."

"I'm on it." Jason wrenched both back doors off their hinges and threw them away. "Nobody fall out, okay?"

Failsafe struggled to sit up, raising his hands and letting his golden energies flow forth from them.

Sally watched him work. "Brace it against the ground. Like a teardrop, pushing us forward and keeping our wheels off the ground."

"I don't know . . . if I could do it on my best day . . ." Failsafe said through gritted teeth.

The back of the van raised up, very suddenly, like it had been grabbed by a crane. Hector yelled something incoherent, and with a loud *crack*, the front end hit something hard enough to rip away the front wheels and axle. Sally saw the pieces go spinning away.

And yet, the van was still moving forward.

Detroit Steel leaned over to look out a side window. "You're doing it, Aramis. I can see the field all around us."

The ride was only slightly smoother than before, but that was due to the irregularities in the ground and the field only dampening them a bit. Hector shut off the engine. Their forward momentum came entirely from riding on a cushion of Failsafe's force field. It was an odd sensation for Sally, rather like trying to balance on a beach ball that wasn't quite fully-inflated or trying to ice-skate with clown shoes. With a lurch, Failsafe forced the van up onto the railroad tracks, making for a much smoother journey.

Failsafe's face had gone pale and he was sweating so hard that steam rose off his head in the cold air. "Don't know how much longer . . ."

Sally patted his arm. "Hang in there, Aramis."

"Yo, there's a bridge comin' up." Hector looked back from the driver's seat.

"That will be the Spuyten Duyvil." Yunbao scrolled through the map on her phone. "After that is Manhattan."

The golden glow around the bottom of the van vanished as Failsafe fell back, eyes shut and hands twitching. The front end dropped onto the rails and skidded, shooting sparks up in twin fountains. "Hang on! I'm gonna—" Detroit Steel threw herself out through the windshield, twisting in midair to face the van in its headlong rush. She punched both hands into the radiator to get a good grip, sending a huge blast of scalding steam into the air, and hunched down to brace her feet against the rails. The van slid to a stop in a few seconds. For a long moment, the only sound was the ticking of hot oil in the van's ruined engine and the whistle of wind around the edges of the broken windshield.

"Is everyone all right?" Sally asked into the silence.

Everyone confirmed they were unhurt, except for Failsafe, who had passed out. They climbed out of the wrecked van and looked upon the destruction they'd wrought upon its humble body. Hector sighed. "This is gonna be a motherfucker to explain to my brother."

Sally squeezed his shoulder. "We'll buy a replacement. Okay, we're hoofing it from here. It's not a long bridge, but we're way too exposed here, and a train could come along at any second. Jason, clear the way, would you, baby?"

A whistle rent the air and Sally turned to see exactly what she'd feared. A train had emerged from Manhattan onto the bridge. They only had seconds to get off the tracks. The driver yanked on the emergency brake but the train wasn't slowing fast enough.

Jason reached underneath the van and tipped it back until he could reach the frame. Detroit Steel grabbed the unconscious Failsafe in one steely arm and held tight to one of the vertical supports. Hector did likewise, while Yunbao scampered up one of the other supports like a monkey. "Sally, I got this. Move." Jason shouldered the van upward, getting his grip secured on the frame.

"But—"

"Go!" He threw the van as hard as he could. The wreck flew through the gap between the rotating center and the fixed Bronx end of the bridge. Sally sidestepped the train just as it whistled past, her perceptions cranked all the way up. Her heart skipped a beat as she thought Jason hadn't gotten clear in time, but then she saw him float out of the way in slow motion. He was beautiful, all laid out the way he was, even with the beating he'd taken from Justice. But as he passed through the air, his face contorted into fear, and Sally realized he'd misjudged his leap, and was going to miss the edge of the bridge. She lunged toward him . . .

. . . and slipped on a patch of ice.

She was airborne for a half a second, trapped in slow motion, unable to get any traction without contacting a solid surface. Jason was going over the edge. By the time she got her feet under her, she wouldn't be able to reach him. "Jason!"

Her right foot touched the bridge floor and she used the traction to twist herself around from her slip and she ran right to the edge of the bridge, afraid she'd see the love of her life plummeting into the frigid river. That was when she realized two things: the bridge was only about five feet above the surface of the water instead of one of the titans that was tall enough for ocean vessels to pass beneath; and Hector had somehow managed to catch Jason's arm, and the two men held each other's wrists as Jason's feet dangled only inches above the water. Sally rushed over to the Man of Nickel as he flexed his metal arm to pull Jason back onto the bridge.

Sally gave Hector a quick kiss—but not so quick that he missed it. His eyes widened in surprised as she stepped back. "*Gracias.*" She turned to embrace Jason. "You asshole. You scared the hell out of me."

"I love you too."

An approaching helicopter drowned out anything Sally would have said. Sirens also sounded from the Hudson as two police boats closed on the bridge. "This is the NYPD," said a voice over a loudspeaker. "You are under arrest."

A glacier appeared in front of the approaching police boats, rising out of the water and forcing them to veer away. Overhead, a brilliant arc of flame made the helicopter circle away. With a roar, a VTOL jet dropped out of the sky to hover on the opposite side of the bridge from the patrol boats. Sally's heart leaped into her throat as she recognized the *Dorothy*. Her jet nozzles made river water flash into great billows of steam, acting as an effective camouflage from above. The side hatch opened and Davey was there, wearing an all-black jumpsuit that looked to be a size or two too big from her. Sally figured she must have borrowed it from Jack's store in the jet. She waved at Sally and Sally waved back.

Snapdragon cruised by overhead, his magnificent flame wings illuminating the steam clouds in gold and orange like his namesake. He loosed another flame jet in the general direction of the thrum of helicopter blades, careful not to get too close. After all, as Sally would have reminded him, the police were not their enemies.

Snowball slid down the end of her ice ramp to touch down upon the bridge. With one hand she fed more ice onto her glacier, spreading it across the Spuyten Duyvil until it touched the banks of each shore. With the other, she made a beautiful, ornate bridge of her own, stretching to the open hatch of the *Dorothy*. Her bridge was almost a work of art, with graceful, swooping curves and inverted icicles giving it a feel of an icy version of wrought-iron. "I know, it's goddamn gorgeous. Ice sculptures are transient things, noted for their impermanence, especially when they're being constantly melted by jet engines. You guys want to get a move on already? This is harder than it fucking looks."

Sally shook herself. It finally hit her that they were being rescued. And on the heels of that thought, she was furious with her teammates for disobeying her orders. And then, at last, she was grateful that they had. "Move it, guys. Shawna, get Aramis."

Detroit Steel hefted Failsafe in her arms. "Got him."

Jason and Hector followed her aboard the *Dorothy*. Yunbao paused at the base of Snowball's ramp. "You must not leave this ice here. It will be a hazard to river traffic."

Snowball nodded. "Yeah, yeah, I got it. Can't let the crunchies be at risk, even though we're all looking at federal prison because of one of them."

"That'll be enough of that, Sara. And Yunbao's right. I want this floe gone."

"We'll get it, me and Nabil. Get on the *Dorothy*, boss. You can write me up for insubordination later."

"Don't think I won't, Sara."

Snowball flashed her a tight smile. "I know. That's why you're a good leader. Juice made the right choice."

Sally headed into the *Dorothy*. "What are you doing here, Davey?"

"Assisting you." Davey's mass of blonde hair was pulled back into a tight bun and she had a shapeless toque over it all. "Minerva and Ment took care of securing Fort Justice while I came here to play superhero with the big kids." She winked. "There are still people at HQ who are loyal to you and Juice and your team, and Ment is making sure those are the people still running the show over there."

"You realize we may be facing an assault from the Feds before this is all said and done. I want you and all civilians cleared off the platform immediately. I won't have you getting caught in a crossfire."

"I don't plan to wind up as a name in a Wikipedia entry about the Federal assault on Fort Justice. Instead, you're going to tell me your brilliant plan to save us all from our inevitable destruction by a jealous and vengeful Senator."

"Not just yet. Has Shillelagh checked in?"

"We just heard from her five minutes before we dropped in on you. She said she's *where you started*, whatever that means. And no, don't tell me. Plausible deniability and all that."

Outside, Snapdragon flew along the top of Snowball's glacier, dousing it liberally with his flame jet, while Snowball broke apart the softened chunks into slush. Some of it might drift back together and freeze, but that wouldn't make anything serious enough to be dangerous. After a minute of work, the two of them flew back into the *Dorothy* and Sally told the pilot, "Hit it, Hurley."

Zach Hurley brought the jets up to full and the *Dorothy* lifted away from the bridge and water. "We have two helicopters shadowing us. One is NYPD and the other is a Sky News chopper. Radio traffic suggests that more are on the way. Orders?"

"We need to swing out over Spanish Harlem to pick up Shillelagh, and then back to the castle, Hurley. It's time to end this, one way or another."

"We're not going to fight the Feds, are we?" Jason yawned. "I mean, I'm willing, but man, I'm beat."

"No. We're going to play our trump card and then we're going to wait for the consequences."

"You think we'll get arrested?" asked Snowball.

"I don't doubt it for a second. But if things shake out the way I hope, it might not be for very long." Sally gave Hurley the address of Hector's brother's garage, and told him, "Don't save on fuel to get there."

"Roger that, ma'am." Hurley opened up the afterburners wide.

* * *

The *Dorothy* had a *quiet mode* for her engines, Hurley admitted it was a very loose definition of the term. "It'll still drown out people's TVs. It just won't shake their pictures off their walls."

"This is the middle of Spanish Harlem." Sally looked at the cityscape below, decorated in shades of gray and white. "We can't land just anywhere."

"Not if you wanna keep your hubcaps," said Hector. "Or whatever this airplane has."

"It's a *jet* . . ." Hurley sounded offended.

"Whatever, *cabron*."

Sally stood up from her seat. "Okay, then, drop me and Hector. The rest of you head back to Fort Justice."

"Yes, ma'am. Curbside service coming right up." Hurley dipped the *Dorothy*'s portside wing and dropped her into a spiraling descent that ended with a hard jolt on the snowy street. A lone snowplow skidded into a fishtail as the driver realized a jet had dropped onto the roadway.

"Minerva, you're in charge until I get back. Defend the castle walls if you have to, but God, don't hurt anybody. If everything works out, this will all be over in a few hours and we'll be back in business." Sally clasped her friend's hand.

"And if it doesn't?"

"We might as well look into countries without extradition treaties."

Minerva smiled. "I hear Croatia's nice."

Hector jumped out of the open hatch onto the steaming road surface. "Hey, you coming or are you gonna stand there and gab all evening?"

"I'm coming, Hector." Sally hopped down to the road and ran to the shadow of a building. As soon as Hector was clear, she ordered Hurley to take off, and was treated to the impressive sight of the *Dorothy* flinging herself back into the dusk sky.

They hadn't been able to land right outside the garage, which was fine with Sally. It gave her and Hector a chance to disappear into Spanish Harlem on foot, attracting far less attention without the jet. By the time they'd walked two blocks from their drop-off site, the orange streetlights were spitting themselves into life, and people came out onto the streets despite the weather, congregating to chat or to share in the serious business of drinking. Sally turned up her collar and pulled her hat down low to hide her face, while all Hector had to do was transform out of his body of nickel to become just another anonymous New Yorker.

"Thanks again for your help, Hector." They crossed a street, hustling to avoid a pizza driver going far too fast for the road conditions. "But I'm sorry we got you involved. I know you were trying to keep a low profile."

"Shit. You didn't have to ask. I'm tellin' you, Martina . . . she was a good kid. She didn't deserve to have her fuckin' head blown apart. You got the shit you needed from that company?"

Sally smiled into the freezing wind. "Yes. Yes we did. And believe me, Hector, we're going to make them pay dearly for Martina . . . and Jack, and Juice, and even Syndicate S, because they were just as much victims as everybody else. Chessboard made them to be patsies for The Militia, and we already know they made The Militia too. It all ties back to Senator Goodwin, and I've put together a case against her that nobody will be able to ignore or sweep under the rug."

"Assumin' they don't bust a cap in your ass first. You're playin' with the kind of people who don't take this kind of shit lightly."

"I know, and I'm doing what I can to watch out for my team."

"You need to watch out for yourself, too, *chica*."

"I've got you to do that, Hector." Sally paused. "I want you to come work for me."

Hector snorted. "I ain't no superhero. I'm an ex-con."

"I've got one of those on my team." Sally smiled. "He's on parole. Look, Hector, I know you're not a front-line kind of guy, and I respect that. You're a hell of a good trainer and you're streetwise like nobody else. I could use someone like you."

"To do what?"

Sally lowered her voice. "There are times when I can't act in an official capacity. Times when I can't ask anyone on my team to do something that is illegal. And there are times that I look at them and say to myself what they all really need is a good table leg upside the head. Know what I mean?"

Hector burst out laughing. "You want someone to do your dirty work for you?"

"No, I want someone who I can trust to watch my back while I'm doing it. If something's got to be done that's going to risk someone getting arrested, I'm the one going to assume that risk. I can't ask anyone on my team to do that. Think of yourself as an independent government contractor. You do a job, you get paid handsomely, and at the end of the day, if you need a good sparring session and nobody else will oblige, I'll strap on the gloves again."

"You really gonna put faith in a fuck-up like me?"

"You're no fuck-up. I could tell that from the first day I met you. I have nothing but respect for you."

"Respect. Yeah. Respect is good. Hey, there's your girl." He nodded his head toward someone beyond Sally's shoulder.

She turned to see Shillelagh crossing the street toward them, her hood low against the blowing snow. Sally halfway expected to hear the roar of an engine and to see the bad guys trying to run her teammate down. That's what would have happened in the movies, but so far, they'd managed to stay one step ahead of their pursuers, and Sally intended to keep it that way. "You all right, Eileen?"

"I'm fine. Can we get out of this weather pretty soon? Jail sounds nice and warm compared to this."

"I couldn't agree more. You still have the USB drive?"

Shillelagh handed it to her.

"Hector, does your brother have a computer in his shop? With internet?"

Hector snorted. "What you think this is, the fucking Dark Ages?"

"Let's go."

"What are we going to do?" asked Shillelagh.

"Knock down the castle walls."

Twenty-One

*"We interrupt the Ken Reichel Show with breaking
news and now go live to our headline news desk . . ."*
—First Choice Radio Network Interruption of the
Ken Reichel Show

February, 2009
New York City, NY

Sally reached out to her friend Vanitha, the parahuman hacker known as Kali, using Hector's brother's computer. The two of them had conducted a high-speed instant message conversation, facilitated by both Sally's super-speed and Vanitha's ability to transmit herself into any computer via a phone line. They'd made a plan together, with Vanitha agreeing to fulfill Sally's requests as they were less about working against Chessboard as a client of hers and more about allowing Sally to transmit her information on a wide-ranging basis when the time came. Sally suspected that once Vanitha saw the data Sally had recovered from Chessboard, she would have agreed to help in even more ways.

You remember the woman who interviewed Juice in Playboy a few months back? Sally typed, her fingers blurring across the keyboard.

Yes. Good interview. But then I only read it for the articles. Honest.

If you can put me in contact with her, I'll give her the scoop first. Then you can open the floodgates.

That's the easy part. I can put her article on the wire. AP, Reuters, Al-Jazeera. Within minutes after she posts hers, every news agency in the world will have it and they'll all want to put it front and center on their websites, and cover it on their networks. This will be legendary. After a brief pause, she added, *I hope you know what you're doing.*

Me too.

After that, she and Shillelagh returned to Fort Justice. It was the middle of the night and despite patrol boats circling around the oil platform, Minerva found a way through the sweeping spotlights to collect Sally and Shillelagh. She used her ability to transfer flight powers to others, and the three of them swooped over the choppy black water in silence. Sally was terrified that she would fall, that somehow Minerva's abilities would fail, but Minerva reassured her the entire flight across the bay and when they touched down on the icy deck with Minerva's cape flowing around them all like a flag, Sally was only shaking from the cold, not fear.

She took a steaming hot shower, luxuriating in the spray for several minutes with her perceptions accelerated, which made it feel like she'd spent an hour in a spa. Afterward, she dressed in a clean costume and joined Davey in her office.

"I can't believe this shit." Davey waved at the flatscreens. She'd replaced the scenic desert environments with dozens of windows from the data contained on Sally's USB drive, as sorted and catalogued by Vanitha. "I'd be shocked if Oswalt isn't already on the run. There's enough information here to send her to Guantanamo for a very long time."

"I don't suppose you've had the time to put together some kind of presentation for me," said Sally, mostly joking.

"Not yet. Sorry about that. It's a lot to sort through. But if your story doesn't jump around too much when you tell it, I think I can find enough supporting documentation to add some local color."

"Are you sure you're not a parahuman after all? Super-information-processing?"

"No. Took the test twice to be sure." Davey smiled. "I'm just that damn good." She touched the omnipresent Bluetooth headset. "Go ahead." She paused, listening. "All right, thanks. Tell her we'll be ready in one minute."

"What, did Van—uh, Kali already track down Ms. Bradley?" Sally dashed over to her desk, pulled a small mirror from her junk drawer, and checked her hair.

"She did, and apparently Ms. Bradley is waiting to take our video call. Your friend moves fast."

"The two of you would make a hell of a team. Um, do I look okay?"

Davey glanced up from her tablet to appraise Sally. "You look . . ."

"What?"

"Heroic." Davey smiled. "Knock 'em dead, boss."

Sally smiled. "Watch this."

A new window appeared on one of the flatscreens, showing a woman seated in front of a computer with an indistinct dim room behind her. She looked a few years older than Sally, and had her hair pinned up on top of her head. Her glasses reflected her computer screen like tiny white windows and she had a large mug of coffee clutched in her hands. "It's really you. I wasn't sure."

"Cheryl Bradley? I'm Salena Tibbets, a.k.a. Mustang Sally. I'm glad you agreed to take my call."

"Your . . . friend made a very convincing case on your behalf. I must say that I've seen some very strange things in my time working for *Playboy*, but having a naked woman appear out of my computer and then set up a video call for me is in the top ten. Maybe the top five."

She sipped at her coffee. Sally was just thinking that she could really use a cup herself when Davey set one down beside her on the desk. Sally nodded in gratitude.

"You're a very popular young woman right now, Ms. Tibbets. There's a federal warrant out for your arrest, and the media's all up in arms over some kind of smash-and-grab that you and your team pulled earlier today. So the fact that you've reached out to me has piqued my interest. I'm recording this interview, so you know. And your friend has apparently set up some kind of transcription software, and I'm watching it fill up pages as we speak. This thing is practically writing my article for me. I may be in love."

"She's good at stuff like that."

"I hope you can arrange an interview with her at a later date."

"I'll see what I can do. Shall we begin?"

Bradley nodded. "Take it from the top and let's see what shakes out."

Sally took a deep breath, gathering her thoughts. She knew she could shift back and forth between accelerated perceptions and normal time, allowing her enough time to plan what to say next, but the more she did that, the more likely she was to forget herself and come across all chirpy like a cartoon character, which was something she didn't need to let get out into the public. "This whole story begins with a promising young MMA fighter named Martina Hladky, who died under suspicious circumstances a month ago. Her death, which I'll go into detail over in a moment, led to an insidious conspiracy involving illegal medical experimentation, murder, framing members of Just Cause and the PRA for crimes they did not commit, and goes all the way up to a United States Senator intending to dissolve Just Cause, strip away parahuman civil rights, and create her own private super-powered army. How's that sound for starters?"

Bradley's mouth fell open. "It sounds like a goddamn Pulitzer Prize. Tell me more about Martina Hladky."

Sally sipped her own coffee and began her tale.

* * *

Two hours later, Sally had talked her voice husky and worked herself up into a bout of real, righteous anger over the events that had transpired since she'd taken charge of Just Cause New York. Bradley had asked numerous canny questions, leading Sally to the next parts of her story without putting words into her mouth. When Bradley asked if Sally thought that Chessboard's illegal human experimentation constituted domestic terrorism, Sally said yes without even having to think about it.

"I witnessed their so-called Touchstone Technology in action. It's Zoe Oswalt's parahuman ability to grant powers to others, but it appears to be completely random and unsafe. She gave a security guard super-strength, only to have his muscles grow so big so quickly that he couldn't move. He couldn't even draw a breath. She killed that man right in front of me. How many others died in the process of her creating Senator Goodwin's private army? And how many more of them didn't die but are now slaves with the threat of having their heads blown off by implanted bombs?"

"You've got as close to an airtight case here as I've ever seen. Data. Reports. Video. Even if you obtained it illegally, it's still very compelling."

Sally took a deep breath. This was where she was walking on thin ice. "I didn't obtain it illegally. We had specific instructions to do so from acting director Sapo of the PRA."

"He's in Senator Goodwin's pocket." Bradley shook her head. "That's practically public knowledge. Why would he tell you to do something that would jeopardize his career like that?"

Sally held up her phone. "I have a recording here of him telling me to do just that. To fight terrorism. To stop the planes before they hit the buildings." She enabled playback on the phone.

"That's fine, Director, but until then, I need clarification on our duties as heroes. Are we supposed to sit around waiting for trouble to start and then respond? Or are we supposed to actively prevent it?"

"I . . . I don't understand."

"Director, I know you're not an idiot. Are we a deterrent or a response force? Do we wait for the planes to hit the buildings and then respond, or do we stop them if we can?"

"Stop them, of course!"

"Thank you, Director."

Bradley's eyes widened. "That's pretty thin. You don't think that will hold up, do you?"

"It will." Sally sat down at her desk, only to stand up again a moment later. She had so much nervous energy it was a fight to keep from pacing too fast to interact with anyone. "Because he's going to back me up on it."

Minerva came into Sally's office without knocking. She looked irritated but didn't interrupt Sally's video chat. Sally glanced at her and Minerva cocked her head and eyebrows in a clear *we need to talk* motion.

"Okay, last question. You've gone over a mountain of data here and built a strong case against Chessboard and against Senator Goodwin. What's next for Mustang Sally and Just Cause?"

Sally sighed. "All we ever wanted to do was be superheroes, and by that I mean to serve and protect the innocent from those threats only we can address.

I've spent my entire life training to do that, and as long as I can still put one foot in front of the other, I'll be the one running to danger instead of from it. I hope the evidence we've gathered here will be enough to let us all get back to doing that, because we can't help anyone from the inside of a cell in Deep Six."

"My article is practically already written. I need about half an hour to get everything finalized and then I can upload it to the server. It'll hit *Playboy* right away. Your friend gave me an email address to send it to after that, and she said it'll populate to news outlets worldwide. You really need to let me talk to her."

Sally smiled. "I'm not in a position to say yes or no to that. She's a friend, not part of Just Cause."

"Okay then. I'll send you a copy."

"Hurry. I have a feeling we're going to need to move very fast on this." Bradley broke the connection and Sally turned to Minerva. "What is it?"

"Feds. They've brought boats and are surrounding the platform. Helicopters as well. Marine gunships. Also, radar says there's an *Arleigh Burke*-class Destroyer inbound."

Sally grimaced. "They're going all out to make sure we come quietly or not at all." She turned to Davey. "I don't think we're going to have time to wait for Bradley's article to come out. Can you summarize my presentation so I have something to send out on my own?"

"Already have. And Kali has sent us a distribution list with some very, um, astonishing names on it. Did you know she's got the President's email address? I mean, his private email. The one nobody is supposed to know."

"I'm not surprised. Send the file to Michael Sapo."

"Done."

Sally still had Sapo's number on her phone. She punched it in and waited. "Sally?" he asked immediately when he answered. He must have recognized her number.

"Hello, Director. We need to talk."

"Sally, where are you?"

"You know exactly where I am. I'm with my team, in our headquarters, and we're surrounded by law enforcement intending to board us and arrest us."

"My advice to you is to let them."

"I think perhaps you'll want to reconsider your position, Director, and I'm going to tell you why. Open your email. We've sent you something. Go ahead, I'll wait while you page through it." Sally covered the mouthpiece of the phone and looked at Minerva. "Do what you can to stall the Feds. Don't let them aboard. Do not engage them under any circumstances. Passive defenses only. Have Snowball freeze shut the exterior doors and slope all the stairwells. Same thing with the helipad."

"Sally, what is all this? This is terrible." A note of real fear sounded in Sapo's voice.

"Yes, it is, and you're going to be stuck in the middle of it unless you do two things for us."

"Which are?"

"You need to announce—publicly—that we were operating under your orders, and you need to contact the director of whatever agency is leading the operation to arrest us and tell them to withdraw their forces."

"I will do no such thing."

"Director . . . *Michael*, you're not thinking this through. This is your career at stake here. It's well-known that you're Goodwin's stooge, and we have a lot of evidence implicating her in the Chessboard operation. I have a recording of you telling me to be proactive and to stop the terrorism before it starts. Do you deny we had that conversation?"

"You . . . recorded it?"

"Legal in the state of New York, Director. If you disavow us, I make that recording public. That will be the end of your career. Chessboard is involved in domestic terrorism, and we have the evidence to prove it. Nobody in the government or the public is going to look very favorably on a politician embracing terrorism."

"But . . . Senator Goodwin . . . she'll destroy me."

"She can't without it looking petty and vindictive and she won't want to tarnish her image further. You throw her under the bus and you come out looking like a hero. You sent Just Cause to break up a domestic terrorist threat. Otherwise, you look like a stooge." Sally winked at Davey, who grinned and gave her a thumbs-up. "This information went to the press a few minutes before you got it. In less than an hour, it will be the top story of every major news outlet on the planet, and by tomorrow morning, the whole world will know about it. You can't stop this, Michael, you can only get out of the way."

"You went to the press with this. Jesus, Salena. You know what this means?"

"It means we won. And Senator Goodwin lost. And you need to pick your side right now. Call whoever's in charge of coming out to arrest us and tell them to call off their dogs. Your phone is going to start ringing nonstop anytime now from reporters wanting a comment. You better figure out what you're going to tell them."

Sapo sighed into the phone. "You've put me into a hell of a bind here."

"Yes I have. I won't have my team wrongly accused of crimes they didn't commit, and won't have them used as political pawns in somebody's bigger game. We're superheroes, Director, and we're going to do our jobs. You can either back us, or you can face the consequences of not doing so." Sally felt like chewing her nails down to the bone. She had her hand hovering over the tremendous house of cards she'd built, the final piece clutched in her fingers. If she laid it down correctly, she'd have a completed construction. But if she'd miscalculated at any point, it would all come crashing down around her.

"All right. You win. I'll call the FBI, and I'll back you up. I don't like it, but the alternative is even worse."

"Very good, Director. I appreciate it. I'll make sure my report figures you in favorably. And one last thing . . . You're clearly not cut out of the right mold to make these types of game-changing decisions. You may want to consider resigning your position. I'm sure James Forsythe would very much like his old job back, and I'm willing to bet he's going to be released shortly."

"Fine, whatever you like. Now if you'll excuse me, I have to make a phone call and figure out how to salvage my career."

"I'm sure you'll do just fine, Michael." Sally felt buoyed as if she were full of helium. "People like you tend to land on their feet."

Sapo hung up and Sally set her phone down.

"Well?" asked Davey. "Did we win? It sounded like we won."

"We won." Sally high-fived her assistant.

"What happens now?"

"We wait to see if Sapo follows through, and wait for Bradley's article to hit the wire. I guess there's nothing left to do but wait."

* * *

Bradley's article hit the news wires with the inevitability of an approaching tidal wave. As it was getting picked up and spread across the world media circuits, the boats and helicopters circling Fort Justice pulled back, and the approaching destroyer turned and headed back out to sea. Sally sat in the medical wing where Jason was recovering from his savage beating at the hands of Justice and the two of them channel-surfed between news sites, tagging each one as it picked up the story.

At last, Sally fell asleep, sprawled across Jason in his hospital bed, lulled into unconsciousness by the droning tones of the talking heads reporting on Just Cause halting a domestic terrorist plot. She was shaken awake some time later by an exhausted Davey. "What is it?"

"It's big. The whole thing's gone viral. I've seen it reported on every network. There are thousands of new links appearing online every minute." Davey laughed. "Chinese and Middle Eastern media outlets have reported on it."

"Is that good?"

"It's not bad, that's for sure. Zoe Oswalt has gone missing, and the Justice Department has opened an investigation into Chessboard. We're expecting the Feds to issue a warrant for Oswalt's arrest shortly. The PRA is holding a press conference in less than an hour, and the President announced he will be addressing the nation immediately thereafter."

"What about Goodwin?"

"She made a statement about an hour ago. She categorically denied any wrongdoing."

"Of course. Is she going to be in trouble?"

"I'm not sure. We're in a gray area here. She's a sitting Senator, and there would have to be a resolution passed by a two-thirds majority in the Senate, and the Democrats don't have that. I doubt they could get more than one or two Republicans to cross the aisle to support it, and that's the only way she gets expelled from the Senate. All we can hope is that her party leadership decides she's toxic and they ask her to resign. They can't afford for this shit to blow back upon them."

"And she still walks?"

"Most likely into a cushy career of speaking engagements or getting a prime gig on Fox News."

"You know that recording I made of her in her office, right? We can't use that?"

"Of course we can, but this is the only way to remove a Senator, unless she resigns. Otherwise, we just have to believe that she can be voted out in the next election. I'll make sure you get your registration updated before that date." Davey yawned. "I've been up for two days straight, Sally. If you can manage to keep things running without me, I've got a hot date with my pillow."

Sally smiled. "You are amazing. Thank you for everything you've done. Take a few days off. You've earned them."

"You're a good boss, you know." Jason's voice was thick and sleepy. "But you're hell at letting a guy sleep."

Sally kissed his nose, making him wince. "I'm just leaving. I've got stuff to do. You stay here and rest up, okay? I'll check on you in a little while."

"You better."

"I love you, you big goof."

"I love you too, Sally."

Twenty-Two

*"Is the Goodwin Act dead in the water? Yes, for now.
But I can certainly see reintroducing a new version of
it in the future. This is only, if you'll pardon the
expression, a speed bump."*
                              —Senator Christine Goodwin (R-NY)

February, 2009
New York City, NY

Jason made enough popcorn to fill a small movie
theater and distributed baggies of it amongst the heroes
and staffers in the Command Center as they got ready
to watch the President's address. Some speeches had
the text released to the press in advance but this one
was largely a mystery to the talking heads and political
blogs. Speculation ran rampant, and a few enterprising
staffers had even put together an insanely complicated
pool based upon mentions of specific names.

Sally put twenty dollars in on her own name and
fifty on Juice's. She could have dropped more; one of
the problems of being part of an organization that
provided room and board and a generous uniform
allowance was she had far more money than she knew
what to do with. She donated sums to various charities,
set more of it aside in a retirement fund, and she and

Jason had discussed the possibility of college funds for the family they'd start someday. It had almost been a relief to pay off Vanitha for her assistance, because it felt like she was actually doing something to benefit herself with it for a change.

The networks all cut away to the President's desk in the Oval Office and the conversations in the Command Center died down as the President leaned forward and spoke in his rhythmic, soothing baritone. "My fellow Americans, good evening. Tonight I want to tell you a story about a group of heroic men and woman who, at no small risk to themselves, uncovered a terrorist plot and halted it before it could be put to use against American citizens. I'm speaking, of course, about Just Cause New York—" Cheers and whoops sounded through the Command Center. Sally snuggled a little closer to Jason, enjoying the smell of buttered popcorn permeating his hair. "—and their leader, Mustang Sally, whom I had the pleasure to meet in person only a few short weeks ago . . ."

The accumulated heroes and staffers drowned out the President's speech for a minute while they applauded and cheered for Sally and for themselves. Sally wished she could run away and hide, embarrassed by the adulation, but knew it would be a poor showing of her in her leadership role. Instead she waved her hands to try and calm everyone down. She really did want to hear the President's speech, because she was hoping for a couple of specific points that had been gathering traction in the political rumor mill. Sure enough, the President announced he was immediately reinstating James Forsythe to his position of Director of the Parahuman Resources Agency, and had asked the FBI to release Jack Raymond from custody, as clear evidence had been presented to show his innocence in the shooting of Senator Christine Goodwin.

Sally smiled. She hadn't spoken directly to the

President, but had taken a call from one of his staffers. The young woman had asked for Sally's input on what she would like the President to bring up in his speech, and Sally had said *free Jack Raymond and reinstate James Forsythe to his former position* without even having to think about it. It seemed the President had agreed with those terms. She pulled out her phone and sent a text to Zach Hurley, asking him to be ready to take the *Dorothy* out to collect Jack, because she wasn't about to make her friend wait for a ferry in the cold and snow after what he'd been through.

"Looks like you won, babe." Jason kissed her palm with his buttery lips.

"Yeah, it kind of does, doesn't it? It feels good to get one after everything that went wrong the past month."

Sally whispered into Jason's ear, "I know something else that would feel good. Go back to our quarters and wait for me. I won't be long."

He almost dropped his popcorn in his rush to leave the Command Center as casually as possible, grinning like a dog about to get a turkey leg.

Sally leaned over to Minerva. "Can you let me know when Jack gets back?"

"Of course." Minerva's nose wrinkled just a little and Sally felt her ears get hot. Surely she couldn't smell *that*, could she? And then Sally realized that she didn't care, and winked at Minerva.

Minerva's face reddened and Sally felt a little thrill of triumph as she sauntered out of the Command Center like a general returning home after winning the war.

It wasn't a bad analogy when she thought about it.

* * *

The following morning Sally awakened to a text from Davey that Jack had returned and he was waiting in her office. *He made you coffee*, Davey texted with what Sally thought was a peevish air. Sally didn't mind; Jack had made her very first cup of coffee all those years ago when she'd been a fresh-faced eighteen-year-old intern with Just Cause. It felt like a lifetime ago, even though it had barely been half a decade. Perhaps her constant acceleration of her perceptions made her life seem like it was blazing past in comparison to that of other people. Or maybe it was just something that happened as people got older.

Nevertheless, Sally didn't want to keep Jack waiting. He'd spent far too long as a guest of the state in the Solitary Housing Unit, and he didn't need to spend more time waiting for her. She dashed through the shower, using a washcloth to scrub down as the falling water didn't hit her fast enough for her patented twenty-second shower—much easier to pull off since she'd cut her hair. She spent an additional minute getting dressed, fixing her hair, brushing her teeth, and was out the door and heading for her office only three minutes after getting her notification. Not too shabby.

The first thing Sally noticed was that Jack had started to grow a beard. "What the hell is that all over your face, Raymond?" She poked at his stubble, surprised at how much gray was mixed into it.

"You like it? I think it makes me look more dashing. Like Indiana Jones in the jungles of Peru."

"You look more like his dad. All you need are the glasses and a tweed walking cap."

Jack smiled. "You're such a nerd for knowing that's what it was called, Sally."

And then they hugged like the longtime friends they were, and it felt to Sally like things were back to normal . . . except that Jack seemed a little standoffish. It was apparent enough that she stepped back. "What is it, Jack? Is everything all right?"

"Yes. No. Kind of."

"Talk to me."

Jack slipped past her to her desk and retrieved a tall hazelnut latte that he'd probably made himself down in the cafeteria. "Here. Special, just for you."

Sally's eyes fell upon the envelope sitting on her desk beside where her coffee had been resting. She looked back at Jack. "What is that?"

He grimaced. "I practiced this all while I was in jail. I got really good at it. It was just supposed to roll off my tongue totally naturally, but . . . Damn, Sally, it's hard to face you and say this."

"Jack?" Sally felt tears start to prick the corners of her eyes. She had a sinking feeling she knew what was coming, and she didn't want to accept it.

"I'm done, Sally. It's time to hang up my pistols for good. I've been doing this since before you were born. I'm . . . shit, I'm looking down the barrel at fifty in a couple of years. The world's changed. Everything's changed, and I'm tired. I'm so tired of being a superhero, Sally."

Sally saw tears in Jack's eyes and it nearly wrecked her for good. "You're always going to be a superhero, Jack, even if you're not in Just Cause anymore. That's who you are, not what you do."

"Don't try to talk me out of it." Jack dashed the back of his hand across his eyes. "I'm not going to be swayed from this."

"Jack, we both know that if I asked you to stay, you'd stay. You'd stay until you died on the job. I mean, I do want you to stay, but I understand why you can't. I'd be lying if I said I didn't think this was on the horizon. Not with Sondra back in Denver and you here." Sally took his hand.

"You sure you don't want to talk me out of it?" Jack put on a brave, hopeful smile. "I'm pretty weak-willed."

"Don't make this more difficult than it needs to be. You're one of my closest friends, and I know that if I ever really need you, you'll be covering my back." Sally smiled at him. "I know Sondra wants to have your baby."

Jack snorted. "Yeah, she's brought that up a few times. And by a few times, I mean pretty much every conversation we've had for the past year."

Sally squeezed his hand. "You'll be a terrific father, Jack. You've been one to me in a lot of ways, and I can't thank you enough for that. You just promise me that I get to be the baby's godmother, and we'll call it even."

"Long as you'll return the favor when you and Jason have a rugrat of your own."

"You can be my baby's godmother." Sally giggled.

Jack nodded toward the envelope. "Those are my forms. They're all signed. It wasn't easy, but I did it."

"I'll notify the troops and file all the requisite bullshit where it belongs. I hope you know that we're going to have a retirement party that will attain such epic embarrassment levels that folks will be talking about it for years."

Jack grinned. "That's more like it. I want strippers in a giant cake. Hookers and blow."

Sally smiled back. "I'll see what I can do. You want to stick around to tell everyone else?"

Jack shook his head. "No, I just got out of jail. I'm going to go buy a new suit and then fly home to see my wife and try to get her pregnant."

"Thanks for sharing, goofball."

"Sorry, didn't realize you were sensitive about suits."

Sally gave him a friendly shove. "You know what I mean. Promise me you'll come back so we can send you off properly."

"I promise." Jack extended his hand. "It has been a true pleasure and an incredible honor to work alongside and for you, Sally."

Sally took his hand. "Likewise, Jack. You've been a great teacher and friend." She drew him into an embrace and he didn't resist. "Good luck, Jack Raymond."

* * *

Sometimes it seemed like the paperwork was multiplying even as Sally worked on it. She'd spent the morning since saying goodbye to Jack wrestling with her reports and documentation of recent events. Her coffee had grown cold twice and she'd had to run to the microwave to reheat it. It wasn't that she didn't want it; she got so engrossed in her work that she lost track of time and by the time she remembered it, it had grown cold again. At last, she made herself drink it lukewarm. Jack had made it for her; it wouldn't be right for her not to finish it.

Davey popped her head into the office. "Anything I can do to help with those reports?"

Sally looked up, surprised at the interruption. She realized that she had pencils behind each ear and was twirling another through her fingers like a propeller. "You want to finish them for me? Then I can pretend that they don't exist, and go back to being a regular superhero."

"Yes, I can wrap them up for you. But before you go back to being a regular superhero, you have a call from the PRA."

Sally's heart leaped. "Juice?"

"Yes."

"Well, put him through."

"Line one on your office phone." Davey paused. "You know how to get line one, right?"

Sally snorted. "I'm not completely helpless." The phone had a lot of buttons and indicator lights on it. One of them had to be line one, right?

"Top left. *Park pickup* and then number one."

"I knew that."

"Of course." Davey's tone made it clear that she knew Sally was full of shit, and she knew that Sally knew that she knew.

Sally pushed the buttons. "Hello? This is Sally."

"Sally, it's James."

"I'm really happy to hear your voice, sir."

"Knock off that *sir* shit. We've had that discussion before." Sally could hear the smile in his voice, though.

"It's just . . . you know."

"Yeah, I know."

"You know Jack just retired this morning?"

"I thought he might. He called me overnight to talk about it. I can't say as I blame him. He ran in the big leagues even longer than I did. Did you know we came up through Just Cause together? We both started in '85. He was in college and I was finishing law school. Your mom helped train us both."

"That's cool."

"I'm hoping that after a couple of months off, Jack gets bored enough that he'll take a position with the PRA. I could use a good assistant director to fill in for me the next time I get arrested for contempt."

"I'm sorry about that."

"It's not your fault in the least. I'd have done it no matter what. Some things are worth fighting for." He paused. "You did really good with this one, Sally. I'm proud of you."

"I never know if I'm doing the right thing or not. I feel like I'm guessing almost all the time."

"With most leaders, that's just the way it goes. The good ones guess right more often than not. You're guessing right, Sally. That's why you're in charge of the big team."

Sally snorted. "This isn't the big team. That's the one back home. In Denver."

"I'm afraid not. New York is the most important city in America, and your team is the one in charge of protecting it, along with the rest of the Atlantic seaboard. Like it or not, yours is the one that people will most closely associate with Just Cause."

"Thanks, because I really need the pressure."

"You thrive under it. I didn't choose you or your teammates lightly. You just keep doing what you're doing and you'll keep making me proud."

"What if I screw up?"

"You will. It happens to all of us. It's not the mistakes that define us, it's what we learn from them."

"That's really profound. You should write that down."

"I'm working on a book, as a matter of fact."

"I'll put it on my shelf when it comes out."

"I'll bring it to you myself. Keep up the good work, Sally. What's next on your agenda?"

"*Once more unto the breach, dear friends.*"

Juice chuckled. "Good luck with that."

* * *

True to Davey's prediction, it was looking more and more like Goodwin was going to come out of the whole mess with no worse than a bullet wound and a slightly bruised reputation. She'd had her own people spinning everything to make it look like she'd been an unwitting participant in Zoe Oswalt's machinations. With Oswalt missing and the Feds hot on her trail, it wasn't hard to convince the public who was really at fault in sound bites between reporting on the Super Bowl and the weather. There was an official investigation just getting underway, but given the complete lack of coverage it was receiving, Sally doubted it would receive more than a footnote in some back-page political blog. A few media outlets and bloggers weren't letting Goodwin off the hook, but the general public's attention span was already focused upon a new scandal involving a gold medalist swimmer and a picture of him inhaling from the wrong sort of pipe.

But Sally hadn't forgotten, and she wasn't going to let Goodwin forget either.

Before, when she'd first visited Senator Goodwin, Sally had worn her stealth outfit, dressed all in black like a super-speedy ninja, and she'd sneaked into the house just like one too. This time, she wore her crimson and gold proudly, and she walked through the Senate building's front doors for all to see. She wasn't afraid, and she wasn't going to let Goodwin intimidate her again. If the Senator pulled another gun on her, Sally would dismantle it before her eyes and let the pieces fall to the floor. She wasn't going to leave until she'd spoken her piece.

Senator Goodwin was in her office with the door open. She sat at her desk with one hand dangling from her arm sling and the other resting atop the desk, not working, but waiting.

Sally knocked on the door frame.

Goodwin looked up at her and made her wait for several long seconds. "Come in. Sit down."

Sally entered the office and sat. She was a little nervous about confronting someone who was every bit as much her enemy as some of the high-powered villains she'd battled over the years. Despite those misgivings, she presented herself as confident. Goodwin would respect confidence more than she would respect anything else about Sally, including her station and her record. "Senator. How's the arm?"

Goodwin's face could have been chiseled from marble for all the emotion she showed. Like Sally, she had her guard up and wasn't going to give away anything. "Improving. Thank you for your concern, Commander."

Sally blinked at that. It was, as far as she could recall, the first time anyone had referred to her by her official rank instead of by her name. She filed that away for future reference. By using it, Goodwin had empowered her further than if the Senator had used her name. It made the conversation feel more formal, more distant, and that was what Sally needed. "Surprised to see me?"

"No, I expected you'd come by sooner or later." Goodwin looked at the time on the cell phone on her desk. "I have a meeting in half an hour. You have ten minutes before I need to depart, Commander."

"I only need two. Senator, I know you don't like me, and you don't like parahumans. You've made no secret of that in the press. But you have said some things to me privately that I don't think you'd appreciate being released to the general public. I'm willing to let those things disappear, but I want something from you in return."

"You recorded me." It wasn't a question.

"I did. It's legal in this state." Sally allowed herself a small smile. "I checked."

Goodwin's smile was equally small, and equally devoid of humor. "What do you want, Commander?"

"I want you off our cases. You want be a racist about parahumans? Fine. That's who you are and I can't change it. But my team, my family, my organization are off limits. Drop your legislation against us. Stop your scheming against us, and I won't release that recording. I can't promise someone else won't tie you to Chessboard, but if you comply with this, I promise it won't come from me."

"I have no ties to Chessboard. You are quite mistaken, Commander. I was as much in the dark about their illegal human experimentation as anyone was. One of their agents even shot me. For me to be involved in any way with a dangerous, terrorist organization such as that would be unpatriotic and unprofessional."

"That's your story and you're sticking to it. Still, I want you to lay off Just Cause. Like us or not, we're still the good guys."

"Or you'll destroy me? I am a sitting United States Senator, Commander. Be very careful who you threaten."

"I'm not threatening anything. Just trying to come to an arrangement."

"I see you've learned something about how the game works. It only gets more difficult from here. I've been doing this for a very long time, Commander."

Sally crossed her arms and said nothing.

"Very well, for the time being, the Goodwin Act is off the table. You can go back to your little island castle secure in the knowledge that you're not about to be evicted from it. I may revisit it at some point in the future, but for the time being, you're off the hook. But if that evidence of yours finds its way to the public eye, I promise you will be at the center of such a shitstorm that you'll never find your way back to the light. You may have battled stronger opponents as a superhero, but you'll never meet one more formidable than me."

"Then we have an agreement, Senator." Sally stood. "I'll consider that as valid as any promise made by a politician." She cracked a smile like Jack would have. "You're safe here in your castle too."

"For now. I have my sights set a bit higher yet."

Sally shuddered. It was as much an admission that Goodwin intended to vie for the presidency at some point. She wouldn't acknowledge it. When the time came to stop Goodwin at a crucial point in her career, perhaps with an election on the line, Sally would be ready. "Good day, Senator." She turned to leave.

Goodwin called after her. "Commander!"

Sally turned, slowly, without fear.

Goodwin smiled. "You're not the only one who can record a conversation. I suggest you remember that. Good day."

Sally departed, leaving behind the stink of the political morass for the fresher air of Washington D.C. in the winter. She knew she hadn't said anything particularly damning to herself or Just Cause in the meeting with the Senator, but Goodwin could have been referring to something else. Who knew, in the long run, what kind of intelligence Goodwin had obtained over the years? As she'd said, she'd been playing the game a very long time, and she was indeed a formidable opponent. Sally expected there would be numerous run-ins with her in the future.

But for now, the sun was shining over Washington, making the accumulated snowfall sparkle and giving the historic buildings a gleam that they deserved. Sally closed her eyes and turned her face toward the sun to let it warm her skin. It was a couple hundred miles back to New York City and Fort Justice, back to Jason. She could cover that distance in half an hour easy.

"Hey, Mustang Sally! All right!" called a man as he shoveled snow, whistling. He gave her at thumbs-up and she smiled back at him. She was pretty sure she'd seen him before. The more things changed, the more they stayed the same. There would always be people who hated parahumans, like Senator Goodwin, but there would always be those who loved them.

Sally trotted over to him. "Do you have a cell phone, mister?"

"Sure, you need it?" He leaned on his shovel.

"Just for a moment."

He dug in his pocket and handed it to her.

She raised it up. "Smile!" She took a picture of the two of them together and then handed the phone back to him. "Keep up the good work, mister."

"Hey, thanks a lot! I'm gonna show this to my kids."

Sally grinned, and then turned to the north and ran.

ABOUT THE AUTHOR

 Ian Thomas Healy dabbles in many different genres. He's a ten-time participant and winner of National Novel Writing Month and is also the creator of the *Writing Better Action Through Cinematic Techniques* workshop, which helps writers to improve their action scenes.

When not writing, which is rare, he enjoys watching hockey, reading comic books (and serious books, too), and living in the great state of Colorado, which he shares with his wife, children, house-pets, and approximately five million other people.

Visit www.ianthealy.com for more information.

ABOUT THE COVER ARTIST

Irshad Karim is a digital illustrator based out of Ottawa, Canada. While largely self-taught, he has reinforced his knowledge with courses at Concept Design Academy in Los Angeles, and studied under entertainment industry professionals such as Kevin Chen, James Paick, John Park and Peter Han. More of his work can be seen on his online portfolio, www.irshadkarim.com.